OREGON

Klamath Territory

Klamath R.

CALIFORNIA
1846

chazaud

Sacramento R.

• Lassen's Ranch

Feather R.

American R.

Fort Ross •

Sonoma •
Sutter's Fort •

Sierra Nevada

San Rafael
The Presidio
San Francisco
Yerba Buena
San José •
Mission Dolores
Pacheco Pass

San Joaquin R.

Mission San Juan Bautista
Hawk Peak
Monterey •

Sierra del Gavilan

Salinas Valley

N

San Gabriel Mountains

R. Porciuncula
San Gabriel •

El Pueblo de los Angeles
San Pedro

Socorro via Gila River

San Pascual •

San Diego •

0   50   100   150   200   250
Miles

THE
BEAR FLAG

Cecelia Holland

A PETER DAVISON BOOK

Houghton Mifflin Company

BOSTON

1990

Library of Congress Cataloging-in-Publication Data

Holland, Cecelia, date.
The Bear Flag / Cecelia Holland.
p.   cm.
"A Peter Davison book."
ISBN 0-395-48886-9
1. California — History — Fiction.   I. Title.
PS3558.O348B37   1990
813'.54 — dc20   89-71670
CIP

Frontispiece map by Jacques Chazaud
Book design by Anne Chalmers

Printed in the United States of America

WAK 10 9 8 7 6 5 4 3 2 1

For

CAROLLY,

because, as the wise man said,
it's not often you find
a good writer who's also
a good friend

"Fair young maid, all in a garden,
Strange young man riding by,
Saying, 'Fair pretty maid, will you marry me?'
This then, sir, was her reply."

The Bear Flag

I 🏵   Beneath a sky as clear as Eden's, Catharine Reilly walked up the dun slope of the South Pass.

The wind was roaring down from the west, a massive tumbling of the air, smelling of blown grass and wet rock. Climbing, she leaned against the force of the wind, and it slapped her hair back off her face and tugged the bodice of her dress tight around her and fluttered her skirts until she had to hold them down with both hands.

She lifted her face to the wind, into the tangy fragrance and the tingle of its furious caress. Her bonnet had already come loose; she held it crumpled in one fist as she made her way up to her husband.

At the height of the slope, in the sun by an outcrop of colored stone, John Reilly sat perched on a rock, his sketchpad on his knees. His coat was thrown over the boulder behind him, and his shirt sleeves were pulled up. The wind had made a riot of his blond curly hair. His pencil stroked rapidly over the white page before him; when she came up beside him, he ignored her, absorbed as he was in his work.

She stood there a moment, looking over his shoulder, and frowned, dissatisfied. The drawing was done well. In a few lines he had laid down on the page the great, broad, smooth trough of the South Pass, and now under his hand fragments of the emigrant camp appeared, the wagons and carts parked square for the night, the little groups of oxen and horses cropping the short brown grass, the figure of a child, in the distance, running with swinging arms down the slope. As she saw the child on the sketchpad she heard the faint screech of the real child's voice.

She turned away from the camp and looked into the north-west.

The South Pass rose in a long, easy grade from the high plains to the Wind River Range. For days, sitting on the wagon seat, she had watched and watched the distance ahead of her; straining forward as if she could jack them up over the horizon, she had waited for the mountains. On the approach they had passed little bits of them, gigantic rocks erupting from the plain, low, sandy hills blocking her sight. Now, scaling the height of the pass, leaning into the wild wind, she came up at last before the peaks.

She drew in a deep breath of the wind; she opened herself up, and the wind filled her. Before her the land dropped away so fast that it was like a door opening on nothing. Mostly air, a world unformed, chaotic, streaming with the pure light of the sun.

Below their blazing crests, the mountains descended to blue darkness, a half-guessed-at valley or plain, to rebound again beyond from the unseeable depth into another steep, notched wave of rock, then fell away again and rose again until the horizon swallowed it all in a hazy blue that was a defeat of vision. The wind roared up from this plunging space as if it were born there, the breath of the rock.

"Why don't you draw this?" she asked, turning back toward John Reilly. He lifted his face, and she leaned down and put her arms around his neck and kissed him. Still holding him, her cheek against his hair, she said again, "Why not draw the mountains? Aren't you sick to death of the wagons?"

He said, "I don't know where to start." Still entangled in her embrace, he lifted his pencil again and drew part of a wagon's familiar, dingy canvas bonnet.

She sank down beside him, her arms around her knees, and returned her gaze to the mountains' tremendous surge. "It's magnificent."

"It's too big, Cathy. Too complicated to draw."

She leaned against him, but her gaze remained on the mountains, which pleased her deeply; she felt for the first time in this long journey that they had reached someplace worth coming to.

The sun was going down. All along the sky's ragged edge the color slowly bloomed, on the low clouds deepening to red, between the clouds forming streaks of pure gold, along the horizon itself turning a delicate pure pink like the inside of a shell. Below this brilliant play of light the earth grew dark and the shapes vanished into the dark, as if the night were gathering them back in.

Suddenly restless, her husband put his pencil away and folded the sketchpad. "Come along, it's getting late." He got up, reaching out to her, and drew her to her feet.

Hand in hand they went down the slope toward the camp. Their wagon, which carried in it everything they owned, formed half the near right corner. Catharine looked up at her husband's face. They were still so newly married that she sometimes found him absorbingly strange.

At the camp he circled toward the pasture to bring their oxen in for the night, and she went into the middle of the square of wagons to cook their dinner. Nancy Kelsey was already at the fire, cutting strips of bacon; Catharine knelt down beside her to bake bannock bread.

Nancy asked, "What's your John want to do — go to Oregon, or California?"

Catharine pressed the bread dough impatiently into the skillet. At first she had enjoyed the camp work, she who had never cooked anything, never cut a carrot or peeled a potato, delighting suddenly in making pan bread. Now she did it as quickly as she could, bored with it. "Is that what they're all talking about?" She could hear the men behind her, gathering together on the far side of the camp, their voices rising, arguing.

Nancy said, "They got to make up their minds." She was a big, broad-hipped girl with capable hands, always working. At nineteen, a year younger than Catharine, she was already a mother; her baby lay on its blanket just beyond her. "Your John talk any to you about it?"

"Not really." She thought John's mind was made up. They had always wanted to go to California, from the beginning.

"Ben keeps fretting at it," Nancy said. "Look, now, Cathy, you got to tip the pan up more, like this, or you'll lose all the good heat." Her voice had a mild edge of amusement. Carefully she propped up the skillet on its side so that the warmth of the fire baked the top of the dough.

Catharine looked over at the growing knot of men. She could see Broken Hand in their midst, their guide, whose real name was Captain Fitzpatrick. His left hand was misshapen. He wore animal hides sewn together like an Indian's clothes; his hair hung in a ropy braid down his back. John Bidwell was there also, and Nancy's husband, Ben, and now Catharine saw her own husband striding up to join the group around the scout. She rose to her feet and went closer to listen.

She and John Reilly had been married only four months. They were both from Boston, but he was an Ann Street Irishman and she was a Mather from Franklin Place, and by rights they ought never to have married at all.

They met at a lecture in New Bedford, where she heard an ex-slave talk about the rights of colored people and women, and then again at a bookstore, where she was buying a book of poetry. She liked his sketches. She liked his overlong blond hair and the square set of his shoulders. When he talked about his dream of moving west, taking land of his own in the wilderness, something wakened in her soul, and the house in Franklin Place seemed like a prison.

He went to her father, honorably, and asked for her hand in marriage, and Edward Mather ordered him out and locked his daughter in her bedroom. She escaped down the servants' stair and with John Reilly fled on the next post coach west. In New York a justice of the peace married them. They went on to Saint Louis, where with the last of his savings they bought a wagon and a team and supplies. They pawned her wedding ring for a dollar to pay their passage across the Missouri River.

John had heard about a party of emigrants, Oregon-bound, assembling at a place called Sapling Grove, somewhere in Kansas. With their wagon and their oxen they reached Sapling Grove in the late spring and found more than sixty people already there, to go west.

Most were farm people, from Ohio or Kentucky, boisterous, heavy-handed, quick-tempered, hard-working. The excitement of the great trek that lay before them seized them like a fever, an overflowing heat that gave itself away in wild, aimless fits of noise and motion. They danced and ran and talked at the tops of their voices, and then, on the morning they were to leave, they abruptly discovered that nobody knew which way to go.

Fortunately they fell in with a party of Catholic missionaries whom Broken Hand was guiding west. So they had gotten this far. But here at the South Pass, the missionaries had to turn north to find the Flathead Indians they had been sent to convert, and Broken Hand was going with them. Now the settlers had to set off on their own.

Broken Hand loomed in the middle of the crowd of men. He had lived on the frontier all his life and looked like a wild creature of this country, with his clothes of hide and his battered, knotted hands. His voice rumbled.

"The trail to Fort Hall is pret' clearly marked from here. You go on down toward Soda Springs, and you'll find the wagon tracks. You follow them west, toward the buttes . . ."

Catharine went up closer to the men, behind her husband, who stood, increasingly impatient, listening to Broken Hand talk.

"Onst you get to the Snake, you got to start looking for the ford."

"Is anybody writing this down?" called John Bidwell, and there was general laughter. Catharine laughed too. Fitzpatrick seemed to be confusing them all.

One shoulder higher than the other, hulking in his filthy worn leathers, the plainsman hawked and spat and said, "Hard part's behind y'. From here to Oregon's pret' easy. Even a bunch of green twigs like you oughta be able to follow the trail from here."

Ben Kelsey said, "What if we don't want to go to Oregon?"

"Shut up," yelled somebody on the other side of the circle.

"Oregon sounds good enough to me." There was a widespread murmur of agreement.

In the group around Reilly, John Bidwell said, "Back in Ohio, when we all started talking about this, it was California we wanted to get to."

Broken Hand drawled, "California's a different place'n Oregon. Damned near impossible to get to, and the Spanish dons don't hardly take to Americans. They'll throw you in chains soon's you pipe up. I heard of white men died in chains in Mexico."

Ben Kelsey said, "The Britishers think they own Oregon. That ain't no sure thing, neither, seems to me."

Bidwell leaned forward, intent. "Listen, I'm telling you, I've heard in California the soil's so good you just spit and grow people. Isn't that worth a little risk?"

Fitzpatrick looked up at him and said nothing. He had the stolid patience of a man who knew exactly what was possible and intended to waste no effort on what was not. Catharine glanced at her husband, sitting quietly in the midst of these men.

Somebody else said, "Hey, Bidwell, you're so sweet on California, show us how to get there."

That was the problem. As at Sapling Grove, nobody knew which way to go.

Bidwell moved in toward the middle of the circle. He was a rangy young man, with a shock of black hair and a restless energy that kept him moving even as he talked. "I've heard, southwest from here, there's a lake —"

"There's a lake, all right," Fitzpatrick said, with a crackle of laughter. "I been that far."

"And a river running from it through the mountains and through California out to the Pacific Ocean. The Rio Buenaventura."

"The River of Good Luck," said John Reilly. "That's auspicious."

Broken Hand said, "Ain't nobody I know ever seen that river. But I seen the lake, and it ain't a fit place for anybody but seagulls or salt merchants."

"What's the trail like to Oregon?" another voice asked.

"It's pretty rough," said Fitzpatrick. "Goin' through the Snake River country — that's murder on beasts and wagons. But the trail's there and it's hard to get lost, which there's something to be said for in this country." His voice thickened momentarily and he coughed. "Indians are mildly unfriendly."

John Reilly leaned forward to catch his eyes. "What about the Indians around this River of Good Luck?"

Fitzpatrick grunted. "I ain't never seen no such river. Out there west of the salt lake there's nothing but Digger Indians. They ain't no trouble — they're too poor to do much."

Kelsey said, "It's just about as far to Oregon as it is to California, ain't it?"

Reilly turned to Bidwell. "Where did you hear about this River of Good Luck?"

"A fellah named, unh, Roubideux, something like that." Bidwell's eager face swung toward him. "He'd been all over this country. He says in California you live like Adam and Eve, it's always sunny and warm, there's no winter there, and the going's real easy. You just ride out ever' day, shoot some meat for dinner, pick the fruit right off the trees."

"You're going for certain, then."

Bidwell shrugged his shoulders. "The damned British are sittin' there in Oregon. We fought two wars already with them and may be headed for a third, and if we fight and lose, all the Americans in Oregon will likely have to give up everything, or go back to bein' English." He nodded to John Reilly. "Kelsey's going. Ain'tcha, Ben?"

Ben Kelsey's deep voice sounded off to Catharine's right. "I got a good mind to. Me and my brother Jack, here."

John Reilly nodded to Bidwell. "I'll go with you."

"Glad to hear that, Reilly. You'll be good to have along." Bidwell gripped him briefly by the hand, turned, and shouted at someone else.

Reilly rubbed his hands together. Abruptly he turned and saw Catharine there behind him, and he backed up and reached his hand out and drew her over to him. She leaned against him and his arm went around her. They enclosed each other. Outside them the men were bellowing arguments, their voices rising like smoke to the starry sky. Reilly said, "We're going to get there, Cathy. We're going to have our own place, soon enough." He squeezed her.

"Cathy!"

Catharine twisted, looking behind her. Nancy Kelsey stood by the fire waving her arms. "Oh. My bread." She went back hastily toward the fire, to rescue their dinner.

2 BESIDES BIDWELL and the Kelseys and the Reillys, a man named Bartleson decided to head for California, bringing with him his sons and a brother and six guns. Largely on the basis of the six guns, he was elected captain of the wagon train. On a big roan horse he rode along in front of them all, shouting orders and waving a stick over his head. The only other woman besides Catharine was Nancy Kelsey, with her baby.

Fitzpatrick had pointed them along a trail that led south and west over a barren plain. There was no grass, only low brush with silver leaves that gave off a wild, woody aroma, like an herb. Broken Hand had told them to watch for horse Indians, saying that the Arapaho sometimes came this far west on raids, but after a few days' travel they grew careless with the fire, sitting around it until well after dark, arguing about whether to put it out or not.

Bartleson grunted. "Fitzpatrick was an old fool. Do you see any Indians? That's because there ain't none." He turned his head and spat. In the fire's blaze his cheeks shone red as war paint. "It's not like I'd mind anyways. I got me a little keg of whiskey in my wagon. A nice pack of Indians could make me rich, at a beaver pelt or a fox fur for a drink."

The men were slumped and easy around the fire. Nancy and Catharine began picking up their pots and knives.

Bartleson leered at the other men. Around him his sons and brother crowded like a wall. "Well? What d'you say?"

On the far side of the fire that still burned high in their midst, Ben Kelsey clapped the meat of his broad hands together. "Broken Hand ain't that old, nor a fool, and you kept it hid from him you got this keg. You know the laws about selling whiskey to the Indians."

"Law. Who said anything about the law? There ain't no law out here. This is God's country." Bartleson began to laugh, his belly shaking.

Nancy got hold of Catharine's arm. "Come along, give them room to rant."

Reluctantly Catharine followed her away from the campfire, down to the edge of the river. Nancy knelt to scrub a pot with a handful of sand.

Catharine stood looking back at the men. "Selling whiskey sounds like a bad idea to me."

Nancy said placidly, "My Ben will sit on that."

Now in fact Kelsey said, "There ain't no reason to make this any more complicated than it already is. No peddling whiskey." He got up, moving toward the fire, and with a stick began to break it up. John Reilly stooped to push sand over the flames. The round glow of light shrank, but the men crowded together, on their feet now. Catharine took a step closer to them.

Nancy came up beside her and held her by the arm. "Stay back, Cathy."

Bartleson said, "Now, hold on! You ain't the captain here, I am!"

Kelsey straightened; the last half-smothered glow of the fire barely lit him to the knees. In the dark behind him, his brother Jack and John Bidwell moved up to flank him. Kelsey hooked his thumbs in his belt and scowled at Bartleson. "You got yourself elected captain, but I figger we can get you unelected."

"You think so!" Bartleson stuck his thumbs in his belt.

"Are they going to fight?" Catharine asked, startled.

Nancy slipped a reassuring arm around her waist. "No, no, just bellow."

Kelsey and Bartleson stood face to face a moment, and then John Reilly strode up and pushed in between them.

"Damn it, what are you doing? Fitzpatrick said we were green, and so we are — here we're stuck out in the wilderness and you're feuding over selling liquor to Indians like you were barkeeps in Boston. Look up there!"

He pointed at the sky, and obediently they all turned and peered up where his arm aimed.

"You see that red star there? That's Antares. That's a summer star, and it's nearly gone. Look around you! The winter's coming. We're out here with no food but what meat we can shoot, with women and a baby — and you want to hang around and make a little money!"

He swept his challenging gaze around the firelit circle of men. Bartleson stood back, not smiling anymore, looking smaller. One of his own men had a hand on his arm, holding him. The fight was gone from Kelsey's look; when Reilly faced him he turned his head away. There was a taut silence. Abruptly Bidwell strode forward and began to kick apart the fire and douse the flames, and several others joined him. The darkness fell around them, and the cold.

"Let's go," John Reilly said, in the night. "Let's get to sleep and get a good move on tomorrow."

"Say hey to that," someone murmured, and they began to head back to their wagons.

In the dark, later, she said, "You're a hero."

He cradled her in the crook of his arm, his breath warm on her forehead. "No hero. Worried, mostly." His beard scrubbed her cheek. "I'm beginning to be sorry I dragged you out here, my dear one, my darling."

"I'd rather be out here with you than back in Boston eating cake," she said.

"We could go back," he said. "We could head up to Fort Hall."

"No!" She stiffened, pushing away to look at him, alarmed. "No, we can't go back." Going back was a kind of defeat, an admission that they had been wrong. She would never admit she had been wrong.

He gathered her in again. "You're brave, Cathy. But you don't know what's ahead of us. Neither do I, and that's what worries me."

"California," she said. "California is ahead of us. Remember that lecture?" During their courtship they had walked to Cambridge to hear a former Harvard student talk about his voyages to the Pacific. His ship had traded for hides and tallow in California, and in his talk he had made it seem peaceful and quiet, cut off utterly from the rest of the world, a sleepy paradise of orange trees and clay houses and slow-rolling surf. "California is out there, somewhere, if we just keep going."

"Is that what you want?" her husband asked.

In the cramped, dark space of the wagon, she lay pressed against his body and wondered what he was asking her. "I'm with you," she said. "That's all I care about."

He said, "You have me, but you still want something. As long as I've known you, you've wanted something, and I wish I knew what it is."

She was still for a moment, startled by this alien view of her. Far away in the desert the quavering howl of a wolf sounded. She put her hand on his chest. "I want to do something great," she said. "Something noble. Like the people who won the Revolution. Or Columbus." Saying it, she could not help but laugh at herself. "But, you know, I'll settle for you."

"Hunh." This bit of humor ruffled him; perhaps he took her seriously. "That's a man's dream. Women are already noble for putting up with us." His arm tightened around her. "Go to sleep, Cathy. Dream like that."

They found a shallow river and followed its course out onto a broad, stony, sagebrush-covered plain. Day by day the mountains slipped behind them. Before them lay broad, flat land, treeless and dry. The animals crowded along the banks of the

river, where the only grass grew. During the day, as they traveled, Catharine watched for patches of grass, and took a knife
and cut the grass and saved it in the wagon to feed the oxen at
night.

The river ran shallower with every mile, foul-tasting and
mucky. Its banks were marshes, studded with reeds like spears.
Two of the wagons sank down to their wheel hubs in the mud,
and the group had to stop to free them while the animals ranged
desperately for something to eat. Catharine sat on the Kelseys'
wagon seat, holding Nancy's baby, while the other woman
sewed her husband's jacket. The men were arguing as they
worked, their voices rising over the gritty clash of the shovels.

"Damn, this country's sour as my mother-in-law. Bidwell,
damn you, where the hell's this River of Good Luck?"

"I say we cut off due west. Make a run for it."

"Make a run, what you'll run is your rat-butt off."

"If we turn north now, we can probably make it to Fort
Hall."

"Yeah, that's you, Bartleson, chickening out."

Catharine said, "They're always arguing."

"They're men," Nancy said. "Men spend most of their time
together pushing each other into line."

Her hands moved with a deft speed that stirred Catharine to
envy. She had never learned to sew. She wished she could play
the piano for Nancy, so that the other woman would find something to admire in her.

Nancy said, "I'll mend that dress for you, Cathy, if you can
change it for somethin' else."

Catharine shifted the baby in her arms. "It's all right." She
did not want Nancy having to work for her, too. The baby was
stirring awake, warm and heavy and faintly malodorous.

"You have such pretty things," Nancy said. "You should take
better care of them." Her smile took the edge off the reproach.

"You show me how, then. She's waking up. What a baby,
Sarah." She loved the baby; nobody at home had babies. Sarah
opened her blue eyes wide and produced a lunatic smile.

"Hey!" A yelp burst from Nancy. "Indians — look —"

Catharine jerked her head up, looking where Nancy pointed. On the next ridge, rising like a wave of sand up from the flat bed of the desert, six little riders trotted boldly along. Nancy snatched the baby out of Catharine's arms and hid it under her shawl.

The men roared, "Indians!" Bartleson grabbed his rifle from the scabbard on his saddle and waved it over his head, and Ben Kelsey loped up from the river muck, his boots filthy, and reached down without ceremony past Catharine's skirts and brought a gun out from under the seat.

"They're gone," Catharine said.

Kelsey's breath left him in a grunt. He was older than Nancy by some years, and he never smiled. His broad, dour face was stubbled with beard like a mown field. "They ain't gone. You just ain't seein' 'em anymore." He walked down toward the other men, who were standing in a line above the mired wagons and staring away to the west.

The Indians did not show themselves again. The men went back to the work of digging the wagons free. In a few moments they resumed their arguing, over something else. The women made the fire and cooked a little bread; Catharine had only a few cups of flour left, but she had a good quantity of beans. Soaking these in the brackish river water left them tough and foul-tasting and made for flatulence, hours after eating. She wondered what the Indians ate. There seemed nothing in this country except sand and sagebrush and vultures.

They freed the wagons and rolled on. The river wound on through treacherous flats of mud, growing wider and shallower as it ran south. Even the animals began to get stuck in the salty, slick marshes that fringed it. Once a flock of seagulls circled over the wagons, screaming at them, and flew away to the south, which meant, the men said, that the salt lake was close by.

Wary of the mud flats and tired of the stinking water, they decided to swing west, across the flat land toward the low ridges in the distance, hoping to find the River of Good Luck. They filled their water casks and cut what grass their beasts had not yet eaten, and they pushed on.

In the western distance the blue ridges of the mountains lay like blades against the sky. There was no shade from the glare of the sun. The oxen plodded steadily along, their knobbed hip-bones swaying. Bartleson on his roan horse and Bidwell on a mule set off to scout the broad, barren plain ahead for the river. The ground was stony and raw, and even the sagebrush grew sparsely here. There was no water.

That night, when they camped and gathered in the cattle, three or four head were missing. The next day, in the evening, a few more were gone, and a mule limped in with an arrow in its leg. So the Indians were there, somewhere.

Bartleson and Bidwell came back; they had found no trace of the River of Good Luck.

Once there had been rivers here. The group followed an ancient gouge through the land where shoals of gravel and sand terraces imprinted with the wind-blurred marks of waves showed that the water had run high there in the past. Strands of grass like inept birds' nests hung twisted in the bleached branches and the exposed roots of the brush that grew out of the bank. The phantom river hampered them as if it were real; it took the men half the day to get all the wagons across a gorge where once another old stream had run into this one, and almost immediately afterward Bidwell's open cart broke a wheel again. The young man packed his food and clothes onto his oxen; they dragged the broken cart off to one side and left it.

The riverbed turned southward, and now a thin layer of water seeped along it. There was grass growing sparse and coarse on the flat sand, but the beasts would have none of it. Walking through it, looking for fodder, Catharine saw the ground ahead of her sparkling in the sun. When she stooped to pick a blade of grass, there were tiny crystals all over it. She touched her tongue to the grass; the crystals were jewels of salt.

She stopped where she was and looked ahead of them, down the gorge of the invisible river. The sun glittered on the grass. Far away in the gray-brown plain, she thought she saw a row of trees and the gleam of water. All was dun, dust-colored, gray-

green and gray-brown; the horizon melted indefinably into the
edge of the sky. She turned and trudged back to the wagons.

John sat on the wagon seat drawing while the other men
argued out their course. Their animals were weak for want of
fodder, and following this old river was taking them deeper into
a barren salt flat. The low mountains that loomed ahead looked
no greener.

"Keep going west," Kelsey was saying. "That way at least
we're gettin' closer."

Bartleson scratched his belly. "We ain't gettin' no wagons up
over those mountains." He jerked his head toward the west.

Catharine looked down at the white page on John's knee. In
a few abrupt black lines, Bartleson's face, framed by his wide-
brimmed straw hat, glowered at her; beside him was John Bidwell, laughing, eternally sunny, his eyes bright. "That's good,"
she said, pointing.

"Oh, is it." John glanced at her, and then beneath his darting
pencil her face appeared, her wide eyes, her little knob of a nose
and sharp chin, her hair tucked demurely beneath her bonnet;
his pencil rose a moment, still, above the little portrait, and then
in an irresistible flash of his fingers he drew a mustache on her
upper lip.

She jabbed an elbow into his ribs. "You devil."

His arm snaked around her and he drew her against him,
and they kissed. From the council going on around them there
was a whoop of vicarious pleasure.

Later, in the dark, they made furtive love, hiding what they
were doing from the others just outside. They tried not to rock
the wagon; they were wedged in between the chest of clothes
and John's toolbox. Pressed against his body, touched to ecstasy,
she clenched her teeth to keep from crying out.

"God," he said, lying on her, "what I'd give for a real
bed."

"Turn around, we'll go back to Boston."

He laughed. Shifting and scraping, they struggled for room
in the close darkness, and the wagon creaked. Out there now,
perhaps, in his blankets, John Bidwell knew the Reillys made

love. Fat, ugly Bartleson knew. She turned on her side and pulled the blanket up.

"A bed," he said sleepily. "A mug of ale, clean water to wash in, to wash you in, paved streets that go where I expect them to, loaves of fresh bread, still warm from the oven, and butter —"

"John," she said.

"Clean clothes, no blisters, no idiot oxen, no Indians —"

She stilled him with a kiss. His hands pressed against her, shaping her, making her real. She needed him, and a wave of gratitude washed over her, that he whom she needed so much was kind and good and clever and full of love, and needed her, too.

This was right; it had to be right. What they were doing, what they had done. In the end it would all be right. Warm and safe in his embrace, she shut her eyes.

3 ✍ IT TOOK HOURS TO FILL their water casks from the slow-seeping river. They hauled the wagons across the streambed and turned due west, across a broad flat covered with thick and tangled sagebrush. The men walked in the front, hacking a trail through this miniature forest; the sagebrush stems, like iron, yielded only to heroic blows.

After a few minutes, Bartleson in a rage shouted the other men out of the way and drove his team hard at the brush, as if he could force his way through by mere temper.

Under the constant cracking lash, the oxen plowed into the sage, hauling the wagon after. The brush sank and creaked, and the wagon wheels screamed, sliding on their iron rims along the stems and catching in the forks of the brush. Even under the wagon's weight the sagebrush would not break but only bend, and once bent the tough, springy stems fought their way back to their original shape. They bore the wagon completely up off the ground, while Bartleson on the seat shouted and swung his whip and the oxen bellowed, until the wagon slowly, with great dignity, rolled over sideways onto the great mattress of brush.

Bartleson and his whip sailed off into the sage. The Kelseys and John Bidwell broke into roars of laughter. While the fat man fought free of the vegetation they all stood around grinning at him. After that, Bartleson swung an ax with the rest of them.

All that day they struggled up a long ridge that rose like a wave from the earth. Near the summit they came on a patch of meadow with tall grass and a little spring. Catharine drank some of the sweet, clear water and stepped back to look on to the west.

This crest was the forefoot of a range of low hills, abrupt, wind-hollowed, sprinkled with puffs of sagebrush. Beyond she could see only the implacable sky.

The wind was cold. She drew her shawl around her. The sun was low in the west, dropping toward a horizon of hazy notches. Off to the north, to her surprise, was a nearby hill that wore a cap of white snow.

"You see that?" John Bidwell said. He came up beside her, but it was to her husband, chopping sagebrush for the fire, that he spoke. "You were right — the winter's coming on. We got to get a move on."

Reilly leaned on the ax. "I've been thinking we could move faster without the wagons." Catharine stooped and began to gather up the chunks of brush he had chopped, their oily aroma like a protest. "You rode down south of here. What'd you find?"

Bidwell's fingers plucked at his thin black beard. "The farther south you go, the drier the country gets. You think these hills here are rough — down south they go straight up like walls, and they're bare as blank walls, too, no trees, no grass, no water." He stopped, staring not at them but through them. "Looks like the devil's stoneyard down there."

Catharine carried the wood away to the fire. Bartleson was sitting by it already, his knees spread, poking with a stick at the flames, while Nancy on the far side was working to make a little bit of bread.

"What a mess. What a mess you got us into!" said Bartleson. He glared at Bidwell.

"Hey," Bidwell said, "I didn't press-gang you. You came along on your own pins." The deepening twilight was driving them all in toward the fire.

The baby wailed. Nancy, bent over the pans on the fire, said, "Get her, Cathy, will you?" and Catharine went to the Kelseys' wagon and lifted Sarah up into her arms.

Kelsey said, "We can't go back. We done ate up all the grass getting this far. Due west is the way to go. Just keep on going west. Get through it."

Bartleson struck at the fire with his stick. "What a mess you got us into," he said, this time to nobody in particular.

"The wagons are slowing us down too much," John Reilly said. "The hills are getting steeper. I say we leave the wagons. Pack our gear on the animals."

Kelsey's head bobbed up and down. "About what I was thinkin'. Slaughter the ones that ain't gonna make it anyway and jerk the meat." He nodded around them. "There's enough grass here to keep us a couple days while we do it."

Bartleson's lips pursed out. "I got a lot of stuff in my wagon." His small eyes squinted from one of them to the next.

"Leave it. Cache it. Maybe you can come back for it." Kelsey gave him hardly a glance. He looked at Bidwell and Reilly. "Get going on it first thing tomorrow."

They slaughtered half their animals, cut the meat off the carcasses, hung it in the sage fires to smoke and dry. After three days the meat had shrunk and toughened like leather. They packed it in sacks left over from their stores of food, took their belongings out of the wagons, and began to strap the meat and their possessions onto the oxen and mules.

The Reillys had slaughtered one of their two oxen. They stood by their wagon trying to decide which of their things were important enough to pack. Catharine took her clothes out of her trunk and stuffed them into a sack with John's clothes. She stroked the pretty paper lining of the trunk, regretful. John touched her cheek. He slid his sketchpad in beside his box of tools and his ax, strapped on top of their remaining ox.

The Bartlesons were gathering up the beasts into a herd, now, on the edge of the meadow. They looked strange, the oxen, packs of goods riding on their knobby backs. Catharine climbed into her wagon, looking around for anything else she could carry.

John leaned in at the back. "It's like leaving home again," he said, and pulled his mouth into a smile, but there was no amusement in it, no humor. "I'm sorry, Cathy."

"What are you sorry about?" She climbed down beside him and put her hands on his arms, exasperated.

"Bringing you out here. You giving up so much."

She slid her hands around his waist and hugged him. "I'm not giving up anything I really want."

"Hey!" The yell came from the crest of the hill, behind them, an angry bellow. "Hey — damn you —"

"We ain't got time to wait around, Kelsey."

"That's our meat, too!" Bidwell shouted.

John swore under his breath. He strode past Catharine, around the back of the wagon. "Stop," he shouted, "stop, damn you, Bartleson!" and began to run.

Catharine went after him, hurrying up the long slope. She could hear the low rumble of animals galloping. The men were shouting again. She scrambled up the slope through the clawing, clutching sagebrush.

Across the trampled meadow the men were fighting and running. At the far end the settlers' animals were galloping away in a tight bunch. At the near end Kelsey, on foot, had hold of the bridle of Bartleson's rearing horse. She stood, her knees quaking, wondering what to do. Twenty feet from her, Bartleson leaned out of his saddle and struck Kelsey across the face with the ends of his reins, and Kelsey let go and stumbled back.

"See you in California!" Bartleson wheeled his horse around and thundered off.

Catharine scurried along the steep slope; she slipped and fell, scraping her knee on a rock. Down the far side of the ridge she could see their whole herd, all the beasts they had not slaughtered, rumbling away through the sagebrush. The packs rode like crazy jockeys on their backs. Bartleson and his men, on horseback, whooped along in their tracks, herding them with sticks and ropes. John Reilly, before her, spun around, and plunged back down the slope, cutting off their ox before it stampeded away with the others.

"What's going on?" Catharine cried, bewildered.

John Bidwell threw down his hat. "Beat again," he said.

Kelsey was glaring at the disappearing Bartlesons. "They had all the meat?" Off at the edge of the meadow, Nancy wailed.

John Reilly came up, leading his ox. Kelsey's brother followed, panting; he had given futile chase to the Bartlesons. He said, "I knew we shouldn't of trusted 'em."

"They took it all?" Catharine asked blankly.

Nancy Kelsey stamped into their midst, her face red, tears on her cheeks. "I hope it poisons 'em."

"Come on." John Reilly reached out and pulled at Bidwell's sleeve. "They can't gallop that stock forever. Let's get after them."

Kelsey grunted. "Right." He turned to his wife. "Get things together. This ain't so bad as that. We'll catch some of that stock, I swear we will. Come on, boys." He grabbed a rope from the tailgate of his wagon, which they had been using for a slaughtering table.

John Reilly turned to Catharine. "Stay here. We'll be back before dark. Make a fire." The others were already going off down the slope after Bartleson and the herd, and he broke into a run after them.

The two women stood there, watching them thrash away through the brush. The baby was cooing and crowing in the shade under the Kelseys' wagon. As the sounds of the men died away the child's murmurs became the loudest noise in the desert.

Nancy said, "We should have cut up Bartleson along with his cows."

"There isn't anything to eat, then," Catharine said. She bent and picked up the baby and joggled her, as if she were crying and had to be soothed. Nancy sat down on the ground, staring away to the west.

Catharine washed the baby in the spring water, as Nancy had shown her how to do, and Nancy came over and sat there, her hands idle in her lap. The sun sank toward the ragged edge of the world. In the blue twilight the men came back.

Nancy with her sharp eyes saw them first, and yelled. The men were only little black figures straggling back across the desert, driving ahead of them a horse, a mule, four oxen. Some of the beasts still had packs on their backs. The women watched them come. Catharine looked for her husband among them, and then counted the men, and counted them again.

"John isn't there," she said.

Nancy said, "He must be riding scout or something." She put her arm around Catharine's waist.

Catharine took two steps toward the ragged little train of men and beasts that struggled through the sagebrush. Her heart began to pound. She lifted her eyes and scanned the empty, hazy desert. He was not there. And then, as Bidwell climbed the slope toward the camp, he lifted his face and saw her, and the expression that came over him hit her like a blow.

"John." She broke into a run down the slope.

Bidwell reached for her and caught her and held her. "I'm sorry," he said. "Oh, Mrs. Reilly, I'm so sorry."

"What?" she said stupidly, watching the other men, and now, as Kelsey came toward her, and his brother, driving the stock, she saw what they had draped across the back of the horse.

"Oh, please." She put out her hands. "Oh, please —"

Bidwell held her; she struggled to free herself, and he held her fast. "He fell into a gorge. His neck's broke. He died right off."

"Oh, God —" She tore out of his grasp and ran down the slope, heedless of the brush, of the broken ground, and flung herself against the horse that carried John Reilly.

His head hung down the side of the horse, the long blond curls matted. He was cold. She jerked her hands back from the dead flesh.

"Oh, God," she said again. She felt, suddenly, the world spinning away. She turned toward Nancy Kelsey, beside her. "What am I going to do now?"

"Hush," Nancy said, touching her. Stiffly Catharine put her hands out again and laid them on John Reilly.

Bidwell said, "We'll take care of you, Cathy. We're all together in this now."

She shut her eyes. Nobody was going to take care of anybody. Here in this indifferent, barren country they would all vanish, and nobody would even know what had happened to them. She felt herself gone already, nothing left but the husk, her soul and spirit trailing after her husband.

Bidwell said quietly, "We got to bury him."

"I have a shovel," Kelsey said.

"Cathy," Nancy was saying. "Cathy, come sit down."

"I'm all right," she said blindly. "I'm all right." She stumbled away tamely in the other woman's hands, although she wondered why she bothered doing anything, now, except die.

With the shovel and their hands, they made a hole in the stubborn, waterless soil, hardly large enough to lay him in, and they stood there around him, nobody saying anything. Nancy was crying. Catharine tore her eyes from her husband's body and looked up; the men were watching her, their hands lowered to their sides. They would not cover him until she was ready.

"Wait." Her throat hurt. She went over to the ox that held the last of their life together, and took the sketchpad out of the pack. At the grave she knelt down and slipped the pad under his head like a pillow.

Nancy asked, "Don't you want to keep that, Cathy?"

"I might lose it," she said. She stroked his hair. He had been so good, so honest, and she had loved him so much; it was not fair. She bent over him, doubled up, stuck in that pain. Nancy

Kelsey lifted her and held her. They heaped dirt and rocks on John Reilly and started away over the desert.

They had recovered none of the meat they had so carefully cut and jerked; Bartleson had gotten away with all of it. They had a little water, but that was soon gone also. In the afternoon they came on a little spring. The water reeked, and on its surface a sheen of color floated. The horse refused the water, but the mule and the oxen drank. Catharine took a single mouthful. Afterward her throat burned and her stomach heaved. Her mind was like a sore, a wound, that throbbed with every breath.

Kelsey had gone off circling through the brush around them, and now he came back. "There's a trail up here," he said, his voice keen. "Let's go."

They plodded after him. Nancy's face was grim, her eyes sunk into pits above her cheekbones. Catharine took the baby from her. Almost at once her arms ached; her legs already ached, her head ached.

The trail that Kelsey had found was worn deep into the dry ground; it was a rut no wider than Catharine's foot. All around them was the tangled brush, its small, hard leaves powdered with dust. Driving the animals ahead of them, they trudged into the west, where now the sun laid long streamers of color over a few faint, light clouds. The baby began to cry in a low moan; Nancy took her and gave her the breast. Nobody spoke.

The mule stopped. Kelsey went around behind it and hit it with a stick, and the mule staggered on for three steps and stopped again. Kelsey lifted the stick, his face contorted, and beat the mule over the bony hip and side. The beast shuddered but did not move.

"Kill it," Bidwell said, his voice a dry croak. "We can eat it."

"I'll get some wood," Nancy said.

"No. Save it." Kelsey lifted the stick and beat the mule until the stick cracked, and the dying beast dragged itself forward again, its head so low that its slack lips nearly touched the dust.

"Ben," Nancy said, "we have to eat." She was sitting down,

the baby at her breast; she pulled the front of her dress over its head.

"Keep going," Kelsey said.

Catharine held out her hands to Nancy to help her up. The baby was still nursing hard, even as her mother stumbled to her feet. Upright, Nancy said, "There's no milk left, there's nothing coming out." Her voice was quiet. She walked after her husband, the baby still in her arms, pulling at her breast.

The baby would die, too. Catharine gripped her fists against her chest. The baby would die next. Something in her contracted, drawing in, away from feeling. She forced herself back up to the surface.

They struggled on, going up, going down, following a dry wash until its course bent away from the west, and then they pushed off through mats of sagebrush, trudging up a shallow slope. Their animals plodded along ahead of them, the mule staggering, its muzzle skimming the ground. The long sundown light shone in their faces. Overhead a vulture appeared, circling, and then another.

"Is it waiting for the mule or us?" Catharine asked, and to her amazement Bidwell laughed.

Kelsey said, "Let's look for a place to camp." His lips were cracked, and when he spoke blood oozed into the dust on his beard. With the coming of night the wind was rising, sharp in their faces.

One of the oxen lifted its head and lowed. Bidwell said stupidly, "What's that?" The horse flung up its head, snuffling the wind. The ox lumbered heavily into motion. Its cavernous nostrils flared. The other oxen quickened also, and even the mule began to walk along at a brisk pace. The horse broke into a trot.

In a raw-throated voice Kelsey said, "They smell water," and began to run after them. Catharine turned to Nancy, and holding her arm and half leaning on her, half carrying her, she scrambled after Kelsey and Bidwell and the oxen down a little slope studded with brush and came out on a tiny trickle of a river.

It was more a long swamp than a stream. The water ran so

slow and shallow and full of sand that nobody could find a place to drink. The horse sank in up to its fetlocks, put its muzzle to the shimmering surface, and sucked up a long draft. Kneeling beside the horse, Bidwell dug a hole. Rapidly it filled with muddy water, and Catharine flopped down next to him and like him scooped up handfuls and drank, the fine silt clinging to her tongue and teeth.

She splashed the water on her arms, on her face; it smelled, but the taste was sweet, and she drank more of it, patient now, willing to let the dust settle to the bottom of the hole, savoring each sip.

Bidwell stood up. "Now, kill the mule," he said. A moment later Kelsey's gun went off.

4 ⚑ THE NIGHT WAS OVERWHELMING, enormous, the sky spattered with silver fire, the wind a continual buffet, its voice sometimes a mutter, sometimes a fretful whine, sometimes a shriek that drove even the men to huddle together. Whenever the wind roared high Nancy piled more wood on the fire, as if she could frighten something away.

Her cheeks were sunken. When she gave her breast to the baby it looked like an empty sack. Cuddling the baby in her arms, she lay down to sleep beside her husband, and he gathered her toward him and cradled her head on his thigh.

Catharine sat before the fire, wearing her jacket and John's, her feet almost in the fire. The people around her seemed farther away than Boston. She could not make real to herself that John had died; she caught herself thinking of things to tell him, listening for his voice, looking off into the desert wondering where he was. Afraid that he would not be able to find them, in the dark.

Bidwell sank down beside her. "Pretty miserable country." He gripped her arm. "You doing all right, Cathy?"

"I can't get used to it," she said. "He was so alive."

He said, "I liked him a lot, and he was a good, solid man; we needed him."

Ben Kelsey sat on the far side of the fire, chewing on a twig. One arm lay across his sleeping wife's shoulders.

His brother tramped over and sank down next to him. "Them mountains look just as far now as they did ten days ago."

"We gotta keep a watch out," Bidwell said. "The fire will draw the Indians for sure."

"Maybe the Indians can point us the way out of here," Kelsey's brother said, and laughed.

Kelsey rounded on him. "You got a laugh in you still, do you? We're dyin' here, one by one, ain't nothin' I can do but watch my wife and child die, and you're laughin'."

"Hey, now," Bidwell said. Kelsey sank down again, his head drooping, muttering to himself.

Catharine said, "I'll help you keep watch."

"Don't you mind about that now, Cathy," Bidwell said. "That's men's business."

"Please," she said, "I have to do something. I can't just sit here."

He put his hand on her arm again. Across the fire Kelsey said, "What difference does it make? Let the bastards come if they want. They'll pick our bones anyway."

Bidwell leaned toward him. "Come on, Ben. You got a wife, a baby, you have to stiffen up. All of you. We can make it. We got rid of the soft stuff when we got rid of Bartleson. There's nothing left here but real hard hickory. If we stick together, we'll make it." He turned to Catharine, his eyes bright, anxious. "Come on, Cathy. You gonna let John die another time?"

She jerked her head up, startled and angry. Bidwell's face shone with desperation, but what he had said struck her deep. If she died too, John Reilly was forever lost. She put out her hand to John Bidwell. "I'll help. Do you want me to stand the first watch?"

His face eased with a smile, and he got her hand and gripped it tightly. "Good girl. What about you, Ben? You take the second watch?"

Kelsey lifted his head, his eyes shadowed in the firelight. After a moment he wiped his hand over his mouth. "Yeah, I'll take the second watch." His voice was listless.

"Good," Bidwell said, and got to his feet, reaching out to help Catharine stand. "I'll show you what to do."

For days they followed the river westward. Mostly the stream was a swath of waterlogged sand through which the current was visible mainly as a faint wrinkling of the surface. Coarse reeds sprouted up along the banks, and thickets of brush. There were black crickets everywhere. Bidwell and Kelsey tried to stalk the lanky, speckled sage grouse; the two men shot several times but killed only one bird.

They chewed up the last of the mule meat; they drank the turbid water of the river and looked over their remaining beasts, wondering which to kill next. Wondering what to eat when the last of the cattle were gone.

Late one day the river took them by an Indian village. At first Catharine did not know what it was. The Indians had gone, perhaps fleeing from the whites long before the whites even knew they were there. On one bank were a dozen little humps that turned out to be huts, frameworks of reeds covered with woven grass; a fire still burned in the middle of the village, and Bidwell, on a quick rampage, found a basket with handfuls of shelled nuts and a skinned rabbit hanging by its heels from a pole. They flung the rabbit onto the fire and devoured the nuts, and then shared the meat, half raw; blood ran down their chins. The oxen and the horse fell to eating the village's grass huts.

The huts seemed tiny, too small for anyone to live in. Catharine wondered if the Indians were small. Into her mind leapt the image of them no bigger than rabbits, hiding around her in the grass. She looked down at the frail bones in her hand and shut her eyes, her stomach clenching.

The river ran shallower and the sand stiffened under their feet until at last the water disappeared and they were walking along a dry wash. They went on toward the west. In the hazy distance the edge of the world was a saw-toothed line of mountains. The land rose and fell in waves under the tough pelt of the sage-brush, and the settlers struggled up one side of each ridge and then down the other side, over the gravel fans of abandoned riverbeds and past banks of sand worn hollow by the wind. The sun was inescapable, a white glare blasting into their eyes.

From each high ridge, through the shimmering clear desert air, they looked out toward the mountains, but the mountains seemed no closer. In between still lay the bleak high desert, here and there patched with the gray-green of the sagebrush, more often only bare sand and rock. There was no water, and no game at all.

One morning, from the top of a ridge, they saw a line of tall trees ahead of them, such as grew along rivers, and gladly and desperately they plunged on, wasting their strength in a reckless charge toward the promised water. As they got closer the trees shrank, falling back into the ground as if the desert were eating them from the roots up, and when the settlers reached them, the tall trees were only a stand of sagebrush on the crest of another ridge.

The group stood there, knee-deep in the illusion of a forest, and looked out over the same world they had looked out over that morning. The baby began to moan. Nancy gave her the breast, but Sarah pulled once and spat out the nipple and cried in a harsh, painful voice, and Nancy turned and thrust the infant into her husband's arms.

"Here — you take her, I can't do anything for her." She sat down on the ground, put her hands over her face, and began to cry.

"Let's go," Kelsey said. He settled the baby in the crook of his arm. She was still moaning. His mouth curling down at the corners, he looked at Bidwell.

Bidwell said, "Maybe we can carry her."

"No," Nancy said. "I don't want to go. I'm tired. I want to sleep."

"Come on, Nancy," Kelsey said, and nudged her, and his brother banged the ground with his stick and herded the animals off. As if his stick had drawn some protest from the earth, there was a distant hollow boom.

"Did you hear that?" Bidwell wheeled. "That was a gun."

"A gun." Kelsey turned and stared toward the northwest. "Sounded like thunder to me, sort of."

Catharine stooped down beside Nancy, her arms around her bent knees. "Are you all right? Can I help?"

Nancy lowered her hands. "I can't stand to see her hurting, is all." Her eyes were red-rimmed but dry, like raw blisters. Catharine leaned toward her, trying to draw off some of her pain.

Bidwell said, "Sure sounded like a gun to me, some kind of big gun."

"Sure."

"Course I was the one who said there was a River of Good Luck."

Kelsey said, "You got to be right sometime. Whatever it was, let's head toward it." Carrying the fussing baby, he started off obliquely down the slope, kicking loose little showers of stones as he angled across the dry hillside. Nancy reached out to Catharine and gripped her hand, and they rose and went after him down into the ocean of the sage.

Perhaps it had been thunder. In the afternoon they walked beneath a roof of cloud, the wind whined, and suddenly large tangled flakes of snow began to drift down from the sky, big as baskets. Catharine gasped; she tried to catch the first flakes in her hands. The snow melted as it reached the ground.

Soon it stopped falling at all. The clouds hovered over them.

Cold, edged in ice, the wind blew up into their faces and stiffened Catharine's cheeks. Her hands were cold, and her teeth
began to chatter. Her feet felt like lifeless lumps; maybe she was
dying from the bottom up.

She could not die. She carried John Reilly along inside her.
She had to get to the end of this.

They tried putting Nancy and the baby on Kelsey's horse, but
the brute stopped and would not move, and she got off and
walked. Catharine tried to hold the baby for her, but the child
knew the difference in their touch and wailed until her mother
took her back.

Late in the afternoon Kelsey's horse caved in. It thrashed
once on its side, its legs milling as if it were running, and then
lay still. Its eyes were dull. Kelsey came up with his gun and
shot it once through the head.

"Get some wood." He pulled the knife from his belt; Bidwell
and Jack Kelsey had already fallen on the horse like tigers. Bidwell plunged his knife into the sunken belly and ripped open
the hide, and the warm, rich stench of blood flowed out. Jack
Kelsey knelt to put his lips to the stream of blood.

Catharine's stomach roiled. She jerked her gaze away from
the men hacking apart the horse. Nancy sat down where she
stood, holding the baby, and Catharine went to the ox with her
pack on it and got a blanket for them. Nancy stared away into
the air, her eyes sunken into grayish pits in her head.

The smell of raw meat reached Catharine's nostrils. Her belly
convulsed again, throwing up a bitter bile into her throat. Her
legs hurt. She staggered into the brush to find firewood.

"Nancy." The harsh cry hurt her throat; she plunged forward
and fell to her knees. Under a tangle of brush lay a thin puddle
of snow. She tore at it with her hands. "Nancy!" Pocked with
holes, the snow was painfully hard to the touch and cut her
fingertips when she tried to break the crust. Jack Kelsey stumbled over and sank down beside her. They dished up the snow
into a pot, scrambled off to find more, gathered a whole potful
of dirty, crunchy snow.

Bidwell had already built a ragged-looking fire. In the first
weak flames they scorched strips of the horse's heart. The

melted snow made a cupful of sweet water. Nancy, her face gaunt, her eyes like black pits, chewed and chewed the soft meat and put bits into the baby's mouth. Catharine could not see if the baby swallowed anything. Nancy drank all the water, not asking permission. No one grudged it to her.

Kelsey said, "We got to cut up this meat and save it."

Catharine looked around at the others, squatting by the fire. She could not get close enough to warm herself; her back was frozen, her hands were stiff, although she hung them almost in the flames. She said, "I'll get more water."

Kelsey said, "Take the pot." He stepped past the fire to the horse, drawing his knife again. His brother was already carving strings of meat away from the horse's ribs. Bidwell stropped his knife on his trousers. For the first time Catharine noticed how the cloth hung in pleats around his legs. There seemed no more meat on him than there was on the horse, who lay there dead, its belly a cave, its white ribs like rafters.

She went back into the brush, looking for more snow. In their first quick foray they seemed to have found almost all of it. Here and there below a bush she came on a damp handful. In the shade of the next rise, snow clung to a heap of round, smooth stones like cobblestones. With her forefinger she scraped the white crust from each separate stone into the pot.

Her hand was wet. Patiently she licked it dry.

In the brush around her she heard the shrill cries of sagehens warning of her approach. A shadow like crossed swordblades drifted across the rumpled gray-blue surface of the sagebrush: a vulture, circling in on the dead horse. On the dying people. There was no snow under the brush on the next slope, which faced west, into the sun. She walked on, through a lowland where the brush grew thinly.

Her nose itched with the smell of burning brush, the stink of scorched meat, and she looked back and saw the smoke of their fire rising dark and thick into the air. She would use that for a marker, to keep from losing her way. Putting it directly behind her, she walked forward into the desert.

Above her the sky was pale blue, but to the west the clouds still lay thick and low. She went that way, carrying the pot with both hands. The iron was so cold that she wrapped her skirt around her hands to hold it. The ground rose steeply under her feet, and the horizon loomed much closer. She climbed the ridge, each step higher than the one before.

Beyond that ridge was another. She stopped, gathering strength, getting her breath back. She felt the vast, indifferent land around her as if it pulled the strength from her. The country before her was folded and rolled into hills and deep gullies, where even the sagebrush grew sparsely. The clouds were bundled back against the mountain peaks. She started down the slope, working diagonally across it; in places along it shards of rock like strange tombstones erupted from the sand, gypsy colors, red and gold. The sun was blazing again; the air rippled.

The ground at the foot of the slope was bare, overlaid with a hard white crust; there was nothing to catch or shelter a drift of snow. She wished she had brought some of the meat. Her belly felt turned inside out. Look for trees, which grew only where there was water. Look for insects, for the trails of animals. Ahead the white earth gave way to a sheer bank, which she climbed.

She plunged straight on through the scattered brush, her legs rubbery. Her mouth and throat hurt, and she drank the table-spoon of water in the bottom of the pot. Her mind swam with images of water, cool and wet. A River of Good Luck. She staggered along to the west, toward the clouds, now breaking up; there would be no more snow. The pot in her hand weighed like an anchor. If she put it down there would be nothing to carry water in. She thought of Nancy's baby, of her wordless, helpless suffering. She climbed another long ridge, stooped as she went, sweeping her gaze under the tufts of brush, the stubs of rocks. A gleam of white drew her through brush that tangled in her dress and gripped her like an enemy, but when she reached what she thought was snow, it was only sand.

The light was bleeding out of the sky. Soon she would have to turn and go back, with her empty pot, her failure. Stubbornly she fought on to the west, through waist-high brush, looking for a riverbed or an animal trail.

A tough, crooked branch of the sage caught her by an ankle, and she tripped. She fell so hard that her senses were jogged, and she lay still, numb, her head refusing to work. Slowly her strength collected.

When she got up she thought she had turned around, somehow; there was the column of smoke in front of her. She made herself straighten up; her mind was dazed, her thinking slow. She was still facing west. The smoke was west of her.

After a moment she turned and looked behind her, the way she had come. In the darkening sky, there was no trace of Kelsey's smoke. She wondered if she had circled blindly through the wilderness, come around behind her friends. Looking forward again, she picked out the thin streamer of smoke, fading away into the twilight, and gathered herself and started toward it.

It was farther away than she had thought, or perhaps it had been a mirage. She climbed another ridge and walked across the broad, flat floor of a wash. Somewhere off to the south, the vibrating night-welcoming call of a wolf spiraled into the air. At the foot of the next slope she stopped, tired, the pot clutched in her hands.

Overhead, now, a single star shone. The wind was rising, sweeping along through the wash behind her, lifting loose dust, crying over the bare rock. She turned and looked back again. It would be hard to find her friends in the dark. A sudden wave of panic struck her; she was lost, alone, hungry, and very cold. When she faced forward again, looking up at the climb ahead of her, her heart quailed.

She had to go on. She could not stop, she could not die. She struggled to strengthen herself as she had before with thoughts of John Reilly, of Nancy's baby, but they slipped off the surface of her failing mind. Yet she could not die. Let them all die; she would live, keep going, come somehow to the end. Slipping on the loose, brittle soil, grabbing hold of the brush around her to pull herself along, she started to climb.

A branch whipped her across the face. Her feet lost their grip, and she fell all the way down again to the bottom of the slope, in a rubble of stones and dirt. The pot came rolling down after her, making a terrific clatter, and cracked her hard on the ankle. There was dirt in her mouth. She tried to get up again.

More dirt cascaded down around her. There was a sudden racket above her. She pushed herself up on hands and knees and fought to raise her head. Something big was coming down at her in a rush.

She flinched, and it grabbed her. "Sweet Jesus, it's a woman. A white woman."

She lifted up the enormous weight of her head and looked into pale blue eyes and a dark face that split now into a wide, wicked, reckless grin.

"Pretty one, too, I'll bet. Luke! Bring some water." She stirred, trying to tell him about the others, and he gathered her up effortlessly into his arms. "Whoa, now, little baby, the old man's got you." Exhausted, she let his strength take her.

5 ✠ LIEUTENANT FRÉMONT stared morosely at the bleak brown slope that rose sheer away from him, shutting off the sky to the west. "Find an Indian."

"I ain't seen the feather off an Indian since we left Klamath," said Basil Lajeunesse. Tall and thin, the scout slouched like an old man in his saddle. "Where you want me to go, Lieutenant? I been up and down every goddamn canyon on this mountain. There ain't no way through. We got to go farther south."

Frémont's gaze lifted, beyond this first, immediate barrier, to the distant scarps, the high, barren ridges of rock that shut off half the sky to the west. He had to pass through this wall, and he had to do it soon, and yet he could not find even the first trace of a trail. He shortened his visual range to take in the scout frowning down at him from his horse. "Find an Indian," he said again, and waved his hand toward the mountains. "Get going."

"Whatever you say, Lieutenant." Basil's voice rattled with exasperation. He rode off across the meadow, toward the gorge where the river ran down.

Lieutenant Frémont marched with military precision in the other direction.

Before him lay the meadow, a broad sweep of grass, wind-blown and sweet-smelling, that covered a bench of some sixty or seventy acres. The river rushed along its southeastern edge, its cold, foaming water spread in a quick green swath over the rocks of the wash. Beyond that a thin stretch of grass fed on some last trace of moisture, and then the merciless sagebrush desert took over.

Frémont's eighteen men had made their campfire on the sunny edge of the bench, where the rising slope sheltered them from the blast of the wind. To its hubs in grass, their mountain howitzer waited in the sun nearby, its tarnished barrel stuck into the air. Their mules and horses were scattered over the ground along the river. Frémont stopped as he came close and ran his gaze over them. What he saw made him draw a deep breath.

These animals were done for. Their heads sagged, too heavy for their hollow necks. Their ribs propped their hides up, and their hips stuck out like doorknobs. Two of them coughed in the brief moment he stood looking them over, and every one stood awkwardly in some position that favored sore feet and ruined legs; the only one that moved at all limped with every step.

The lieutenant looked off past the howitzer, toward the campfire, and saw the same conditions among his men. All but a few were slumped in their blankets by the fire, although there was still daylight and work to be done. They were thin and weak and spiritless.

Somebody yelled, "Hey! That's Kit. Kit's come back."

The men around the fire stirred out of their dull silence. Frémont himself squinted toward the east, out over the shallow swing of the river. Beyond, the land rose steep and barren into a wave of hills. He put up his hand to shade his eyes. Out there in a fold of the vast rolling plain, among the silver-green of the sage, the small, dark figure of a horseman was riding out of the mouth of a draw. That would be Kit Carson, his chief scout and best hunter, who had gone off two days before to find some game and more grass. After him came another tiny figure.

And another. Frémont's frown deepened.

The men around the fire had seen them, too, and now one gave a yell of disbelief. "Hey, lookee there."

"What's all that?"

Kit had a horse, and Luke Maxwell, who was with him, had a horse, but across the broken, brush-covered valley before Frémont came many more beasts than that, some oxen, and more people, too. The men around the campfire were walking down toward the river, their voices bubbling up. The first of the strange oxen were reaching the river, their sides sunken, their bellies tucked up to their loins. In their stretched walk, their swaying heads, he recognized a desperate energy on the verge of giving out. They plodded out toward the water and plunged their muzzles into it. Frémont went a little closer. Kit on his bay mare rode up to the top of the eastern bank of the river.

He had someone behind him on the mare, and now this person slid to the ground and went to help another climb down into the river. A grunt exploded from Lieutenant Frémont. Those two were women.

His mind went in opposite directions: first, a surge of rage that any man would subject members of the tender and gentle sex to such hardship; second, a leap of the heart that after months of hardship he was now to have the company of members of the tender and gentle sex.

His stride lengthened. By the time he reached the near bank of the river, he was half running, and he was not alone, as the rest of his company rushed forward, roaring with new vigor, to welcome the first white women they had seen in months.

At the river's edge one of the women waded out into the stream, her skirts floating; with her hands she reached out and poked the bubbles of cloth down below the surface of the water. Behind her the other woman gave the bundle in her arms to a

big man with a black beard and forged out into the rushing
stream.

Kit rode his horse in after them, moving along above them
to break the current. The newcomers' oxen were shouldering
through the deeper water and now reached the shallows below
the bench, and with a long, low bawl they put dry ground under
their hoofs and began to struggle up toward the grass and the
other cattle.

Frémont's lips tightened. A tingle of alarm passed down his
spine. He turned and cast a wide look across the meadow behind him; his own mules and horses had already consumed
most of the grass here. There was nothing for these beasts to
eat.

His men were yelling, high-spirited and excited for the first
time in weeks. They broke from their line along the top of the
bank and rushed down to meet the women as they waded
through the river, to their thighs now in the rushing blue-green
water.

The first of them walked up out of the water. Her hair swung
loose, a long black tumble of curls over her shoulders. She wore
a ragged man's coat and huge boots like buckets on her feet.
Her dress, soaked through, clung to her body. On the bank the
line of Frémont's men all together gave a long, lusty call of
greeting.

She came straight at the lieutenant, shivering. Her hands
clutched the dripping coat around her. She looked gaunt and
exhausted. Her cheeks were red from the cold wind. Frémont
leaned down from the top of the bank to help her, and she
looked up, taking his hand, pulling herself up the bank, and his
gaze met enormous green eyes, flecked with paler hazel, in a
face thin as a waif's.

"Thank you, sir," she said. "God bless you for being here."

Her voice was low, flavored with the broad vowels of New
England. A cultured voice. He said, "Miss, I do believe I'd come
the whole way all over again just to be able to make your acquaintance."

"Well," she said, "I don't think I would." She turned away

at once, going toward the fire. The men trailed after her, rushing to get her warm, to feed her.

Kit jogged his horse up the bank. "Got you a few more problems, Lieutenant," he said, and laughed. Swinging his mare around, he loped out into the meadow.

Basil Lajeunesse was coming back, trotting up from the direction of the western canyon. He stopped by Frémont. "What's going on? Well, now." He was looking at the black-haired woman standing by the fire, eating a half-raw strip of mule meat. "Where did that come from?" His voice was a croon.

"Kit found her," said Frémont.

"Oh, that figures," said Basil. "Still want me out scouting, Lieutenant?"

"I'll send Kit," Frémont said.

"Good." Basil went to join the rest by the fire.

The brass howitzer sat in its iron-bound wooden trucks a little way from the campfire. When Kit saw green-eyed Catharine Reilly walking over that way, he got himself over there too.

He had saved her from the desert, which gave him a proprietary interest. She had no man. She was gaunt as a longhorn, but she had beautiful eyes; he thought that when she ate right she was probably a looker. He came up on the far side of the howitzer, and she started in again thanking him, in her low, pleasant voice, and he let her, grinning at her, enjoying the speckled green eyes and the sound of her voice.

He leaned his forearms on the howitzer. "Somewhere in there maybe you told me your name, but I don't remember it."

"Catharine Reilly," she said, and smiled, looking tired.

"Christopher Carson," he said. "Everybody calls me Kit. What d'they call you?"

"Cathy," she said.

"Cathy. I don't like that much." She had a nice mouth, too, with wide, well-shaped lips. "That's a city girl's name. You ain't in the city no more. I'm gonna call you Cat." He leaned a little closer to her, thinking about kissing that big, sweet mouth. "Cat, Kit. Got that?"

She was watching him steadily, with a smile she was trying not to let him see. The green eyes glinted. "Oh, yes."

"Good." He jerked his head slightly toward the campfire and the other men. "You somebody's sister? One of these goats got you spoken for?"

At that the smile vanished like a candle blown out. Her face shrank into a haggard grief. She looked away, toward the east. "My husband died."

He said, "I'm sorry."

"He fell over a cliff," she said, toward the river. "His neck broke."

He reached out and turned up the collar on the heavy, shapeless coat she wore. "Hey, now. Don't cry, now, I'll help you."

She said, "You already did, Kit. Thanks." But she did not look at him; she went on staring at the river.

Lieutenant Frémont was striding up toward them, shoulders squared in a paradeground bearing, his hands tucked behind his back. Kit straightened, getting his hands on his side of the howitzer.

Frémont smiled. "Well, Kit, I've always said you could find anything in the desert, but you've surprised even me this time."

Kit said, "Cat Reilly, this is Lieutenant John Charles Frémont, U.S. Army Topo-something Corps."

Frémont moved in like a cow horse, his shoulder to Kit, edging between him and the girl. He said, "A pleasure, Miss Reilly."

"Mrs. Reilly," she said. She glanced past him at Kit, her gaze unreadable.

"Well," Frémont said heartily. "A pleasure, in any case. I detect a Massachusetts accent, do I?"

"Boston," she said; she sounded tired. Kit went away to take care of his horses.

"Well, Mrs. Reilly," Frémont said, uncertain. "And where are you trying to get to, out here in this godforsaken wilderness?"

"California," she said. She lifted her eyes, looking up at the mountains behind him, and then lowered her gaze to him.

"What are you doing here? Didn't you say you were in the army?" She looked doubtfully at his buckskin coat.

"Topographical Corps, as Kit pretends not to know. We're mapping the West, so that settlers like you can find your way out here."

Her mouth kinked with some dry amusement. "Really? You know your way around, do you?"

Frémont cleared his throat. "We will when we're done. We've already been up to Oregon. Tried to get down to California from there, through the Klamath country, but that's impossible." He shook his head. "It's as if there's an enchantment around California, you know, as there are in tales, some spell on it we can't get through." He smiled at her, apologizing for this fancy.

"Now you're trying to get over the mountains? So are we." She sounded eager. She lifted her gaze again to the harsh rock barrier that loomed beyond them.

"Kit will find a trail," Frémont said. "He always does."

"Can we go with you?" she asked.

"I —" He slid his hands up the flat, oily front of his hunting shirt, wishing he were wearing his uniform coat, which would impress her more. "This is an army expedition, Mrs. Reilly. But I suppose, under the circumstances . . ."

"We'll help," she said. "We'll do our part of the work."

"Of course," he said. "We aren't going to abandon you in the desert."

She smiled at him, and his chest expanded. Suddenly he wanted her to know that he was more than a buckskin bumpkin like Kit.

He said, "And we're far from Washington. Here, I suppose, I'm the general."

"Well armed, too." She laid her hand on the dingy brass barrel of the howitzer. "Did you shoot this off yesterday? We heard something."

"Yes, we did. It lifts the spirits of the men. And keeps off the Indians." He slapped the howitzer. "A little firepower puts the fear of God into them. God and the United States."

"Virtually synonymous," she said.

She was teasing him. He warmed under the gentle feminine
attention. "Actually, when General Kearny — my commander — found out I had this gun, he tried to take it away from
me. I left early to avoid getting the order to return it."

Her eyes widened and her long mouth twitched. "Lieutenant.
How bold. Won't you be in trouble when you're home again?"

Casual, unperturbed, the general here, he shrugged one
shoulder. "I have powerful friends. My wife's father is Thomas
Hart Benton."

Her black eyebrows rose. "Senator Benton? Of the Senate
Foreign Relations Committee?"

Gratified, he smiled at her. "The same."

"Well," she said, "that's interesting." Her look was sharp
with lively, unwomanly curiosity.

"Do you know Senator Benton?"

"No, no. But my grandfather was the ranking Whig on the
committee for years. My grandfather was in the Senate." She
shrugged her shoulders, her body shifting, going back to the
main purpose. "As you say, that doesn't matter here. How are
you planning to go over the mountains?"

He twitched, irritated at her insistence; she should leave
things like this to the men, but she was staring at him, expecting
answers. He cleared his throat again. "However Kit finds us a
way to go."

"Good," she said, and her gaze left him and scanned the
meadow; she was looking for Kit.

Annoyed, Frémont searched his mind for something to say
that would bring her attention back to him. Then, off by the
fire, the baby let out a howl.

She smiled at him. "Thank you, Lieutenant," she said, and
went off toward the baby. Frémont leaned on the howitzer,
staring after her, and then turned again and looked up at the
mountains.

Catharine bounced the baby. "Ooooh, Sarah." She rubbed the
tip of her nose on the tiny cold tip of the baby's nose, and the
child giggled.

John Bidwell sank down beside her. "All right, Cathy, everybody's talking to you. What's going on here?"

She laid the baby in her lap. "They're a bunch of army mapmakers. They're trying to get over the mountains, and they'll take us with them."

Ben Kelsey and his brother dropped down on their heels on the other side of her from Bidwell. Nancy had gone down to the river to wash the baby's clothes out. Kelsey said, "Look, these fellahs ain't in any better shape than we are. Do they know where they're going?"

Catharine said, "No."

Bidwell's fingers scrabbled in his beard. "The ones I've talked to say they've been wandering around here for weeks trying to find some way west."

Kelsey grunted. "I say we keep going on our own."

"Where?" Catharine said.

His head twisted to stare up at the blank, enormous mountains. Bidwell gave a snort of weary amusement. "Yeah, you see. Now, look, the one scout was sharp, you know, finding Cathy and then finding us. As long as they're willing to take us along, let's go."

Catharine nodded. "I don't see we have much choice."

Kelsey glanced at his brother, who laughed and said, "I ain't stopping here, that's for sure."

"Right," Kelsey said. "But we stick together, we take care of each other, first and last."

Catharine hugged the baby. "That's what's gotten us this far," she said.

6   RUST-RED AND YELLOW and creamy white, the cliff to his left lifted straight to the hard blue sky; it dribbled small stones and dirt like an old man drooling. Where the deep shadow lay, there was a patch of snow, frosted red with dust.

The cold was sharp. Maybe it was going to snow again. Out there over the slope to his right, which ran more gradually to the horizon and lay in the sun, a high-flying hawk wheeled in the flat blue space.

Ahead the canyon pinched to a crack, the river bolting through in a white crash. He swung his leg over the mare's neck, slid to the ground, and walked in behind a loose jumble of boulders, where a dent in the cliff face marked a trail. The rock smelled slightly sour. At eye level a vein of glittery white ran through the roan-red stone. In the still cold between the biggest boulder and the raw cliff face was more snow, crystal-line, pocked with holes from water dripping down into it.

At the very edge, where Kit was about to put his foot, the snow was indented in a curve that he traced with a forefinger. The ice was cold and smooth where something had pressed it firmly down when it was loose snow. He stepped there; his foot fit perfectly into the curve in the snow.

He went quickly up the trail, glad of the footprint; Indians didn't go to nowhere, not even Diggers. On all fours he scaled the last vertical stretch of the cliff face to a ledge, where he stood up and looked out to the west.

The land broke all up and down, the sheer, eastward-facing rock cliffs falling away into longer, flatter slopes, each ridge climbing steadily higher into a massive crown of crags and plummeting gorges through which there was very little rea-son to expect a trail. Yet he had to find a way; he and his party were running out of time and chances. He knew — not in the way Frémont guessed, with his instruments measuring like some doctor, but because Kit knew this country better than any other white man alive — that south of here the mountains were higher yet and the desert dry as the sand in an hour-glass.

The ghost of a trail he had followed up the cliff led off over the jagged, dusty rocks before him. He slid back down the way he had come, collected his mare, and circled around the cliff and scrambled through a ravine to pick up the trail he had seen beyond the gorge. The river's bed widened out a little, forming a pocket where the sun had warmed the air and some grass grew. In the mud along the edge of the river he found tracks of rabbits and birds and part of another human print.

They certainly knew he was here. Probably they were watching him. He went along the river's gorge a while, letting the mare pick her way through tumbled red rocks and tufts of grass, and again the cliff face closed against him. The river bounded out of a deep cleft in a rock that rose up straight into the sky; at the top a single pine tree sprouted, a twisted trunk, a single crazy curling branch with a tuft of needles. He worked his way up and down the foot of this cliff for a while and found no way through.

Giving up, he moved off to the north, taking what the land gave him, skirting the slopes, following a dry wash up the side of a pan of gravel strewn with the rubble of an old landslide. Sprays of grass and brush sprouted like stray hairs on the rock and sand. Here again, in a loose sandy slope, he crossed signs of game, and after an hour's patient stalking and waiting, mostly waiting, he shot a rabbit.

In the draw above the gravel pan he made a small fire, putting on enough greasewood to make smoke, and spiked the rabbit's pieces on sticks and hung them over the coals. The mare grazed on a few stalks of late grass. The air was tingling now, sharp with coming snow. The sky was still mostly blue, but some big clouds were sliding down over the mountains and drifting into the east, piles of white, darker at the bottom, trailing their shadows after them like skirts. He sat down with his back to the rocks and waited.

The draw opened out before him onto the desert. From here he could see all the way out, past the little fire and the mare nosing up the last of the grass, down over the sweep of the gravel, and over land that rolled off to the east in long, rolling waves. The sagebrush gave it mostly a silver-green color, but as his gaze rested on it other colors appeared to him, the bloody red of the rocks that weathered away into softer pinks and oranges. At the eastern edge of the sky the hills rose, blue and gray and dark blue.

As he sat there he felt things loosening inside of him. Living in the camp with other people knotted up his gut sometimes.

He let the wild country soak into him, and Frémont's arrogance and fear and the fear and softness of the other men lost their grip on him and he felt whole again, not picked to bits by all these people around him.

They hated it here, the harsh intolerance of it, the white blast of the sun, the bitter aftertaste of alkali, the howl of the wind. Yet Kit, sitting before his fire, his gaze stretched out over the desert, treasured the endless delicate gradation, the broad horizons and the swiftly upreaching rocks. He felt good here. A man alone, who knew what he was up to, could make his way here, and a man alone could sit and stare across the desert to the curve of the earth, and forget himself and where he ended, and be that silence, that space, that infinite blue distance.

While he sat there, romancing himself with these thoughts, there came from behind him, above his head, a small crunch, stones and earth grinding together momentarily under some passing weight. He waved with his hand at the fire and said, in Shoshone, "There is food enough here for two."

Nothing. He waited a little longer, but the rabbit was getting overdone. Moving slowly, he took a quarter from the fire, holding it still by the stick, and laid it on a rock some way off, and then sitting by the fire got the other pieces out of the flames and began to eat.

The mare was standing hipshot at the far side of the draw, broadside to the sun, her head down. Abruptly she jerked her head up, snorting, her nostrils flaring. Behind Kit, again, there was a grating of stone and dirt, and then a naked man sprang lightly down before him.

Kit lifted his head. The Indian glowered at him across the fire, his knife raised. Kit nodded to him and to the piece of meat on the rock. "Eat."

The Indian was making faces at him. Maybe he spoke no Shoshone. Slowly he backed away to the rabbit, his gaze steady on Kit, and he stowed his knife in a sheath on a thong around his neck. He wore a rabbit skin over his privates. He picked up the piece of cooked meat, then came back to the fire and squatted and ate.

Neither of them tried to speak until the rabbit was gone.

Then Kit spoke again in Shoshone, saying his name and asking the other man's, but the Indian only shook his head, frowning. Kit began to use his fingers.

That worked better. The Indian's name was Melo; his people were called the Washo, and they lived all around the desert here. He asked if Kit had come from the big camp of the whites — he made the sign for white men by pulling at his chin, pretending a beard — and when Kit admitted to that Melo nodded, his face keen.

He leaned forward over the fire and his hands moved and his eyebrows rose, asking: Where the hell do you think you're going?

Kit grinned at him. He pointed: West.

Melo's eyes popped. His mouth fell open. He turned and looked the way Kit had pointed and faced the white man again and shook his head back and forth, back and forth.

Kit pointed west again, and again to Melo, and made walking with his fingers: Have you gone west?

The Indian sucked his face long, and his slow head-shaking began again. He turned and pointed to the mountains, and his hands made shapes in the air: The mountains are high, rock on rock, snow on snow. There is no passing over these mountains, not now, with the winter coming.

Kit nodded. In American he said, "I get the idea." His fingers smelled of rabbit and he licked them. The fire was going out. Melo was staring at him steadily. Kit went to work with his hands again: How far to the other side?

The Indian shrugged. By the expression of his eyes and mouth and a quick gesture of his hands he conveyed the opinion that perhaps there was no other side. He dusted his palms together and rose.

Kit sat watching him; the conversation seemed to be at an end, and the Indian went off, across the draw.

But then he turned, at the foot of the next little slope, and looked back, and with a circling of his arm he called Kit after him. Hastily the buckskin man got up, kicked apart the fire, and followed.

7 ⚐ NANCY LED ONE OF FRÉMONT'S MULES, piled
up with their packs; Catharine came after her with the baby.
Single file, the train of packed beasts and men straggled up
through the canyon, into the teeth of a harsh, cold wind.

Kit's Indian was leading them into the mountains. Already
the walk was a struggle, the climb so steep that her legs ached
from lifting her feet. The baby murmured, heavy in her arms,
watching the sky. The two days in Frémont's camp had revived
Sarah; her skin was pink again, her eyes were bright. She rode
in Catharine's arms like a mandarin, looking calmly around her
at the scenery, while Catharine staggered up the rough trail.

Frémont's men went first, dragging the howitzer; she could
hear them swearing when the gun wedged a wheel in between
the rocks and would not move. The narrow floor of the canyon
was a tumble of sharp boulders. Nancy's mule slipped and blun-
dered over them and stopped, and Catharine, behind it, the baby
slung over her shoulder, struck it first with one hand and then
with her belt, forcing it into one more step, one more step. John
Bidwell, behind her, called out, "Keep it moving, Cathy, that's
a girl."

She struggled on after the mule, her eyes lowered, not looking ahead, at the looming height above the train. She had heard
the men talking; she knew how they feared these mountains.
But they were moving, they were going, one foot after the other.
As long as they kept walking, they were winning.

The train struggled up over a ridge and into another canyon,
climbing higher with each stride. Kit, short, square in his blackened, fringed buckskin shirt, with his long red-brown hair
hanging loose on his shoulders, rode back down the line and
circled behind them, shepherding them along. His gaze swept
over her, impersonal, seeing her only as another charge; he
nudged his horse into a fast trot back to the head of the train.

They camped that night on a broad meadow where there was
grass and water, and the argument sprang up among the men
that they should wait there a few days, let their animals gain
strength. Kit would not listen to it. In the morning he drove

them on. Catharine watched him furtively. His ceaseless, purposeful energy gave her heart. With the other settlers, struggling along in Frémont's wake, she worked to keep up with the scout, to match him.

At the edge of the flat meadow the mountain heaved up again in a wall of naked stone that towered a thousand feet high. There seemed no break in it, no passage through it, but the Indian found a crease in the rock that led diagonally up across the blank face of the mountain. The howitzer banged and rattled over the rocky ground. It took all the men, swearing and heaving, dripping sweat in spite of the cold, to drag it up the trail; even the women went to help haul it the last hundred yards. When they reached the exposed height, the night was falling, and Catharine, looking back, could still see where they had camped the night before.

They cooked on stones, they slept on stones. The wind was cold as frozen iron. Catharine saw the Indian at Frémont's fire, huddled almost on the coals; she thought he looked terrified.

Perhaps she had read him right. In the morning he was gone. Kit went out to scout the way on, Frémont's men followed with the gun, and the settlers trudged along after, pushing blindly forward. They were climbing into a dank evergreen forest where trees hung over them, their branches interwoven webs. Another steep-sided, stone-filled ravine led them around the base of a pointed peak whose top blazed white with snow in the sunlight.

The ground began to rise steeply again. Brush barred their way. The mules balked and the men lashed them on, beating them until blood sprang from their matted hides. The howitzer jammed its right wheel between two rocks and could not be moved.

With picks and branches they pried the wheel loose. Frémont said, "Maybe we should dismantle it, try to pack it on in pieces."

The other men's voices all rose at once, protesting, and they settled down to argue. Catharine went on up the trail a little, picking her way over the tumbled rocks that slipped and rolled under her weight. The men made her angry. They were always doing this, wasting their time arguing. Her shoulders hurt. Ahead, now, this dry watercourse rambled through stands of tall pine, between sheer hillsides, toward another snowy peak.

Behind her they had convinced Frémont not to take the cannon apart; they were trying to haul it forward again. She went back to help Nancy with the baby. Abruptly the wind came up and struck her and thrust her forward.

She wheeled, looking back up the trail, and saw a whirling gray fog sweeping in out of the west. The sky was still blue above her, but westward it was dark and lowering. The wind rose higher, screaming through the pine trees; their supple tops bent over and the branches began to sway and dance.

The white peak in the distance vanished behind a dense descending curtain of gray. Amazed, Catharine stopped where she was as the oncoming storm buried the mountainside before her in flying snow. Kelsey came rushing across the rocky canyon toward his family. "Come on. Hurry! We have to get under cover!"

Frémont bellowed, "Leave the gun. Run!"

The men struggling with the howitzer fled from it before the words had formed on his lips. Abandoning the gun there, square in the middle of the trail, they broke into a dash for the lee hillside just ahead of them. Nancy held the baby; Catharine stumbled along after them, her shoes coming apart again. A stone wedged itself under her toes. The wind came straight into her face, laden with flecks of ice that stung like tiny darts, thickening to a wall of icy snow, blinding and cold, that swirled around her and pushed her around.

She could see nothing. The wind banged her forward and backward and the snow pelted her cheeks. Someone yelled, somewhere. With her hands outstretched before her, she rushed on through the white blizzard, fell, got up again, fell again; then from behind a hand gripped her under the arm and half carried, half pushed her across the uneven ground, thrust her on into the pitiless snow.

She scrabbled with her feet on the ground and then suddenly

was in out of the snow. She lifted her head, dazed. Beside her stood John Bidwell, brushing snow off the front of his coat. "You all right, Cathy?"

She put her hand on his arm. "Thanks, John."

They had reached the shelter of a cliff; the snow blew madly past them, leaving here a tiny pocket of windless, snowless ground. The men were crowding into it, carrying firewood; Frémont was already lighting a fire. Catharine's legs hurt. In the shelter of the cliff, Nancy was sitting, the baby in her arms.

Kelsey joined them. They wrapped themselves in their coats and huddled together, looking out at the driving snow. A few minutes later his brother and John Bidwell came in, dragging pine boughs behind them, which they tipped up against the hillside to form a lean-to.

Frémont's men were still trying to bring in firewood. Kit was nowhere. Catharine tucked her frozen hands into her armpits and went toward Frémont's fire. It leapt up, the flames six feet high, roaring, but just beyond, the flying white fury walled off the world, and the snow was drifting steadily into this sheltered spot. Frémont's men were clustered around the fire; some had brought in branches to make a sort of tent. One of them squatted to put more wood into the flames. Catharine tore her eyes from the roughened blue-gray skin of his fingers. Her hands must look like that also.

"Where's Kit?" she asked. Sinking down on her hams, she leaned into the warmth.

The men sagged around the fire. She knew some of their names. Basil Lajeunesse, tall and bony-faced, said, "He was out there looking for the trail. He must be on ahead of us."

Alarmed, she swung toward the blinding white wall of the storm. "Will he be all right?"

Their leathery faces turned toward her, and one of them gave an incredulous laugh. "Kit?" This man smirked at her. "Kit's a wolf, lady. Don't worry about him." He turned to the man beside him, who was also leering at her. "Ain't that sweet, she's worried about Kit."

She backed away, her ears burning, and went back to her friends.

In the morning Kit was there. The storm had passed. Only a few inches of snow lay on the ground. Their cattle, many still carrying packs, stood in a wretched, wet, stinking mass just up the draw against whose bank the people had sheltered. The cold was bone-cracking but the sky was blue and cloudless. Frémont and his men went back to get the howitzer, and the settlers started off along the trail west.

The wind had drifted the snow deep along the trail. As the settlers fought and dug their way through it, Frémont caught up with them.

He had not brought the howitzer. No one said anything; Frémont's cheeks were bright, which could have been from the cold wind. Beside him his men looked innocently unconcerned, as if there had never been a howitzer. After that, though, they seemed to make better time.

That night Frémont boiled water and took its temperature and determined their altitude to be above six thousand feet. Kit brought in an elk, and Nancy cut holes in the hide and wore it for a coat. The cold was like a steadily closing grip around them.

The next day they came into a great flat valley where the dark trees stood packed in the laps of the snowy peaks. Beneath the crusted snow the ground was a frozen marsh that their feet slipped on and broke through. The jagged ice slashed the legs of the animals. The glitter of the sun gradually blinded the people struggling along through it. The snow on the ground was becoming deeper, although no more had fallen. All day they fought through the thickening layer of it. Nightfall sent them on a frantic search for firewood. During the night more snow fell.

Frémont's men led the way, battering a path. The Kelseys and Bidwell joined them, each man taking his turn at the head of the column to beat and claw the way forward a yard at a time through the waist-high snow, opening a trail for the others. The leaders tired within minutes and dropped back, and the next few took their places.

Frémont would not let the women do this work. Nancy and Catharine gathered firewood, the train moving so slowly now that they had time to build a fire and heat water and steep pieces of jerked meat in it for a broth to warm the exhausted men when they staggered back to the end of the column. Each time the front of the train pushed too far ahead, the women would abandon the fire and go make another.

At night Frémont's men and the settlers no longer camped in separate groups. Now they bedded down together, as close as they could, for the warmth of one another's bodies. All night Catharine shivered, barely asleep; her dreams were tangled images of roasted meats, potatoes, flagons of foaming milk. She woke trembling in the blue dawn, hearing Frémont shouting everybody awake, driving his men on. Her body so stiff with cold she could hardly walk. Chewing on souring mule meat that made her stomach heave. Drinking melted snow.

Frémont took another measurement and told them they were above seven thousand feet.

Their packed food gave out and they shot a mule. Nancy mended shoes for the men out of pieces of the hide. By mid-afternoon of the next day snow was falling again. Catharine was collecting pieces of firewood for the night's camp; she stopped when she saw the first snowflakes, and straightened and looked around. The snow drifted down out of the sky, deepening the gloom of the coming night. The pine trees standing thick around them hissed and groaned in the wind. The sky was settling closer and closer over her, driving out the light.

She hurried around gathering firewood, packing it on the dying mule that staggered ahead of her in the line. Her breath came short. The night was falling in on her, around her, burying her, and the other people had gone on ahead of her, leaving her behind. She flogged the mule after them. She could see nothing but the beaten trail leading away into nothing. The trees stooped around her, hissing in the wind, their tops bent under loads of snow. For a moment, in the cold, she shut her eyes and stopped, and she felt around her the numb oblivion, waiting.

She opened her eyes. She would not die. She had been close before and had not died, and she could not die this time either. She lifted one foot and put it down, and then the other, and ahead of her she saw the glow of a fire, flickering in the gloom. Her legs grew stronger. She pushed on, toward her friends, her people, and the warmth and light they made in the dark.

The next day they dragged themselves up toward a saddleback, with Kit ahead of them, urging them on, and fought through snow high as their shoulders to a great stand of pine trees. In the morning, for the first time, they were moving downhill, into a forest so tightly grown they had to hack apart the intertwined branches with knives.

When they camped that night, Kit came up to her. "How you doin', baby?" he said. "You feelin' hale? Come on, I got somethin' to show you."

"What?" She followed him away from the Kelseys, and he led her off toward the black-trunked, dripping trees. When she saw he was leaving the camp, she stopped, uncertain. "Where are we going?"

He came back beside her and got her by the arm. "I want to show you somethin'." The wide grin flashed across his face. "It ain't that far, and the tough part's all going out. I'll carry you if you get too beat, I promise." He gripped her sleeve and pulled. "Come on."

She could not deny him, and now she was curious, and gratified at his attention. He led her straight up the hill, through the forest. The stiff climb hurt her knees and she began to gasp for breath, and he put his arm around her and half carried her on. They walked out of the trees and faced a snowfield, tipped steeply up into the sky.

"Come on," he said. She forced herself to plod after him; if he could do it, she thought, she could too. He stopped every few moments to wait for her. With her arm over his shoulder he dragged her up the last hundred yards, through snow that weighed down her feet, and led her out on a steep, sheer ledge.

"There you go," he said.

She sank down onto the ground, fighting for breath, her lungs on fire and her legs quivering.

Before her, below her, lay the gaunt ridges of the mountains, wave on wave of rock. As high as they were now, the sun was still above the horizon; the last light tinted the snow. Kit sat on his heels beside her, pointing.

"You see that tabletop, in the north, there?"

At the limit of her vision one mountain humped up over the rest, flat like a loaf. The sun gilded it to a blade of gold. She was still trying to breathe. "Yes."

"I was to California once, with Ewing Young, when I was a nit, and I seen that mountain. That's California there."

She stared across the distance, the understanding coming as slow and hard as her breath, and finally she turned to him. "We're going to make it," she said.

When he grinned his eyes crinkled. She realized with a guilty start that she was half in love with him, and John Reilly was not even dead a whole month yet. He said, "We'll make it, all right." Still smiling, he looked out toward the mountain in the distance, and she drew her attention from him and put it on the land around her.

Before them the land swooped off into a vast snowfield, stretching down to the edge of another dark forest; down there the night had come, and the snow was blue like an icy ocean. Across it ran a dented line, a string of darker blue dots. "What's that?" she asked, pointing.

"Tracks. A wolf pack went by there couple minutes ago," he said. "They're down by the trees, now, see?" He nodded.

She strained her eyes, trying to make out what he saw. The blue snowfield ended in a surge of trees, black and thick.

He said, "The fourth one from the front is the leader."

Now her eyes picked out what he was showing her, so far away she could see only that something down there moved. "The leader doesn't go first? How can you tell?"

"Carries his tail up. Only the king wolf has a high tail." His voice thickened with some hidden joke. "The one in front, he's just the scout." He laughed, facing her again. "You glad I brought you up here, Cat?"

"Yes," she said. "Thank you."

"I knew you would be," he said. "Come on, let's get back."

The next day the snow was thinner, and the day after, it lay around them in patches on the ground. Kit led them down along the canyon of a creek running thick and brown with melt, the defiles choked with uprooted brush and broken rocks. They crept across the face of a sheer cliff where the trail pinched down to a crack. Below, the pine trees gave way to oaks, their knotted branches hung with fluffy balls of mistletoe. Here there was game. The grass looked weary and dead, but the last of Frémont's mules plunged into it ravenously. They moved out through rounded, soggy hills into a broad valley.

Catharine was worn to nothing now; during the day she stumbled along helping Nancy, or maybe Nancy was helping her. Her arms felt heavy and limp, and she carried the baby propped against her shoulder, afraid of dropping her. At night she slept without resting; when she woke she was just as tired as when she had lain down. Her teeth were bleeding and the skin of her fingers was raw and oozing. With her friends she staggered on.

In the western distance, low hills poked into the sky. Kelsey said, "There's always one more mountain range. This country was made for goats."

Kit went on ahead of them and did not come back to that night's camp. They started out across the broad, flat valley, its grass winter-dead and dry, toward a lone two-headed peak that seemed midway to the hills. The air was warmer. In the distance they could see elk and deer, dark against the yellow grass.

Frémont's last thermometer had broken and he could not measure the altitude, but he guessed it to be still some thousands of feet above sea level. A dry streambed led them down toward a thin trickle of a river. Catharine waded out into it and scooped up a handful to drink.

"Hey, look!" Bidwell croaked.

She straightened, her hands dripping, looking back. The other settlers were gathered along the bank, staring away down the valley. She went toward Nancy and Sarah.

A horseman was galloping toward them over the brown grass. He wore leather pants and a great cartwheel of a hat; when he swung his horse around before them, looking them over, his spurs clinked. The settlers gawked at him, stupid.

Frémont went forward, pulling his ragged shirt straight, his shoulders squared. "Good evening to you, sir —"

The rider shook his head, his dark face splitting into a white toothy smile. He rattled off a string of incomprehensible words, and Luke Maxwell lunged forward and began to talk back to him in the same tongue.

After a few moments Maxwell wheeled. "California!" he cried. "This is California! He says we're two days' ride from a place called Sutter's Fort. We made it!" He flung his hands up over his head. "We made it!"

The men howled so hard that the rider's horse spooked. Catharine turned toward Nancy, and the other woman held out her arms and tears popped from her eyes. They embraced, laughing. Abandoned on the grass, the baby gave an indignant howl. Nancy turned to her husband, sobbing and smiling, her arms out.

Catharine moved aside, turning her back on the others, looking around her. The broad valley stretched away to the north, to the south, beyond the reach of her eyes. Under the gentle sun it lay like a place of dreams. She had struggled to come here, she had lived through agonies to come here. And yet, now, what was there for her here? The wind rose, blowing the grass over, curling lasciviously around her ankles. The empty land seemed no home to her, only another temporary stopping place on this perpetual journey. Suddenly downcast, she went through the rejoicing settlers to the river and knelt down to splash cool water on her face.

8 🔨   CATHARINE HAD NOT BEEN inside a building in months. She kept ducking her head under the beams of the ceiling, although they cleared her by two feet. She went around the long room, looking at the tools and gear hung on the walls, amazed at the smooth wooden floor she walked on.

The other people came in the door behind her, and their voices rose, exuberant. John Bidwell walked up to her. "Well, Cathy, here we are!"

She laid her hand on his arm, smiling at him. "I can't believe we don't have to go on tomorrow. Look." Tugging on his sleeve, she pulled him over to the window. "Isn't it beautiful?"

He gave a shake of his head, his gaze traveling over the broad, golden stretch of valley beyond the window. "Well, it's big, anyway. How much land do you have here, Captain Sutter?"

The master of this place, John Sutter, crossed the room toward them. He was shorter than Bidwell, with long side-whiskers and bright dark eyes that poked at Catharine; he had a courtly, European manner as he inclined himself toward her with a bow. "I have something here in the area of fifty thousand English acres, Mr. Bidwell, all granted to me by charters of the government of Mexico." He flexed, standing up taller, as Bidwell pursed his lips and blew a soft whistle. Sutter's smile broadened, taking in Catharine and the rest of the room. His skin reddened with a regal pleasure. "Would you care to sit down, Mrs. Reilly? Our humble repast awaits."

At the table they crowded together on benches, elbow to elbow, as at a great family feast. In her father's house there would have been white linen and silver; here there were tin plates and belt knives and raw wood. A brown woman served them; Catharine thought she was an Indian, her body swathed in shapeless cloth, her face placid as a full moon. When she lifted the lids on the dishes the contents sent up the steaming odors of beef and beans. Catharine reached for a pear from a bowl of fruit. Her mouth streamed water.

Sutter himself, sitting at the head of the table, cut a piece of bread and handed it to her. "Would you care for a glass of wine, Mrs. Reilly?"

"Thank you, Captain." At home she would not have been offered wine, either.

"Lieutenant Frémont, a glass with you?"

She ate steadily, tasting everything, greedy. Pear juice ran down her chin; she slathered butter onto one of the warm, delicious corn flatcakes, and the butter melted and dripped all over her. She wiped her hands on a cloth. Looking around the table, she saw the rest of them also stuffing themselves; Nancy's chin was shiny, and even Frémont's cheeks were full as a squirrel's. The brown woman poured coffee into Jack Kelsey's cup, and he held it under his nose and breathed in the aroma and shut his eyes.

John Bidwell gave a whoop. "Hey, these little red things bite back!"

"Chilies," Sutter said, his voice broad. He sat back, surveying them with an air of pride and fatherly indulgence. "I do advise you take them little by little, too, until you're used to them." He turned to Catharine again. "Mrs. Reilly, you are enjoying our fare."

"Captain Sutter," she said, "I have never eaten so well in my life."

Frémont leaned his elbow on the table. "Captain, this lady has earned her enjoyment — both these ladies: hardy as the men, they were." He nodded solemnly to her. "Kit agrees."

"Well," said Catharine, "if Kit says so, it's the gospel." She reached for the butter again, for another of the warm cakes, to celebrate Kit Carson's praises.

Sutter was saying, "I've heard of your scout before. I wish he had joined us at this table."

"Kit's uncomfortable indoors," Frémont said. "If you want to meet him, go out where his horses are tethered."

"An amazing feat, to guide you across the Sierra in winter. I don't believe anybody has ever done it before." Sutter reached for the squat-bellied clay jug of liquor and poured some into his cup. "Mrs. Reilly, Mrs. Kelsey, let me warn you in advance about our aguardiente. You may prefer the wine."

Nancy said, "Even the wine's too strong for me." She was fighting down a yawn.

"I'll have some," Catharine said, and held her cup out.

Sutter rose and came to serve her. Above her head he spoke to Frémont. "It is in fact a drought year. The snow may not have been deep in the high passes."

"Deep enough," said Frémont. "We had to abandon our howitzer."

"A howitzer!" Sutter sank back into his chair. "You brought a piece of ordnance! How sad you had to leave it. I was a captain of artillery in France. I have always loved the big guns."

"Have you guns here?" Frémont asked.

"Some cannon. Ordnance is very scarce in California."

"Yes. What is the situation here? Are the Mexicans effectively in control of the country?"

The liquor was very strong, setting Catharine's head afloat. Nancy leaned toward her. "Don't you think you're getting a little drunk?"

"Oh, certainly," Catharine said. She looked into Nancy's face. "I want to, Nancy. Don't you? I want to eat everything. I want to touch everything. We're alive, Nancy — alive! We did it. We came all that way, after everybody said it was impossible. And we're alive."

Nancy shook her head. At the corners of her mouth a smile suddenly twitched. "I'm just gettin' sleepy. Look at my men."

Frémont and Sutter, leaning forward over the table, were arguing fiercely about politics. Bidwell was listening, his face keen, but Ben Kelsey and his brother sat like lumps, their faces stupid with overeating, their eyes glazed.

Nancy said, "I think I'll be getting these babies to bed." She stood up. "Come on, Ben. Jack." Her hands fell to her husband's shoulders.

Frémont was saying, with force, "It is the American destiny to control this continent. The United States shall reach from the Atlantic to the Pacific, one nation, forged in the crucible of freedom."

Sutter said, "I think you'll find some minor obstacles in your way, sir. Such as the British empire, which wants Oregon, and California too, perhaps."

"We shall have to fight, certainly," Frémont said. "The United States is like the bastard son among nations — no one will give us what we deserve, we must shoulder our way up to the table and take what is rightfully ours."

Catharine gave him a long, curious look; she wondered if he was illegitimate. The Kelseys were trudging out, weary, contented, and they all called good-nights back and forth. Sutter turned to her.

"We must be boring you, Mrs. Reilly. Perhaps I should let you go to your rest."

"No, not at all," she said. "You said you were in France? Are you of French origin? How did you get here?"

Under this volley of questions he expanded, his elbows cocked, his head back. He said, "No — I am Swiss by birth. But I served in Paris, in the Swiss Guards of King Charles the Tenth, as an officer of artillery. The lure of new lands brought me here, although, like you, I had a lot of trouble reaching California. I went to Oregon first and could not fight my way south through the forest."

"Like a wall," Frémont murmured.

"We were hauling our mules up and down the precipices on ropes," Sutter said, "which struck me as the wrong order of things, that we should carry the beasts." He held out his cup, and the brown woman brought another potbellied clay jug over and poured the clear liquor for him. "So I sailed over to the Sandwich Islands and took a ship in from there." Reaching out, he swatted the brown woman's behind. "Which is of course where I found Manaiki."

Manaiki presented them all with a bland, unfocused smile. She went off, clearing the dishes. Catharine's eyes followed her, another woman who worked and worked and worked while men talked.

Bidwell asked, "What do you do with this place, Captain?"

"I am hoping to settle some families on it. Families like yours." He nodded, looking from face to face around the table. "Let me extend the invitation to you, here and now. Join me in

New Helvetia, help me build a new country here. The government of Mexico has conferred on me the power to write passports and residence permits. I can give you your papers tomorrow. By tomorrow noon you can be landholders in California."

With a gusty sigh Bidwell sat back. "That's what I'm here for."

Catharine rubbed her palms together. She wondered what she should do now. Their voices rose, arguing again about the right of the United States to the western lands. John Reilly had wanted land, had wanted a farm. She knew nothing about farming. She owned nothing to start with, not a tool, not even a good change of clothes anymore.

She could marry again. Probably she could marry John Bidwell, this good, steady, kindly man who had saved her a dozen times, whom she trusted utterly, whom she did not love.

She pushed that off. That was the safe, the easy way to live. She had not come all this way to live like that. Here, in this untouched and innocent country, she would find some way to make a life of her own, one moment at a time, as she had gotten here.

Her stomach fluttered. Getting here had nearly killed her. Had killed John Reilly. She reached for the cup of liquor, thinking of him, and drank deep.

9 ✍ UNDER AN OAK TREE just beyond the wall of Sutter's Fort, above the American River slough, Kit was sacking out one of his new horses. The rest of Frémont's company was still down on the broad yellow plain of the valley, roping horses from the herd they had collected and breaking whatever they could catch. The dust they were raising hung in the air like dirty snow and drifted in clouds across the Sacramento.

Kit used his saddle blanket on the red mare, waving it around her head and swatting her sides and flanks with it and then rubbing her all over; she stood trembling under his touch, snorting, her ears pinned back. When he socked her with the blanket again she reared. He laughed. Grabbing the halter in one hand, he blew his breath into her flared nostrils. She tossed her head up, violated.

"Whoa, there, little baby." He rubbed his face against her muzzle, getting her used to his smell. Out there on the yellow grass, Cat Reilly was walking down toward him from Sutter's Fort.

He hung the blanket over the mare's back, his eyes on the woman coming through the wintery sunlight toward him. The wind blew her skirts in a flutter around her. She walked not with a dainty, swaying, ladylike walk but with the all-out, mile-eating stride she had learned in the Sierra. And with other things she had learned in the Sierra — a watchfulness, a head held high, eyes alert, wary. She was looking better after only a few days of steady eating, the body under the threadbare dress rounding out into smooth curves that made the palms of his hands tingle. It was too bad he had to go.

"Hey, there, Cat," he said. "Come to say goodbye?"

She walked up under the shade of the oak tree; it was cool out of the sun, and she hugged her arms around her. "I guess I am. When are you leaving?"

"Tomorrow, if I'm lucky and these goats get their outfits together." He scrubbed the blanket along the mare's side; she stood planted, her ears switching back and forth. Cat leaned against the oak trunk, a frown tucked between her eyebrows.

He could appreciate that she was looking at some problems. He said, "What're you gonna do now, Cat?"

"What should I do?" she said eagerly, as if he could give her some answer, and he shook his head, grinning at her.

"Whatever you want." He watched her sideways, pretending to work on the horse. "You scared?"

"No," she said, looking away, and then, "Yes." She faced him.

"When I was a little nit they 'prenticed me to a saddle-maker." He tossed the blanket onto the mare's back and leaned on her, his arm over her withers. "I hated it. Sittin' around all the time, doin' the same thing over and over. Ran away with a wagon train on the Spanish Trail. The first night out I was so scared I wet my britches. Didn't have no dry pants so I nearly went back to Howard County."

Her mouth curled; her eyes were merry. "I don't believe you," she said. "You've never been afraid of anything in your life."

He slapped his hand on the mare's side and she jumped. "Come along with us," he said. "We're going south. You think the Sierra is hard — there's places down in the Gila River country where the rock's so hot it'll burn your feet off right through your boot soles."

"God," she said. "What an invitation." Her eyes snapped with high humor. "Thanks, Kit. Thanks for everything."

"Hey, baby, you ain't done with me yet. I'll be back." He reached his hand across the mare's rump to her, and she gripped it and shook it, like a man. "You just be here."

"I'll certainly try," she said. "Take care. I'll think about you."

"Good. You do that."

"Goodbye to the others," she said. "Tell them."

"I will."

She waved one last time and went back toward the drab clump of huts on the valley floor. The long, rangy stride took her rapidly away from him. She would have to be tough to get along here. He thought she was tough enough. He turned back to the red mare and slugged her again with the blanket, to toughen her up too.

10 AFTER FRÉMONT LEFT, the fort seemed much smaller. John Bidwell went to work for Sutter. The Captain gave Ben Kelsey and his brother each a mule to ride, and they went out into the valley and found homesteads, which Sutter marked out on the big map in his office.

This map hung on the whitewashed wall that divided the big main room of the office from the cell at the end, where the desk was. Inside the cell, at the desk, John Bidwell was writing something in a ledger, his back to the room. He had glanced up when Catharine came in but then gone straight back to the work.

The sunlight spilled in the window in a dazzling arc, but most of the room was dim. Out here in the main room the only furniture was the long table down the middle, two benches on either side of it, some stools. There was a wooden shelf hanging on the long wall opposite Catharine, and some pieces of harness and a crosscut saw blade.

The map of New Helvetia seemed just as bare as the office. Down the expanse of yellowing paper on which it was drawn, the great river coursed in a fading purple trace of ink, with other streams running down from the east, out of the Sierra; just below the Y where the American River came into the Sacramento, a patch of overlapping penciled squares marked the fort. Scattered over the paper, mostly east of the great river, were five or six other faintly drawn, widely scattered squares, the homesteads of Sutter's settlers.

Into this blank the Kelseys were about to vanish.

Now Sutter was turning toward her, facing her across the table. "Yes, Mrs. Reilly, you wanted to see me?"

She went to the edge of the table and laid her hands on it. "Captain Sutter, I want to thank you for taking us in and helping us . . ." Her voice was dribbling out, saying nothing that got her nearer to her goal. He stared at her, his mouth half hidden behind his drooping mustaches, giving her no help. She stopped.

"Is that all?" he said, tolerant.

"No." She flung herself straight at this. "Please. I need work. I'll work for you. I'll do anything."

"You will," he said. He pulled back the stool in front of him and sat on it and continued to stare at her. His courtly manner had vanished; he looked her over like a plantation owner buying a new slave. "What can you do?"

"I can . . ." Play the piano. Recite Coleridge and Keats. "I can read and write. I can . . ." Nothing. "I can learn." Feeling worthless and humiliated, she could no longer meet his eyes; she gazed down at the riven blackened wood of the tabletop.

"Can you cook? Can you sew?"

"No," she said, to the tabletop.

"Where will you sleep?"

"Can't I sleep where I am now?" She had not thought about this. She and the Kelseys had been living at one end of the long shed that quartered the rest of Sutter's men, on the west side of the compound. Lifting her eyes again, she saw his eyes fixed on her breasts.

Slowly his gaze rose to meet hers again. "If you stay here alone the men will be all over you." His lips widened into a smile that did not warm her. "You can sleep with me."

She swallowed. A wave of shame climbed through her. In her memory John Reilly lay close beside her, his hands on her body, his breath in her face. She straightened, backing away from the table. "No," she said. "I won't do that."

Behind him, suddenly, John Bidwell said, "Captain, she can keep the books. I'd rather do anything than this."

Sutter's head swiveled toward him. Bidwell had come into the doorway of the little clerk's cell to talk to them; the sun flowed past his head and shoulder, leaving his face in a hood of shadow. Sutter asked, "What makes you think she can do that?" He swung toward her. "Can you figure?"

"Yes," she said, relieved; she was good at arithmetic.

"Give her a chance, anyway. She can do anything she puts her mind on," Bidwell said.

"Show her how," Sutter said. He was staring at her again, his gaze traveling slowly down over her. Clearly his elaborate European courtesy was something reserved for his equals, not his underlings. He said, "You'd better do a good job or I'll put you to scrubbing floors."

She went around the table, picking up a stool as she went, and went ahead of Bidwell into the cell to look over Sutter's ledger.

11 🖾   NANCY SAID, "I wish you'd come with us." She
turned, lowering her hands; the bag she had just put on the cart
slid down deeper among the few sacks and sticks of the Kelseys'
goods. Sutter had given them a few farm animals and two mules
and this cart, with an ox to pull it, some tools, seed, supplies,
even cloth. It seemed like nothing.

Catharine said, "I can't farm, Nance. Besides, Sutter has
given me work. I'll do better here." There was enough to do in
Sutter's office to keep three people busy. She held her hands out
to Nancy. "I'll miss you."

"I'll miss you, Cathy." Nancy swung her arms around Catharine; the warm brown mass of Nancy's hair pressed against her
face. "We'll come in as often as we can." Under Catharine's
palms the other woman's back was rigid and bony; she still
looked thin as a crane's legs.

Catharine reached into the front of the cart and lifted up the
baby. "Goodbye, Sarah." She put her nose to the baby's nose,
and the child, used to this game, gave a fat, milky cackle of
pleasure. Abruptly Catharine was half in tears; she held the
baby against her shoulder, her hand on the back of Sarah's head;
her eyes met Nancy's, and the other woman patted her arm.

"You'll have babies of your own someday."

On the edge of the slope, the two men had the mules saddled,
the cow and her calf and the two sheep and the pig all gathered,
and they came over to say goodbye. Reluctantly Catharine let
the baby's mother take her back. Jack began to shake her hand,
then said, "To hell with that," and pulled her against him and
slapped his arms around her. "You be careful."

"I will."

Ben kissed her forehead. "Any of these —" His head jerked
toward the fort. "Anybody gives you any trouble, you let us
know."

"I will," she said, wondering whom she was comforting; they
would be days away. She glanced toward the fort, where in the
morning sun a few of Sutter's dozen or so men were working.
For them she had no feeling; for these people, who were leav-

ing, she felt everything she knew of love and trust, and she searched their faces with her gaze, remembering. "Goodbye."

"Goodbye," they said, turning, and left her. "Goodbye." The men went off to herd the stock away, and Nancy got onto the ox cart and clicked her tongue and called. Over her shoulder Sarah's round face bobbed. The cart rolled off down the long gradual slope toward the river, along a path already rutted by other wagons. She watched them go until they were far up along the Sacramento's eastern bank. Slowly she trudged back across the plain into Sutter's Fort.

Most of Sutter's men were Kanakas, tall people with dark, smooth skin who had come with him from the Sandwich Islands. They kept to themselves, speaking their own language. The two women were Kanaka also. One of them, Manaiki, slept with Sutter, and the other slept in the crew's quarters with one or another of the men, sometimes several. The rest of Sutter's crew were white men, Americans, mostly, tramps and backwoodsmen.

With a piece of canvas and some old lumber Catharine closed off a space to one side of the kitchen, in its own spacious building on the other side of Sutter's office from the crew's quarters. She made a bed of planks and a straw tick. For a few days after the Kelseys left, nothing happened, and she began to feel safe there, but then one evening when she went in to go to bed a man walked in behind her.

He came at her fast, and she had no warning; he enveloped her like a great black rag flung around her. Her scream was muffled against his arm. He lifted her up as if she were a baby and carried her toward the bed while she thrashed and kicked helplessly. The rank smell of sweat and horses and urine and wood shavings burned in her nose. A hoarse voice growled into her ear, "Now, come on, lady, take it easy, we're just gonna have some fun."

She whined in her throat. Her temper popped like a boil. In a blind rage she drove her elbows into him, swung her fists, while he struggled to pin her arms and stretch her on her back in the bed. She made no sound; anybody who heard would be on his side anyway. She threw herself to her right, doubled up her legs, and kicked at him hard. One heel skidded off his chest, and he got hold of her ankle and pulled her leg past him and fell forward onto her between her legs.

Her breath whooshed out of her. Her head spun. She beat her hands on his shoulders, gasping with breathless rage.

"Come on, lady." He wallowed on her, crushing her under his weight, his breath stinking in her face; she could feel him working her dress up over her hips. She wrenched one arm loose and got a hand in his hair, then pulled his head down and sank her teeth into his face.

He yowled. He hit at her, trying to knock her away, but she hung on, grinding her teeth together; she wanted to hurt him, even if he hurt her back, even if he got her in the end. His hand palmed her face and he ripped her away from him and flung her against the wall. She scrambled toward the corner, where there was a little stool, and held it in both hands, ready to hit him.

In the darkness she could see nothing. There was silence except for his harsh breathing on the far side of the room. He said, "You know, lady, you takin' the fun right out of this."

She said, "Get out." Her voice squeaked out, fluty with panic. She could still smell him.

"Now, now. Maybe I been goin' at this wrong." His voice softened to a syrupy croon. "You come over here and sit and we'll get friendly."

"Get out! This is my room." That he should be there, hulking in the dark, in her room, ignited her to a feverish rage. She banged the stool on the floor. "Get out of my room!"

"All right, all right." Unhurried, grumbling, he lumbered heavily across the room, his feet padding on the floor. "Stupid bitch." The door banged. He was gone.

She groped her way back to the bed and sat down, her heart pounding, her skin prickling and hot, the stool beside her. At every sound she started. She sat there most of the night, unable to quiet herself enough even to lie down.

When morning came she went out to the kitchen and found most of the men sitting at the split-log table, eating bread. Sutter was not there; John Bidwell was not there. The palms of her hands were slick with sweat. She could feel their feral interest on her. At the big covered hearth, where the coffeepot hung, she poured herself a cup of the thick black stuff, and then forced herself to go over to the table.

The five white men were sitting in a row on one side of the table, and she sat down on the side opposite them. They ignored her, their eyes elsewhere, talking to one another in a low rumble of voices. She held the cup of coffee in both hands and blew on it, her gaze traveling from one face to the next down the row before her. At the third man her gaze crossed a pair of hard dark eyes staring back at her.

She did not have to look for the marks of her teeth on his face; she knew him. She even knew his name: Zeke Merritt. He was twenty years older than she, an ex–mountain man, burly in his greasy leather shirt, his black hair a mop that blended down into a tangled beard that hid all his face but his eyes. Into the middle of this mass of hair he poked a piece of bread, his eyes steady on her. His brows were like black caterpillars.

"Something the matter, lady?" he said. The other men looked around at him; the low drone of conversation faded into a rapt silence.

"No," she said. "Nothing's the matter." She lifted the coffee cup to her lips, looking away. The other men were staring at her now. She could barely drink the tarry coffee, but she sat there until all the men had gotten up and left.

She went into Sutter's office and worked on the books. He had not kept the ledgers current but had only made diaries, and now the books were three years behind. The desk was too small to open all these books at once, so she dragged the ledger out onto the big black table, where the morning sun came in through the side window. She opened the diary and, as John Bidwell had shown her how to do, began to translate Sutter's day-to-day work into debits and credits.

Sutter came in. Short, loud, he made the room seem smaller, and with him there was always a steady stream of men moving in and out of the office, getting orders, picking up tools or advice, and reporting problems and successes. Bidwell entered the room and came over to her. His beard was growing out; he looked older, more solid. "Are you all right?" he said, low. He bent over the books, running one long finger down a line of figures. "You've got a much better hand than I have. You're doing a good job, Cathy." He looked quickly into her face. "Did anything happen to you?"

"Why do you ask?"

"Just . . . I heard — overheard — something."

"No," she said. "Nothing happened." She could not expect him to take care of her.

Sutter called, "Bidwell, over here."

His hand clapped her shoulder; he went down toward the Captain, and they stood talking. Beyond Bidwell, among some other men, Zeke Merritt was staring at her. She lowered her eyes to the books, her cheeks hot.

Bidwell said, "Zeke, you come with me. Captain, I'll take Merritt."

Sutter said, "Good, yes." He came up the room past Catharine, who raised her eyes to see Bidwell leaving, the black-haired mountain man tramping after him. He had helped her again. A rush of gratitude filled her, for his unselfish caring. She dipped the pen into the ink; the nib was fuzzy and she dried it on the edge of the well.

The amount of work that Sutter did was beginning to amaze her. In this vast, parched valley it all seemed to dry up and blow away. The diary reported fields plowed and planted, lost to the drought; thousands of bricks made, hundreds of feet of lumber brought in from somewhere on the coast, and yet all that stood here were the low, rude shacks, which the baleful wash of the sunlight seemed to crush down into the bleached landscape and the wind wore to dust.

Sutter had vast herds of cattle somewhere out in the empty haze. He fished, or the local Indians fished and sold their catch to him; into the wasteland of his debts the tiny profit vanished like a trickle of spring run-off. Sometimes he brought in herds and slaughtered them for the hides and tallow. In one of the shacks huddled in the angle of the fort's unfinished wall, blankets were woven, which he used to pay the Indians for the fish. In another shack Sutter's men made kegs, to hold the fish when it was salted. All this she entered into the ledger under the appropriate dates: so much fish, so many hides, so many bags of tallow.

Sutter came up the room to her and tapped her hard on the shoulder, imperious. "Go down to the forge and bring Pablo here for me."

She went down the stairs to the yard and crossed it to the forge, on the far side of the squat-trunked oak tree that filled the northwest corner. She knew who Pablo was, small and brown as a hazelnut. In front of the forge he was shoeing a mule. The mule was resisting, and two other men held it, one twisting a long, hairy ear down and the other braced on the halter. She waited until Pablo had tacked on the shoe and let the hind hoof go, and then she said, "The Captain wants you."

Pablo started silently across the yard, and she followed. Behind her, one of the men said, "Pretty skinny."

"Sharp teeth, though," said the other, and they laughed. She hurried up the stairs after Pablo, her neck and cheeks roughening with a harsh heat.

When she went into the office Sutter was talking to the blacksmith; she went back to her work with the ledger, but for a moment she did nothing, her mind stuck on the jeering and lust of the men. They would be just as ready to hold her down as they would the mule. It occurred to her that Sutter would protect her if she slept with him, but she thought it was a bad bargain. What she needed, she decided, was a knife. She turned over one long page of the ledger and wrote the date at the top.

"Here," Sutter said, pulling the book out of her hands. "Get up. Go down and find me something to eat." He pushed against her, crowding her out of the chair, and took her place, bent over the book.

"Captain," she said, "you have to stop interrupting me."

His head swung toward her, and his lips pulled back off his teeth. "I don't have to do anything! You're the one who has to do as I say. I'm hungry — go get me something to eat."

"If you want me to finish this work, I can't —"

He lunged up out of the chair, got hold of her arm, and pushed her back against the table. His face came down an inch from hers. "Damn you, you want to be a man, you can be like my men. You do as I tell you, right away, no back talk, no second guesses. Understand?" As he let go of her arm, he wrenched her wrist, shooting a bolt of pain up into her shoulder. "Get me something to eat!"

She backed up, every nerve ajump, her stomach fluttering. She was dimly aware that someone had come into the room behind them. Sutter stepped back, saying, startled, "Well. What are you doing here?" She turned and walked out of the room, encased in her humiliation, and ran down the stairs and across the yard to the kitchen.

She had no choice; she had to obey him.

In the kitchen the cook was sitting in a corner, drinking; pots of beans and beef stewed on the great, slow fire. The hot air reeked. She found a wooden plate and put food on it and poured a cup of coffee and carried it all back across the yard and up to Sutter's office.

He was still sitting in her place, talking to a man she had never seen before, who stood beside the table with his hat in his hands. Sutter sprawled loosely in the chair, his voice booming.

"I thought you were going back into the Russian navy." He nodded to her. "Here, put it down." He slapped the table in front of him. She set down the plate and the cup of coffee and he leaned forward over it, taking his belt knife in one hand.

"I decided I liked horses better than ships," said the other man, in a harsh, throaty accent. "California better than Sitka. Do you give me a job or not?"

"Yes, I'll hire you." Sutter was brisk. "She'll write you in. Catharine, put him on the payroll." His head jerked toward her, but his attention remained on the man he was hiring. "Still play whist, don't you?"

"Not since you taught me how at Ross."

She circled the end of the table, going to the shelf where the other ledgers were, and brought down the big buckram-bound payroll ledger. The residue of Sutter's abuse lay on her like an old dream. The stranger walked up the room toward her, into the sunlight coming in the window. Sutter still sat where she usually sat, now wolfing his meal, and she put the ledger down on the table a little way from him and pulled the inkwell closer.

"What's your name?" She turned the pages over, looking for the last entry.

"Count Sergei Timofeievitch Sohrakoff," he said.

Startled, she lifted her head and laughed, and he smiled at her. For the first time she saw him clearly. His hair and beard sprang out around his head in a wild, crinkly red-blond mass; his eyes were a brilliant dark blue. He wore a serape and leather pants laced up the sides. Under her stare his smile widened.

"Oh, la, your lordship," she said. "What's your real name?"

Sutter looked up, his jaws moving, and spoke through a mouthful of food. "Tell her the story later. I want you to come look at these Russian lathes."

She bent over the ledger again. "Wait. I'm sorry. Tell me again." He said his absurd name again, and she wrote it, as well as she could, last on the list of Sutter's men, just below her own.

Sutter ate as he did everything, in a hurry; he was done now. He put the coffee cup down and pushed the plate away. "The next time," he said to her, "put sugar in the coffee. Come on, Count." The two men went out. She watched them go, feeling better, useful, part of something, not the last name anymore, and plunged back into the diaries and the ledger.

12 🦫 SUTTER'S KANAKA WOMAN, Manaiki, helped Catharine make a new dress from a length of white cloth out of the storeroom. The brown woman watched her put it on for the first time, and her face broke into an approving smile.

"You pretty now," she said. "When you come, so skinny, so

tired, you look like old woman, now you pretty, young, nice, in you new dress. I see why Zeke Merritt want you."

"Damn it!" Catharine tugged fitfully at the sleeves of the dress, which pinched her under the arms. She had come to enjoy swearing. "Does everybody know?"

Manaiki's smile widened into a horizon of teeth. "Everybody make fun of him. You watch out, he bad man, they call jokes on him, he maybe blame you."

On the table lay the scraps from the piece of cloth. Catharine gathered them up to make a belt for the dress. The Kanaka came around the table toward her.

"Sutter want you too, you know."

"I don't give a damn." She ripped up the cloth into strips and braided them together. "My husband is dead. He was a better, sweeter, finer man than all of them together." She stared hard into the brown woman's shrewd dark eyes. "And he is still my husband, and I don't want anybody else." She wrapped the belt around her waist and tied it.

Manaiki beamed at her, her cheeks round as apples. "You good, good." She patted Catharine's arm and went out.

Catharine gathered up the scraps of cloth, even the shreds. Somewhere over the Sierra she had lost the ability to throw away anything. Manaiki returned, her arms full of more white cloth.

"You use this," she said, and dumped the cloth onto the table.

"Silk," Catharine said, disbelieving. She plunged her hands into the mass of glossy fabric, lifting it up, and pieces of it fell from her hands in a soft, luxurious shower. "God! Manaiki — silk underwear!"

The Kanaka stood nodding at her, pleased. Sleek dimples tucked in the corners of her mouth. "The don send. For Lady Sutter, back in other world."

"Sutter is married?" Eagerly Catharine climbed out of the baggy new dress; the soft glow of the daylight shone in the silk like a buried fire. "Does he know you're giving me these?"

"He forget them, maybe," Manaiki said. "They be here years. I wear them, he look on me, he know." Her plump hand pushed back the hair by her cheek. Her voice quavered. "He pay no matter to anything but New Helvetia, Catharine." She pushed at the clothes. "You wear them, you pretty, pretty skin, like silk."

"Where did he get them?"

"Don Vallejo send. They make gifts to each other. Make them look strong, have something to give away, better present than come back."

Catharine pulled silk panties up over her thighs. The sleek fabric stroked her hips. In her groin, her body clenched slightly, answering the soft, sliding touch, betraying John Reilly with a pair of silk underwear. Manaiki was smiling at her. Manaiki would be her friend because she was no longer a rival for Sutter. The Kanaka held out a chemise, beautifully sewn, hemmed in a froth of lace.

"No outer clothes," Catharine said regretfully. She put on the chemise and then had to pull the rough dress over it; but she felt better suddenly, almost triumphant.

"No. Clothes hard to find," Manaiki said. "You need a man, Catharine. Get a man soon." She turned, shapeless in the long waistless drift of her red dress, and went out of the kitchen. Catharine gathered up the rest of the silk underwear and took it into her room.

13 ✠ THE NEXT COW HAD a broken horn. As it lumbered along it hooked the jagged stump at Count Sohrakoff's horse, racing beside it, and then veered suddenly away toward the open plain and the freedom of the distance. Sohrakoff steered his horse to head it off. The horse was green and stubborn and he had to crank it around by force, and the cow got ahead of him by two strides. He leaned out and whacked it with the butt of the killing knife, and it swerved back toward the river.

They had been running cattle here all day long now, stirring up the dust into a drifting pall that turned the sunlight a molten yellow. The air stank of blood and tallow. Sohrakoff had a rag tied over his face, but still his mouth was full of grit, his eyelashes glinting, his throat sandy.

In his left hand he gripped the long knife, spike-tipped like a barbless harpoon; he spurred hard until his horse lengthened out and caught up with the galloping one-horned cow. He headed the cow back toward the two he had already killed, and bending down across his horse's shoulder he drove the point of the knife deep into the groove along the cow's neck.

The knife stuck and the butt twisted out of his hand. The cow thrashed on a few strides, slowly collapsing, spraying blood and dust through the butter-colored air, and at last sank flopping into the sparse grass. Sohrakoff slowed the horse to a walk.

The trick to this was keeping all the kills close together, and he had dropped this cow a scant thirty feet from the last one. A crew of cutters and skinners was already closing in on it to peel off the hide, to hack away its fat. He jogged the horse over toward the river, where there was some shade.

This was also closer to the tallow vats, where the Kanaka women were melting down the fat. Sohrakoff pulled the scarf down off his face, trying not to breathe the stench, and watched the other men out in the sun, struggling and swearing.

He was up here to look around, and already he had seen a lot. Sutter had big plans, but they were still mostly dreams. His crew was smaller even than when Sohrakoff had first worked for him the year before, at Ross, the old Russian colony on the coast. Ross was the weight dragging Sutter down. The Swiss had bought the colony from the tsar for thirty thousand dollars, none of it, so far as Sohrakoff knew, paid yet. Now he was scrambling for money. The drought had burned up his wheat crop, and he was driven into the hide-and-tallow business, the dirtiest, cheapest work in California.

They had bunched up the cattle into a bend of the American River, north of the fort, and two groups of men were killing and butchering. A cart rolled steadily back and forth collecting the chunks of fat and the carcasses and hauling them back to the fires and the tallow vats. Short-handed, Sutter was using everyone he had: the Kanaka women were skimming the tallow into leather sacks, and the white woman, her head covered by a huge, floppy sombrero, walked alongside the oxen, driving the cart.

On the flat valley floor, the carcasses they had already stripped lay in great heaps of guts and bones, half buried under the churning bodies of the carrion birds. Vultures, too fat to fly, their naked heads damp with offal and blood, crowded in circles around each kill and jeered at any man who rode too close.

They were the only ones thriving at this. Sohrakoff lifted his reins; the mosquitoes were eating him. He picked up his horse into a quick gallop out into the dusty sunlight.

The steer he had just killed was in pieces now. Two men on foot heaved the smoking red chunks of meat and bone up into the cart; the other man folded the hide in half and tossed it onto the pile on the ground behind them. The cart rolled away, the wheels grinding, the white woman walking beside it driving the ox with a switch. Sohrakoff rode up past her, in among the other men, looking to see what had to be done next.

"Hey, Zeke," said one of the cutters, a tall man named Christenson. "You need some help with that woman?"

"Ah, shut up," Zeke Merritt said. He had been herding up stray cattle; in the midst of the other men he slid down heavily from his horse. "Somebody else ride. Where's the jug?" By the stack of hides was a can of water; he stooped for the cup. Sohrakoff's throat was gritty, and he went over and waited his turn to drink.

Christenson was staring after the cart rumbling off down toward the stinking tallow fires. "I could hold her for you." He said this loud, so that the woman would hear him; his tongue licked a white leer across his face.

"Hell," Zeke said. "If I really had to have her that bad I'd get her, and no help from you rope dicks." He cast a truculent look around him at the other men, who had been gaffing him about this the whole time Sohrakoff had been here. "She don't want me. Ain't no way to have fun with a woman don't want ya." He held the cup out toward Sohrakoff. "Here you go, Count."

"Thanks." Sohrakoff leaned down for the cup and drank. He liked Zeke. He did not like Christenson, who was a shirker.

"Where's the next 'un? Jesus! Half the way to Texas!"

They trudged away down the cracked brown earth toward the next dead cow.

"Hold it — hold it —" Zeke spread his arms out. "This one's branded." He twisted, his eyes sweeping the brown landscape for Sutter. The other men stood back, glad to do nothing. The steer lay on the bloody ground, sizzling with flies; there was a huge ornate mark burned into the hide of its tick-bitten brown shoulder. Sohrakoff sat back, looking to see what Sutter would do now.

The Captain was down by the tallow vats, but when Zeke hailed him he came at a gallop. The cart rolled back up toward them, the steady shrill scream of its wheels growing louder.

"Vallejo," Sutter said, bent forward to stare at the brand. He reined in, took off his curly-brimmed hat, and wiped his forehead on his sleeve. "Well, it's dead now, can't help that."

"Vallejo." The white woman had reached them, her switch in her hand, her feet caked with yellow dust; she looked up at Sutter on his horse. "Who is Vallejo?"

"You stay here long enough, you'll find out." Sutter glared around him at the men. "Get to work, damn you. Cut it up — it won't hang you. I'll pay him for the damned cow." He swung his horse around behind the cart and rode away.

The white woman pushed her sombrero back; her nose was sunburned. She kept a wary look out for the men around her, especially Zeke. Ignoring her, the old mountain man tramped up past her, toward Sohrakoff, and held out the long spike of the killing knife.

"You do the killin', you're good at it. Don't nail us no more of Vallejo's stock."

"I'll watch out," Sohrakoff said. He stuck the blood-soaked knife down under the fender of his saddle, alongside his thigh.

The woman gave him an oblique, inquisitive look. He turned and smiled at her, which set her tongue working. "Who is this Vallejo everybody's so afraid of?"

"The don of Sonoma," he said to her. "The Vallejos own everything west of here."

Zeke muttered, "Damn greaser devils."

"Everything?" she said, surprise in her voice. She turned to look west, across the Sacramento. "How much is everything?"

"A lot." Christenson cackled.

Sutter gave a bellow, down the way, and hastily the woman raised her switch and beat the ox into its short-legged trudge. As she went by, Christenson reached out and swiped at her and she dodged his touch. He gave a harsh laugh of excitement.

By midafternoon the hides were piled high under a buzzing fog of flies, and the stench of blood and raw meat and tallow thickened the air like a soup. Sohrakoff rode over to the cart and stepped down out of his saddle. He had been killing cattle for hours; his mouth tasted like metal and his arm was sore. He peeled off his shirt, hung it on the corner of the cart, and bent down for the tin cup in the water can.

Zeke Merritt stamped up next to him. "Likely Cap'n ull let us quit for the day, once we get these last steers hacked."

"I'll give you a hand cutting."

"Good. I wish these other pilgrims worked as hard as you."

"I'll do anything to get this over with."

Zeke swilled up a loud mouthful of the water and spat and made a face. "God damn. How can anybody drink this stuff?" His small, shrewd eyes gave Sohrakoff a quick scan. "Where you been since Ross?"

"Around."

"Yeah?" The cup dropped with a clang into the pail. On Zeke's face above the black wire of his beard the crescent-shaped bite mark was a lump like a raspberry. "Horses or cards?"

"Both." He wanted Zeke off this trail; he put down a false one. "Ever been to Honolulu?"

"Naw. I hear the women there are real easy."

"Easy come, easy go." The four steers remaining to be butchered all lay close together; he went to help flay the next carcass, and Zeke followed him.

John Christenson was supposed to be working with them, but mostly Christenson stood by watching. While the other men slashed and hacked at the carcasses he folded up hides with his feet and kicked them casually toward the heap. Sohrakoff and Zeke heaved the quarters of the steer up into the cart while the woman went around picking up chunks of fat off the ground and pitching them in over the side.

As she drove the cart off by him, Christenson stepped in and put his hand on her again. Sohrakoff wheeled on him. "Leave her alone. She's working at least."

Christenson was taller than he was, with lank yellow hair down past his ears and a chest that caved in under the breastbone. "You got an interest, Rusky?"

Zeke Merritt barked a deep, hoarse laugh in his throat. "Naw, not the Count — he likes 'em a little darker, right, Count?"

Sohrakoff jerked his head around toward Zeke. "You talk too much."

Christenson said, "Yeah? You like Indians or niggers?"

Sohrakoff said nothing, but his skin tingled. He knew he was getting into a fight. He and Zeke stooped over the next cow, and Zeke plunged the knife into its belly; a gush of stinking green fluid poured out across the ground. Christenson hung back again, doing nothing, while the other two men hacked off the hide, one tugging the skin back and the other slicing it free of the flesh.

While they were chopping the carcass into quarters Sutter rode by and Christenson made a show of being busy. They hauled the quarters up toward the cart, waiting on the dry beaten bunch grass.

The white woman stood there watching them. Christenson gave her a leer and turned back to Sohrakoff, his voice booming. "Ain't nothing wrong with a colored woman, and the best thing is, when you get tired of her, you can always sell her to somebody else." In the yellow dusty mask of his face, his teeth showed. "How much you get for yours, Rusky?"

Sohrakoff turned and sank his fist into the hollow below Christenson's breastbone. At the impact his own belly tightened to a knot. The tall man wobbled back three steps and fell, and Zeke grabbed Sohrakoff's arm. "No fighting! Captain's orders. Leave him alone — he's always a stiff."

"He wants a fight I'll give it to him." Sohrakoff wrenched his arm out of Zeke's grasp, and Christenson jumped on him. They went down hard, Sohrakoff on the bottom, and he hit the ground on his back and Christenson butted him.

He yelled; a white blaze filled his mind. He flung Christenson off, and the tall man lunged away, almost under the wheels of the cart. In the powdery dust the killing knife glinted, and Sohrakoff grabbed it.

From behind, something struck him hard and knocked him sprawling. He rolled over and looked up at Sutter's horse standing over him, Sutter leaning out of his saddle, shouting at him.

"No fighting. I have rules here. You pull a knife again I'll throw you out!"

Zeke Merritt stepped forward. "Captain, Christenson was hazing him."

"I don't care! He pulled the knife. Take him up and lock him in the calabozo. Two days, Count." Sutter nodded to Zeke and jerked his thumb toward the fort. "Get him out of here."

Christenson gave a derisive hoot of laughter. Sutter rode his horse straight at him, and the tall man dodged a few steps away. "Cap'n, Cap'n —"

"Work, you bastard!" Sutter leaned over Christenson and roared at him. "Flay and cut those last three steers yourself. Work here or you'll skim tallow! Got that?"

"Cap'n, yes, Cap'n."

Zeke prodded Sohrakoff on ahead of him. "Getting me off early," he said, with a grin. "Thanks. Nice quick temper you got there."

Sohrakoff growled at him, his mind lowering, and let Zeke pilot him away toward the horses.

14 ✒ THE CALABOZO WAS an adobe closet built against the opposite side of the kitchen from Catharine's new room. She set the lantern down on the ground by the door, put the big iron key into the lock, and shook it and twisted until the lock opened. When she pulled the door open the lantern's light leapt into the narrow space beyond.

There, sitting with his back to the wall, the Russian gave her a sullen look. "What is it?"

"Sutter wants you to play whist."

He shifted, his head swiveling away, his gaze aimed at the wall. "The hell with him."

"Would you rather stay here instead?"

He faced her again, his pride yielding to a grudging relief. There was just enough room in the calabozo for him to sit. The heat from the kitchen filled it even now, with the sun down, and his bare arms and chest shone with sweat; dirt streaked his forehead. He stared out past her into the yard, where the air was fresh and cool, and finally he got up and came out the door past her.

She had brought his shirt; she held it out to him.

"Thanks."

By the rails of the corral there was a water trough, and he walked straight toward it. Picking up the lantern, Catharine started after him and then stood there while he plunged his head into the water, slicked his bushy hair back, and sighed. She could sense his mood ease. He put his shirt on. As he walked toward the central building she went along beside him. He had talked to her once before, which gave her the courage to ask him something. "What happened to your wife?"

"Nothing," he said. "She was a good woman. I wish I had her back. When the tsar sold Ross she went to live with her own people."

"Was she an Indian?" she said.

"Kashaya. They lived near Ross. They're really close with each other, they need each other more than we do." They had reached the foot of the stairs. In a low voice he said, "Anyway, she needed them more than she needed me."

Going up the stairs after him, she said, "What's Ross?"

He stopped on the landing, in the light of the lantern over the door. "A place. On the coast, west of here." He looked down at her two steps below him. "What's your name?"

She paused, only for an instant, and said the name she liked best. "Cat. Cat Reilly."

Sutter put down his glass. "Now that there's been another revolution in Mexico City, they'll send a governor up here, and then you'll see Vallejo and Castro and the rest bowing and bobbing like the Chinee." His eyes followed the slap and whisper of the cards falling on the table. "There's the king of diamonds. I knew you had it, Sohrakoff."

Sohrakoff took the trick and led a low club. "They've appointed a new governor, a man named Micheltorena. He hasn't left Mexico City yet and the dons are already plotting against him."

The American John Bidwell gave him a sharp look. "How do you know that?" Beyond him, at the far end of the table, at the edge of the lantern light, Cat Reilly was watching them, her chin in her hands; she was not doing the work she was supposed to be doing.

"I'm just guessing," Sohrakoff said. "But I know the dons."

To his right Zeke Merritt was fumbling with his cards, his lower lip stuck out like a flap. "Unh — what's trump?"

Sohrakoff put his hand up to hide his smile; across the table he and Bidwell exchanged a look of amusement. Sutter bristled. His head thrust toward Merritt. "Diamonds! Diamonds are trump. How many times are you going to ask?"

Merritt played a diamond on the trick. "I forgot," he said, with dignity. He reached for his round-bellied jug, his hand unsteady. In his small, red-rimmed eyes there was a glitter of resentment.

"I thought you knew how to play this game," Sutter said.

Zeke mumbled something below the level of words.

Bidwell shifted restlessly on the bench. Sohrakoff liked him; he was a quick, keen man, hard-working, a few years younger than the Count. Sutter was making great use of him, since Bidwell would work just as well when Sutter was not there as when he was. Now the American turned again toward Sohrakoff. "These dons — who are they? How can they throw a governor out?"

Zeke was musing over his cards. Sohrakoff wondered if he had forgotten that now he had to lead. Across the table from him, Sutter lounged on one arm on the table, expanding in the heat of the brandy, and rushed in importantly to answer Bidwell's question.

"In California the dons are like kings. The first white people up here were the friars, you see, and not many of them. Maybe eighty, ninety years ago, they came up here from Mexico and built the missions. Rather, they made the Indians build the missions. There wasn't anybody else, just the friars and a couple of soldiers and a lot of Indians. They tried to bring in some settlers, but it's just as hard to get here from Mexico as it is to get here from anywhere else."

"The place is a fortress," Bidwell said.

Sutter went on, "Anyway, when Mexico revolted against Spain, twenty, thirty years ago, the generals grabbed off the missions for themselves. They say Mariano Vallejo supervised the laying out of San Francisco de Solano at Sonoma because he knew it was about to be secularized and he intended to take it."

"So the generals became the dons? How many are there?"

"Five or six aces," Sutter said. "Vallejo in Sonoma, and Pico and Carrillo in the south, Alvarado and Castro around Monterey, a few others; they control thousands of acres, thousands of head of cattle, hundreds of vaqueros. Then there's a few hundred smaller landowners."

"Like plantations. What are vaqueros?"

"Riders. Cowherds, what the word means. They're mostly Indians. Little better than slaves, actually."

From the far end of the table Cat Reilly asked suddenly, "Aren't there any cities?"

"Cities!" Sutter slapped the flat of his hand on the table. "No cities in California, except maybe El Pueblo de los Angeles, down south. How many people down there, Count? Are you going to lead, ever, Merritt?"

Sohrakoff shrugged, in no hurry to play cards. He wanted Sutter flowing in this direction. "Eight, nine hundred people, maybe, in El Pueblo. Not counting Indians." Zeke twitched; he took a heart from his hand and dropped it on the table.

Sutter won the trick. "There are no people here," he said to Bidwell. "In California a major army is forty men with ropes and willow lances. This Michelena fellow can do a lot, if he brings himself some guns. If he doesn't, he can't do much at all." He led the ace of clubs, Bidwell followed suit, and Zeke Merritt, with a look of utter concentration, played a trump on it.

The Swiss let out a howl like a wounded man. "You fool, Merritt!" He bounded to his feet so hard the bench rocked over with a crash. "You stupid fool. You trumped my ace!"

Zeke's face contorted, his features screwing up tight in the clearing between his beard and his hairline. "Damn you, I ain't takin' this. Play by yourself, you're so goddamn smart." He slammed his hand down on the table, got up, and walked unsteadily toward the door. Halfway there he wheeled and came back and grabbed his jug, fired another glare at Sutter, and tramped out.

Sutter ripped out a string of words in German and flung his cards down. "Why can't I find three other people in this godforsaken country with the wits to play whist?"

Bidwell shrugged. "I guess that does it." He opened his hands and the limp cards splattered onto the table.

"I'll play," said Cat Reilly.

She came up to their end of the table, into the brighter light. To Sohrakoff she seemed small and finely made, even for a woman; her unruly black hair was tied up on her head in a bit of cloth.

Sutter leaned back and frowned at her. "Have you ever played?"

"No," she said, "but I've been watching. It doesn't look difficult."

"Sit down," Sutter said. His voice quivered with leftover anger. He picked up the deck and blocked it in his hand and fixed her with an unblinking stare. "Whist," he said, in a voice like an oracle, "is a demanding game, I warn you, not to be taken lightly, a game as subtle and as violent as life itself." Sohrakoff put his elbows on the table, smiling; Bidwell gave a little shake of his head. Sutter's gaze switched, narrow and condescending, from one to the other. "Played, unfortunately, by mindless louts as well." He nodded to her. "We'll give you a try at it. Count, deal."

The deck was old and the cards stuck to one another. Sohrakoff shuffled them and began to spin them out. Bidwell leaned on the table. "Well, if there are so few people here, then I can understand why they try to keep everybody else away."

Sutter said, "They can't go on doing it forever. You got in, and Cat, here, walked right in over the Sierra in the dead of winter."

Startled, Sohrakoff glanced at her again. "You came over the Sierra?"

"We both did," she said, and nodded toward Bidwell. "Kit Carson brought us over."

She had strange eyes, green with flecks of pale brown, almost yellow. Sohrakoff liked her voice. He wondered what had driven her here, what drove her now, pushing her forward into this man's game. The cards sailed across the table into four little heaps, and he flipped the last one face up before him: the queen of clubs.

In Sutter's fist his cards splayed into a fan. "The dons can't keep California sealed up like this forever. Things are changing, all around us. There's Oregon, for instance. There will be a war for certain over Oregon, the way the British and the Americans are moving in there."

Bidwell said, "I hope not. We were lucky to get through the last war with them, and Andy Jackson's too old to fight, God save us."

"We won't go to war with them over Oregon," Cat Reilly said. She picked up her cards.

Sutter chuckled in his throat. "Do women vote now in the United States? There will be a war. Do you understand what trump is, now?"

"Clubs," she said, and the Swiss looked surprised. Sohrakoff picked up his cards. So she had been paying attention.

"Yes." The Captain began to sort out his hand, picking the cards one by one out of his fist like a bird pecking corn. "You mark my words, whoever wins Oregon will win California too. And that will be the British, who have built Fort Vancouver on the Columbia, and who drove Astor out, and the other fur trappers."

"They have the rest of the world," Bidwell said. "Might as well take Oregon too."

"I think you're wrong," said Cat Reilly. "We'll get Oregon."

Sutter's eyebrows sank down over his nose. "What do you know about anything?" He plucked a card from his hand and tossed it onto the table.

She said, "The British won't give up all of Oregon, but they're really only interested in Vancouver Island and the coast along there, which is their access to the Pacific. The Americans are all south of Vancouver Island. There's an easy compromise, and they'll make it."

Sohrakoff lifted his head and stared at her. This made sense to him, even in a woman's voice. Clearly it did to Sutter, too, against his will; he fussed with his cards and squirmed in his place and burst out, "How do you know that?"

"My grandfather was Grimes Mather," she said. "He was in the Senate from Massachusetts when they negotiated the original treaty with Britain back in the twenties. The subject was an active one at our dining table from the time I was a little girl."

Bidwell swung toward her, a wide smile on his face. "Your father was a senator?" Finally he played to Sutter's lead.

"My grandfather. My father teaches history at Harvard University." Calmly, without hesitating, she put a card down on the trick, and Sohrakoff played under her; she pulled the four cards toward her.

Sutter reached across the table and took the trick away from her and laid it down in front of himself. "She's lying. She can't prove it and we can't disprove it — she's making it up." He glared at her. "Everybody who comes to California was a king in his own country. You wonder why anybody ever left. Lead."

She led the ace of trumps. Sutter squawked, "Not that, you idiot! Damn it!"

"If there's a war," Bidwell said quietly, "it will be over Texas, anyway, not Oregon."

Sohrakoff twitched. This talk now was heating up: a war over Texas would certainly involve California. He played low on the trump trick while Sutter groaned and rubbed his hand over his face.

"I don't understand what I did wrong," Cat said mildly, when Sutter had collected the trick and added it to the one already in front of him, and smooth as a shark she led the king of clubs.

Sohrakoff gave a yelp of laughter. "She's a hustler, Captain. You got yourself a grafter in skirts." He dropped his trapped queen under her king. "Do you have the jack, too, girl?"

"No," she said, and led low. Sutter, silent again, played the jack to win the trick and continued with the last of the trumps; suddenly he had the intent look of a man going for big stakes.

Sohrakoff aimed his gaze across the table at Bidwell. "Why would there be a war over Texas? It's been years since the trouble there. Why fight now?"

"Mexico won't fight over Texas," Sutter said scornfully. "Mexicans don't fight. You know that. Texas is lost to them."

Bidwell said, "Americans who took over Texas in '36 made it an independent republic. Sam Houston's been smart — kept neutral and quiet, so the Mexicans could pretend it wasn't really lost. But there's more fire under him all the time to bring Texas into the Union, and Mexico will never tolerate that." He glanced at the woman. "Isn't that right, Cathy?"

"Not much they can do," Sutter said crisply. "The Americans have all the guns." He was playing out a string of hearts, squeezing Sohrakoff down to his last three cards; needing to slough something, the Count dropped a spade, and then lost his unguarded queen to Sutter's ace.

The Swiss crowed. "Got you there," he said. "Pinched you till you screamed, hah, Sohrakoff?" Bubbling with satisfaction, he counted the tricks. "Small slam!" He lifted his head and spread the unction of his approval on Cat Reilly. "Not bad for a beginner. Of course I had a howitzer of a hand."

"Well," Bidwell said, "I've been gunned down, anyway. That's the rubber, finally, and I'm going to bed. Cathy, shall I walk you over to your place?"

"Thank you, John." She was facing Sutter, her hands on the table, her face sweet and pliant. "Is that all, Captain?"

"Stay. I want to talk to you."

"I'll wait," Bidwell said, and Sutter wheeled on him.

"She can manage on her own. Go to bed. Sohrakoff —"

"I'm not going back in the cooker," Sohrakoff said.

The Swiss nodded. "Just don't pull a weapon. I can't have my men killing each other."

"Make Christenson work more than he talks."

Sutter heaved up a humorless laugh. "Tell me how and you can be my overseer. Get out of here."

Bidwell went through the door onto the landing of the staircase. Sohrakoff started after him; he glanced over Sutter's shoulder at the American woman. "Good night, Mrs. Reilly."

Her strange eyes turned toward him; she did not smile. "Good night, Count." He went out into the dark and the wind.

Sutter leaned his arms on the table, facing her, his expression intensely serious. For the first time she had his interest, almost his respect. His voice was crisp. "You have a rudimentary instinct for the game. Let me tell you a few things. First of all, never lead off an ace of trumps like that."

"I had the king," she said.

"Shut up and listen to me. Lead the king, then the ace. Always play second hand low. Cover anything above a ten if you can. Lead low from a long suit, high from a short one." He picked up the deck and blocked it. "Tomorrow, before we play, I'll talk to you about signaling." He nodded, dismissing her. "Go on, go to bed."

She swung her feet across the bench and got up, tired. In a few hours they would be out on the valley floor again, killing animals and turning them into money.

She started toward the door, and he said, "Cat."

She turned. "Yes, Captain."

"Any of these men gives you trouble, tell me, I'll throw him in the calabozo."

"Captain," she said, angry, "I'll handle it." She walked out the door and down the steps into the blue moonlight.

15 🚩 BIDWELL SAID, "I wish I were half as good at anything as Sutter thinks he is at everything."

Sohrakoff laughed.

They were walking across the yard toward the shed where the crew slept; Bidwell had found some tobacco and was packing a pipe. Moths swarmed, glinting in the clear, faint light of the full moon, and the looping flight of bats coursed through them, laced with high squeaks.

"When Zeke trumped his ace his face went the color of raw beef," the Count said. "He has a knack for the cards, though; he knows the game." He was tired of Sutter. It was the Americans who interested him now.

They had reached the long, low adobe building where Sutter's riders slept. Bidwell stuck a straw up into the lantern over the door and brought the flame to his pipe. "You know, until I met you I never knew there was a Russian colony here."

Sohrakoff turned away from him. He leaned against the wall beside the door, reluctant to go inside. "You Americans do everything backwards. We came east to find the land, and you came west to find the ocean."

He did not want to remember Ross, the failed dream, the redwood kremlin on the sea cliff, where he had been born.

Which belonged to Sutter now. Around him now were the bones of Ross — the shakes on the roof, the framing of the adobe walls, the floors. Bidwell held the pipe out to him.

"Thanks." He took a long pull of the sweet, head-spinning smoke. Handing back the pipe, he threw a curious look into the American's face.

"Your accent is different from Mrs. Reilly's."

Bidwell shook his head. The lantern behind him framed him in a rim of light. "Cathy's from Massachusetts." He laughed, his face pleasantly lively. "Actually, Cathy's from another world. I never knew that before, about the senator, but it fits — she couldn't boil water when she started out with us. I'm from New York state. Taught school a while, moved down to Missouri, tried to farm, came west."

"Why?"

Bidwell turned toward him, and the lantern light washed over his cheek, one eye, the edge of his smile. "I don't really know. I felt it out here. The space, the size. All my life I listened to stories about the west. You stand at the edge of the plains at Kaw's Landing and look and look until your eyeballs pop out, but you can't see an end to it. So you have to come find it. And I did."

In his voice there was a rising note of satisfaction. Sohrakoff got the pipe back and took another drag on it. The Americans gave off a boundless certainty, an innocence, for all their toughness and will, that what they wanted was what everyone should want. They knew nothing larger than themselves. He let out the blue burst of smoke into the starry air.

"You play a pretty good hand yourself, Count," Bidwell said.

"It's not that hard a game." Sohrakoff could hear the men inside snoring; his back tightened, resisting. "I'm going to go sleep in the stable. Thanks for the smoke."

"Good night," said Bidwell.

On the south side of the fort, outside the row of stones that marked Sutter's planned front wall and below the squat little cannon that stood by Sutter's planned front gate, Manaiki grew a garden. Most of the things that relieved and made palatable New Helvetia's endless diet of beef came out of this plot of worked earth — squash and onions, three kinds of peppers, melons and corn and red beans.

She complained all the time that nobody helped her, and one day in the late spring, when most of the men had gone off with Sutter to gather cattle on the American River, Catharine went out to haul water from the well to the garden.

Sohrakoff was in the fort still, the only man left; he was working over near the end of the unfinished wall, building a shop for the three huge lathes Sutter had gotten from Fort Ross. While she cranked up the bucket from the bottom of the well he walked across the yard toward her.

"Can I get some water?"

She set the dripping wooden bucket on the rim of the well. "Go ahead."

He dipped up the water with his hand, splashed his face and his springy orange hair, and drank, then leaned on the well, watching her fill the big buckets on the yoke that she would carry down to the garden. His sweat-soaked shirt was plastered to his chest; one of his knuckles was a mashed scab. "Are you really the granddaughter of a senator?" he asked.

"Are you really a count?"

"No," he said. "Which is why I think to ask."

She laughed, looking up at him, knowing she would catch a smile on his face, and did. When he smiled his blue eyes blazed. She said, "My grandfather was a senator from the Commonwealth of Massachusetts for eighteen years. That's not, you know, like being a don." She dropped the bucket and crouched to fit herself under the wooden yoke, balanced on the stones of the well.

"I'll do that," he said, and moved up behind her, and took the heavy yoke up off her shoulders. For an instant while he stepped into the weight his chest brushed against her back. She moved away, reaching down for the other bucket.

"Where did you get your name, then?" she asked, and followed him away down the grass toward the garden, lugging the smaller bucket with both hands; the wire handle cut into her fingers.

"My father was Timofei Sergeievitch Sohrakoff," he said.

"I've never heard of him."

"No, nobody has, nobody will. But what Alexander Baranoff thought, my father did, and between them they built Russian America from Yakatut to Ross."

"Why did they sell Ross, then?"

"The tsar lost interest. My father told me once, 'Watch out for the men in the blue coats. And watch out for the people who obey them.'"

He walked easily under the yoke, holding the buckets still; she had to stretch to keep up with his rangy stride. The hands on the buckets were big and long-fingered and flexible, with square, bony wrists. He spoke over his shoulder to her.

"My father and Baranoff used to sit around the kremlin in New Arkangel getting drunk and telling each other they were the real nobles, and one night Baranoff wrote my father a patent."

They had reached the end of the garden; three rows down, in the young corn, Manaiki stooped in her billowing red dress, pulling weeds. The Russian slid his hands up under the yoke, easing the weight on his shoulders. He smiled at Catharine.

"When he died, everybody started calling me Count, and my father would have liked that, so I stayed with it."

The garden was a lush green island in the plain burned blond by the drought. Outside the ditch that edged the plot, the straw stood up in clumps, pale as spun gold, above the bare, crusted earth. Inside the ditch the plants rose smooth and full. Among them a few wildflowers had caught hold of the reliable water, and Manaiki let them stay, a little round cluster of white daisies, a stand of wild radish in extravagant shades of purple, even a poppy, its silky orange skirt of a bloom rimmed with pure yellow. Walking along the edge of the garden, her bare feet sinking into the loose, loved soil, Catharine began to spill the water slowly into the neat little ditches Manaiki made along her chili plants, now knee high, their glossy green leaves curling down a little in the heat, their plump fruits hanging from the stems like organs.

Sohrakoff sat on his heels, chewing on the stem of an onion green, watching her. She went back to fill the bucket again.

"Washington has always tried to keep Americans from moving west," she said. "We don't listen to them."

"I don't think you people listen to anybody."

She dunked the bucket into the big pail on the yoke, irritated at that, insulted, perversely, since it was true.

Across the garden, Manaiki waved to her, commanding. "Here — the peas need more drink. Bring all water."

Sohrakoff stooped under the yoke again and bore the water away to the far side of the plot. Catharine walked along by him. He set the pails down on the grass where Manaiki pointed, and the Kanaka woman filled her bucket.

"Catharine, there." She pointed to another little bucket lying in the grass, and then went off down a row of beans. Sohrakoff stretched his shoulders, his hands rising above his head. He picked up the long tail of his shirt and wiped his face with it.

"Were you rich, in Boston?"

"Rich." Catharine stooped, the can of water in her hands, and dumped the water along the plants. The wet bulge ran one or two feet along the dry soil and abruptly collapsed into it. "No, we weren't rich. Brilliant, is more the word. We all had to be brilliant. We did everything better, we were prettier — or handsomer, in my brother's case — and we played the piano better, and knew more, and said cleverer things."

"Than who?" he said.

"Than anybody who wasn't a Mather," she said. She went back to the yoke for more water. Boston seemed unreal to her now, like a painting on a wall somewhere. "Of course my sisters and I weren't supposed to be better than my brother."

He laughed, and she smiled at him, pleased with her own wit and with him for appreciating it. He bent down and got the bucket out of her hand. "You play the piano? The commandante's wife at Ross had a piano." He gave her a quick sharp look. "In fact Sutter probably has it."

"A piano? Here?"

"It was at Ross after the Rotchevs left," he said. "Sutter took everything movable. It must be here somewhere, in one of the storerooms."

"A piano," she said. Manaiki was coming toward them, her round brown face beaming.

"You see how my peas grow? Come look."

"I have to go back to work," Sohrakoff said, and started away; then suddenly he stopped still, staring away down the plain. "Oh-oh."

Catharine twisted to see where he was looking. South of the fort the valley stretched away in a long, low yellow trough, dotted with the round dark green heads of the oak trees. Through the haze the river wound in a tangle of dusty willows, the water's surface filmy with wind ripples. Down there, two days before, Sutter had gathered a herd of cattle, and they were moving, stirring up the dust. Catharine shaded her eyes, trying to make out the forms that slithered through the distant murk.

Sohrakoff said something in a language not English or Spanish. His hand closed on her arm. "That's the Vallejos. Come on."

"Vallejos," Manaiki said. Her round brown arms rose, her eyes wide and her mouth falling open. She gaped down toward the churning fog of dust on the southern plain. "The Vallejos come!"

Her voice was a high wail. The red dress flapping around her, she wheeled and ran toward the fort.

"The Vallejos! The Vallejos!"

"What's going on?" Catharine cried.

"Move," Sohrakoff said, and pushed her toward the fort.

With his hand on her back shoving her on ahead of him, she ran up past the little cannon and the row of stones. Manaiki was disappearing into the kitchen, her wails sounding muffled through the open door; the door slammed. Sohrakoff towed Catharine past the steps of the central building and shoved her toward the dark open stable.

"You go in there," he said, "and crawl into a corner, somewhere dark, somewhere nobody can find you, and don't come out until I get back here with Sutter." Turning, he ran two steps to the corral and vaulted over the top rail; the horses dozing in the shade spooked at his sudden appearance and trotted nervously around the pen.

Catharine hurried after him. "What is it? What's going on?"

He got one hand over the nose of a bay horse, his other arm around its neck, and muscled it to the far wall, where scraps of leather harness hung. "Those riders down there, they're Vallejo's men."

"How do you know? They're so far away —"

"They can't be anybody else! The river's fallen so low they've forded it somewhere, they're going to try to drive those cattle off, and they'll be up here, too, to see what trouble they can make."

He pulled the crown of a bitless bridle up over the horse's ears. Catharine stood where she was, uncertain, her heart thundering against her ribs. He dropped the top rail of the corral and led the horse out and whirled toward her, shouting at her.

"Go! Hide, girl — get the hell where they can't find you!" He vaulted up onto the bare back of the horse and galloped away down through the yard, past the central building, and swerved out of sight to the north.

She walked a few steps after him, her middle knotted and her throat dry. Manaiki ran around the end of the central building.

"Catharine, Catharine, come and hide in the kitchen with us." She held out one pink-palmed hand, the fingers splayed. "Catharine —"

Catharine ran up the steps that led to Sutter's office door. From the landing at the top she peered to the south, where the yellow dust hung in the air. In the drifting haze she could see only a mass of moving forms. The cattle were bunching together; she knew enough about them now to realize that they did not crowd up into packs unless they were herded, and suddenly, her throat constricting, she saw a line of horsemen cantering across the long, bare plain toward her.

"Here they come," she said.

At the foot of the stairs Manaiki screamed and ran around

the front of the central building, headed for the kitchen again, where the other Kanaka woman probably already huddled in the dark. Catharine went into Sutter's office.

In her gut there was a rippling like nervous wings, and the backs of her hands itched. She walked up and down the room twice before her panicky thoughts would settle enough to be put in order. She was not going to hide. She lived here, this was her place, nobody could make her cower and hide in her own place. Finally she went into the little clerk's office and opened the drawer under the desk, where she knew Sutter kept a gun.

On top of a pile of papers lay a two-barreled flintlock pistol. When she picked it up the weight reassured her. She hoped it was loaded. She had never loaded a gun or fired one. The wooden grip was cool and smooth; there was a brass plate on the butt, and the action was brass and steel, cold to the touch. Some of the panic stilled in her blood. She wiped her hand over her face, stroked back her hair, and went out to the landing of the staircase.

The horsemen were closer now, jogging in a wide rank over the grass; there were six or eight of them. They wore sombreros and close-fitting jackets and leather pants. She stood on the landing, holding the gun by her side, watching them ride up.

They came in past Manaiki's garden, circled the little cannon, and trotted their horses through the row of stones into the yard below her. They rode superbly, as if their bodies grew up out of their horses. They ignored her. Swiftly they scattered through the yard, looking into the shops and banging on the doors.

The last of them rode up toward the staircase.

This one was different from the others. His hat and jacket were black; silver glinted on the brim of the sombrero and the front of the jacket. On his saddle shone plates of chased silver, and his reins were covered with little silver beads. When he reined up below her, he swept off his sombrero.

His face was round and hard, red as an apple, his eyes like stone. His slick black hair clung to his head in feathery curls. He made a flourish to her with his hat and bowed and said something in Spanish.

"I don't speak Spanish," she said. Her heart jumped into her throat. She had forgotten the difference in language; if she could not talk to them this would be much harder.

Across his florid face a wedge of a smile flashed. "Yet I do speak English, if not perfectly. I am Don el General Mariano Guadalupe Vallejo, at your service. And you —"

"My name is Catharine Reilly," she said.

"And you are a guest of Don Juan Agosto Sutter?" Slowly his men were collecting behind him, looking up at her, their dark faces lean and unsmiling under their battered dusty hats. Two of them had ropes in their hands, the loops already dangling, swaying open. She tightened her fingers around the butt of the pistol and moved closer to the wall, under the eaves of the roof.

"I am Captain Sutter's clerk," she said to the don below her. "Where is Captain Sutter?"

"He's coming," she said. "When we saw that you had decided to pay us a visit, Don Vallejo, we sent to him, and he will be here very soon."

The black beads of his eyes surveyed her, traveling slowly up and down. "Perhaps," he said. "But Captain Sutter, I believe, is well up on the American River, hours away." His tongue licked pink and wet over his bottom lip. He was staring at her as if she had no clothes on. Abruptly his head jerked up toward the office. "I am going up there now, Señora Reilly. You may open the door for me."

A thrill of alarm jagged through her. She could not let him into Sutter's office, to spy on all Sutter's papers, Sutter's books and plans. Her mouth was dry. She fought off the urge to look away to the north. The don below her spoke in Spanish to his men, who fanned out, surrounding the foot of the staircase with their horses, and Vallejo himself swung down from his saddle.

Upright as a chess piece, his walk springy with arrogance, he paced to the foot of the stairs and came up two steps, and she swung toward him and lifted the pistol.

"Stop there."

He stopped. His black brows arched up, and his mouth curled with a semblance of humor. "Ah. Tender me the gun, señora, lest you harm yourself." He put out his hand and took another step up the stairs.

She put her thumb on the right-hand hammer of the action and cocked it back. "I'll shoot, Don Vallejo," she said. "Don't come any closer. I am not letting you into the office."

He fixed her with the stare of his brilliant black eyes. He gave off a radiance of power and certainty. "Since you are Sutter's clerk you must know he has stolen cattle from me."

She licked her lips; her mind leapt to the cow they had killed by mistake and rendered into tallow. His authority was wearing on her and she felt her joints loosening, her resistance going soft. Then behind her, below, there was a singing in the air, and she ducked.

Something like a whip whacked her hard across the back of the head. A loop of rope slid over her shoulder, fell limp at her feet, and slithered away. She let out a yell, startled, and the gun in her hand went off.

The explosion raised every hair on her body on end; she nearly dropped the pistol. Below her Vallejo bounded backward off the steps. She pressed her back flat against the wall of the building behind her and wheeled around, seeing the riders in the yard shaking out their ropes, their eyes pinning her, the nasty whirring of the ropes like little voices. She crouched down into the angle of the landing rail, where they could not get a loop over her.

"I'll shoot again — go! Get out!" She struggled with the second hammer, trying to cock it; it was much stiffer than the first.

Vallejo barked an order, his voice strident. He was standing well back from the stairs, ready to dodge. "Señora, I advise you to surrender at once, and I shall be gracious."

She was stooped down in the shelter of the stair rail. Through the railing she could see his riders, their ropes ready in their hands, the horses skittering nervously sideways. She aimed the gun straight down the steps at Mariano Vallejo and said, "I'll shoot, damn you," and he backed up another step.

Finally she got the second hammer cocked. He scuttled back from the foot of the steps. His voice rang out, yelling orders.

Half the riders abruptly broke away and trotted around the central building. There was another door over there; they would break in that way, come at her from two sides. She thought, I'm not getting out of this, and pushed that useless, cowardly idea out of her mind. She raised the pistol in both hands.

"Leave or I'll kill you right now!"

From one of the men below her came a high shout of warning. Another horseman was galloping up past Manaiki's garden.

It was Zeke Merritt. His horse dropped down to a jog and carried him, slack and hulking in the saddle, up to face Vallejo's men. "What's going on here?"

"Zeke," she shouted, "watch out."

Around the corner of the building the rest of Vallejo's men charged in a flying wedge. Zeke wheeled toward them, and a rope spun out and dropped over his head. It jerked tight around his chest, and Zeke flew backward out of the saddle and hit the ground with a thud.

The rider galloped his horse straight toward the row of stones. The rope snapped taut. With a howl of sudden pain Zeke skidded across the ground after him. Catharine thrust the gun out between the posts of the railing and shot the horse.

It went down like an avalanche, plowing headfirst through the dust; the rider pitched off in a heap. Zeke rolled onto his feet, bellowing. The horse got up again, staggered a few feet, and fell, blood gushing from its neck.

Vallejo's men scattered through the yard, their voices a chorus of high-pitched derisive screams. With the gun useless now, Catharine lunged for the door to the office and darted inside, and a moment later feet pounded on the stairs. She leaned against the door, her hand on the latch.

"Lemme in!" Zeke roared, and she flung the door open. He bulled past her into the office, running toward the far wall where Sutter's guns were hanging. "Lock that door."

She slammed the door. "God, am I glad to see you!"

"I'll bet you are. What are you trying to do, you stupid bitch — start a war?" He brought a long rifle and a powder horn across the room; his back was coated with dust, his hair

sifting dust; the seat of his pants was ripped, showing half a
filthy, hairy buttock. "Get out of my way!" He thrust her
roughly off to one side and pushed the door open. "Waugh.
They're going." His voice wheezed with relief. He lowered the
rifle and went onto the landing.

She followed him, her knees quivering. The horse she had
killed lay sprawled across Sutter's line of stones. Vallejo and his
men were jogging away out of the yard, two riding double. As
they passed by the cannon, they all swerved to ride through
Manaiki's garden. Catharine brushed a tangle of hair back off
her face. Below the pulped and trampled garden, the Californios
swerved away, spreading out across the plain, going back down
toward the distant yellow haze and the milling cattle.

"They're stealing the cattle," she said.

Zeke grunted. "Let 'em." All the tense purpose in him was
gone; he seemed suddenly almost jovial, the gun barrel tipped
up toward the sky, and he gave a booming laugh. "Sonsabitches
can pick on a lone woman, but once a man shows up they run."

"Once you got to the arsenal," she said.

Suddenly a surge of joy took her, lifting her up like a wave.

She had won. She had driven them off, she had defended her
place against them. As if she exploded outward from every
boundary of her body she reached across New Helvetia and
gathered it in, hers, transformed from mere earth and grass into
a sacred place, enspirited with her love.

She trembled with the force of this passion; she had never
loved anything so much before.

Another rider jogged into the yard: John Christenson. He
circled the dead horse and goggled up at her. Across his saddle-
bows he had a musket.

"What's going on? Sohrakoff said there was trouble."

"You're too late," Zeke said. "I run 'em off." He slapped
Catharine's backside, companionable, as if she were another
man. "Cat took the only scalp. Sure glad you plugged that horse,
lady." He swiped at her again, more exploratory, and she sidled
out of his way.

16 ✠ SHE FOUND THE PIANO, a battered spinet, in one of the storerooms along the north wall, packed in between strange Russian engines and covered with heaps of moldering rugs. When she mentioned it to Sutter, he shrugged.

"There's no place to put it. Besides, it's probably broken. You're about to have a hell of a lot of work to do, Cat; you're not going to have time for a piano."

She took a card out of her hand and dropped it onto the table. She and Count Sohrakoff were playing together in the fifth rubber of the night against Bidwell and Sutter. The light of the lantern overhead showered them in its fuzzy yellow glow; the silence of the fort at night surrounded them like a negative space.

"We could move it up here," she said. The cards slapped down on the wooden tabletop. Sutter won the trick and took it in and laid it carefully in front of him, paying utmost attention to his cards. His voice rang like something metal dropped on the floor.

"Forget the piano. I have work for you to do. For everybody. I want to finish the wall before planting time. Now that Sohrakoff's got the carpentry shop done, I want people making chairs and tables." He led the ten of hearts and Catharine played the queen over it. "I want you two" — his hand wagged back and forth between Bidwell and Sohrakoff — "to go over to Ross and ramrod another load of lumber back here for me."

Bidwell murmured under his breath, staring at the half-played trick on the table before him. Clearly Sutter's lead had gotten his partner into some trouble.

The Swiss tapped his fingers impatiently on the tabletop. "Just play the card, Bidwell. When you hesitate, you give it all away."

"I didn't give it away," Bidwell said, and let the king fall. Sohrakoff won the trick with the ace and led the jack and then the nine.

Sutter said loftily, "Whist is like life. You have to take things in the order that they come to you." He reached for the jug. He had already had a lot to drink, which perhaps explained his bad play. "I'm going up to that Indian village near the peaks and give some pretty presents to the chief there. Maybe I can get him to send me some of his men."

"Why don't you leave those people alone?" Sohrakoff said.

Catharine glanced up at him, startled by the angry undercurrent in his voice. Bidwell said, "I don't see what good a bunch of Indians will do you, Captain. You got to get some more whites in here, to do the things you want to do."

"Those Diggers are just sitting around up there doing nothing. I'll pay them. Damn you, Count, have you got anything left but hearts?"

Sohrakoff spread his hand; every card in it was a winner. His gaze rose hard and unblinking toward Sutter. "There's nothing you can give those people that they need. Nothing they can do for you, as Bidwell says. Leave them alone."

Sutter's shoulders moved. His gaze slid away into the vague distance, his face sulky. "I shouldn't have brought it up. Whose deal is it?"

Catharine looked from him to Sohrakoff; the Count was still staring at him, his sunbleached eyebrows drawn down. She flung a fog of words in between him and Sutter. "At least let me dig it out of the rubble. It'll rot where it is." She shuffled the cards; she was learning how to do it properly, mostly by watching Sohrakoff, but now in her tense fingers the deck stuck together in mid-riffle and refused to bridge.

"What are you talking about?" Sutter asked, exasperated.

"The piano," Bidwell said. He leaned his elbows on the table, one hand up, hiding his smile. "She's going to keep on you until you let her have it, Captain. You might as well give up now."

"Deal," Sutter said to her. "Forget the piano. You'll never get it up the steps, you'll never get it in the door."

Sohrakoff said, "I'll bring it up here for her." He was sitting back on the bench, his elbows cocked up, still staring at Sutter; a shadow of bad temper lay over his face, but the edge was off. Relieved, she blocked the deck and put it on her left, for Bidwell to cut.

The Swiss grunted at Sohrakoff. "If you can get that piano up here, do it." He picked up his glass and drank, his eyes shut. She said, "Thank you, Count," and dealt the cards.

Breathless, Zeke said, "I got it — I got it —"

"Cat," Sohrakoff said, "pull."

In the yard below the steps, she gripped the halter of the mule and led it forward. The rope shrilled in the pulley, and the piano rumbled slowly up the steps. They had lashed a board to its side for a skid. Above, on the landing, Sohrakoff stood in the doorway, one hand on the rope, which ran on past him through the sheave he had fixed on the roof beam and down to the mule below.

"Come on, Zeke —"

"I got it," Zeke roared, and the piano moved, and the mule, snuffling, leaned against the rope and pulled. With a rattle of wood the piano banged up to the steps to the landing.

Zeke howled, triumphant. "Hey, we're dancin' tonight!"

Sohrakoff leaned down over the rail, waving to Catharine. "Slack off — we're done with that part." He straightened, his gaze looking beyond her, and his face settled. She turned.

Up the long, gradual slope from the Sacramento River people were walking in a line. They were naked brown young men, with lank black hair. Sutter had brought back the Indians.

Catharine led the mule to the corral and unharnessed it, and went over to watch the Indians come into the yard. She cast another look up at the landing, to see if Sohrakoff still watched, but he and Zeke were muscling the piano in through the door; she could hear the scream of wood rubbing on wood, and Zeke said a strange obscenity. The Indians walked up toward her.

Behind them came Sutter, on his gray horse, shooing them along with waves of his arm, as if they were sheep. "Go on, get in there. We're going to feed you now. Raphero, tell them." He leaned down to tap one of the young men on the shoulder and rattled off a string of Spanish. The young man looked up at him, wide-eyed, and moved faster; he caught up with the rest of the Indians and talked to them in their language.

They all gathered in the east yard. Sutter jogged his horse by, bellowing for Manaiki, for the cook. His face was round as the sun, and as bright.

He reined in beside Catharine. "You see? Their chiefs told them to come, and they came. This will be good for them. They'll learn how to work. In the meantime —"

Manaiki and the cook came out of the bakery, dragging between them a big basket full of round loaves of bread. They set it down before the little mob of Indians and stepped back.

The brown men stared at them, stared at the basket, did nothing. They were smaller than white people. They wore almost no clothes, a scrap of hide around their privates, a string of beads. They stood close together, their arms folded up before them, like little children, and their eyes were wide and dark with fear.

They smelled strange, like fish or wet leaves. Their skin was shiny. Their long hair was braided with beads. Their voices were soft and high-pitched.

Catharine went over to Sutter, who was standing in the shade of the oak tree by the corral. Along the rail behind him, Pablo Gutierrez had unsaddled his horse and was rubbing it down with a hay swath; Sutter, his head high and his arms out, leaned against the fence of the pigpen. On the far side, the six pigs snuffled and rumbled through the muck, certain he was going to feed them. A trotter hit the fence with a bang.

"Captain," Catharine said, "these people aren't going to be much use to you."

Pablo glanced at her over his shoulder. Sutter made a sound at her, remarkably like the noise the pigs made. "Why aren't you up there playing the piano?"

She twisted to look back at the Indians. "Captain."

He put his hand on her and shoved her toward the central building. In her ear he hissed, "You interfere with this, I'll run you out of here, you understand? You wanted that goddamn piano — now go play it!" He propelled her hard toward the steps.

She walked fast, getting away from him; as his hand left her, her steps slowed. Her insides were churning. All her life, around the dinner table, in the streets, in lecture halls, she had heard of the evils of slavery. She had always known that she stood on the right side, against evil, against sin. Even running away from home she had seen as a struggle for freedom against debasing servitude. She had always known that when the time came she would be on the right side.

She had reached the bottom of the stairs. She put her hand on the railing, struggling with herself. She wanted desperately for Sutter to be right. The Indians would learn. They would be paid, they would work, learn honorable labor. But these thoughts skimmed the surface, they attached to nothing real, they winged back and forth, trying to weave air into truth, but the truth lay under it all, like a rock, which she could not reach to change.

She could not leave New Helvetia, not now.

She went up the stairs and into the office. The piano stood against the far wall, below the rack of guns. Its paint was peeled away and the raw wood was scarred. She pulled the bench over and sat down and put her hands on the keys, and played a C major scale the length of the board.

The instrument was out of tune, but all the keys sounded. She could tune it reasonably well later, and even now it was close enough to play. The music made an order, a space, a sanity, and she plunged gratefully into it, remembering a sonatina of Mozart's, neat and bright. Her fingers were stiff and awkward at first but the old skill returned; she grew more confident with each note. Someone came in behind her, and in the doorway to the next room Zeke Merritt appeared, listening. She kept her eyes away from them. She pinned her gaze to the bare, gouged wood before her and played the music of civilization.

Vallejo's visit convinced Sutter that he had to finish the wall around the fort before he did anything else. He put the white men to building it and the Indians to making the bricks. This went along well enough, the Indians enjoying trampling the clay and slapping it into molds, and the wall went up quickly;

by midsummer it was done, only two gaps remaining where the gates would hang. Sutter thought he could bring the gates from Fort Ross. Then he set the Indians to rendering tallow, which they did not like so much; after two days of that, all the Indians disappeared.

Sutter tramped up and down the east yard, kicking the dirt and swearing in English and Spanish and German. The sun was already fierce, even this early in the morning, and the six white men watched him from the shade of the long wall. He wheeled toward them, decisive.

"Saddle up. We're going after them."

Cat was watching from the stair landing. All the men turned to obey him but one. Sohrakoff stepped forward, his hands on his hips. "Let them go. If they don't want to work here, don't make them."

"I need them," Sutter said. He marched up and down the yard, his arms swinging. "They promised me they would work."

"They don't understand that," Sohrakoff said. "You go out there and drag them back, it's like bringing them into slavery."

Catharine gathered in her breath, her chest constricted. "Captain." She went forward to the rail. Her throat was tight, as if a fist clutched her there, trying to keep the words inside. "Maybe he's right."

The other men were strung out along the east side of the yard, staying out of the summer sun; they had begun to get their horses out of the corral, but now they were still, silent, watching.

Sutter swept them with a look, shot a frown up at Catharine, and strode toward Sohrakoff. "I need those men! This isn't slavery. I'll pay them, they told me they would work — and they're only Indians, damn it!" His voice rose toward a yell. "Get your horses!"

The other men, knowing him, began to move off toward the pole fence beyond the oak tree. One of the rails dropped with a clatter. The horses stirred, shifting, their hoofs pattering on the hard, dry ground. Catharine went down the steps into the yard, headed for Sutter, who was face to face with Sohrakoff.

The Russian was planted in his tracks, his hands on his belt. "I'm not running Indians."

"Then get off my place," Sutter snarled at him.

Catharine reached him. "Captain, he's right."

He whirled on her, his face dark red, and shouted into her face, "They're only Indians!"

"Captain —" From the shade, John Bidwell came forward. "You know, this doesn't sit too well with me, either."

Sutter's eyes widened; he lifted his head and cast a broad look around him, and he took a step toward Sohrakoff, his hands fisted. "Get out of here before I shoot you."

Sohrakoff said, "I'm leaving." He walked over toward the corral. Sutter glared after him.

Catharine put herself in Sutter's way, her heart hammering. "Captain, even in California, there are moral laws."

"Damn you," he said; he thrust his face into hers, his breath blasting her. "Go, then. You go, too."

She licked her lips. In the fierce glitter of his eyes she saw that he meant it: he would drive her away from New Helvetia, she would lose everything. And nothing would change. He would do what he intended, no matter what she did. Down through the middle of her resolve a crack opened like a tear.

Behind her, quietly, Bidwell said, "Well, Captain . . ." He was caught in it too.

Sutter collected himself with an obvious effort. The color drained from his face. His mustaches drooped limp in the heat. He said, "I am paying them. Feeding them. All I ask is some work out of them. And I have to have the work. John, Cat — you know that. What we're making here takes work." He nodded to them. "You work. It doesn't hurt you."

She said, "If I left, you wouldn't haul me back by force."

Abruptly, behind her, a horse galloped away out the space in the wall where a gate would go. She started. She felt the drumming of the hoofs like an assault along her nerves. The sound faded; she did not turn, she did not look after Sohrakoff. Her eyes stung, suddenly. She wondered what she wanted to weep for.

Sutter said, "This is not slavery. This is pure necessity."

Bidwell sighed. "All right, Captain. You'll do it anyway, I guess." His feet milled in the dust.

Unsmiling, Sutter nodded to her. "Is it all right with you, Mrs. Morality?"

She lowered her eyes.

In the night she woke suddenly, knowing there was someone else in the room with her, and a hand came down over her mouth.

She lurched up, the blanket clutched to her; all over her body the hair stood on end. He said, "It's all right, it's me."

"Count." In the dark she could just make out his shape, hunkered down beside her bed.

"I came to say goodbye to you," he said.

"I thought —" Her voice was ragged. She thrust her hair back off her face and tried again. "I thought you had gone."

"Sutter can't run me off. I was going anyway, I'm tired of him. But I wanted to say goodbye to you. I'll miss you, Cat."

"I'll miss you," she said, and put out her hand toward him. "Goodbye, Count."

In the dark he moved, and then suddenly his hand went around behind her head and he kissed her. His mouth was soft and sweet, his beard shaggy against her cheek. His tongue slid in between her lips. He turned and walked out of the room.

She sat up still in the bed, gripping the blanket against her breasts. Her nipples tingled; in her groin her sex tightened with desire. Her mind stopped, too full to think, jammed with her feelings, with a blind, almost overwhelming urge to call him back.

He would not come. He was gone now. She lifted her head, her eyes dry, her throat clogged. After a long while she lay down again and shut her eyes and tried to sleep.

17 ❧ SOHRAKOFF RODE into Monterey late at night; everything was dark and quiet, even along Cockfight Alley in the ruins of the old presidio. The little town lay in the laps of the hills above the beach, a scatter of square adobe houses, their whitewashed walls pale under the moon. Out in the bay three or four dark ships rode at anchor. The surf churned a white froth along the beach, its hiss and sigh and roar the constant music of Monterey, its salt tang the perfume.

He went past the old customs building to the big, rambling house that belonged to Don José Castro, commandante-general of California.

There was a light in one of the windows in the side wing of the house. He had intended to go in through the stableyard and sleep there until the morning, but instead, seeing the light, he put his horse up and went around to the door and knocked.

A drowsy cadet opened it for him, jerked awake at the sight of him, and stepped back to let him in. "You want Lieutenant Orozco? I think he's asleep."

"The light's on in his room." Sohrakoff went in past the boy and walked through the house toward the side wing. There was no light except the glow escaping around the edges of a door midway down the corridor. Sohrakoff knocked once, sharply, and went in without waiting for an answer.

The light hung from the center of the ceiling. Under it, the commandante of Monterey, Lieutenant Jesús Orozco, was seated at the big sand-covered table that took up most of the room. He watched Sohrakoff come in without a flicker of surprise on his face, although the Count had been gone almost six months.

Orozco was in his early thirties, tall, slender, his lancer's uniform impeccable even now, when he was off duty and in his own room. His jet-black hair and black eyes and plowshare jaw and high, flared cheekbones were all evidence of his Indian blood. He had gone to the military academy in Mexico City, where he had learned the war game kriegspiel, which he was playing now on the sand table; he had already shaped the sand into ridges and lowlands, a miniature world, and now he was sticking bits of twig into the sand to make trees.

He said, "You've been gone a while, Count. I was beginning to think you weren't coming back."

"I told you I'd do a good job," Sohrakoff said. "What's that?"

"The battle of Austerlitz." Orozco bent down under the table and brought up a leather box, in which he kept a variety of toys he used to signify soldiers. "You've spent all this time in New Helvetia?"

"That's where you told me to go, isn't it." Sohrakoff pulled a chair around into the blind corner opposite the door and sat down in it. He said, "I found out what you wanted to know. Sutter has no foreign connections. He's uninterested in anything but building his ranch." Sprawling in the chair, the Russian put his left boot up on his right knee; Orozco's rectitude always made him deliberately sloppy.

"There was some talk he'd call in the French." The lieutenant was putting pieces out onto the game table.

"All the while I was there I saw no sign of anything between him and any other country." He let himself relax in the chair after the long ride; this was as much of a home as he had now. His next business was making sure he stayed here. "What he's doing that's dangerous is letting in the Americans. He has two or three families there already."

Orozco's mouth stretched into a smile. "A virtual army of Anglos."

"That's how they took Texas, that's how they're taking Oregon. They leak in and fill the place up."

"I won't worry about two or three settlers, especially in the north valley, which is a desert. What else?"

"Sutter and Vallejo are like dogs along a fence. Sutter is enslaving the Indians. He's behind in his payments for Ross, and his crops have failed two years in a row."

"You certainly took your time accumulating this relatively foreseeable information."

Sohrakoff wore a spur on his left heel; he played with the

rowel, spinning it around with his forefinger. "I met a woman up there I was really getting to like. But Sutter is a swine."

"As long as he isn't going to sell us to the French or the British," Orozco said, "he can be the biggest pig in California, with my blessing." He put a black chess knight, the figure he used to represent Napoleon, on one of the hills on his sand table. "Will he support Micheltorena?"

"Probably, yes. He wants his charters confirmed. Especially the secret charter on Ross. Did anything interesting go on here while I was away?"

"I had a short, unpleasant discussion with General Castro on the subject of artillery that convinced him of precisely nothing and will doubtless hold up my promotion for another year. He signed your papers."

"Good." Without papers Sohrakoff could not stay in California; he had made himself useful to Orozco in the first place to get legal papers. Flicking the rowel back and forth, he watched the Indio soldier putting pieces onto his game table in neat European rows.

"Does Napoleon win this one?"

"Of course. The emperor's greatest tactical achievement. Heavily outnumbered, he appeared to be giving up, drew the Russians and Austrians into his center, and crushed them with flank attacks."

"If he'd lost he'd have looked like a goat."

"He didn't lose."

"It was his soldiers who won his battles for him. They liked to fight, they thought they were saving the world. When they stopped believing that, anybody could beat him. One-eyed Russians. One-armed Englishmen."

"Spoken like the cannon fodder you are." Orozco hunched forward, his eyes on the game table, one hand to his chin. He was always clean-shaven; Sohrakoff had never seen him with even a shadow of a beard. His voice flattened, emotionless. "Are you here now for a while?"

"As long as I've got papers."

"Very well. I can use you. There's nobody in the room you were in before you left."

"All right." Sohrakoff stood up, pleased; this had been easier than he had expected. Obviously, in spite of his complaints, Orozco thought he had done a good job. Now the lieutenant was locked in his game, fighting old battles from half the world away. Sohrakoff went out to the corridor and down four doors to the corner room.

18 ♛ CATHARINE COULD FIND no music for the piano. She remembered many of the pieces she had learned in Boston — Beethoven, Mozart, Purcell, exercises of Czerny's, Scarlatti sonatas adapted from the harpsichord. She sat at the piano whenever she could, and as she played more, other things came back to her. Sometimes if she stopped thinking her hands went on by themselves, spinning out music she thought she had forgotten utterly. Feeling her way through a Chopin waltz, she ignored the steps pounding up to the door behind her, until it flew open with a crash and John Christenson roared in.

"We got guests, lady — Cap'n says we roll it out tonight!" He let out a whoop that she felt inside her ears.

"Guests." She turned. "What do you mean?"

"Wagons!" He danced around the room, more energetic than she had ever seen him, his yellow hair flying. "There's a train of wagons coming down from the Sierra."

A thready excitement quickened her blood. She went through the next room to the stair beyond and stood on that landing, which looked east, and peered away down the valley.

The sky burned a pale, gilded blue. The long, dry summer had dusted everything with a thin layer of grit. Along the river the willows lay in limp clumps, their leaves grimed the same color as the soil. The haze in the air obscured the flat snowtable of Mount Lassen, at the northern end of the valley, hid even the peaks of the Sierra. She stretched her eyes into the distance, seeing nothing.

"There." Christenson came up beside her, pointing.

Her gaze strained. The vast emptiness confused her; her vision slipped off the fine details, tricked into looking farther than things were, and then, off by the American River's willow-shaggy bank, something white crawled into her view.

She caught her breath. Her hands gripped the railing. Down along the far side of the river against the sunbleached grass she could make out six, eight, maybe more tiny wagons, settlers' wagons, a thin line of bonnets, lost in the huge sweep of the valley. They crept on, almost invisible in the sun's blaze. They hardly seemed to move at all. She remembered that: how sometimes the wagons hardly seemed to move at all.

Yet they had moved, inch by inch rolled a continent behind them.

"Americans," she said. "Settlers."

"Pretty much can't be nobody else." The tall man spoke in a voice vibrating with excitement.

"Well," she said, "I think the Captain's right, I think tonight we celebrate." Light-footed, quick-hearted, she ran down the steps to find the cook.

The news of the arrival of more settlers brought the Kelseys down to the fort, with the other two families who lived up the river, and even some people from farther away. Every night for a week, when the sun went down, the yard of the fort erupted into dancing and drinking and fiddle playing, gambling and gaming and exuberance.

Sutter gave all the newcomers residence papers and land, and he turned their starving stock out on the valley grass and supplied them with fresh oxen, teams of mules, harnesses, plows, seed. He sent some of his men off with them to make sure they found their homesites and to help them raise their cabins. And one by one each family vanished into the vast distance.

A few of the single men in the train did not take up farms

but stayed at the fort and went to work for Sutter. There was plenty of work.

John Bidwell left for Ross to bring back lumber; the Russians had built their fort so well that it would take him months to tear the buildings apart. Zeke Merritt abruptly moved out of the fort and into a cabin of his own, half a day's ride away, saying he would rather slave for himself than for Sutter. To her surprise, Catharine missed the old mountain man as much as she did Bidwell.

The autumn drifted on, but no rain came. In the yard the leaves of the great valley oak hung like bats from the black branches. In the dwindling days before the solstice huge herds of elk churned through the north valley, stirring up dust clouds that stalked along the river bar in whirling towers. The river itself ran a thin trickle, clear as a mirror when the wind died, jade green from the dust when the wind blew, a puny rivulet mocked by the vast ridges of gravel and sweeps of sand, the huge undercut banks on either side, like the ruins of a bygone majesty. In the low places on the valley floor dense fogs formed like frozen cotton.

The winter wore by. In spite of the drought Sutter drove them all to furrow up the wheatfields again, struggling with the awkward Russian plows, with Spanish plows made from curved branches tipped in iron. The Indians refused the hard, boring work and ran away again, and Sutter rounded them up and brought them back. When they did not work he whipped one of them almost to death; after that they obeyed him. Catharine had tried to stop him, and he had laughed. She made herself stand there and watch the flogging, wondering why she could not make any difference in this. Through January and February it did not rain.

Then the sky darkened and the wind rose out of the south in a hot blast, and for half the month of March it did rain, day and night, and the wind screamed. The two yards of the fort turned into swamps. The thatched roofs of the new saddlery and the carpentry shop fell in. Part of the wall washed out. There was nothing anybody could do but huddle around a fireplace and wait. Wrapped in an old buffalo coat Catharine played the piano all day, her hands freezing, while Sutter paced up and down the room behind her, swearing and peering out the window.

The rain stopped; the sky cleared. Now the Sacramento River surged half a mile wide, a roaring, leaping palomino slop that carried whole trees along in its vigorous rush. Every lowland was a sea. Every hillside leapt with muddy creeks. What grass remained was pounded flat to the ground and slimed over with pale brown mud. Dirty, bawling herds of cattle and horses, elk, and deer stood packed onto the islands of high ground. Stacked driftwood paralleled the riverbanks in long, tangled mounds that marked the highest rising of the flood. The willows along the river bar were snarled with brush and trash, grass stems swept like hanks of hair around every twig.

The American River, which flowed into the Sacramento on the north side of Sutter's Fort, had climbed its banks and cut a new course much closer to Sutter's hill. Another new channel had run down over the south side of the fort, ripped through Manaiki's garden, and gouged a ravine ten feet deep through the yellow soil on down to the Sacramento. Where Manaiki's melons had plumped, a dead calf hung intricately twined in the fork of an uprooted tree. The wheatfields were gone, the seed swept off, the furrows washed away, the scalped ground below drying in the sun like a scab.

Sutter asked, "Can you ride a horse?"

"No," Catharine said.

"You're about to learn," he said.

He gave her an ancient, wind-broken mule, and she went out with the men to drag hay to the stranded animals, to drive them to feed when the water dropped, to bring in the driftwood for the fires. Riding was easier than she expected, especially in a huge Spanish saddle like a chair, on a mule too sick to trot. After the first few days her legs stopped hurting. On the fifth day she rode over to see Zeke Merritt.

Since the rain stopped, the sun had been blazing down and the whole valley was a vast steaming puddle. The mule, wheezing and groaning, carried her along past tangles of driftwood and little herds of gaunt cattle. Overhead the vultures stitched the air with their curved flights, drawn by the rotting corpses of drowned animals. She rode by a tree where a flock of birds of all kinds fought over something hanging in the upper branches.

The air smelled deeply, richly, of wet soil and wet grass. Along the high ground, the wildflowers were prizing their mud-laden leaves up off the drying film of the muck. On the stems blooms were popping out, their color shockingly pure, covering the yellow mud with rugs of red clover, with blazing patches of wild mustard, with the purple minarets of lupine, tipped in white.

Around the great puddles on the rolling plain, the flowers gathered in concentric rings according to their need for water, the lupine and wild mustard around the outside, then the magenta blood-drops of the nettles in their venomous fur and the glossy yellow of buttercups and the tiny rosettes of blue-eyed grass, and in the water itself masses of white starwort and popcorn flowers and the royal blue of lobelia like a piece fallen from the sky.

Zeke's cabin was totally surrounded by brown water. Some half-submerged willows, through which a fleet of ducks paddled, marked where the creek was supposed to be. Two cows and a horse stood forlornly in what remained of the yard. Zeke himself was up on the roof, a jug in his hand, slouched back against his chimney.

When he saw Catharine, he let out a yell. "Lady! What're you doing on a horse?"

She rode up as close as she could get to him, holding on to the horn of the saddle in case the mule slipped. "Hello, Zeke! Do you need rescuing?"

"Hell, no! I got my jug. Got an excuse not to work." Zeke rumbled out a laugh. "You swim over here, lady, we'll have ourselves a party."

She called, "We could use some help, Zeke."

"Go on, now," he shouted, and waved his arm. "Now you're sounding like Sutter. I'm in hog-wallow heaven here, I ain't movin'. Everything square back at the fort?"

"No," she said. "Everything is a damned mess. Please, Zeke. We need you."

He spat. With the heel of his hand he thumped the cork into his jug. "You askin' me, or is Sutter askin' me?"

"I am, Zeke. What the hell do you think I rode all the way over here for?"

He cradled the jug in his arm, his head swiveling, looking around at his homestead. A duck waddled out of the open door of the cabin into the muddy brown water and glided away. "All right," he said. "Let me get my horse saddled." Massive and ragged, he lumbered down along the side of the cabin roof and dropped to the ground; his bare feet sank into the mud up to his ankles. His shoulder-long hair was turning grizzled. She settled down to wait for him; then they rode together back through the valley, past the wildflowers and the gluttonous vultures.

Sutter and his crew rebuilt the roofs that the wind had blown down, patched the adobe, ditched around the outside of the fort, and dug a new well. In the late spring John Bidwell came back from Ross with twenty carts of split redwood lumber, and they finished the cobbler's shop, the saddlemaker's shop, the second forge.

The fort was busier now. Sutter kept the Indians inside the fort to prevent them from running off; they had a room of their own, but they roamed loose around the fort when they did not work, which was whenever Sutter did not watch them. Otherwise they made blankets and chairs and hats. The settlers came in often to use the shops and equipment, to shoe mules, to mend harnesses. Manaiki bore a baby, and the other Kanaka woman had two children now, fat and happy.

One of the older settlers died, and Sutter promptly married John Christenson off to his widow. This gained some savor for Catharine when she found out Christenson had been married eight times before. The whole valley came in for the wedding. They danced all night, slept through the next day, and danced the whole night following.

June began with baking heat. There was no wheat crop to reap and thresh, and they finished rebuilding the fort, even hanging the gates. This made it look much better, somehow, permanent at last. Sutter let the Indians go back to their people for their midsummer dances and sent most of his men out to the brush, to their own places.

"Come on," he said to Catharine. "It's June in California. There're better things to do than work."

"Where are we going?" she asked.

"To Yerba Buena," he said. "To the merienda."

19 ☙ CATHARINE AND MANAIKI found a piece of cloth from Ross in the storeroom, and they made Catharine a new dress for the merienda. When she wore it out of the Hudson's Bay post, where they were staying in Yerba Buena, Sutter swept her with a look and said, "We have to find you some good clothes, Cat."

"Thank you," she said, between her teeth. The dress was crude, but she loved the soft old material; its newness alone was a pleasure. "You know, Captain, under the circumstances it's surprising I have anything on at all."

"You should talk up. If you don't tell me I don't know what you want." He got hold of her hand and towed her down toward the beach. "Come watch this."

It was midmorning. The last of the night's fog was burning off, trailing in feathers and rags over the still surface of the cove. Out in the middle of the bay the hump of an island sheltered the harbor, which was crowded with ships. Sutter's sloop *Sacramento,* its sails furled, was anchored in the deeper water, broadside to the beach, its shadow painting the surface before it. Nearby lay a broad-beamed, single-masted boat with a black-painted hull and fancy gilt trim along the railings; several little rowboats nuzzled like puppies around this one, and Catharine could see men working on the deck.

Two other ocean-going ships sat closer to the rocky point. Small boats toiled busily back and forth: a little open boat with a lateen sail was running in toward the shore, heavy with baggage, wallowing through the water. Two square-sterned row-boats were making their way out again toward a ship just be-yond the *Sacramento*. Around them all the white gulls swooped and dipped.

A dozen people from Yerba Buena stood along the beach watching and talking. Sutter and Catharine went up to the edge of the little curling waves.

"What's that?" she asked him.

On the shore a quarter of a mile away, a flat barge lay in the slosh of the bay's edge; men were leading off horses. Sutter grunted. "Vallejo's vaqueros. If they could shoe their horses with pontoons they'd ride across the bay."

With a crack of hoofs on wood a horse bolted off the barge; dragging the man who clung to its halter, it lunged on up the beach into the salt grass, spraying sand. The sun gleamed on its mahogany flanks. Catharine said, "That's a beautiful horse." High-headed, tossing its black mane, it reared against the three men trying to calm it.

Sutter made another sound in his chest. "Look, now, look at this." His hand closed on her arm, pulling her attention around.

On the ship with the gold trim, they were struggling with a big, awkward object, trying to lift it up over the rail to the boats waiting below. The strained voices of the workmen drifted across the water. From the crowd on the shore rose an amused hum of talk. The object tilted down over the side of the ship, roped into a web of cable, while the men on the boat below lifted their arms toward it.

"God," she said. "It's a carriage."

"It's Micheltorena's," Sutter said, his voice starting up in his nose somewhere. "The new governor. Isn't that a joke?"

With ropes and hands and high-pitched pleading voices the men lowered the square, ungainly shape of a topless surrey down toward the waiting boat. Catharine shaded her eyes with her hand; the morning sun came straight across the bay toward her, turning the water painfully bright. The sunlight gleamed on the side of the governor's fancy carriage, with its padded seats and spoked wheels.

The coach was too large for the boat waiting for it. The men rested it, teetering on its axles, on the boat's gunwales; its wheels hung over on either side. Clearly they had done this before. Another rowboat was already moving briskly into place to tow the first boat and the surrey to the beach. From the crowd there rose a ragged, ironic applause.

Catharine said, "He didn't ride that up here from Mexico City."

Sutter guffawed. "Yes, certainly, right through the Yumas and the Mojave." The flat of his hand whacked her shoulder. "He sailed up from Guaymas with it. Sailed it here from Monterey. If you ask me he'll have a lot of trouble getting it over to the beach."

The merienda would be held on the ocean beach, two hours' walk across this humpy, narrow peninsula from Yerba Buena. Catharine turned to look behind her, at the drab, treeless hills, the slopes shaggy with chaparral and sawgrass.

Yerba Buena was a mere scatter of shacks and gardens on the eastern side of the peninsula that shut San Francisco Bay off from the Pacific. The biggest structure was the Hudson's Bay post, a two-story adobe building reinforced with redwood beams and roofed in red clay tiles. The trails that ran off from Yerba Buena toward the presidio to the north and the Mission Dolores to the south were footpaths and horse tracks. She turned to judge how wide the carriage was.

The governor's surrey had reached the shore, rocking and swaying on the rowboat, a man in the stern holding it still, another in the bow extending two oars out into the water to steady it all. The boat's keel growled aground in the shallows. The two men leapt out, seized the long yellow shafts, and ran up onto the shore, and the carriage slid off the boat's gunwales into the bay and rolled up to the beach, spinning sheets of water off the wheel rims, the spokes a yellow blur.

With a roar of approval the crowd split to let it pass and then closed in around it. Sutter, his hand still on Catharine's arm, pulled her back out of the way.

"That's how Mexico City is," he said. "They come up here

with things and ideas that won't belong, and then blast us because we can't use them." With long strides he drew her along to the back of the crowd, to a short, burly man. "Here, Mr. Rae."

She recognized the name from Sutter's correspondence: he was the Hudson's Bay factor. He swung around, only a few inches taller than she, with a round red face and popping eyes that gave him a look of surprised rage. His upper lip was a short, stiff thicket of graying bristles.

Sutter said, "Here. Sell her some cloth, will you, so she can make herself some decent clothes." He let go of her, his hand trailing down her arm in a vague caress. "Put it on my account." He drifted toward the surrey, to which the governor's men were now attaching the cloth top.

Rae blinked at her, swept her from head to foot with a measuring look, and said, "You're Cat Reilly."

"Yes."

"Wait here a moment, if you please." His voice was a Scots growl, buried back in his throat somewhere. Briskly he walked away around the crowd toward his post, on the slope above them.

In a few minutes he returned, striding toward her. "Come along," he said, without pausing, and she followed him down the beach to a warehouse just above the high-tide wrack. He unlocked the door and took her inside and there lit a lantern.

The warehouse was long and dark and smelled of must, of dry things and dirt and creosote. Across it wooden shelves ran from floor to ceiling, row after close-set row, packed with bales and crates and kegs; many of the shelves were curtained off. She followed Rae back into the far end of the place, where he set down the lantern on the floor between two shelves and reached up into the dark.

"This isn't a drygoods store I run here," he said. "All I have is some trade stuffs. You want me to, I can try to smuggle you up something." While he talked he was rummaging through what looked like piles of shoes and boots until suddenly he began to pull bolts of cloth down from the shelf to the floor.

She said, "Wait — you'll get it dirty." She stooped, stroking her hand over a red calico. Heedlessly he piled the cloth beside her.

"Get what you want and come tell me up at the post. This is the merienda; I have thousands of things to do." He went away into the dark, his footsteps harsh on the dirt, fading, gone as he rounded the corner. She turned the lantern up.

There was linsey-woolsey, the red calico, some blue calico, a heavy cotton twill, and behind it all, on end, a bolt of sprigged muslin.

"Oh!" She seized it, lifting it up out of the dust, and laid it carefully on a shelf. "Oh, how beautiful." Slowly she ran her hand down over it, relishing the smooth, supple touch of the cloth; in the lantern light it was hard to see the colors of the tiny flowers, maybe blue or purple. There was a lot of it, too, yards and yards of it, and she was going to take it all.

"Cat."

Startled, she wheeled, twisting to look around, and was face to face with Count Sohrakoff.

"Count!" Gladdened, she reached out her hands. He came toward her, his hair a nimbus in the lantern light, and took her hands and pulled her forward a step. She looked up into his face. "How did you know I was here? Where have you been?"

The lantern shining up from the floor struck only the glitter of his beard, the line of his eyebrows, the edge of his nose. "I heard just this morning you had come with Sutter." He sounded awkward, unsure, as if there were something wrong. Or going to be.

She let go of his hands, warned. "Where have you been?"

"Monterey." He moved, and the light shone more on his face. "Look, I'll tell you this up front, before you find out sideways. I have an arrangement with an officer of General Castro's."

She took a step backward. Castro was the don of Monterey. Sohrakoff was in the Califomio army. Startled, she blinked at him, slowly understanding what he was telling her. "Were you working for him when you were at New Helvetia?"

"Yes. That's why I was up there."

She said, "You were spying on us."

"You could call it that." His voice was steady now, soft in the stillness of the warehouse, in the dark. "Orozco had to know if Sutter was riding point for the British, say, or the French. I found out he wasn't; I left. In the course of it I did a lot of work and got nothing for it but my keep. I think Sutter and I came out even. And we had to know what was going on up there."

"Are you spying on us now?" she said. Her voice quivered; she felt, suddenly, as if he had struck her in the face.

He backed away, his gaze leaving her. "I was afraid it was going to happen like this, but I thought I'd give it a try anyway. Have a good time at the merienda." He turned and walked away into the dark.

"Count," she said.

Just at the rim of the lantern's power he stopped and looked back. She wanted him, it hurt to see him walk away, but he had spied on New Helvetia, he had betrayed them, he was working for the dons.

She said, "Goodbye, Count."

He left. She leaned back against the shelves behind her, a sharp pain in her side like a knife. After a while she took the sprigged muslin and went out of the warehouse.

20 🦅 CATHARINE WAS GLAD OF her broad-brimmed hat, which shaded her face; the June day hummed with a robust heat, the sky like a hard blue arch. She kicked off her shoe and dug a toe into the hot sand. Sutter had ridden a horse out of the Hudson's Bay stable; from his saddle beside her, above her, he was waving to someone else across the beach.

"That's Livermore," he said. "He has a little place, out east of here, bad Indian country. Nice fellow." Getting away from New Helvetia and the endless grinding work had made Sutter vigorous. He looked younger, taller, much happier. "And there's Richardson. That's the man who's going to own Yerba

Buena someday." He threw his arm up, hailing at the top of his voice, waving until far down the beach, over a hundred anonymous heads, an arm waved back, another voice hallooed. Then Sutter turned to her, sharp, his horse snorting and pushing with its nose at his tight hold on the reins. "Why do you have your shoe off?"

Catharine took off the other shoe, bent down, and picked up the pair. She was watching a young Californio who was digging a hole in the sand a few yards away; beside him on the beach lay a sack that thrashed and wriggled.

Sutter rode up beside her and nudged her with the toe of his boot. "Put your shoes back on. Act like a lady; everybody here thinks you're with me."

Catharine ignored him. The Californio pulled a chicken out of the sack. As soon as it saw daylight, it let out an ear-cracking crow. The man stuffed it feet first into the hole, held it down with one hand, and shoveled sand in over it with the other, the coarse grains sprinkling the chicken's glossy dark green wing feathers.

She said, "What are they going to do?"

Sutter bent down, got her by the arm, and pulled her off down the beach, swerving to avoid a crowd of small naked children running down to the surf. "Don't get involved in things like that. Nothing you'd be interested in." He stopped her. "Put your shoes on."

"I don't want to," she said.

Behind them the cock crowed again, but when she turned back to see, Sutter rode around into her field of vision. "Stay out of it. Don't get up on your pulpit here, you'll embarrass me, yourself — everybody — and do no good."

He pushed his horse against her, herding her away up the beach, and she let him, feeling like a coward; but he said no more about her shoes.

The beach here ran wide and white for more than a mile between the surge of the ocean and the steep slopes, gashed with ravines, of the inland hills. There was already a huge crowd here, all along the stretch of sand and in the little sheltered benches where the ravines that gouged open the sea cliff flared out onto the beach. More people were steadily arriving down the several paths that came over the hills, in *carretas,* on horseback, on foot, carrying great hampers and rolls of canvas and small children.

Someone somewhere was playing a guitar. There were fiddlers, too, and she saw a huge old bass violin, nestled in a silk shawl in the back of a cart. The sweet smell of strawberries scented the air, and the seaward slopes of the cliffs, where the fruit grew wild, swarmed with people gathering them, like a milling hive of bees runneling through the green fluff. A flock of screeching children played on a tremendous stump half-buried in the sand, the broken roots that radiated from its dark bulk dangling small brown bodies.

Catharine wrinkled her nose, catching a sudden whiff of dirty animals. Up ahead a corral of ropes and poles held a restless, stirring mass of white wool. On the bare sand before them, a vaquero on a bay horse had his rope around the neck of a bawling red and white steer; another vaquero had the steer by the tail, and as Catharine and Sutter came up even with them, a third man swung a sledgehammer squarely into the broad, triangular forehead. The steer collapsed. The men fell on it with knives.

"There, see?" Sutter's horse jogged back to her. "They'll roast it on a spit for anybody who wants some. All day long you can walk along here and eat." He smacked his lips. "Chili and beans and beef, strawberries and cream, fresh hot tortillas —"

The steer was now a flayed carcass lying on a crust of red sand. Spread raw side up on the ground nearby, the hide still twitched and jerked. An old Indian woman came up to cast a handful of salt over it.

Catharine lifted her head. In the corner of her eye, she had seen, down the beach, a sudden movement. "What's that?"

Sutter turned. Up the narrowing wedge of sand between the sea and the brushy slope of the hill, among the throngs of ebullient children and slower grown-ups and the scattered tents and spread picnic cloths, the governor's black surrey was hurtling toward them.

People fled out of its way, opening a steadily growing lane ahead of it. Two horses drew it, but they were no proper team in harness, hitched sedately to the shafts. Instead, vaqueros rode the horses, each carrying one shaft tucked under his inside arm while he spurred along at the customary dead gallop.

Sutter roared. "That's the way to travel!"

The carriage was coming right at them. She stepped back to give it room to pass and Sutter reined his horse around, but as the rig neared them it slowed and stopped. Under the fringed top a thin man in a black coat lounged across the back seat, his arms spread languidly wide.

In the front seat, the driver half rose and took off his hat. "Please, your gracious pardon, sir — have I the honor of addressing Don el Capitan Juan Agosto Sutter of New Helvetia?"

Sutter stepped forward, touching his hat brim. The carriage was drawing a crowd of the nearby people. Catharine stepped back, away from the press. "Cat!"

She went up through the curious onlookers around the carriage; Sutter leaned down from his horse to stretch out one arm to her. His face was flushed with the excitement of impressing somebody new.

"Excellency, I present Señora Catarina Reilly." He pushed her up toward the surrey. "My dear, this is His Excellency General Manuel Micheltorena, the governor of Alta California."

The smiling man on the back seat of the carriage reached his hand out toward her without moving his body at all. "Señora, I am ravished with delight." His grip was cool and flabby. His skin looked translucent. He brought her hand halfway to his lips and kissed at it.

"Your Excellency is very gracious." Sutter had given her a few phrases in Spanish. Micheltorena looked too young to be a governor, too young and too sick.

"I shall be joining His Excellency in his tent," Sutter said. "You may expect me sometime later this afternoon, Catharine."

The pale man sprawled on the seat of the surrey lifted his head, giving Sutter a wide-eyed look of indignation. "Of course if your most beautiful wife would accompany us also, I would be overwhelmed."

Sutter let out a yap. "My wife." He looked her over as if he had never seen her before. "Certainly. She'll come. Get in, Cat."

"I'd love to," she said. "How?"

The governor did not move; he took up the whole of the back seat. Even in the lusty warmth of midsummer he looked clammy. While she was looking for a step to climb, Sutter reached down and got his hand under her armpit and boosted her up over the wheel. The carriage rocked under her weight.

She crouched uncertainly under the carriage top, wondering where to sit, and the driver got up and jumped out. The governor of Alta California waved her casually toward the empty seat. She lowered herself to it, sweeping her skirts in around her.

Micheltorena raised his voice in an order. The vaqueros hardly needed to be told; before the words were out they were charging away down the beach. Their abrupt start rocked her almost over the low back of the seat. The governor lolled in his place, smiling at her. He said something, which drowned in the racket of wheels and hoofs.

Sutter was cantering along beside them. He and the governor began to shout back and forth in Spanish.

Catharine faced forward again, her hand clenched on the rail on the side of the seat. The panorama of the beach sped by her like a streamer: a snatch of fiddle music and a whirl of red cloth, a huge firebed, studded with iron pots, over which a spitted carcass hung, a tide of small children scrambling through a patch of strawberries. The sweet smell of the crushed fruit cloyed in her nostrils. Abruptly the carriage left the sand and jounced and banged off through high grass that spanked against the floor of the carriage like flails, up over a low slope, toward a huge peaked tent.

She braced herself with her feet on the dashboard of the surrey and snatched down her billowing skirts. The carriage bounced giddily along, its wheels whining, the top swaying from side to side on its flimsy wire piers. They raced at full speed toward the tent, which stood in a wedge of sand below the sheer pitch of the hill; above it, between two black boulders, a string of horses was picketed, and out in the sun stood another pen of sheep and cattle.

The vaqueros slowed to a trot, the surrey bumping over the grass, and then to a walk, and dropped the shafts. When the tips hit the ground they dug sharply into the sand and the whole surrey jounced up into the air and hung, halfway to disaster. It fell back on its wheels with a jolt. A guard in a red and green uniform walked forward, expressionless, with a salute to greet them.

Micheltorena, long and thin in his black clothes, climbed down to the ground; Sutter was dismounting, letting his reins trail, ignoring the groom who quietly took his horse away. The governor sauntered toward the tent; its door flap was hooked up on a pole, like an awning. Over his shoulder he said, "Would that I could offer you the sort of hospitality customary in Mexico City, but, alas . . ."

Sutter went after him, brushing past Catharine. She remembered her shoes, which she found on the floor of the surrey, and she put them on and went after the men.

As soon as she was inside she began to sweat. The tent was full of people, their voices a low rumble; the light was dim, the air stale and hot. Against the back wall of canvas there was a table laid out with plates and cups, ewers of wine, silver platters heaped with strawberries, and baskets of tortillas covered with linen napkins. A servant carried in a platter of stewed meat and laid it down on the splashed linen.

Sutter was just vanishing through another raised tent flap, in the side of the canvas wall, and she went after him.

This next room of the tent was cooler and much quieter. A man in a green uniform coat stood just inside the flap. Micheltorena was crossing the room toward a chair, into which he collapsed as if he had run all the way from Yerba Buena.

"Captain, a cup of wine?" He lifted his hand, and a servant crept out of the corner.

In this room also there was a table, but it was covered with papers. The major paper seemed to be a large map of California. Catharine started toward it, but Sutter got her arm and held her back, saying, in a low voice, "No, no. Get out of here. Go eat something." The Indian brought him a cup.

When she passed back through the flap in the tent wall, the provocative aromas that met her nose flooded her mouth with water. Many more platters now filled the table. She went up to it, wondering how to be served.

In the crowded room the man who approached her was so unobtrusive she did not notice him until he spoke. "Excuse me," said a mild voice, as Bostonian as her own, "I think you must be Catharine Reilly."

She turned quickly. She faced a slight, immaculate man in a merchant's dark coat, with thin side-whiskers and pale hazel eyes. He held out his hand to her.

"My name is Thomas Larkin. I am the United States consul in Monterey."

"A pleasure, Mr. Larkin."

"No, the pleasure is quite distinctly mine. Let me assist you at the table." He looked dapper and official, but his gaze was direct, and she saw that his mildness derived from an amazing self-confidence, which gave him a more persuasive air of authority than Micheltorena. She had not known there was an American consul in Monterey.

She said, "Good. I'm starving."

He laughed. "A healthy appetite is a blessing in a woman."

They went to the table, found dishes, and served themselves from the stews and roasts and chilis laid about. While Catharine was spreading butter on a warm tortilla, Larkin, smiling, turned toward her with a little dish of strawberries.

"Here, you must try these." Proud as if he had picked them himself, he ladled some of the sweet red mash onto the tortilla.

The berries were delicious. They went outside and sat under an oak tree and stuffed themselves with roasted meat and tortillas and strawberries. Larkin watched her with a steady, avuncular interest. The skin of his face looked smooth and fine as candlewax.

She said, "You must be an old neighbor of mine, by your accent, Mr. Larkin."

"I was indeed. For the last ten years, however, I have been a Montereño, a citizen of Monterey, and proud of it." He wiped his lips with a napkin, smiling, and said, "You're wondering how I know who you are."

"I admit to being curious."

He folded the napkin and put it neatly down. Everything he did had a finicky precision. "I heard about you from Lieutenant John Charles Frémont." He clasped his hands together before him. As the sun climbed, the shadow of the oak tree slipped up over his feet toward the knees of his fine gray trousers. "He gave me to think you might want some help getting back to Boston."

"Boston," she said, astonished. "Why would I want to go back to Boston?"

His eyes widened. "You don't want to go home?"

"Mr. Larkin," she said, "I am home."

"You mean," he said, his curiosity fighting his decorum, "you've made a home with Captain Sutter?"

"I mean, I find myself at home in New Helvetia. I am not Sutter's mistress, although you seem to have leapt to that conclusion. I work for him, the way, say, Zeke Merritt does. I keep his books and manage his office." She put down her plate, and a white-coated servant came up at once to remove it.

Larkin picked crumbs from his trousers. His smile pleated his lips at the corners. "Clearly both Lieutenant Frémont and I myself have made some unwarranted assumptions." He signaled to another man in a white coat, who was passing by; he brought over a tray of cups and a jug and served them wine. Catharine watched the rough brown hands at their work. The Indian shuffled away, stoop-shouldered. A dark understanding tugged down on her mood: these people were slaves.

Larkin was watching her, his cup untouched beside him, his expression vague as a painted angel's. "I understand Sutter and Mariano Vallejo have had some disagreements."

"A neighborly dispute," she said.

"General Vallejo will officially arrive tomorrow," Larkin said, "although he is undoubtedly here now. It's the custom of the merienda to defer all feuds, however vital to the maintenance of personal honor."

She gave him a long look, wondering what he had heard. "I'm not that bloodthirsty. Vallejo will obey this little custom, too?"

"General Vallejo is a man of devout custom." Larkin looked away, his hands still on his knee, edging into something. He said, "The June merienda is the biggest gathering in the north of Alta California. Soon every powerful man in the area will be here — Sutter, the governor, General Castro from Salinas, and General Vallejo from Sonoma."

"Do any of these generals actually have armies?"

He laughed, facing her again. "Of course. Don't make quick assumptions yourself, Mrs. Reilly."

"Thank you for the advice."

"It's well known that Governor Micheltorena faces opposition among some of the dons."

"I've heard something about that." She rubbed the bridge of her nose, remembering where she had heard that the dons were plotting against Micheltorena. Larkin was another spy, she realized, a man sent to lie abroad for his country's good. She did not want to think about Sohrakoff, who was a bruise in her mind, painful to touch; she looked away, down the sprawling clutter and noise of the beach.

A column of horsemen was riding up toward the governor's tent, a line of painted leather jackets and upright lances, with little pennants on the tips. She watched their jaunty procession through the camp. So there were real soldiers after all.

Larkin said, at length, "I don't believe Micheltorena fears any opposition from Sutter."

She turned toward him. "No. Captain Sutter is supremely loyal to the government that granted him his charters."

"Yes. An admirable position. Has Sutter brought many of his men here?"

"A few. Five, counting me."

Larkin shrugged one shoulder. "That's modest."

"You just said something about this being a peaceful gathering, Mr. Larkin. Why should he have a lot of his men here?"

He smiled again, a ripple on the surface of his concentration. "Dear Mrs. Reilly, since you believe they're all generals, you should have no difficulty understanding that the Californios love a show of force."

She said, "Mr. Larkin, you are not being particularly straightforward with me." She reached for her cup of wine, and he put it into her grasp. His small hands were smooth as the sprigged muslin, the nails sleek.

"I'm a diplomat," he said. "To your health, Mrs. Reilly."

They drank together, their thoughts separate. The column of mounted men wound in through the campfires toward the tent, and their leader swung down from his horse.

He was trim as a tin soldier. His tight blue uniform coat fit without a wrinkle over his shapely chest and shoulders; his high boots reflected the sun. He stood pulling on spotless white gloves, tugged down the brim of his shako, snapped a salute to the green-coated sentry, and went inside.

Larkin said quietly, "Castro is here now. That is his man, Lieutenant Orozco." His voice sank to a murmur, as if he spoke to himself. "Best soldier in California, whatever the rank."

The name rang in her ears. This was Sohrakoff's officer. She said, "Why?"

Larkin turned his calculating gaze on her. His voice came slowly, as if he thought out every word. "Orozco is one of the few men in California who sees the thing whole, and square. Unfortunately he's on the wrong side."

"Which is the right side?" she said, startled.

He watched her a moment before he spoke, spare, neat, careful as a craftsman. "I shall be straightforward with you, Mrs. Reilly, and see what it gets me. I have a good deal of interest in knowing what is going on with Sutter, and would be willing to pay for the information."

She said, "Mr. Larkin, no."

The consul's pale eyes measured her. Ruminative, he said, "Well, there, you see the value of candor." There was suddenly in his face a brilliant, unstated hilarity, like a flame leaping behind a smoked glass. "Of course now I see no reason to go on feeding your curiosity. Good day, Mrs. Reilly." He got to his feet, his trousers dusty, his coat hitched up in the back, and strolled off into the bright sunlight. Catharine picked up her cup and drank the last of the wine.

21 ✍ MICHELTORENA SAID, "Captain Sutter, I have reviewed your charters, and I find some irregularities with the papers to do with the title to Fort Ross."

He slouched in his chair, looking exhausted; in the cool, dim light of the tent his skin seemed gray. He fingered the charters on the table in front of him with long, tapered hands. Sutter straightened himself up into a military posture, his fists behind his back and his chest square.

"The charters were very clear to me, Your Excellency, when I signed them."

"I would like to make them so," said Micheltorena. "To everyone involved." He laid his hands flat before him and stared at Sutter. "Captain, I shall confide in you, since I am convinced of your loyalty. The new government in Mexico City sent me here with specific orders: to break the power of the dons. We mean to reorganize the government entirely, around a popular assembly, and move the capital from Monterey to El Pueblo de los Angeles." For the first time since Sutter had met him he seemed vigorous, although still pale, as he leaned forward on his arms. "Have I your support for this?"

Sutter said slowly, "I am loyal to Mexico City. Perhaps I question whether this reorganization is any more a solution to the country's problems than the last one. Have you got a good weight of metal to back up this revolution you're proposing?"

The haunted face in front of him was dimming like a dying lantern, and Micheltorena slumped down again in his chair. He said, "Alas, I have no real army. A few Sonoran peasants, whom I was forced to leave in the south. I am hoping, Captain Sutter, to appeal to reason."

He followed this with a wide-eyed stare at Sutter, who said nothing. At last Micheltorena nodded to him.

"I am asking you, Captain, for example, to end your feud with Don Mariano Vallejo. Three days hence I am calling all the great men of this part of California together, in a council, to settle the issues that divide you." Abruptly the governor raised his head. "Yes?"

Sutter turned, following Micheltorena's gaze. One of the two green-coated sentries was saluting in the open doorway. "Lieutenant Orozco, Your Excellency."

"Yes, let him come in." Micheltorena gestured. "With your permission, Captain Sutter." As if the effort were enormous he pried himself up out of his chair and strolled around the desk toward the middle of the room.

The Swiss murmured something and moved away, to get off by himself and think this over. Micheltorena's attitude was annoying — he wanted to come into California and rearrange it like a child's set of blocks, and yet he had no army. The dons would not give up their absolute power here for the grace of God and the benefit of Mexico City. All the government ever did was toss things upside down; they put nothing back together again. Now Micheltorena was issuing a summons to his *consejo,* which sounded suspiciously like a court. On the other hand there were Sutter's charters, lying on Micheltorena's table.

A tall soldier with an Indio look to his face came into the room and saluted the governor. Sutter cast a critical eye over his uniform; Castro outfitted his officers in European-style tunics and crossbelts, but they were too plain — they needed some braid or epaulets or frogging. This one at least kept his boots shined. Micheltorena turned to Sutter.

"May I present Lieutenant Jesús Orozco. Don Captain Juan Sutter, of New Helvetia. Captain Sutter was an artillery officer in Switzerland."

"France," Sutter said.

Orozco's dark eyes stabbed at him. "You served in the French artillery? In which regiment?"

"I was in the Swiss Guards at the court of Charles the

Tenth," Sutter said. "In 1830 we defended the Tuileries against the mob."

The long, dark Indio face twitched. His gaze burned into Sutter's a moment, a mocking light in his eyes, and with a start the Swiss saw that Orozco did not believe him. Before Sutter could even look indignant, Orozco was facing Micheltorena again, correct as a painted toy.

"Governor, I hope to have the pleasure of talking with you about the presidio, before the merienda is over."

"Yes, perhaps," said the governor, uninterested. "Now I am in conference with Captain Sutter, if you please."

"Governor, this is a matter of a certain urgency, and I would like to have a commitment from you."

"You're dismissed, Lieutenant."

Orozco straightened, saluted, and left. Micheltorena sighed. He dragged himself away toward his chair again. "A presumptuous man, Lieutenant Orozco." He collapsed into his chair, his hands on the charters. "Now."

"Yes," said Sutter, crisply. "On the matter of my charters for Ross."

"An issue that will depend very much," said Micheltorena, "on your reconciliation with General Vallejo." He sat back. His black eyes seemed lusterless, like charcoal. "Good day, Captain Sutter."

Craning from side to side above the flat sand, the chicken's head squawked and stretched, its bright eyes blinking. Up the beach sounded the triple beat of galloping hoofs, rolling closer, closer, until the horse flashed by and the vaquero leaned down out of the saddle, grabbed the chicken by the head, and ripped it out of the ground.

There was a bored patter of applause from a few of the people nearby. Nobody was even watching anymore. The vaquero loped back up the beach on his horse. Its neck broken, the chicken flopped on the sand, too stupid to know it was dead; its clawed feet ran in the air, its wing opened, the red eye stared desperately outward.

She folded her arms around herself, holding the shawl firmly against the wind off the sea. She had been watching the vaqueros at their chicken-killing game for more than an hour. Her own fascination with it repelled her. She wished she had stayed up at the dancing. Grimly she turned away, forcing herself back toward her friends.

They ate the chickens later, and probably the death was painless, and compared to the ordinary brutality of life, what did it matter? She was the one who was wrong, who had lost her sense of balance. In the Sierra she would have torn the chicken apart herself.

"Cat!" John Bidwell beckoned to her from higher on the beach.

A wild cackle of fiddle music sang across the sand. John made space for her in a ring of people. In their midst was an old man, his gray mustaches drooping extravagantly, who put a fiddle up under his chin and began to spin out dancing music, his head and shoulders wagging. There was a yell from the far side of the crowd.

John turned to Catharine, his hands out and a smile blooming in his curly dark beard. "Ma'am?"

She laughed up at him. His merry, guileless look outshone her gloom, and the idea of dancing raised her spirits. That was what she needed, some fast moving to music. She flung her hair back, took his hands, and joined him in the circle.

Later she stood back and watched them spin by in a *ronda* and drank a cup of strong red wine. Pablo Gutierrez came up a little way from her, his cheeks bulging and his hand filled with a chunk of beef wrapped in a tortilla, and she sidled over toward him.

"Eh, *chica,*" he said, and swallowed. "You have a new dress."

"Thanks, Pablo." He was the only one who had noticed. He smiled at her, his homely brown face like a cow's as he chewed. She said, "Teach me some Spanish."

He gave her a sideways look. "I can't teach you nothin' fast enough to talk it here."

"Tell me anyway."

Between bites of his reeking, dripping piece of barbecue he

taught her a collection of phrases. He had been with Sutter the longest of any of them, having joined him on a disastrous venture to Santa Fe before Sutter ever came to California. The dancers whirled in pairs and spun in the larger circle of the dance, a pleasing piece of harmony. Behind her, suddenly, like cats singing on a fence, a whining chorus of voices went up.

"Eh, gringa, gringa, gringa!"

She wheeled around and saw five or six horsemen passing by; they leaned toward her and hooted and jeered. She put her back to them.

"Vallejo's men," Pablo said. "Don't pay no mind." He patted her arm.

"What does that mean?" The nape of her neck was prickling up, like a rake running backward through her hair. " 'Gringa.' "

"Unh . . ." His dark eyes looked her over. "*Norteamericano* woman. Only, you know, not nice. Like 'nigger.' "

"Oh." She hugged her arms around herself.

"You want to learn some more Spanish?" Pablo asked. He stuffed the last of the tortilla into his mouth.

"No," she said. "That's plenty."

Orozco asked, "Have you ever fired any of these guns?"

"We have no powder," said the cadet. His voice was edged with amazement that Orozco even bothered to ask. He was in his first year in the army, his cheeks soft as chick down. The governor's visit, with two generals and a lieutenant, was the greatest event of his year here; possibly it would be the only event. He was trying to suck his stomach in; his gloves were dirty, his belts crossed backward.

Vallejo and Castro were walking off down the wall after Micheltorena. Vallejo's voice rose again, sharp.

"Monterey is the capital of California, and has always been. To move the capital after so many years is folly. To move it to El Pueblo is dangerous folly."

Micheltorena turned, his black coat distinct against the creamy yellow of the adobe wall at his feet, the hot blue sky, the clump of wind-torn cypresses to his left. "El Pueblo is the only city in California, and the assembly is there."

"The assembly," Castro said, with a grunt, and walked briskly forward, past Vallejo and Micheltorena, as if he could end this tour simply by getting around the circuit of the wall quickly.

El Pueblo was El Pueblo de los Angeles, hundreds of miles to the south. The assembly consisted of the five most powerful men in the south, its dons. Between north and south, *arribeño* and *abajeño,* there was an endless war, and Micheltorena's reorganization was only another battle in it; it would solve nothing, drive the country apart rather than bring it together, deepen the dons' fixation on their own feuds.

Orozco walked along the top of the adobe wall to the next gun, an old ship's gun, lying on a broken truck like an afterthought, its tackles rotted, its trunnions rusted out. Orozco shoved at it with his foot. "Where are the tools?"

"The tools," said the cadet blankly, glancing from side to side as if someone else would answer.

"The sponges and ramrods, the training quoins — such things," Orozco said, "as are required to shoot off artillery."

"Sir," the cadet said, and stopped, his lower lip between his teeth.

Vallejo was snarling into Micheltorena's face. The governor stood expressionless, his arms folded over his thin chest, listening. Orozco continued to poke at the useless gun with his foot and looked widely around him.

The presidio stood in the constant wind on the hillside above the straits. It was a square of low, vine-covered crumbling adobe walls enclosing a few badly kept buildings. The clump of cypresses screened it from the worst of the wind. White herons roosted in the black-green flattened heads of the trees; in the long grass a thrush began to shrill out its spiraling cry. The vines that grew up over the walls grew over the guns too, and there were trapdoor spiders nesting in their bores.

The women, of course, went on as always. In the yard below, an Indian girl with a red kerchief on her head was milking goats, and another hung wet linen out to dry. Orozco went after his superiors, on down the wall.

Micheltorena was saying, "You will of course send delegates to the assembly."

"In a pig's ear I'll go to the assembly," Vallejo roared.

Orozco turned to look out at the straits. The fogbank had drawn back out to sea, a long, low gray gap in the fabric of the world. The black shapes of the offshore rocks showed at the edge of it, like broken teeth. The blue sheen of the Pacific stretched in through the sunlight, toward the shore, barely wrinkled by the long oceanic swells.

In the straits, between the little strips of white along the thin brown beaches on both sides, the wrinkles on the water were like glaze crackling. Beyond, widening out into the broad arms of the bay, the rippling surface resumed its order, spreading fanwise toward the shores on all sides.

Ten guns could hold those straits against an armada, if they were good. If they were loaded.

Micheltorena said, "General, you are not listening to reason."

"Reason." Vallejo wheeled. Across his cheeks the hot red color shone. His black eyes found Orozco. "Does this sound reasonable to you? To give us all to the *abajeños*? Should we agree to that?"

Orozco stiffened to attention. "No, General."

"You see," Vallejo shouted. His hand slashed up through the air, seizing his triumph. He glared into Micheltorena's face. "Even he agrees with me!" He turned on his heel and strode away down the top of the wall.

Micheltorena watched him go a little way and then turned toward Orozco, who was still standing there waiting, since he was only a lieutenant and Micheltorena was a brigadier general. The governor said, "These people are beyond argument."

"Yes, Governor."

The long, pale horseface studied him a moment longer. Slowly the governor turned and ran his attention over the presidio wall, the guns, and the straits below. He said, "What a disgrace. The defenses of the country are literally in ruins. California is at the mercy of the first man with a sword who rides across her borders. Something should be done about this."

"Yes, General." Orozco stepped forward, a sudden hope spurring him to quick talk. "I will be happy to assume —"

"After," Micheltorena said, "we have settled these larger issues. You're dismissed." His hands clasped behind his back, he walked away down the wall. Orozco followed him, grim.

Catharine had drunk more than she should have and sat down to let it wear off. From the darkness behind her came a jeering voice.

"Gringa! Gringa!"

She ignored that; she had been hearing it all night now. They were bellowing and jeering at the other Americans, too. The rest of the crowd all seemed very friendly, very drunk. Their arms draped around one another, her friends went off to watch a cockfight.

Hungry again, Catharine walked along the beach toward the nearest bonfire, where there would be food. The night lay deep over them, but on the beach the merienda roared on. Every few dozen yards a great fire crackled and leapt, casting up sparks, throwing off showers of quaking orange light, in which people shouted and danced, ate and drank and roamed. Between the fires lay deep pockets of shadow.

She wandered wide around two people making love in the sand, barely out of the lapping fireshine. She heard a dog barking, somewhere, insistent; the stench of garbage reached her for an instant and vanished into the tang of the ocean breeze.

The dark cliff hemmed one side of the beach, a half-visible wall, and on the other the ocean growled and rumbled; the merienda ran down the middle like a ribbon of fire and fiddle music. She stepped across a body lying sprawled on the ground and walked up to the next fire, where a cauldron stood on the coals, an Indian behind it with a ladle and a stack of tortillas.

He gave her a tortilla full of meat, and she stood eating it, watching the dancers in a *rota*. The Californio women were all beautiful; they made her feel homely as a half-plucked chicken. She watched a girl of no more than fifteen or sixteen who danced by with an awkward stick of a partner. In the girl's upswept dark hair there was a red rose, and red ribbons accented the black lace of her bodice; her cheek was a pure, flawless creamy velvet, and the curve of her lips seemed borrowed from some former life, too old, too knowing a smile for such a child. Her eyes were more beautiful than the rose. Catharine went on toward the next fire, looking for the other Americans.

As she crossed a dark stretch of sand she realized suddenly that a horse was keeping pace with her, and she stopped and turned. Mariano Vallejo looked down at her from the back of a magnificent bay stallion. The firelight sparkled red-gold on his embroidered jacket.

Her heart galloped. She held out her hands, palms up. "I'm unarmed today, General."

She meant it to be friendly, but he made no friendly answer. His eyes drilled into her. She drew back a little, but he only put his hand up to the brim of his hat. He said, "Señora Reilly," and his horse broke into a lope and carried him away.

Her back tingled with warning. She turned to go in the opposite direction, to get away from him, and walked down the dark beach.

The air was still and heavy and moist. She looked at the wet sand ahead of her. Her feet sank into the cold dampness. Behind her there was a sudden crash, a gay howl of voices. Her back to it, she stood facing the darkness.

It seemed all dancing and feasting and merriment, the merienda, but underneath it there ran something else, a rushing dark current, something bad and black. Or maybe she was only imagining it. She gave an uncontrollable shudder.

"Cat!"

She lifted her head. A white wisp rolled by her; the fog was moving in, silent, more dense than smoke. Off to her left, suddenly, she heard the ocean crash, and a wave was sweeping up toward her feet, reaching for her. She wheeled, unnerved, and could see nothing in the fog.

Then through the drifting opaque air Zeke came up to her,

a cup in one hand. "Hey, we're all wondering where you are. We're goin' back to Yerba Buena for the night. Come on, now. You look pretty done."

"Sometimes I hate people," she said. But she was relieved to see him; she reached out toward him.

He crowed. His arm went around her, gathered her against him; he was vast and warm and smelly. She slid her arm around his waist, comforted.

"You're certainly a good dancer, Zeke."

"Sure am. A long difference between that and the first time we danced, you remember that."

"Yeah." She brought her arm back to her side. He reached behind him, grasped her wrist, and firmly pulled her arm around his waist again.

"Any chance we could ever dance that way, you know, sometime?"

"Zeke, you're my friend."

"You been dancin' with your friends all day. Hey!"

From the fog on either side came swarms of men closing on them. Catharine yelled. Something hit her, and she fell to her hands and knees on the sand. Her head whirled. A moment later a weight landed on her. She lashed out and then realized it was Zeke, crouched over her; she struggled free of his encloaking arm and stood up.

Whoever had attacked them was gone. Dim in the darkness, in the faint far light of the collapsing fires, the bare sand spread around her, dimpled from thousands of footsteps, scattered with bits of firewood, scraps of food. Rags and banners of the fog drifted noiselessly inland, blotting out everything beyond a few feet away.

Zeke gripped her elbow. "You all right, lady?"

"Yes. What was that?"

"I don't know." He put his hand up to his head and brought it down before him and looked at it, and she gasped; his fingers were slick with dark, shiny liquid, he was bleeding. She put her hand on his arm.

"You're hurt."

"Hell," he said, contemptuous. "No damage. Ain't no greaser

can hit hard enough to hurt me. Come on." Flinging a quick, furious glance away down the beach, he got her hand and towed her along after him, up toward Sutter and the others.

Sutter said, "You didn't see them at all?"

Catharine swayed in the saddle, exhausted. Her head was pounding; there was a soft, painful lump above her ear. Beside her John Bidwell reached out and put his coat around her. "Thanks, John," she said.

"Listen," Sutter said. He rode his horse around in front of them and spoke to them all. "Don't anybody do anything. Is that understood? I'll talk to the governor."

"That bastard Vallejo," Zeke muttered.

"Don't do anything!" Sutter glared at them. Pablo Gutierrez behind him had a torch in his hand, to light their way back across the hills. His round face was clenched into a frown. Sutter lifted his voice, harsh. "I'll deal with this. You stay together and keep out of trouble."

"Sure," Zeke murmured. "Just the same, I'm packing a gun from here on in." Among the other men somebody grunted in agreement.

Catharine nudged her horse forward. "Let's go back now." She rode on past him up the trail, and the other men crowded after her, toward Yerba Buena.

22 ✒ CATHARINE WOKE in the gloom before dawn. Above her the planks of the ceiling, hung with cobwebs, were just beginning to catch the pale light rising through the window. She was in a room on the second floor of the Hudson's Bay post, having slept in the room's only bed; Zeke and Bidwell were rolled into blankets on the raw pine floor next to her. Sutter had the adjoining room, with Pablo and Christenson.

Bidwell lay with the blankets over his head, his face to the wall, and had reason. Zeke was snoring out great rips of noise, half roar and half honk, so vigorous it was hard to believe he was getting any rest. On his forehead the skin was split into a wide ugly gash. She got out of the bed and stepped across him to the packs stowed against the wall beside the door, found her second dress, and changed her clothes. Zeke's monstrous lullaby sawed steadily on. She went downstairs.

The huge public room of the Hudson's Bay house looked bleak and empty in the gray morning. Overhead the lamps still burned, thin pale flames like ghosts suspended in the sooty chimneys. The tables were pushed off to one side, the benches heaped on top; an Indian woman was sweeping up the sawdust and another was cleaning up around the hearth. Their dark faces were impassive, wider at the jaw than across the eyes, even the whites of their eyes brown. Catharine walked out through the back.

The air was moist and cold; a flock of seagulls flapped and shrieked on the midden beyond the back fence. She followed a worn, thin path down through brambles and dew-spangled nettles as high as her head, out beyond the low gray kitchen building to the privy. Afterward she came back to the kitchen to wash her hands and face at the inside pump.

The kitchen was already steaming. In the dark the windows were rectangles of gray; the fire banked on the hearth cast out no light. At the back of the room sat an old woman slapping tortillas. The cook walked in, yawning, drying his hands on his apron.

A pot of coffee boiled on a hook over the fire. Catharine poured a cup of it, so strong her stomach churned, and drank as much as she could. She took a warm tortilla from the stack on the table and went out into the rising dawn.

The air was turning clear silver. The tortilla was deliciously chewy, and she enjoyed the nutty flavor of the corn. She walked down between the Hudson's Bay house and the fence, where the grass grew tall. The hem of her dress soaked up the dew, swung heavy and cold around her ankles, rough as if it were dipped in sand. She went out through the gate in the fence.

The vast bay stretched out before her, its edge folding and curling along the beach; like a rippling sheet of pewter the broad water ran off toward the lumpy, steep islands, still black with the rising sun behind them.

She thought about the men leaping on her from the fog, at the merienda, and kept a watch around her. A man in a sombrero trudged off past the front of the Hudson's Bay post, a hoe over his shoulder; before a small adobe house a woman stooped down for the wood stacked by her door. Catharine walked on toward the beach.

In a blaze of light the sun broke the dark notched edge of the eastern hills, and immediately she felt its warmth; the day steadily brightened.

She struggled to make sense out of what was going on here. Larkin had said the merienda was peaceful. Then he had said that Sutter had not brought enough men. Everybody thought that the men who leapt on her and Zeke were Vallejo's, retaliating for the fight at Sutter's Fort. She remembered meeting the don on the beach, his cold arrogance, when she had tried to be friendly.

Yet maybe she had misunderstood him. Maybe he had misunderstood her. Certainly, if his men had meant to hurt her and Zeke, they had done a bad job of it; she had been walking alone on the beach all that evening, and surely they would have attacked her then if they meant to hurt her. If they did not mean to hurt her, why attack her at all?

The day grew bright and strong around her. She went back toward Yerba Buena. She had tried to talk to Sutter, but she had gotten nowhere. He was chafing over something Micheltorena had said to him and would heed nothing else. The other men were already loading their pistols; their minds were made up.

The town had wakened. In the harbor now the boats sailed busily back and forth from the wharf to the ships. In front of the Hudson's Bay post three unshaven, filthy men slumped, staring with dull red eyes out toward the harbor. She went up past them into the public room.

The two Indian women who had been sweeping when she left now sat at the end of one of the tables, eating beans and tortillas. Half the length of the table from them the Hudson's Bay factor himself was reading a newspaper.

Catharine had not seen a newspaper in more than three years. She sat down across the table from him and said, "Excuse me, Mr. Rae."

He lowered the paper. His pop eyes glared at her.

She said, "May I read your paper when you're done with it?"

"Certainly." He folded the paper up and laid it before her. "Go ahead."

"Do you get newspapers from the States often?" She opened the paper, which was the New York *Sun* from May 23, 1842; a box on the left side offered a passage to Albany for a dollar on the steamboat *Commerce*. Down the middle ran a long story about public drunks. She looked it over as if she were actually reading it.

"Fairly often," he said. "Every couple of months."

"I'd appreciate it very much if you'd save them for me."

"I will, Mrs. Reilly."

"Also" — she laid the paper aside — "we have a common acquaintance."

He stared at her, suddenly stone-faced. "I don't know what you mean."

"I think you do, since you told him I was alone in the warehouse the other day."

Behind the hedge of his mustache his lips tightened.

She said, "Tell him I want to see him."

He said, "When?"

"He'll arrange it," she said. "If he's interested." She got up, the paper under her arm, and went toward the stairs.

23 ✠   SOME OF CASTRO'S VAQUEROS had caught a bear
in the heap of garbage accumulating at the back of the merienda; on horses, with lassoes, they dragged the snarling, snapping animal down to the beach and tethered it to a redwood
stump. Since it was morning and the horse races had not yet
started, most of the crowd at the merienda drifted down to
watch.

The bear was a big one, for a black bear, with shoulders like
paddlewheels, and it was a fighter; one tusk was broken off.
The vaqueros' dogs darted in and out around it, yapping and
howling, doing no damage except to the onlookers' ears.

Catharine watched from the edge of the water. She had come
down the beach with John Bidwell, but he was working his way
in through the crowd, trying to get closer to the bear, driven as
always by his deathless curiosity. A little naked child, slick from
the waves, ran by her. Across the crowd she saw General Vallejo
on his beautiful bay horse, a black sombrero on his head. She
moved around behind the mass of people, heading along the
margin of the wet sand.

The mob let out a roar that raised her hackles, and suddenly
everybody was leaping back, pushing her away down the beach.
Through their milling and rushing she saw a vaquero with a
spear in his hand. His horse fought in a mad terror against the
rider's hands and spurs, its eyes white and its nose in the air.

The bear reared up, its broad arms spread. Its tongue slob-
bered out of its mouth, and it gave a growl that sent the crowd
recoiling again. The horse shied and kinked in a tremendous
leap into the air, and the vaquero hurled his spear, which
missed.

A howl of derision rose from the onlookers. The rider loped
away. Catharine started off again, and from behind her a hand
closed on her arm.

"Back up."

Obediently she backed up, out of the crowd, away from
everybody, until he said coldly, "All right. What do you want?"

She stopped. They had reached an empty part of the beach,

away from everybody. Sohrakoff stood just to her left, a little
behind her, scowling at her, hostile. She rubbed her hands together; down the beach, the crowd's voice rose in a shriek of delighted terror.

She said, "Somebody jumped me last night. Me and Zeke."

"Jumped you."

"Yes. Vallejo's men have been ragging us since we got here,
yelling, calling us names — nothing serious until last night.
Something's going on here, and I'd like to know what it is."

"What do you mean?"

"I don't know."

"Well, a lot is going on here. You didn't see who attacked
you."

"No."

"Were you hurt?"

"They knocked us down. Cracked Zeke's forehead open."

"Then what happened?"

"They ran off."

"Hunh."

There was a thunderous howl from the crowd around the
bear. He turned to look around him, over his shoulder, wary.
She lowered her gaze. Between them lay some dead space. She
could not meet his eyes; her tongue felt awkward making
words. He faced her again.

"What is Sutter doing about this attack?"

"He says he'll talk to the governor." She glanced at him. He
wore a sombrero and canvas trousers like a sailor's and a long,
loose shirt, not Californio, maybe Russian. His feet were bare.
He turned and stared at her, his pale, bushy eyebrows drawn
down.

"Don't do anything. Keep Zeke and the others from doing
anything."

"Oh," she said, "we're angels. It's just getting a little hard to
keep the haloes on."

"There are six of you and Vallejo has fifty men. Don't do
anything, under any circumstances. I'll look around."

"Thank you," she said.

He made a sound something like the bear's growl. The crowd let out a whoop, and Catharine turned to look. Down beyond their waving arms, another vaquero rushed in on the bear, reined down, cast the spear, lost his balance, and suddenly was in the air himself, his horse spinning out from under him.

The crowd shrieked with excitement and lust. The bear lunged forward. It hit the end of the tether and its body jerked violently backward, but with a flailing paw it raked the vaquero across the ribs and arm; the man rolled away to safety, leaving stripes of blood on the sand.

Catharine glanced to her right; Sohrakoff was gone. She swung around, spreading her gaze as wide as it would reach, but there was no sign of him. She folded her arms together. A wave of doubt rolled over her; she felt suddenly unfaithful to New Helvetia for talking to him. And when she had told him what had happened to her and Zeke, it had seemed like nothing.

"Cathy!" John Bidwell came trotting up to her. "Come watch this." He pulled her off to see the bear fight.

Governor Micheltorena was sitting up in the back seat of his surrey, peering forward to watch the bear baiting. Beside him on his horse General José Castro glanced around him at the crowd steadily filling up the beach around him; some of his lancers moved in to hold them at a distance from him. Lieutenant Orozco sat on his restless bay horse, off a little toward the water, watching the bear.

The crowd screeched; like a single creature, much vaster than the bear, it surged and charged and packed together in a tight ring around the arena. At the center was the stump to which the bear was tied. Another vaquero was now edging his horse out into the open circle of sand around it, his lance tucked under his arm; his horse was fighting every step.

The bear lumbered back toward the stump, its glossy rusty black summer coat leaking sand. The half dozen dogs closed on it, yapping and darting in behind it, and the bear wheeled and struck. One paw collided with a leaping dog and flung it out over the crowd, halfway to the surf. The pack shrank back, snarling and slavering.

To the delighted scorn of the crowd, the next rider could not even force his mount into a charge. A chorus of whistles and jeers rose, and he backed away, hunched down like an old woman. Left momentarily alone, the bear in a frenzy wrestled and heaved and scrabbled at its bonds, and the redwood stump moved.

Castro murmured, "Watch out there."

Micheltorena sighed, leaning back. "Such a brutal and difficult way of life, here in California. Tomorrow is my *consejo,* General. Remember: you may bring six men only."

Castro drew his gaze from the wan face of Mexico City's man, back to the bear growling and fending off dogs by the stump. The *consejo* was not a favorite notion of his and he disliked Micheltorena for mentioning it, especially the six men — to him, who went nowhere without twenty. It was an insult to his prestige, one more sign that Micheltorena did not understand the ways of California and had no respect for its masters.

Then suddenly a big gray horse was trotting up to the surrey, barging in past his guard.

The lancers closed to bar this rider, but Orozco, wheeling in his saddle, was calling them off. An instant later Castro saw why. The man on the gray horse was Captain Sutter. The Swiss don swung around through the midst of the lancers and rode in between Micheltorena and the bear.

"Get out of my way," Micheltorena said.

Sutter leaned down from the back of his gray horse. "I want you to stop Vallejo from attacking my people!"

The governor lifted his fish-colored face. "General Vallejo has been attacking you?"

Castro nudged his horse forward, his attention snagged. Sutter gave him a brief look and a nod and bent again toward Micheltorena.

"Yesterday a gang of men jumped on Mrs. Reilly and Zeke Merritt. They didn't do much damage, but these are my people, and I won't have them worried!"

Castro sat back. Micheltorena's voice rose, velvety with concern, again making mention of his *consejo,* the need for peace and reconciliation. Castro turned and stared away, toward the ocean, to sort out his suddenly tumbled thoughts. Whatever his faults, Mariano Vallejo would not allow such a violence against the peace of the merienda. Someone then was stirring up trouble here, mixing up a plot, and General Castro knew that if there was a plot cooking in California that he did not know about, he was certainly its target.

Beside him, now, Sutter said, in a mollified voice, "I will, Governor, if you wish it. After all, the *consejo* is tomorrow."

The *consejo.* Castro turned to look hard at Micheltorena, still leaning forward over the side rail of his surrey to talk to Sutter. The governor said, "I am sure we can find common ground here, to unify the country, if we keep the good of all foremost in mind."

Castro's lips tightened. Every instinct crackled with alarm. He lifted his reins, turning to call to Orozco to get out of here, and abruptly his horse reared straight up.

He swayed and struggled for his lost balance, his arms swinging, bringing the horse to a trembling stop. His silver-trimmed hat fell off. Around him people were screaming, and Sutter's horse was bounding sideways, banging into the surrey. The bear was loose.

Its roar shook the air, sounding almost in Castro's ears. He fought for control of his horse as the crowd scattered and the great brute ramped up before him, the ropes flying loose around it, the fur of its chest matted with blood and sand and garbage. Sutter was fleeing. In the stranded surrey Micheltorena sat helpless, clutching the side rails, his body rigid, his eyes like peeled grapes.

Castro lunged his horse in between the governor and the bear. "Lieutenant!" he shouted. "Get rid of that!" His arm swept toward the bear lumbering down on him across the empty sand.

Lieutenant Orozco rode forward, his horse collected. He showed no more excitement than the redwood stump. He turned, calling out, and one of the lancers tossed him a spear.

The bear stopped, its head low, swaying from side to side. Its eyes were tiny, piercing. Its tongue hung out over the broken tusk. It stuck its muzzle forward with a snort and charged.

Orozco lifted the spear in his hand, gathered his horse up on the bit, and drove the weapon down to meet the bear. The great black brute reared up to slash at him and the horse spun away, wheeling past the bear's flank, and the rider leaned out of the saddle and drove the spear into the black shaggy side.

At the bear's howl Castro's horse flung itself madly into the air again, fighting for its head. The crowd was screaming a wall of sound around him that damped everything into its uproar. He steadied his horse and glanced at Micheltorena and saw the governor sitting tense as a drawn bow, his jaw hanging loose. Castro swung toward the bear again.

Lieutenant Orozco's charge had carried him into the ocean, his horse to its shoulders in the foaming surf, and the bear pursued and attacked him. The lance jutted from its ribs. As its back turned, a vaquero with a rope charged in and got a loop over the bear's head, and when the animal swerved toward this new threat, Orozco charged out of the breakers, bent down from his saddle, and scooped a spear off the sand.

His horse had caught the fighting fever. When he reined its head toward the bear it flattened its ears down and charged without the spur. On all sides the vaqueros were closing in with their lassoes. A rope uncurled in the air and settled over the bear's head. The bear surged up on end, the lance protruding from its body, the ropes biting into the fur of its neck and shoulder, and Orozco flung his horse against it, the lance level.

The beast reared back to strike at him, and another loop fell over its head and slipped down over its shoulder; when it swung the four-inch sabers of its claws at him its arm was caught a moment, and Orozco went straight at the bear, so close its shadow fell on him, and drove the lance into its throat.

The beast's great paw slashed the air where Orozco's horse's head had just been. Another rope whirled down over the brute's shoulders and jerked taut. It was dying anyway. Heavily it sagged down on all fours, the lances jutting from its throat and side. The crowd closed in, smelling death. Orozco dismounted, led his horse off to one side, and felt it over for damage.

Castro settled his own horse. Its shoulders were black with sweat, and with every twitch and prance the reins shaved foam from its neck. The crowd screamed, triumphant. The bear was dead; they closed in fearlessly to pummel it.

Castro turned to Micheltorena, sitting stiff in his surrey, his face still sleek with excitement and terror. The man from Mexico City let out his breath as if he had held it for long minutes. The stare he turned on Castro was glassy and overwhelmed.

"You see, Governor," Castro said, low-voiced, "you may think you have your bear roped and staked, but the California bear is a rogue, and smarter than he seems." He nodded to Micheltorena. "Good day, Governor." Turning his horse, he rode off across the beach, his lancers trailing after him.

Another of the lancers came by, murmured something admiring, and offered Orozco a salute. At the soldier's approach Sohrakoff had moved back under the shade of the stunted orange tree; after the other man left he drifted up closer again.

"So you're going home before the thing is even half over. One bear's enough for you?"

Orozco was saddling his trail horse; he hooked the stirrup up over the horn and reached down for the girth. "General Castro has an excellent nose for a bad situation. What you just told me confirms it. He's going back to Monterey, and he's ordering me back to Monterey too." He threaded the girth through the saddle ring, his head down. "I have to obey orders. Fortunately, you do not."

Sohrakoff looked around them. General Castro's men packed the little side courtyard at the Mission Dolores, getting ready to leave; a steady parade of the family's servants carried trunks and bags and cushions out through the side door to the carts waiting on the road. Three women marched out, carrying dresses on hooks at arm's length overhead to keep the hems out of the dust.

"I realize you have a private interest in what's going on here," Orozco said.

"Somebody asked me for help."

"Yes. That's important to you. What's important to me is that Micheltorena is worthless, and I want him undermined."

Sohrakoff faced him. "I'll do what I can."

"Well, do it properly — I don't want to have to explain anything or fish you out of another jail. Are you alone in this now?"

"There are people here I can use."

"Good. Report to me in Monterey when you're done." Orozco put one shining boot into his stirrup and swung aboard his horse, every move neat, precise, under perfect control. He disdained the flash and show of the vaqueros, but he was the best horseman Sohrakoff knew, as he had just proven, riding at the bear. In his saddle, he put his hand to the brim of his shako. "Be careful, Count."

Sohrakoff slapped his boot. "I'll see you in Monterey."

The lieutenant reined around, going toward the front of the courtyard, where the lancers were forming a column. Sohrakoff backed up, into the shade of the orange tree.

The Mission Dolores had never been large; now, ten years after the secularization, its honey-colored walls were crumbling like the presidio's. The dons used it now and then, and their sporadic generosity kept a few monks there, a handful of Indians. Behind him, the old herb garden still grew, smelling of mint and basil. He thought about Catharine Reilly, who had sent him away and then called him back again as if he were on a tether.

She was only a small piece of this, inconsequential to anybody but him. She was in more danger than she knew, and she had asked him for help. Not many people mattered to him, and he had to take care of the ones who did, whenever he could. If he could do something for Orozco, too, that polished it.

Castro had come out of the mission; his lancers moved off with a jingling of spurs and bit chains. Sohrakoff went along the wall behind the orange trees to the little gate onto the hillside, where his horse was, and rode back to Yerba Buena.

24 🏴 ZEKE GROANED. "I ain't goin' nowhere. My head hurts." He buried his head in his arms.

Catharine pulled her blankets off the bed. "Come lie down over here, then." She patted the mattress. Zeke moaned, rolling on the floor, and she nudged him with her foot. "Zeke, take the bed."

"Leave him alone, Cathy," said Bidwell. He was dressing himself with great attention, since they were going to the *consejo,* brushing his hair and his beard and putting on a shirt he had saved for an occasion. "If he can't hold his liquor, let him suffer."

Zeke whined. Catharine stepped across him toward the door, looking for her shoes. "Nobody could hold that much liquor. I'm surprised he's alive." On the shelf by the door was a flintlock horse pistol. "Sutter promised we'd go unarmed."

"Look, Cathy, there's a hundred of Vallejo's men."

"But he's only being allowed to bring six, because there's only six of us."

"Castro's men will be there and who knows who else." Bidwell took the pistol and bent and pulled up the leg of his trousers; he stuck the pistol down into the top of his boot. Straightening, he faced her, solemn. "You know me, Cathy. I won't start anything. But I'm not standing there with — excuse me — with my cock in my hand when things get difficult." He nodded to her. "You ought to take one of Zeke's guns."

"The hell with that," Zeke bawled.

"No," she said. "None of us should take a gun. The Captain gave his word."

Bidwell picked up his hat. "If you're right, nobody will ever know I have mine." He put on his hat, evening the brim with both hands. "Let's go."

Micheltorena flexed in a stiff little bow. "How delightful of you to have come, Señora Reilly." He looked hard at Sutter. "Captain Sutter, this is after all a meeting of men."

"I never considered not bringing her," Sutter said; he wiped down one side of his mustaches with his thumb, smiling. "I said six of us, and here we are, Governor, ready to talk peace with General Vallejo."

"Very well." Micheltorena gave her another look. His cold gray lassitude today was geared up to a nervous fidget. His long, pale fingers twitched. There was a fine sheen of sweat on his colorless cheeks. He waved his hand around him at his camp. "Please be as free here as in your own sitting room." His voice was off-key with insincerity. Clearly it vexed him that she had come.

Catharine glanced around. The governor's campsite teemed with white-coated servants swarming in and out of the tent, carrying platters and jugs, firewood and baskets. On the open sand between the tent and the creekbank stood some tables made of redwood slabs, with benches beside them, where the *consejo* would sit. Servants moved around it constantly, putting down cups and moving them here and there and fussing over the seats.

Castro would sit in the *consejo,* also bringing six men. She wondered if Sohrakoff would be one of them and guessed not; Sohrakoff wore no uniform, was a spy, not a regular. She fought against thinking about him, wanting to clear him out of her mind, to suspect him, dislike him as she was disliking all the dons. She wished she had not talked to him again.

She walked slowly up toward the big, squat-trunked oak tree that filled the upper end of the broad apron of sand where Micheltorena's camp lay. The sheep pens at the foot of the steep yellow cliff were less full than they had been three days before; she circled around the roasting pit, smoking in the ground, giving off a dry baking heat that seemed to crisp her skin. On an open fire between the oak tree and the sheep pens a cauldron steamed, scenting the air with the sharp reek of chilies. Two men sat beside it plucking chickens and ramming them onto spits. The aromas of searing meat and peppers made the air seem thicker.

There was a yell behind her, and she turned.

On his splendid mahogany-red horse General Vallejo trotted up toward the camp. The horse's black forelock was braided with roses. Half a dozen vaqueros followed him, dressed in tight-fitting jackets and gaudy long trousers split up the sides and sewn with brocade.

Micheltorena came out of the tent, trailed by his two green-coated soldiers, and with outstretched hands greeted General Vallejo as if they were brothers. Catharine went back to the table, where the other Americans were all sitting along one bench, and took a place at the end, beside John Bidwell. Sutter had gone down to welcome General Vallejo, partaking of the flowery ceremonial falseness of the dons.

"He brought six," Christenson said, on Bidwell's left.

"He has no Zeke," said Pablo Gutierrez.

"Yeah, well," said Bidwell, "right now we haven't got a Zeke."

Catharine was looking down the widening fan of the camp, watching for General Castro. In spite of herself she enjoyed the dons' magnificence. "A Zeke at the post is worth two Vallejos." They laughed as if she had said something clever. There was a cup before her, and one of Micheltorena's numberless servants had come up to pour aguardiente into it, clear as water. Then, to her amazement, General Vallejo walked up to the opposite side of the table and sat down across from her.

His black eyes glittered. His vaqueros did not sit at the table, like Sutter's men, but grouped themselves behind their master and stood there, their faces blank and dark. They were Indians. She realized with a start that Vallejo too was part Indian.

He was gorgeously dressed, as always, his sombrero brim heavy with shredded gold. He took the hat off and handed it backward; a brown hand removed it. His smooth, hard arrogance focused its beam on Catharine.

"Señora Reilly. I am pleasantly surprised to find you here."

"Good morning, General," she said.

He jerked an impatient hand at the servant who approached him with a jug. Micheltorena's man backed off, and one of the vaqueros behind General Vallejo took the jug from him and served the don. Vallejo smiled at Catharine. "If I were Sutter, I would dress you in green, to match your eyes."

Affronted, Catharine stared back at him, one hand on the top of the table, her throat and her cheeks warm. "General, Captain Sutter is my employer, not my lady's maid."

"Ah," he said. "Yes, indeed, your eyes are remarkable. Then there is a husband? Señor Reilly?"

"He's dead."

"And you are faithful to his memory. Charming. Nonetheless you are alive, and very pretty, and you should wear green." He lifted his head; his voice rang. "Governor, I do not see General Castro — when does he arrive?"

Micheltorena was taking his place at the head of the table. Sutter came quietly to sit down to the governor's right. The opposite side of the table was empty, except for General Vallejo, who moved into the middle of the space, his men ranged behind him.

The governor put his elbows on the table and tipped his fingers together. "General Castro has left the merienda."

Sutter said, "What the hell?" General Vallejo exploded in a grunt.

"Left! What do you mean, he's left?"

"Last night," said Micheltorena. His fingers were tapping together, jittery. "He had stomach trouble. He has an old stomach ailment."

Catharine reached for the cup of aguardiente. Sohrakoff was gone, then, also. She had trusted him for nothing. She smothered down a small treacherous sense of loss. The servant leaned in between her and Bidwell, setting down a platter of beef and tortillas on the table.

Vallejo leaned forward, his face flower-red. "And you let him go! What can we do here without him? You let him go!"

Micheltorena said, "I'm not in a position to force General Castro to do anything. If you two gentlemen would reconcile your differences and join me, together we can deal with him."

Vallejo's gaze swung toward Sutter. "My differences with Captain Sutter have one word: Ross. Let him give me Ross —"

"Give you Ross," Sutter said. He leaned forward over the table, his face fierce. "Ross is mine. If you want to be friendly with me, General, you can send back the herd of cattle you stole from me last summer."

The hard, round red face of Mariano Vallejo shifted its attention from him to Governor Micheltorena, and the don of Sonoma folded his arms over his chest. "If you can't compel General Castro, I see no reason to let you compel me."

Micheltorena lowered his hands slowly to the table. "I am the governor of Alta California. Is that not reason enough?"

Sutter was glaring across the table at Vallejo. "Two thousand head in that herd!"

"You lie." Vallejo's eyelids drooped, his lips tight at the corners. He folded his arms over his chest. The two men stared at one another, nose to nose.

Micheltorena said, "I had hoped to do this by the use of reason and patriotism."

He lifted his hands up from beneath the table, and in each he held a pistol. Around the table an abrupt silence fell. Micheltorena rose to his feet. The right-hand gun he aimed at Sutter, and the left he turned on Vallejo.

"However, I will use force if I must. Gentlemen, you are under arrest."

Catharine started once and sat still, her heart pounding. Sutter's face went pale behind his thick mustaches. Across the table Vallejo jerked upright, his eyes darting from side to side, the color hard and bright in his cheeks. The men behind him moved up a step closer, and he raised his hand.

Micheltorena said, "If you look around you, gentlemen, you will see that my soldiers surround this place."

Catharine lifted her eyes. At first she saw no soldiers; all she saw around them were Micheltorena's white-coated servants, tightly packed. Then she realized that these were the soldiers, that each had a knife, and some had long knives, sabers. She heard feet behind her and knew they were all around her. For a moment she could not move even to breathe, as if the knives were in her already, nailing her to the bench.

"Gentlemen!" Micheltorena gestured with the pistols in his hands. "Rise to your feet, please, and tell your men to remain where they are. You and I shall go to my tent and talk there."

Beside Catharine, Bidwell murmured, "Cathy, watch me."

She glanced at him, saw his hands move in his lap, and looked down; he lifted his hands up under the edge of the thick slab of the tabletop and pushed.

He could not move it himself. She slid her hands off the table and pressed the palms up against the underside. The table did not yield. He was murmuring now to Christenson. She put her hands in her lap.

Sutter said loudly, "I'm going nowhere." He jerked up onto his feet, flung his arm out, and pointed at Vallejo. "You got us into this." He wheeled toward Micheltorena, his arm still extended at Vallejo, his finger shaking. "Arrest him, not me — I'm on your side. He's —"

Vallejo bounded up, roaring, and Bidwell shouted, "Now!"

Catharine heaved at the table with her whole strength, Bidwell pushing also, and then the other Americans joined them, and their combined force threw the table over sideways.

The dishes clattered off. Vallejo leapt away, and Micheltorena at the table's end staggered back. One of his pistols fired. The sound beat in Catharine's ears; she ducked down behind the upturned table, looking around her.

Bidwell crouched beside her, his flintlock in his hand. "That way —" He pointed toward the creek. "Run!"

A wall of white coats was rushing at them. Another gun went off, and another. Somebody somewhere was shrieking in Spanish. Catharine got her skirts in her hands and ran toward the creek.

Six white coats veered to follow her. A gunshot blasted in her ears. She raced toward the creek and the open beach beyond, and somebody grabbed her from behind and sent her sprawling.

She rolled over, kicking out, dirt in her mouth. Another hand clutched at her, and she struck at it. She scrambled to her feet, facing a man five feet away who raised a knife at her.

Behind him she saw only Micheltorena's men. But they were running, not fighting. Something was chasing them. Down through the canyon behind Micheltorena's camp there sounded a steadily rising thunder. The ground was quivering rhythmically under her feet. Behind her a horse neighed. The man with the knife wheeled around, his mouth falling open. A wail went up from the crowd running past him.

"Stampede!"

Catharine took two uncertain steps back. Up there, out of the mouth of the creek's canyon, a river of horses was pouring.

Their hoofs pounded the ground into a steady drumroll. A curtain of dust rolled along with them; through it the horses hurtled, their shapes blurred, their colors lost in the yellow veil. The first few swerved to avoid the sheep pens, but the animals coming behind them were packed shoulder to shoulder. They tore through the sheep pens as if they were spider webs. The dust rose in choking waves under their hoofs. As they pounded down into the camp, they spread out, their manes and tails flying. The fires, the spitted chickens, the heaps of firewood, disintegrated under their impact. The cauldron of stew rolled bouncing down the slope into the creek, horses careening around it.

She could not outrun them; they were already around her, swerving to avoid her, more and closer all the time. She looked ahead of her for some shelter.

The widening wedge of the camp before her streamed with running men. Nobody was shooting now. Vallejo and his vaqueros were running like quail along the open sand. She saw Micheltorena ahead of her, his black ungainly figure crane-stepping through the thickening haze of the dust. He ran past his surrey, sitting in front of the tent, and darted toward the cliff.

The horses reached the surrey. The first two veered off, but the third struck the carriage a glancing blow, and then a wall of bay and chestnut bodies plowed into the black lacquered wood. The surrey rolled over, one shaft kicking up into the air, a wheel spinning, and vanished under the hoofs and the dust and the flying wild manes.

Catharine dashed into the shelter of the tent's outside wall, where an ox cart stood full of wine tuns. Each gasping breath sucked the dusty air into her lungs. She choked and coughed; tears ran from her eyes. The ground under her was quaking. Horses streamed past her. The tent shook; it was yielding to the stampede. The peak with its bright flag bowed slowly forward and dipped and collapsed, and over it a horse sailed, shied in midstride to avoid her, and pounded on. The tent churned away steadily into the dust. A mountain of horseflesh loomed over her. She whirled and fled away, looking for shelter and seeing nothing.

She headed for the cliff. Running horses cut her off. She stopped, panting, surrounded. There was nowhere to go. Facing the charge, she began to wave her arms around her, trying to turn them.

A tail lashed her face. She milled her arms over her head; the heaving bodies loomed up out of the smothering dust and split to streak by on either side of her. Through their relentless press another horse was fighting its way toward her, the rider on its back forcing it across the current, banging and plunging through the river of horses.

She flung her arms up to him. He had a cloth over his face against the seething dust; above it his blue eyes blazed at her. He reined in, his horse throwing its head wild-eyed against the bit, and bent and slid his arm around her waist. His fist gripped her dress. Gracelessly he heaved her up across his saddle, and his horse bolted.

Her face was pressed to filthy cloth. Her skirts were up around her waist. She clutched him, one arm around him, the other hand gripping the saddle. Her hair flew across her face. She threw it back with a toss of her head, twisting to look ahead of her.

They were galloping out toward the beach, loping along behind a vast cloud of dust through which horses moved. On the hillside where all week long children had scrambled for strawberries, now crowds of people stood huddled together, taking refuge from the flood of horses. She could see no sign of Sutter or General Vallejo or John Bidwell or Micheltorena. The governor's coup had failed; the stampede had shattered it; the chaos of the merienda had swallowed it up.

Sohrakoff's horse turned and stopped. In her ear his voice asked, "Are you all right, Cat?" She lifted her head and with one hand pulled the cloth down off his face and kissed him.

His arm went around her. His lips were gentle, the bristles

of his beard tickling her upper lip. Abruptly his horse strode forward again, walking back the way they had come, back up toward Micheltorena's camp.

"Where are you going?" she asked. She sat crosswise on his thighs, her arm around his waist; she pulled her skirts down over her knees.

He nudged the horse along into a slow trot, passing a few strays that cantered along in the wake of the stampede, up by the oak tree and the broken sheep pens, into the narrow mouth of the draw. "Zeke can handle the rest of this."

"Zeke!" she said.

He laughed. "I couldn't herd all those horses by myself." His arm was around her; she gripped the front of his shirt. The horse loped back up the draw, where the air was still filmy with dust. The cliff loomed up and he swung the horse off the trail and forced it at a fringe of dense fir trees, and the horse put its head down, snorting, and pushed in through the branches. Catharine pressed her face against his chest, down out of the way of the slapping green spines.

Beyond, the gorge of a feeder creek was a steeply climbing, narrow slot in the cliff wall, its floor tumbled with rocks. It was dark here, the sun not reaching the ground. He clicked his tongue to the horse, which struggled over a fallen limb, splashed through the creek, and climbed a bank. They rode up through a stand of redwood trees, and he stopped.

"Let's get clean."

She slid down from the horse. Here the enormous trees rose dense and dark toward the faraway sky, but off a little way there was sunlight. She went along the gorge to the brightness.

Where the sun shone the creek turned a corner under a bulging gray rock, and a pool had formed, deep enough to be blue-green in the middle. Along its edge was a patch of gray sand. Sohrakoff walked down beside her.

He took off his hat and his shirt. He gave her a sideways look and began to unbuckle his belt, and she turned her back to him. "Help me get out of this dress." He undid the buttons down her back. She said, "How did you find out what was going on?"

"It wasn't that hard, once you told me what to look for. Micheltorena had the whole thing set up from the beginning. His men attacked you, not Vallejo's, to make sure everybody stayed enemies." His hands pushed the dress down off her shoulders. "I watched him; I could see he had dozens of men, and they didn't look like servants to me."

She pulled the dress off and slid her underpants down to her ankles. He went past her, wading out into the pool, and stooped and splashed the water over his face. He was naked. He looked bigger with his clothes off, his upper arms thick with muscle, paler than the sunbrowned skin of his hands and forearms. She pulled her gaze from the flat curve of his buttock and walked down into the water toward him, her skin thrilling, her mouth dry.

The water rose cold around her thighs. He turned toward her, and their eyes met for a moment, too intense; they both looked away. He bent down and began to sluice water over her, washing the dust from her arms, and she stooped to rinse her hair, shivering, not with the cold. She straightened. The cool water streaming down over her, she stood still while he bathed her body.

His hands sleeked over her breasts. He bent down and sloshed water onto her belly and his head moved and he tongued her nipple and she whimpered; she put her hands on his hair. When he stood up she reached between them and touched the velvet skin of the serpent in his groin.

His breath left him in a gasp. His hand pressed up between her legs, and his mouth came down on hers. The cool wetness of their skin was like a barrier between them. They moved to the flat sand along the edge of the pool and lay down, his arm around her, holding her in the curve of his shoulder. She still could not look at him and she closed her eyes, and when his hand slid down over her thigh, for a moment her legs stiffened together. His hand lay still on her thigh.

"Touch me again," he said. His lips grazed over her cheek and his tongue made a light trace of the rim of her ear. She curled her fingers around him.

Under the delicate skin it was hard, not like bone but like a honeycomb, packed with sweetness. His fingers slipped down between her thighs; he unfolded her, opening her, touching a new hot eagerness into her. She wanted that sweetness, that hardness. She moved against him, but he held off, teasing her, his fingers barely touching her while she strained to push herself against him.

"Oh, please —" She lifted her hips to him, and he rolled onto her and plunged into the middle of her.

She felt him all the way up, an alien spike. She surrounded him, she took him in, swallowing him. He said her name in a thick voice. He said, "I love you." He said it again, while her body filled and fountained, overflowing, one cascade after another, each one higher, clearer, until she sobbed in the resistless surge and clung to him, and he yelled in her ear, and they lay still, wrapped together on the sand.

She said, "That was good."

"I wanted you so much, that time at Sutter's." He lifted his head and kissed her hard, his teeth on her lip.

"I didn't even know I loved you until you were gone," she said.

He moved off her to lie on his side on the sand, and his head sank and he kissed her breast. "You have really pretty tits." He stretched out on his back in the sun, his arms over his head, and groaned with a luxurious animal satisfaction.

She sat up; there was sand all over her back. They had made a deep print in the beach. His head turned, he was looking at her; she could look at him now, his arms sprawled over his head, his long legs and well-shaped feet, his penis lying limp in its nest of red-gold hair.

He said, "Do you play the piano?"

"All the time. Whenever I can. It's wonderful, like letting everything go, especially after a bad day."

"What do you play?"

"Mozart, Beethoven, Chopin. Anything I can remember. I wish I could make up songs of my own, but I'm not that good." She put one hand out, diffident, and touched his wiry, damp hair. "What do you do in Monterey?"

He pushed his head into her caress, making it stronger. "Break horses, play cards. Run errands for Orozco." His hand closed over the back of her hand.

"Do you have . . . anybody else?"

"No," he said. He let go of her, and his gaze veered away, pushing her off. "All I have is papers to live there, until they throw me out. I can't, you know, have a life there. It's just a job."

She burst out, "Why do you stay with those people? They're treacherous, cruel —"

"Orozco isn't a don. And they're more than that. All you know is the merienda." He gave her a quick look, almost shy.

"That's enough," she said.

He lowered his eyes. His hand moved along the sand between them, drawing his fingers through it. "New Helvetia is a paradise, is it? This is politics, not morality. Of course to an American they're the same thing."

Jabbed, she backed away from him, one knee raised. He was watching his hand dig in the sand. The silence spun out between them.

He said, finally, "I'm sorry. I shouldn't have said that."

She said, "This doesn't really make anything different, does it. Between us."

"Not much," he said.

"I love you."

"I love you," he said. "But it doesn't change much. I'm going back to Monterey, you're going to New Helvetia." He raised his eyes to meet hers. "We were on the same side this time, but things will change." She looked down at his hand, stroking restlessly back and forth. In the beach between them he had drawn a long, deep line.

He said, "There's going to be a war someday between the United States and Mexico, and California will be the prize. I love this country, Cat. I don't belong here and I have no place here, but I love it anyway and I'll defend it. Against anybody. Even you."

She looked away, across the creek, her mind churning. The silence stretched and thickened, and the longer they went without speaking the harder it was to find something to say. Finally she heard him get up.

"Goodbye, Cat."

"Wait," she said. She turned toward him, unwilling to let him go. He was pulling his pants up over his hips. She found her dress and put her feet under her. "Help me get this back on."

He came over and fastened the buttons for her. When the dress was done up the back his arms slid around her and he held her against him, her back to his chest, and they stood still; she turned her head and pressed her cheek against his chest. Around them the giant trees creaked and groaned in the wind.

He said, "Somebody's calling you."

She moved, and he let go of her. She lifted her face to him and they kissed again; his hand ran once roughly down over her hair.

"Goodbye, Cat." He went up through the trees, his shirt over his shoulder, looking for his horse. She went on down the gorge, toward the beach, where now even she could hear somebody calling her name.

25 ▞ ZEKE WAS THE HERO of the merienda, taking all the credit for the stampede. Sutter's conclusion, and that of most people, was that the trouble had sprung from Vallejo's measureless arrogance. Catharine fended off the few questions they thought to ask her. It came on her almost at once that she might be pregnant; for two weeks she thought of nothing else, terrified, concentrating on every twitch and stir in her belly, working out what she would say to Sutter, imagining what they would say to her, answering them in her mind, and then the blood came and the terror ebbed and left behind a deep-drawing grief, that even that was gone.

She gave herself up to work. New Helvetia was endless work. The summer simmered on; toward the end of it another little flood of settlers arrived, nearly sixty of them, starved and exhausted. Sutter took them in, fed them and housed them until they were hale again, and set them up on land in the north and east of his grant, in the wet side of the great valley. Other people drifted in, not settlers but strays, worn-out mountain men and trappers, drifters, and they made their camps down outside the wall, between the fort and the river. Their camps and common meeting grounds spread around in disorder, and Sutter began talking about laying out a town.

"Why don't you put them to work?" Catharine asked.

"They work. They went out and rounded up those Indians for me last week, didn't they?"

"Oh, yes," she said. "What a noble task that was, too."

"Don't start in with this, Cat." They were in the office, where she was trying to reconcile his books. "The Indians do very well with me. I pay them, teach them, clothe them, feed them — come here." He strode off to the window, and she followed him.

In the yard below, some of the men were lining up horse troughs in a straight line. A file of Indians stood along the side of the yard watching. They wore long shirts of cloth woven on the looms of New Helvetia. Their hair hung down over their shoulders.

"What have they been doing?" she asked.

"Making hats, half of them. The other half making blankets." He sounded pleased. "Now things are starting to go well, Cat, in spite of all. Sunol, that merchant in Yerba Buena, bought all those chairs, and he's sending me new distillery equipment, and he'll buy the whiskey. I can sell the hats in Yerba Buena and pay off some of my debt to Sunol and still have a little for the Russians. It's all a matter of having many things going at once."

The cook came out of the kitchen, two of his boys hauling a big iron pot after him. Under his direction they poured a white mush into the wooden ditch, a half-liquid slop that flowed swiftly down to fill the trough entirely.

The Indians broke from their lines. Rushing forward, they

fell on their knees by the trough and began to shovel the white glop into their mouths with their hands. Some of the white men had come out to watch and stood in the corner of the yard, laughing.

Catharine drew back from the window. Sutter was smiling at her. "See? That's probably the first time in their lives they've been able to eat all they want!"

She shook her head slightly, watching the Indians feeding like pigs. "They're better off starving."

"You're utterly perverse. They learn to work here. It's good for them. We'll civilize them, as much as possible." He paced across the room to the wall and took down his coat. "I'm going down to the embarcadero. Get the books done; I want to see them when I come back."

She grunted at him. Taking the quill pen from its inkwell, she bent over the books that showed he owed everybody more money than there was in California. He went out; she heard him a moment later, in the courtyard, yelling for Zeke Merritt and his horse.

She helped the Kanaka women do the cleaning and kept after the cook, she worked on the books and wrote Sutter's letters begging for more money and credit, she mediated disputes and problems the settlers brought her while he was elsewhere, trying again to build a sawmill, herding cattle and rendering tallow, building a distillery, driving gangs of Indians into the fields.

In the fall there came a letter from Micheltorena.

The governor had come into hard times since the merienda. Returning to El Pueblo de los Angeles he had run into trouble with the people there. Most of his army, recruited from Sonoran jails, had deserted into the sunshine and easy life of California, and now José Castro, prudent and patient and remorseless, was summoning up an army of his own, more than enough to drive out the governor.

Micheltorena could do two things, the letter said. He could return to Mexico City, tell the new government there that the dons were warlords and bandits who could be mastered only by an iron hand, have them declared outlaws, raise an army, and march to destroy them.

Or, the letter said, Micheltorena could call on the only man in Alta California he knew he could trust, Don el Capitan Juan Agosto Sutter of New Helvetia, to bring an army of his famously well armed Missouri men to the support of the rightful governor of the country.

"You're not going to do it," Catharine said.

In grateful recognition of the value of this service Micheltorena was prepared to confirm all Don el Capitan Sutter's charters in perpetuo and to award him the rank and uniform of a colonel in the Mexican Army.

"You're not going to do it," Catharine said again.

Sutter put the letter down, gave her an Olympian stare, and said, "I didn't ask you for your opinion."

"I'll give it to you gratis. This is a disaster, Captain. You're a farmer, not a soldier. Planting time is coming, you owe the Russians thirty thousand dollars; are you going to take every man off New Helvetia and march them away to get killed?"

Sutter grunted at her and walked into the next room, where Manaiki had put out a dish of beans and bread for him, and then came back. "You don't understand California politics. The dons don't fight. They just march around a while, until somebody gets tired and goes home." He thrust the letter at her. "File this and make a copy of it — I don't want him to forget that part about in perpetuo."

She batted the letter with her fingers. "It's the colonel's uniform, isn't it. That's why you're going. All these years of lying about being an army officer and now you'll really be one, and a colonel, too."

His neck bulged. A red hue glowed in his cheeks, and he cranked himself forward, rigid, his face close to hers. "Shut up!"

"Don't be a fool, Captain!"

He flung out his arm, striking at her, the paper forgotten in his fingers. "I was an officer! In the Swiss Guards!" His eyes shone; his face pulsed with hurt and rage and shame and guilt. "Get out! Damn you, this is my place. Get out!"

She straightened, abruptly cool. Under her the floor seemed

to tilt and slide away from her. She mastered herself. He stood on widely braced legs, his face twisted, his eyes murderous.

"Get out."

"No," she said, quietly. "I've given up too much to be here, and I'm staying."

Their gazes met and locked. He hesitated only a moment before he found a way to be right. "Stay, then," he roared, triumphant. "Just get away from me!"

He turned and strode the length of the room again and flung the paper down on her desk, where she would copy it later. She left the building, going out to the heat and the sunlight, and walked once along the whole circuit of the fort's wall before her temper let her slow down.

She expected some of the men to refuse to go, after the disaster of the merienda, but they all went. The newcomers were especially enthusiastic, and the men in the camps. Even a lot of the Indians entered Sutter's army, dressed up in old uniforms salvaged from Ross, and armed with sticks and knives. Late in the year, around the time they should have been planting, they marched away toward the south.

Sutter had left in charge a man who had shown up only a year before, Charles Flugge, who was German, spoke German to Sutter, got him drunk and sang old German songs with him, and played whist well enough to amuse the Swiss don but not well enough to beat him. Probably he also believed that Sutter had once been a captain of artillery in the Swiss Guards. As soon as Sutter left, Flugge took a jug and cornered Manaiki in the Captain's bedroom, and after that he did no work at all.

The rainy season began. A lot of the families living up the valley, their men gone to the war, came down to stay at the fort, women and children in flocks and droves. It had been a long while since Catharine had spent so much time with families. Nancy Kelsey sewed up the sprigged muslin into dresses for her; the other women took over parts of the fort and did the weaving, the shoemaking, some of the carpentry, and made candles, made soap. Catharine taught Sarah Kelsey and some of the other children how to read, using a stack of newspapers Rae sent her from Yerba Buena. Sarah played the piano a little, although she would not practice and therefore did not learn to use her fingers properly. It astonished Catharine how this annoyed her. In the evenings, all the people came up to the central building and sang, mostly hymns, while Catharine picked out the tunes and tried to make harmonies.

In the spring the men came back.

They drifted in a few at a time, first some of the settlers, tired, unwilling to say much; they took their wives and children out of the fort and went back out to their homesteads. Finally Sutter reappeared.

Catharine went out to meet him, walking down from the gate of the fort toward the river. He rode along on his gray horse, leading a straggling line of his men, keeping no order. Catharine stopped on the path, just below Manaiki's garden. Their weary column stretched back into the distance; they seemed to have just enough energy left to reach home.

"John!" She saw Bidwell coming after Sutter. "Zeke —" She threw her arm up. They headed toward her. Sutter reined in a little way from her. He looked older, his mustaches limp, an inch of stubble on his chin. John Bidwell jumped down from his horse and strode toward her, and Zeke Merritt came after him; she flung her arms around Bidwell and pressed herself to his coat, half in tears, and then turned to Zeke and hugged him too, the vast, stinking, bearlike mass of him, and his arms went around her and he muttered something in his throat.

He backed up; beyond him, Sutter sat slumped in his saddle, staring at her. She turned to him and held her arms out.

"Captain —"

He swung down from the saddle and she embraced him. His arms tightened around her and his hand held her face against his shoulder and in her ear he said, "You were right, Cat. You were right." Turning away roughly, he walked out of her arms, his face gaunt. "Come on, now, we're almost there, now, there's work to do." He led his horse up toward the fort, which squatted dirt-colored and solid on the plain before them.

Zeke and Bidwell told her later what had happened, how they marched here and there, chasing Castro's army, but never caught them until one morning when they found themselves lined up over a canyon in the desert near El Pueblo.

"I could see guns aiming back across the way," Zeke said, "and I'm over my rifle, right, sightin' her up, and then one of them snakes across the way calls me a dirty greaser!"

"What?"

Bidwell coughed. They were leaning on the railing of the stair landing, just outside the central building, waiting for Sutter to give them orders.

"That's right. Called us greasers, in English. U.S. English."

"Who were they?" Cat cried.

Zeke said, "Well, we sung out, and it turned out they was all Americans, bunch of trappers wintering over in the Pueblo, Castro just recruited them to have some fun shooting up the greasers. So we couldn't fight. Went off and got drunk instead, and came home."

"What happened to Micheltorena?"

Bidwell laughed. Zeke scrubbed his hand up over his graying beard.

"Him and Sutter, they had it a little rougher, they got captured. You know the dons. They put Micheltorena on a ship back to Mexico, and they teased Sutter a little, cat-and-mouse stuff, but in the end they let him go, and here we are."

"Yes," she said. "Here you are. Now will you please stay here —" Her hands rose, shaping the air between them; she looked into John Bidwell's slow, gentle smile. "Stay here," she said, again. Her eyes stung. He reached out and gripped her hand, holding her tight, the old connection between them strong and sustaining.

"Bidwell!" Sutter called.

He went into the office. Zeke stood looking down at her.

"You know," he said, "that-there, getting those trappers in to fight against us, that reminded me right smart of Sohrakoff."

She twitched, the name like a lash on an old, healing wound. "What do you mean?" It was the first time he had ever mentioned Sohrakoff to her.

"Just something he would think up. Or maybe not; maybe the dons are smarter than I make 'em."

Sutter bawled from the office, "Zeke, get in here!"

He smiled at her. "Gotta go to work, lady." His foot scraped on the landing; he went inside. She stayed where she was, looking out over the broad valley into the deep golden springtime haze.

Sutter's Indians had run away; he sent Zeke out with some of the other men to round them up and bring them back.

This time, for the first time, there was trouble. The Indians tried to fight, and Sutter's men shot some of them. When the Indians were marched back up to the fort many of them were weeping. Catharine could not play the piano after that, not for days; she sat on the bench in the evenings, her hands in her lap, staring at the broken, yellowing keys, while the men played whist behind her. Finally Sutter got tired of her brooding and sent her down with the launch to Yerba Buena, to sell chairs and hats and candles to the storekeepers there.

There was a British merchantman lying at anchor in the harbor, and when she went into the Hudson's Bay post the public room was full of British sailors in their blue shirts and strange round hats. At her entrance, alone, they gave off a lascivious chorus of whistles and jeers, which she ignored. The man who strode across the room to meet her, holding his hand out and smiling, was not William Rae, the pop-eyed Scots Hudson's Bay factor, but an American named William Liedesdorff, whom she had met once at Sutter's.

"Mrs. Reilly. Excellent to see you. I saw your launch arrive — I have just now been making arrangements. Come along, I have a room ready for you."

"Thank you, Mr. Liedesdorff. When did you start working for Hudson's Bay?"

He carried her bag up the stairs ahead of her. "This is no longer the Hudson's Bay Company post." His voice was sleek with pride. "I've taken it over. I intend to run it as a hotel. You see my first guests down there in the public room." He led her along the corridor at the top to the end room and opened the door.

"What happened to the Hudson's Bay Company?" she said, startled.

"Mr. Rae blew his head off, so the company gave up here."

"Blew his head off!" She imagined the little round eyes blasting like cannonballs out of Rae's skull.

"Evils of venery, Mrs. Reilly." He turned, brisk, red-faced with importance. "I trust this room will be satisfactory. I feel the corner rooms are the best, with the two windows."

"Yes, it's fine." She was still struggling with the extraordinary notion of Rae's suicide.

"We will serve dinner when the bell rings." He left, pulling the door shut after him.

She took off her coat and hung it up on a nail sticking out of the wall. The room was still only a box of raw redwood, with a bed and a straw mattress. She looked for a water basin and found none and was going out to tell Liedesdorff what a bad innkeeper he was when there came a knock on the door.

It was Liedesdorff again. "I remembered — Rae told me about sending you the newspapers." His voice swelled with satisfied pride at his own efficiency; he dumped a heap of newsprint on the bed.

She put her hand on the door, holding it open, holding him there. "I need some water. And what happened to William Rae?"

Liedesdorff rubbed his hands together. "Not a nice story for a lady."

"Tell me anyway."

"He fell in love. Unfortunately he was already married. His wife found out and he killed himself."

She stared at him, wondering if he was lying. "Why would the Hudson's Bay Company pack up and quit because of that?"

"Nobody to mind the store, Mrs. Reilly." He left.

She sat down on the bed and picked up the newspapers. Most of them were copies of the Honolulu *Polynesian,* whose focus tended to be more Pacific than continental. In the middle she found a copy of the Baltimore *Sun,* less than a year old.

That put it squarely in the middle of the 1844 American presidential campaign. She read through the three articles that dealt with the candidates. Either Henry Clay of Kentucky or somebody named Polk had been president for months now. Probably it was Clay, as she had never heard of Polk. Halfway through the second article she came on his campaign slogan: *Fifty-four Forty or Fight!*

She lifted her eyes from the paper. From thousands of miles and a year away the world closed in around her, no larger suddenly than the redwood room.

That was Oregon, what Polk wanted to fight for. And the British were yielding, or at least the Hudson's Bay Company thought they were. That was why they had given up on Yerba Buena — not because William Rae had exploded his head but because they were expecting to surrender Fort Vancouver and the Oregon Territory to the United States. Without them this little post here was worthless. She sat staring at the wall, the paper in her hands.

She got up and went to one of the windows that Liedesdorff was so proud of, and looked out over San Francisco Bay.

She thought she had never seen it the same color twice. Today it was a virginal blue, spread sweet as the sunlight off toward the east, the green meadows and slopes and the golden marshes basking in the day's warmth like some great beast that had curled up around the bay and gone to sleep. She put her hands on the windowsill, amazed at the sudden violence of her feelings.

This was her country. This soft, warm sunlight, the exuberant wind, the broad bay, the hills beyond, the redwoods, the teeming valley — this was her country. And California was the next prize. Taking Oregon, swallowing Texas, the men in Washington would surely turn on this place. In her mind suddenly she saw the map, the great, curving upper jaw of the Oregon Territory, the yawning lower jaw of Texas, with California a morsel ready to be devoured. Sohrakoff had told her the truth.

Liedesdorff was back, knocking, a jug of water in his hand. "Is this all, Mrs. Reilly?"

She looked at him wildly until his eyes widened, nervous, and then she jerked herself away from the window. "Yes," she said. "I suppose." She took the water and went to wash her hands.

26 🗶 IN THE HAT SHOP two Indians were nesting the hats and stacking them in a crate; Catharine counted them and wrote the number on a sheet of paper and with a piece of charcoal wrote the number also on the outside of the crate. Standing back, she nodded to Raphero, the chief hatmaker, who put the lid down and tacked it on.

The sound of his hammer was lost in the general uproar of the fort. Out in the yard the carpenters were trying to mend a wagon, and both the blacksmiths were clanging out horseshoes. The Russians had brought them six pigs of iron when they came for their money in November, and Sutter was using it as fast as it would take the heat of the forge. Raphero and his brother carried the crates out to the yard, and Catharine followed, circling past them and past the cart that would carry the hats to the embarcadero to be shipped.

As she walked across to the bakery to watch the bread being put into the ovens, Zeke Merritt sauntered up to her. He was chewing a wad of tobacco the size of an egg, his silvered hair on end, his eyes bloodshot. Clearly he was suffering from a hard night's drinking in the camps. "Where the Captain?"

"Down at the mill." They were trying to build a mill on the American River. "What's the matter?"

"Your friend Frémont's here," Zeke said, and jerked his head back toward the office.

"Frémont! The army mapmaker?" A small tingle of suspicion went down her spine.

"Same fellah." Zeke's jaws muscled through the tobacco wad. His cheeks ballooned, his lips pursed, and he rocketed a long jet of brown juice into the dust. "Him and Kit Carson's up top."

She started across the yard as fast as she could walk. "Go get John Bidwell." She went up the stairs two at a time to the office.

The room with its whitewashed walls and windows open to the sun was drenched with light. The two men were standing at the end of the room where Sutter kept his liquor. When she came in they swung toward her — Frémont the taller, trim in an army uniform, his hat jaunty, and beside him Kit, smiling, hooking his thumbs in the waistband of his blackened buckskins; he wore moccasins fringed to the knee, and in his belt there was a bowie knife like a small sword.

She said, "Well, I never thought I'd see you two again," and went up to them, both hands out. "Welcome to New Helvetia. Sutter's up on the river. I've sent for John Bidwell, who's in charge while he's gone."

"Cat Reilly," said Frémont, "you're more beautiful even than I remembered." He gripped her hand.

"Yes — also the first white woman you've seen in months." She turned to Kit, who was half sitting on the table, grinning at her. "Where have you come from? Get yourselves a drink."

"We were just doin' that." Kit took the hand she offered him and pulled her forward for a loud kiss on the mouth. "Captain's right. You look a lot better'n when I found you pickin' flowers in the desert." His hand was rough as a brick. Touching him, she felt his restless, willful strength, felt, again, the pull he had on her. She lowered her eyes, trying to get some distance.

Frémont was pouring brandy into three of the whiskey glasses. Kit took one. "Here's to California." The air thickened with the smell of alcohol.

Catharine asked, "Where are you coming from?"

"Through the northern Sierra," Frémont said. "A much easier route, I can tell you, than the one we took, Cat."

"Straighter, anyway," Kit said.

Frémont shifted, pushing his chest out, and stroked down the front of his uniform, becoming official. "We're here to get some mules, supplies, gear — we have to meet the rest of our party in the south. We'll need passports, too. What's your opinion? Is Captain Sutter reliable?"

"Reliable," she said. "How can you ask that? He built this place. Do you remember what was here four years ago?"

Kit said, "It's surely a hell of a lot bigger. Dirtier, too." He reached for the jug of brandy.

She surveyed their worn boots, the gaunt look in Frémont's face, the crack in Kit's hat and the rawhide mending his belt. Still, they looked fit enough. "This isn't all of you," she said. "Where're the rest?"

"Camped outside." Kit jerked his thumb vaguely over his shoulder. In his sun-darkened face his pale eyes were clear as water.

Frémont said, "We heard Sutter was hand in glove with the Mexicans."

She took a step back from them, looking from one to the other. "Oh, so that's how it is. What are you doing here?"

Kit began to say something, but Frémont grabbed his arm and silenced him. "Requisitioning mules, as I said. We need packsaddles, also, and other supplies."

"We're very short of mules," she said. "A dozen families arrived last fall, and Captain Sutter gave each of them a team of mules. And we have the planting season coming on."

Frémont said, "I expected some resistance." He paced away across the room, into the light from a window, and stood looking down on the fort. "He certainly has accomplished quite a lot here; I don't remember it was half this size."

She crossed her arms over her chest; there was work to do and the day was rushing on, but she could not leave them alone in Sutter's office. Everything about them had her on edge. Kit was watching her, the perpetual grin on his face; she felt transparent to him. She was glad to hear quick steps on the stairs outside. John Bidwell came in.

"Lieutenant Frémont. No, Captain Frémont, I see." They shook hands. "I hope Cathy has made you welcome?"

"Yes, very well." Frémont glanced from him to Catharine and asked her, "Are you sure I should be talking to him? Where's Sutter?"

On Catharine's left, Bidwell tightened like a strung bow. He stepped forward, between Frémont and Catharine, and said, "Captain Sutter will be here when he's done at the mill. In the meantime, what can I do for you, Captain Frémont?" He looked over at her. "You can go, Cathy. Thanks."

Kit stood. "I'm gonna get my hooks on some real food."

He went out the door after Catharine and at the foot of the stairs walked up beside her, crossing the yard to the kitchens.

"I heard you had a little excitement," he said. "Like a revolution."

"Not really."

She led him off by the clutter of the troughs, past the Indians waiting by the kitchen door for their dinner, and into the warmth and dark, the smell of bread baking and the tang of roasted chilies. The cook was out. A pile of unshucked ears of corn covered the end of the table. She stopped to swing the coffeepot out onto the fire.

Kit stood behind her. "You gotten married or anything?"

"No," she said, and turned, and he grabbed her. "Kit. No." She put her hands on his chest, leaning back away from him. "Please." Her heart was galloping. A lot of her wanted him. He gave her a long look and let go of her and backed up, his open hands out to his sides.

"Whatever you say."

"Thank you." She let out her breath, wiped her wrist over her forehead, and nodded to the table. "Sit down and I'll bring you dinner."

He slid onto a bench at the table against the wall. "You a nun now? I seen nuns in Saint Louis. They just dry up like leaves."

"I thought you were a married man."

"Baby, it's a long way to Taos."

She brought bread, cheese, a slice of beef, a bowl of chilies, a mug of coffee; he began to tear chunks off the loaf and stuff them into his mouth. She went to find the cook, who was in the next room cutting up a beef carcass hanging from the ceiling. When she came back Kit was prowling around the kitchen.

"Where's the sugar?"

She brought him sugar for his coffee. "What are you doing in California?"

The look he gave her was wide and empty. He slid down onto the bench and dumped half a cup of sugar into the coffee. "Making maps. Frémont draws pictures of flowers."

"How many men do you have?"

"Only twelve of us altogether. Ain't no harm in twelve men, is there?" His hand darted across the tabletop and gripped her wrist. "Cat, we're all Americans, right?"

"Well, no," she said.

He discarded that with a wave of his free hand. "All but Sutter." He squeezed her wrist hard. The smile crinkled the corners of his eyes. "You want to go out, show me around the place, later?"

"I'd love to."

"Good." He went at the food again.

She watched him eat, letting what he had just said settle in her mind. With his trail-stiffened buckskins, his ragged hair, he looked rough as a mountain animal. His hands were small and square, slabbed with calluses. She struggled once more against her attraction to him; if she gave in to him once he would have her forever. She forced herself to think about what was going on here.

Frémont had only twelve men, he had said. But he had mentioned another party.

"Where are you meeting the rest? Down south?"

"San Joaquin Valley," he said, around a mouthful of bread. He drained his coffee cup and she filled it again.

"How many of them are there?"

"Twenty. Thirty. Depends on how many get lost." He glanced at her sideways. "You sure a curious cat. I'll trade you: what's going on here? Was there a revolution or not?"

"They threw the governor out," she said. "It wasn't much."

"But Sutter was on the Mexican side."

"Yes. That taught him something. Now he's staying out of their wars. The dons are having a big fight now about where to have the capital. Of course a big fight with them means a lot of proclamations back and forth, canceling one another's orders."

Kit reached for the coffeepot. "Any trouble with the Indians?"

"People in the San Joaquin have trouble with those Indians. Ours are all pretty peaceful."

"Seems like there's a lot of folks around."

"Oh, yes. More all the time. We're settling the whole valley."

He was swirling the last of the coffee around in the cup, a thick goo of half-melted sugar. "A lot of these fellahs hanging around here, Cat, they don't look like they're settling down."

She said, "That's Sutterville."

"Sutterville."

"That's what he calls the camps. He's talking about building a town."

Kit set the cup down. "Come show me the sights."

She took him through all the shops, showed him all the work, even the little room where she slept. He kept his hands off her, respecting her. She had a lot of power here; he saw it in the way everybody else talked to her, in the way she moved among them. That night, in a fine rain, he went out by himself for the real look around.

In the dark the long, gentle slope between Sutter's Fort and the embarcadero on the riverbank was dappled with campfires. The thin shrill of fiddle music rose from one side. Slippery in the rain, worn paths threaded between the camps, clogged with men, with stray dogs and garbage.

As she had said, there were no families in Sutterville. With a steady flux of other men, Kit went from fire to fire, drank a little, listened a lot.

Sutter made his own liquor now, a stiff, fiery spirit with an immediate effect on a man's sense of reality. There was a lot of it in the camps. By the light of a lantern men played cards in the mud or threw dice. Two long lines waited in front of a round Indian hut, which meant two whores; the lines moved along at a fairly brisk pace. Kit went the other way, not liking any of this. Sutterville reminded him of Rendezvous at its worst.

Short of midnight he happened on Zeke Merritt, whom he had met before, and about whom, now, the evening's scouting had gleaned something for a prod.

He said, "I hear you had a little run-in with the greasers."

Zeke growled. "Sons o' bitches. Ain't a one of 'em straight enough to pull a cork with."

"Hell, you know, Zeke, I don't see how you boys all stand it, them dons whuppin' up on you all the time."

"They never whupped on us."

"That's not what I heard," Kit said. He had emptied his cup, and he drifted off toward the next fire to get some more. Zeke trailed after him.

"Listen, Kit, you heard wrong."

"I don't blame you, you know, Zeke." In the crowd around the next fire he stopped to watch two men priming dogs to fight. "Country like this, it makes a man soft." Held face to face, the two dogs snarled and snapped and slavered at one another, their eyes rolling wildly, their bodies pinned in the handlers' arms.

Zeke said, "You got it wrong. The dons don't fight like Americans, they do things sneaky, real underhanded. They ain't even got any guns. They just decide to have a battle and show up, and the one with the most men wins." He shook his head. "They can ride, though, I'll give 'em that."

The dogs hurtled toward each other, growling and sobbing for breath, while the men roared around them. Kit backed up, out of the way. He hated these crowds; he hated this place, with its stench and noise and filth. Frémont had spent the day telling him what a marvel it was.

Cat Reilly had given Frémont that idea. The Captain saw nothing until somebody else told him where to look. Now he had all California lying in front of him, and he would miss that, too.

Kit went up toward the fort again, where his horse stood in a line of other horses hitched against the gate. Inside the wall the bell struck and somebody called the time. He mounted up and rode off north, toward the American River, where they were camped. It was time, he thought, for John Charles Frémont to get his eyes opened.

Frémont did not wait for Sutter to come back and issue passports for him and his men, but left in a drizzling rain as soon as he had all the mules he could find shod and packed. The rain continued. Sutter finally reappeared, and Catharine told him about Frémont's visit.

Sutter looked tired. He had planted his wheatfields just before the wet weather began, and now the winter was on him, the rain finding every leak in the roof, every crack in the walls. He passed one hand over his face. "What do you make of it?"

She said, "He's snooping around looking for whatever trouble he can make."

Sutter's hand hovered near his cheek. "You think twelve men can take over California?"

"I think they may have come here expecting to find us at war, and in the course of a war, anything can happen."

He was still for a long time, thinking that over. Finally he said, "Well, Cat, maybe if the United States did move in here, it would be better. The dons do nothing but fight and steal the revenues."

"It's their country," she said. "Your country. You're a Mexican citizen, remember? You have all these charters from Mexico City. You're a colonel in the Mexican Army."

"That was the wrong thing to say." He reached off to the sideboard and got the deck of cards. "Go call Sinclair and Flugge."

"John," she said.

He was unknotting the bit of rawhide that held the deck together. "You just reminded me that I am no good at war and politics. Whatever Frémont is up to, I don't care. If there's a war with the United States, it will be fought in Texas and Mexico, not here. And then we'll talk." He began to deal out four hands of whist. "Call Flugge and Sinclair. And you play with me. I'm tired of them missing my signals. Insist on it; they always let you have your way."

The winter storms swept by in waves of cloud and rain that broke for an hour's blazing sunshine and then rushed in again. The wheat sprouted. One of the year's crop of settlers, William Ide, had brought a sawblade over the mountains, and they had built a mill around it, which was flooded out, all the work wasted; they almost lost the sawblade in the river. With the year's September wave of settlers there were enough women in the valley to have a quilting bee. In January Sutter performed three marriages. There was some talk of building a church.

In February, Frémont came scurrying back up the valley, drenched and hungry and missing half his mules. In his six-week ramble through the southern valley he had not found the second party of his men, but he had located numerous Indians, who had picked off his mules and harried his camps. Sutter took him in, as he took everybody in, and fitted him out again and sent him down to Yerba Buena on the launch. From there, they heard, he went to Monterey.

27 ☙ THE FRENCH CONSUL'S WIFE said, "Well, Mr. Larkin, you've made quite a difference here."

Thomas Larkin murmured something self-deprecating. They stood to one side of the fandango room in Monterey's new customs house, which he had designed and built, mostly with his own money, and watched the exuberant and elegant crowd that whirled around the polished wooden floor. The fandango room was the central room in the building, and the largest — which was fitting; somebody had said once that if the great Congress had been held in Monterey instead of Vienna, even Talleyrand would have danced.

Nothing decorated it but its newness. He would have to find something to hang on the whitewashed walls, screens perhaps for the windows. Some plants in jars to soften up the corners.

He said, "Have you met our guest from the south, madame?" Colonel Andrés Pico, splendid in a tight brocaded jacket and slim black pants, spun by them with a girl giggling uncontrollably in his arms.

The French consul's wife said, "The *abajeños* are so arrogant." Her face drooped. "If they do move the capital to Los Angeles, Mr. Larkin, will we all have to live down there?"

"I'm afraid so, madame."

She sighed, a long descending note, raised her fan, and waved it briskly.

Larkin said, "And of course you have met Captain Frémont." The American officer was crossing the floor toward them.

"Yes. What a lovely gentleman." She slapped her fan closed and put out one white, ringed hand, the prerogative of a married woman, who could safely be a little forward. "Good evening, Captain. What a splendid evening Monterey has arranged for you."

Frémont bowed over her knuckles. He had a knack for assuming the manners of the people around him, and suddenly he looked very French. With a murmur of excuse, Larkin backed away from him and the consul's wife, circled around the end of the room where the musicians played, and near the front door came on the commandante of Monterey.

Jesús Orozco, who had no family, no patron, and no ability as a sycophant, had been a lieutenant for ten years; in the course of the Micheltorena war he had wrung two promotions out of General Castro and was now a major. The rank had brought with it no more men or arms, and the garrison of Monterey still consisted, officially, of Orozco himself and three cadets. He stood straight as a guardsman, his dress uniform immaculate, his homely olive-skinned face impassive. He did not dance. When Larkin greeted him he seemed to come back from somewhere else to answer.

"You've met Captain Frémont, Major?"

Orozco said, "We were introduced." He spoke no English; Frémont spoke no Spanish. It was the least of their differences.

Larkin turned to watch Andrés Pico in his swooping flight around the dance floor. "This is General Pico's son?"

"The younger brother," Orozco said. "Born a general." Larkin, who knew him well, could hear the acid envy in his voice. The black eyes moved, locating Frémont, who was now dancing, and Orozco said, "This Anglo, what is he doing here?"

"He's a mapmaker," Larkin said blandly. His hands slipped behind his back. He was a head shorter than Orozco and aware, beside the Californio officer, that he was a dumpy, soft townsman who talked for a living. "He was here some years ago — perhaps you remember."

"Yes. If he's a mapmaker and was here years ago, I see no reason for him to be here again, where he has already mapped. I want him out of Monterey."

"He needs to resupply. We're waiting for his licenses to buy goods here."

"General Castro is at San Juan Bautista."

"I know that. I was hoping you might hurry things on."

"General Castro is at San Juan Bautista and I have no power over such matters." And no interest, his flat voice added. The music climbed to a skirling climax; the dance ended with a burst of shouts and applause.

Colonel Pico strolled toward them, short, stocky, handsomer than the usual run of his family. He barely glanced at Larkin; to Orozco he said, "Isn't there anything else to do here? In El Pueblo at least I could see a bullfight."

Larkin asked, "You're bored with Monterey, Colonel?"

The don gave him another quick, condescending look. "I like a little excitement now and then." Half a dozen vaqueros followed him everywhere; they had been grouped around the table at the other side of the room, where there was food and drink, but now they drifted closer to their master. He jabbed his chin at Orozco. "Come show me some excitement. Major."

Orozco was staring across the fandango room at Captain Frémont. He turned to Larkin and said, "Resupply him now. When the licenses get here I want him gone."

Pico twisted, scanning the room. "Whom are you talking about?"

Larkin said, "I'll do what I can."

"I expect that, Mr. Larkin. Come along. Colonel." He started out the door, and Pico followed him. His men slunk at his heels.

Larkin took a glass of wine from a passing servant; the musicians were playing a schottische. A few couples moved out onto the floor, gliding into the seductive rhythm, the long hem of a satin skirt brushing the polished wood, the sleek of a smile quickly hidden behind a fan. Larkin went looking for Captain Frémont.

He found him at the far end of the room contemplating a plate of long pink crab legs. Hesitantly Frémont picked up a piece of shell, and Larkin said, "Here, now, Captain, don't be timid." Taking one of the stemlike legs, he sucked out the meat, making more noise than he had to. "Thus." He waggled the empty shell and dropped it on the plate.

Frémont said, "I suppose it's like crayfish," but he made no effort to eat any of it.

"Exactly," Larkin said. "I just talked to Major Orozco, who says you may arrange for your supplies in anticipation of the arrival of the licenses from General Castro."

Frémont grunted, turning his back on the crab, and stared out over the room. "I can't stomach these dons and their arrogant condescension."

Larkin raised his eyebrows. "In California they are absolute masters. It would be unreasonable to expect them to be servile."

The mapmaker grumbled at him; he had no interest in people who were different from him. He said, "The real news, of course, is the word from Washington." His voice rang hollow with importance.

"Is it," Larkin said. He glanced around them; a good three yards of shining floor separated them from the crowd. He moved to a place where he could see anybody who might approach. "Didn't you just come over the Sierra? I don't see how you can have had much correspondence with Washington."

"Well — I hoped you had heard something." Frémont swayed from his heels to his toes, his hands moving up and down his uniform coat with its ranks of brass buttons.

Larkin smiled at him. He picked up a piece of crab claw and fished out the succulent pink meat and dipped it into a dish of salsa. "What exactly are you expecting to hear?" Deftly he got the fiery tidbit into his mouth.

"Why — the war! The war must begin soon. Texas has rejected the Mexican proposal and accepted our offer to enter the Union. Mexico City has repeatedly said —" Frémont leaned forward suddenly, covert, his voice dropping to a rasp. "Are you ready to strike, when the moment comes, Mr. Larkin? Strike for your country?"

"Strike at whom, Captain Frémont?"

"At our enemies!"

Larkin looked around, his gaze moving over the room he had made, the men and women dancing the waltz, and brought his attention back to Frémont. "There are no enemies here, Frémont. Not yet. And by God I mean to see it stays that way."

In the brilliant lantern light Frémont's face was harsh, the eyes bright with fervor, his cheeks hollow above his whiskers. "The United States will have California."

"Yes. I mean that. I want that. But peacefully, voluntarily, and without destroying the people who are already here."

The mapmaker's face slipped; his noble fervor was a pose, something he struggled toward but could not attain, and he tired quickly in the effort. Now he looked confused. Larkin, who was never tired and seldom confused, advanced into this uncertainty.

"The people here are impatient with the dons' mismanagement. Nobody can do business here, nothing gets done; in the middle of great natural wealth we struggle just to keep a primitive existence, because of the dons. If we offer these people something better they will take it. But we have to let them see it for themselves, come to it themselves."

Frémont shook his head. "While you waffle and waltz with your diplomacy, Larkin, the British are getting ready to make off with the pie."

"I don't believe the British are interested."

"They've said themselves — no worse thing could happen to them in the Pacific than that the United States take California!" Frémont's voice rose, too loud, and through the room heads turned. Larkin got him by the arm and pulled him around so that his back was to the dancers.

"That's true. But the British say many things they never act upon. Even they have their limitations."

"How many ships have they in the Pacific now?" With the lights above and behind him Frémont's gaunt face was a pattern of shadows.

"Right now, I admit, they are maintaining an enormous fleet in the western Pacific. But they have many concerns here."

"One ship of that fleet, one single British man-of-war, could sail tomorrow into Monterey Bay, level its guns on the presidio, and demand the surrender of California."

Larkin said, "Yes. Which would be a disaster, whether the ship flew the Union Jack or the Stars and Stripes." He glanced over his shoulder; nobody out there was listening. The dance was ending and they were all pleading with the musicians for a reel. Larkin lifted his eyes to Frémont. "Captain Frémont, do you have any official instructions I don't know about?"

Frémont said, "I am here to map a trail to the Pacific."

"Very good. Then I shall work to provide you with licenses to buy what you need. Tomorrow you can come into my store and get your supplies, which I will hold for you until the licenses have been signed and delivered."

Frémont said, "Mr. Larkin, I meant no disrespect."

"And showed none, Captain. We should argue these things, especially these things, until we understand each other."

The mapmaker fiddled with his brass buttons again. Larkin reached for another piece of the crab. Uneasily Frémont fidgeted a few more moments and finally wandered away, down the table, looking for more familiar food.

Larkin moved toward the corner of the room, his shoulders

slumping. The window beside him was open, and he could hear the surf on the beach, as if the ocean were breathing. The scent of the blooming lemon trees in the garden sweetened the air. Grimly he forced himself to contemplate the likelihood that Frémont was lying, that he did have secret orders — if not from President Polk, then from Frémont's powerful father-in-law, Senator Benton. That in fact the war had already begun.

Frémont was a mapmaker, not a soldier. If he was here to fight an independent action, somebody had chosen a poor instrument. Which made it all the harder to predict what he might do. Larkin's shoulders moved under his serge coat, adjusting to this shift of balance, and he went up to the table for another piece of crab.

28

PICO RODE a tall palomino horse; his men trailed after him at a little distance. He jogged up beside Orozco and said, "What I had in mind maybe was some quick risk and, you know, women I can do more than dance with."

"General Castro told me to escort you around Monterey." Orozco backed his horse up and turned down the street, away from the customs house. "He gave me no orders to pander."

The big yellow horse strolled along on his left. "I'm sure you'd never do anything that obliging. Major. Are there whores here? Maybe a gambling house?"

"I have a friend who games," Orozco said. "I want to talk to him anyway. I'll introduce you, and the two of you can wallow off together." He glanced back at Pico's retinue, wandering after him along the street. "The eight of you." He lifted his horse into a lope down through Monterey.

There was a light in front of Larkin's massive house, with its extravagant verandahs, and another light outside Castro's house, where Orozco lived; otherwise the little town was dark. The sea growled and chuckled along the beach down to his left. A high fog veiled the sky. He rode across a stretch of sand and grass into the plaza and led Pico along the edge that ran parallel to the beach, past the litter of the day's market, heaps of baskets, the stink of crab and rotten fruit. It was Lent, and many people were in the church at the far side of the plaza.

Beyond the northwestern corner, between the stone-lined bear pit and the leprous ruin of a barracks wall, there was a long, narrow lane. Here torchlight shone, and lanterns, the light breaking and dimming and shooting forth again as people milled around the sources of it. Pico murmured under his breath, "This is better now, I like this." There was a roar from the crowd ahead of them, and the sudden savage screeching of birds. Orozco slowed his horse to a walk and rode into Cock-fight Alley.

Most of the men were gathered around the pit at this near end of the alley, under three lanterns, where now a white cock was slashing up a red one, all bloody feathers and squawks and battering wings. The crowd saw Orozco; their howling voice abruptly hushed to silence, and they moved back and waited. He accepted the deference; when he made no threatening move they turned to the pit again and the uproar picked up. They were laborers, servants, farmers, people who worked too hard to waste themselves on cockfights. Orozco went on down the alley.

The whores were gathered on the far side of the bear pit, where the low wall sheltered them from the blast of the sea wind. At the approach of the riders their voices lifted in sirenic wails and cries. Pico and his men veered off toward them. Orozco rode a dozen yards on, to the last lantern.

This one hung over a card game, six men squatting in a circle, four or five more standing behind looking over their shoulders. They were all intent, fixed on the game, so still the slap of the cards sounded louder than anything else.

"Hit them," said Sohrakoff, sitting on his heels, his back to the wall. There were four cards on the ground at his feet.

One of the other men glanced at Orozco and nudged Sohrak-off. "Hey, Count."

"Shut up! I see him. Hit them."

Four cards dropped, face up, one on each of the four in the row in front of the Count, and with each card the little crowd let out a yell, steadily louder, until Sohrakoff himself shouted, flung his hands over his head, and shot to his feet; the man he played against dove for the money.

"Some nights I can't win with a miracle." The Count walked away from the game, out toward Orozco, who eased his horse away a little, into the dark. Sohrakoff followed him and put one hand on his horse's withers.

"Who's that?" He nodded toward the bear pit.

Orozco let his reins slide. "The younger brother of General Pico. He was at the *consejo* at Carmel and as a friendly gesture General Castro invited him to Monterey and imposed him on me. Tell me about the gringos."

Sohrakoff pushed his hat back off his head, his wild hair haloed in the lamplight behind him. "They're camped up on a meadow about three miles north of here, on the coast. There are twelve of them, all armed. They're in good condition over-all, their stock is in nice shape. They'll have to move in less than a week, when the grass is gone where they are. They put up sentries around the camp but no patrols or anything." He scratched Orozco's horse's neck along the crest of its mane, and the horse bobbed its head. "Anything else you want to know?"

"What are they eating?"

"They bought some steers from a rancher up there. They have supplies with them, too."

"I met the officer tonight. He seems unimpressive."

Pico rode up to them, the gold stitching twinkling on his jacket. "These women will do, Major."

Orozco said coldly, "The doors of my house close in an hour or less."

"Don't expect me," Pico said. He looked down at Sohrakoff, who stood between them, one hand tangled in the mane of Orozco's horse. "Is this the gambler?"

Orozco said, "Colonel Andrés Pico, Count Sohrakoff."

Pico laughed, snagged like everybody else on the title.

Sohrakoff said, "You play cards?" He stepped back, his arm falling to his side.

"I'm looking for a little excitement," Pico said. "Major Orozco here seems not to know much about that."

Sohrakoff's face broadened when he smiled, his eyes going to Orozco. "Excitement is too frivolous for him." He moved over toward Pico; at his side one long hand flexed. "If you have money, Colonel, I'll give you a game."

"I have money," Pico said.

"I'll get my horse."

Pico had more than money — he had a name that in California brought him whatever he wanted. In less than an hour he commandeered a house down the street from Orozco's that belonged to Abel Stearns, a southern merchant who was a family friend, and moved into it with his men and half the whores and flunkies in Monterey. Sohrakoff spent the next eighteen hours playing cards.

Early in the morning after the game ended, the Count went out to the courtyard of this house and sat in the sun. He had won some silver pieces from Pico, and he played with one, walking it back and forth through his fingers and whirling it up off his thumb.

After a little while Pico came out, half-naked, and sauntered up toward him. He had obviously just gotten out of bed. One of his men rushed over with a chair for him and he sat in it, his back to the sun. Somebody else brought him a glass and a bottle of wine. Pico stretched out, his arms over his head; his armpits were stuffed with black hair.

"You don't like women?"

"Not the kind that expect to be paid," Sohrakoff said. He spun the silver real up and down through his fingers.

"Every woman is a whore when it matters," Pico said. "Why are you doing that?"

"Keeps my hands soft."

"Give it to me."

Sohrakoff flipped the coin to him. Pico balanced it carefully between his knuckles; when he tried to turn the coin over it slid off his hand. He swore and tried again. Behind him an old woman came into the courtyard with a broom and began to sweep up; most of the house's servants were here, now waiting on Pico. One of the don's own men brought him a dish of eggs and beans and red chilies. Pico ignored this, struggling to manipulate the piece of silver, his face intense, his hands inept. Abruptly he flicked the coin back over his shoulder to the old woman with the broom. "Eh. *Vieja*. Light a candle for me."

The old woman picked up the money and put it away in her apron; she murmured, her eyes gleaming, and went on with the broom. Pico took the dish of eggs and devoured it.

Sohrakoff said, "Maybe you pay somebody to eat for you, too."

Pico smirked at him. Red sauce dribbled down his chin, and one of his men came forward with a cloth. "What more do you have up here? Any hunting?"

"If you try hard you might find a bear somewhere. Puma, up in the Gavilan."

Pico made a face. "That doesn't sound promising." His men moved around him, gathering up his dishes and bringing him a clean shirt and jacket. He paid no attention to them, his gaze on Sohrakoff. "How does that altar boy Orozco know you?"

"I break horses for General Castro."

"That's all? Are you in the army?"

"I spent three years in the Russian navy," Sohrakoff said. Pico's questions made him restless. "If you write me that piece of scrip I'll be going."

"Stay here," Pico said. "Make yourself comfortable, use the house, the women, the servants, whatever you need, I'll pay for it. I might want a game later."

"No, I'm going." Sohrakoff rose to his feet. "I have other things to do."

"Where do you live?"

"Just send some kid for me. Write me the paper for what you owe me."

Pico shrugged, his eyebrows going up and down. He turned his head slightly, and one of his men scurried up with a slip of paper, which Sohrakoff took. He went out to the yard of the house and collected his horse out of the corral there.

He knew he was being stupid; if he whored around with Pico he could make a lot of money, especially since the don had a mirror for a face and no patience for close judgment. He ambled his horse down to the beach, away from Monterey. He was sick of cutting himself to fit.

He had never fit anywhere, even at Ross. His mother died when he was born, and his father lived at sea; they found him a wet nurse among the Kashaya, the Indians who lived near Ross. She took him down to the village, in the meadow across the cypress-choked ravine from the gray walls of the fort. He grew up with the Kashaya boys, who made fun of his hair and eyes, his pale skin, his size.

He was bigger than they were, stronger, slower, especially with his hands. The Kashaya were great gamblers, with hands so fast and deft some of the Russians thought they used magic, and called them demons. Clump-fingered, they would have said to see him playing with Pico's silver real, and would have wondered why he did not juggle a dozen at once, two-handed.

The Kashaya lived with the land, not on it. When they needed something they took what the land offered and replaced it with a song or a prayer. They killed no people, not even in self-defense, because no song, no prayer, was strong enough to replace a human soul. They divided what they had by gambling for it, not trading or robbing or buying. They fit together, in their families, their clans, as smoothly as a wall of stones; he had no place with them, he was always outside.

They were better than he was at fishing, at hunting and running and games, at everything but horses. They only ate the horses; he rode them, almost as soon as he could walk, which again set him apart from them. Then he discovered card games.

The Kashaya took a while to catch on to card games, and he could finally beat them at something. He learned every game the Russians knew. His father's American mate, laid up for a season with a broken leg, taught him English and casino and poker. He was very good at poker, as Andrés Pico had just found out.

The Russians disapproved of his closeness with the Kashaya, who went naked, had lice and ate acorns, and were the Russians' slaves. His father said, "Do as you please. They're as good as we are. And horses are as good as ships."

The old man, who had served the Russian American Company before the tsar took it over and who spoke Aleut more often than Russian, hated the navy, which now administered Ross. He spent one month a year there. More than once, when he came back from a long voyage, his son failed to recognize him. But Ross was so much his creation, his spirit so sustained it, that the people there talked about him constantly, and the boy knew everything that old Sohrakoff had ever said or done, as if he had been a witness.

When the old man died, the Russians wept, rang the church bell, shot every cannon and musket in the fort. The Aleuts hacked off parts of their fingers and flung them into the sea; the Kashaya danced for four days straight, to guide old Sohrakoff's soul to heaven, because, they said, so potent a spirit would devastate the living if it remained among them.

His son was fourteen when he died, and already circumstances were forcing him out of the Kashaya village, back to the redwood kremlin and the imperial navy. Still he kept close to the Indians his age. When he was sixteen and joined the Russian navy, he married the sister of his best friend. But the tsar had already ordered Ross to be sold.

For years there was no buyer, until Sutter. When he heard that the Swiss don had bought Ross, Sohrakoff went up to the commandante and struck him across the face. He spent the next three weeks in irons, flat on his back in a second-story room of the fur barn. One night as he lay there he heard his wife call, outside the window.

"Seroja," she said, "Seroja, we are going."

"Echai, what do you mean? Where are you going?"

"To hide from the white men. Seroja, goodbye." But she did not leave, not for hours, only stood under the window and wept until her brother came and dragged her away.

He never saw her again. When they unchained him he deserted and went into the hills searching for the Kashaya, but he could not find them, and he came to realize they were hiding from him, too. When the last of the Russians had left, he went back to Ross and tried to work for Sutter, but he hated the Swiss, and his temper got him into trouble.

He drifted south. He worked for a while for a Russian rancher near Rumiantzev Bay, which the Californios called Bodega, but he fought with Vallejo's men, who drove him out of the Sonoma don's territory and then out of Yerba Buena. He had no papers, which got him arrested in Monterey and hauled in before the commandante, Lieutenant Jesús Orozco. While he was talking his way out of prison, he talked himself into a job of work for Orozco, who needed somebody who did not look Californio to spy for him.

Now he rode into the courtyard of Orozco's house, the only home allowed him. The black mood dogged him. The three cadets who made up the garrison of Monterey were grooming their horses against the far wall. At sundown they had to appear at the customs house to stand inspection and take the flag down, and Orozco's inspections lasted more than an hour: the cadets had to be perfect, because they belonged here. Sohrakoff went in past them, to a corner of the yard, and dismounted.

At once a short dark man in chaparejos came toward him across the dusty yard from the doorway into the house.

"Conde, I need your help."

Sohrakoff knew him, a local horse dealer. They had done some trading. "What kind of help?" He led his horse toward the corral behind the house, and the other man followed him.

"You know those gringos, up on the coast? They have a horse of mine and they won't give it back."

"Really." With the front cinch halfway out of its knot, he stopped and stared at the horse dealer. "You mean Frémont? Have you mentioned this to Major Orozco?"

The other man shrugged, apologetic. "I'd sooner talk to you, you know."

Sohrakoff jerked up his cinch again. Here at least was something he could do. "Let's go out there."

Frémont said stubbornly, "I was hoping to reach California to find that war had been declared. I have to have a declaration of war before I can do anything."

Kit tramped away from him, into the shadow of the trees, and wheeled. "Why? It's three thousand miles to Washington. Why wait for them?"

"Because the United States is an honorable country," Frémont said. "We're honorable men. We can't — My orders are to be here, when the war breaks out, to take advantage of the situation." His hands rose and fell to his sides again. "So far there's no situation to take advantage of."

"I was there when the senator went through all that." Kit turned, his hands on his hips. Frémont's balkiness surprised him. "It seemed to me he was suggesting we do a little of the work."

"Besides, Father Benton is only a senator, not president. Not the commander in chief," Frémont said. "His remarks are not — cannot be — official orders. Suggestions, perhaps. Advice."

A senator was high enough for Kit, especially a senator from Missouri. He walked a few steps away from Frémont. It was late in the day; the wind was rising, cool and damp, out of the thick black rags of the cypress clumps, out of the deep grass. Frémont's camp lay north of Monterey, near the ocean, in a grove of black pines where the trees made the air rich as a heady subtle wine. Below, in the open green meadow, the rest of the men lolled around a campfire. They would need the fire soon; the fog was drifting in. Luke Maxwell was walking up toward them.

There had to be some means of forcing Frémont into this. Kit tried to think himself into the mapmaker's frame of mind, but indecision always baffled him.

Luke Maxwell came into the shade under the trees and waved his hand in a casual salute. He spoke to Kit and Frémont together, aiming his voice between them, a nice solution to the current problem of authority.

"Captain, that horse dealer is back again. He's got somebody else with him, and he says he can prove the sock-footed sorrel horse is his."

"Send him away," Frémont said sharply. "I've got no time for that now."

Kit walked forward again, restless, itchy. "You're just going to ride on out," he said to Frémont. "California is right here in your hand, and all you have to do is close your fingers."

"We have to go back to San Joaquin and find Kern and the others." Behind the thin shag of his mustache Frémont's lips hardly seemed to move.

"You don't need any more men!" Kit glared at Maxwell, who was watching them with a little frown, and then, lengthening his gaze, looked down beyond him, toward the meadow. "Who's here? That Peralta fellah?"

"And some other horse dealer," Luke said.

This was as good a way as any, Kit thought. He nodded to Luke. "Tell them we're coming down there."

Frémont jerked, his neck thrusting up, gawky, like a startled chicken. "I gave orders to send them away."

Kit smiled at him, not friendly. "I say we go down there, Captain, and show them they can't fool with Americans."

Luke Maxwell stood before them, his gaze shifting from one to the other, his mouth small and soft. When Kit gave him a pointed look he struggled his face into a noncommittal expression and his throat worked. "I'll go tell them you're coming," he said, and went off through the short grass.

Frémont rubbed his hands together. "Kit, what are you trying to do?"

"If they jump on us, then we got all the right in the world to shoot back. Defend ourselves. Come on, Captain."

He walked on down the high side of the meadow. Here the rolling grassland fell in slumping terraces toward the distant sea; the spring was greening everything up, the old straw like gold, the new grass growing up through it green and blue-green and purple, so that when the wind blew and bent the straw back the hillside rippled in waves of changing colors. There was a road worn into the grass, leading up from Monterey; by this road, now, where it passed along the edge of Frémont's camp, two strange horses waited.

Frémont walked down past Kit, his back straightening; he was trying to appear in command. Kit dropped behind him a few paces, content to let him do it all as long as he did it right. Frémont went down toward the Californios waiting by the road.

Sebastian Peralta was the short brown man on the right. He had been here before, twice, claiming a white-footed sorrel gelding they had bought from an Indian at San José. Before Kit and Frémont came to a stop, the little Californio went at the captain like a gamecock, shouting at him in Spanish. Frémont called for Luke Maxwell to translate. Kit drifted off to one side, watching the other Americans amble up across the meadow and range themselves around the argument.

Peralta was saying doggedly, "It's my horse." He turned around toward the man who had come with him. "He's my witness."

This man wore chaps and a sombrero, but he did not look like a Californio. His hair was a brassy blond tangle, his eyes bright blue. Like Peralta he was unarmed. He was looking around at the camp with a sharp interest that did not confine itself to horses. His gaze came to Kit and their eyes met; Kit hooked his thumbs in his belt. The muscles tensed across the back of his shoulders. This man was more than a horse dealer's friend.

Frémont was saying, "All our horses came with us from the States." His voice quivered; he was lying, as everybody knew. He loomed over Peralta, who was much shorter than he was. "We are on official American business, and I will not endure to be harassed. Now get out of here before I run you out by force."

The blond Californio said, "It's his horse." He spoke English, rough with some odd accent.

Frémont jerked his head up. "Who are you?"

"I'm a horse dealer in Monterey," said the blond. "I know it's his horse because I sold it to him." He moved, drifting closer, and his gaze shifted toward Kit again. He spoke to Frémont again. "It's his horse for certain. If you need proof, I haven't gone near the horse since I been here, but I know there's a scar on the inside of its off foreleg, just above the chestnut."

Frémont's lips pressed together tight. He glanced at Kit, looking for help, and Kit stayed where he was and said nothing. Frémont's voice rose, too loud. "I have papers for every horse we brought. This is a time-honored trick of you greasers, this horse-stealing business —"

The blond Californio ignored him. He had seen Frémont glance at Kit, and he walked up two steps closer to the scout and said again, "It's his horse." Now he was speaking to Kit.

Peralta looked from one to the other, his face quizzical with incomprehension, and he began to shrill at Frémont in Spanish. Luke Maxwell went up to translate again.

The rest of the Americans were gathering in close, smelling trouble, and the blond Californio took another step toward Kit and said, "It's his horse."

Kit lifted his head. He saw in a glance that while Peralta and Frémont were having their own little yelling match, everybody else was watching him, waiting to see what he did. He shook his head at the Californio.

"Don't talk to me, talk to the Captain." He wished Frémont would get this under control.

The Californio's shaggy white eyebrows jerked up and down. "Why? You're the don here, aren't you?"

So that was what this was about. Kit spun around, his muscles bunched and his temper sliding like an avalanche. Basil Lajeunesse was standing three feet away, a flintlock pistol in his belt. Kit took one step to him and yanked the pistol out and leveled it at the blond Californio. "Get out." He aimed the pistol into the Californio's face. "Or I'll make a hole in you big enough to ride that goddamn horse through."

The blue eyes glittered at him. For a moment the other man did not move. Kit cocked the pistol. Peralta backed up a step, his hand on the blond man's arm, pulling him. "Conde, let's get out of here."

The blond Californio turned and walked away down toward his horse, Peralta beside him. Kit lowered his arm, the gun aimed at the ground, and pulled the trigger. At the thunder of the explosion the two quickened their steps. Kit laughed, angry, and turned back to Basil and held out the gun to him.

"If they were Americans," he said to Frémont, "that would be enough, there'd be a pack of them out here by sundown. Since they're greasers it may take something more."

Frémont said, "We're riding out of here in the morning."

Kit lifted his head, staring at him. "Captain, we can't just turn and walk out on this."

"I'm in command," Frémont said.

"Captain —"

"I'm in command!"

Kit said nothing for a moment. Slowly he rubbed his hands down his thighs. "All right," he said, at last, angry, and went off through the pines and the fog.

29

ANDRÉS PICO SAID, "Give me twenty lancers and I'll take care of them for you, Don José!"

General Castro sat in an upholstered chair behind his desk, the two lamps on the white plastered wall behind him casting showers of light past either shoulder. He favored Andrés Pico with half a look and directed the glare of his disapproval back toward the commandante of Monterey.

"I doubt that will be necessary. Major Orozco, this Captain Frémont is leaving California, is he not?"

"He broke camp this morning," said Orozco. "My information is that he is headed east again. With Señor Peralta's horse."

Pico said, "This is outrageous, Don General. You can't let a hostile army ride through your territory." He spun to throw an eager look at Orozco. "Can he."

Orozco ignored him, his gaze on the wall.

Castro said, in a flat voice, "You're dismissed, Don Andrés."

Pico hesitated. Castro's head swiveled toward him, laid over with orange candlelight, and his voice snarled.

"You're dismissed, Colonel!"

Pico turned on his heel and left.

There was a brief silence. Orozco stood at attention, his gaze on the wall above his commander's head. Finally Castro said, his voice constrained, "What is going on here? Is there a war on?"

"Thomas Larkin assures me we are not at war, sir."

"Then what the hell is going on?"

"I'm not sure, sir."

"Well, Major, you had better find out, and very quickly, because if this turns into trouble it will be your fault, and if you embarrass me in front of this *abajeño* Pico upstart I will make you wish you were a lieutenant again."

"Yes, sir."

"You're dismissed, Major."

"Yes, sir." Orozco backed up three steps, turned, and went out of the room.

In the dark passageway, back by the stairs, Sohrakoff came up beside him. "This is, you know, what you like to call a situation," said the Count.

"Yes, and becoming more so all the time, with your help."

Orozco led him on quickly back into the other wing, where Castro never came. Sohrakoff followed him, jumpy, his back still up from his brush with the Anglos. In the passageway Orozco beckoned him up beside him.

"You're sure they are leaving."

"They're riding east," Sohrakoff said. "Not fast. I followed them up into the valley and they camped there near the old *ranchería*."

"Keep a watch on them. General Castro will go back out to San Juan soon." The don's favorite place was his house at the

Mission San Juan Bautista, at the east end of the Salinas Valley; he had come down to Monterey only to deal with this matter of the Anglos. "Don't engage in any more privateering."

"He was looking for trouble. I didn't do that much."

If the Anglos kept going east they would cross the mountains just south of San Juan. "I'll go to the mission with the general. Report to me there."

Sohrakoff said, "What do you think of this?"

Orozco took his helmet off; his hair was damp and creased, and he ran one hand over it. "I wish I knew what was happening right now in Mexico City and in Washington. Did you spend any time with Pico? How does he play cards?"

"Straight up the middle," Sohrakoff said. "When he loses he doubles the stakes."

Orozco grimaced. He felt an iron pressure all around him, keeping him small. What Castro had said to him was beginning to weigh on him, in spite of his discipline, and he fought off the urge to blast Sohrakoff for stirring up trouble. He went through the door into his apartment.

Sohrakoff came along close on his heels. "What are you going to do?"

"That depends on Frémont," Orozco said.

"I don't think Frémont's in command. The scout is — Carson."

"Yes," Orozco said. "So you said." He went on through to his bedroom, dropped the helmet on the bed, and lit the lamp. "Follow them. When they change direction come to me at San Juan." He set down his tinderbox and put the chimney on the lamp.

He carried the light back into the front room, where his game was. In San Juan there would be no sand table, no quiet room to himself, no ocean with its long purling music: a barracks full of other men, hours spent idle, his hands trapped. He sat at the table and began to smooth the sand down, thinking about Frémont, trying to piece out what Sohrakoff had told him with what he himself had seen.

Sohrakoff drifted around the room for a while, making too much noise. Certainly he had overheard Castro's scolding. The scout had threatened him, and he would be looking for a chance to retaliate; his temper was one more thing to worry about. Finally he went out.

Orozco sighed. The sounds around him faded away into the distant murmur of the surf. In the stillness, the emptiness, that was settling around him like a balm, he began to put a battle together on the sand.

Pico said, "Let's go after them and jump them."

Sohrakoff shook his head. "My orders are to follow them, nothing else." He laid his saddlepacks across the back of the horse and lashed them to the saddle.

"Look, Ruso." Pico went around to the far side of the horse and spoke to him across the saddle. "You work for Castro, right? More than breaking horses. Does he pay you?"

Sohrakoff laughed.

"I'll pay you. Work for me. Starting now. We can take these gringos."

"Are you going out to San Juan?"

"Yes. There's going to be a fight, and I want some of it."

"Well, then," Sohrakoff said, "I'll see you there." He mounted his horse and rode out of the courtyard.

Behind the wide blue bay of Monterey, the land spread out in a long green valley, measured out in orchards, in plowed fields, in the neat gardens and the small white adobes of farmers. It was March and the apple trees were beginning to bloom. Frémont and his twelve men rode on steadily through the soft and lovely land, on to the east, where the sky came down against the edges of the Sierra del Gavilan, at the far end of the valley.

Sohrakoff followed, staying well behind; he had read the look on the scout's face when he got the pistol in his hand.

He knew who this man was, this scout. This was the man Cat Reilly and John Bidwell both talked about as if he were made of something more than flesh and bone. What he had done was working itself into Sohrakoff like a barbed hook.

Orozco had told him to do nothing. He had gotten into the habit of doing what Orozco said.

The Americans rode up through Pacheco Pass, through the scrub oaks and the outcrops of gray rock like wind-worn heaps of skulls, and on toward the San Joaquin Valley.

This now was wild country. The Californios left the long inland valley to the Indians, with its rivers and marshes and great herds of horses and antelope. After the winter's rains every lowland was flooded; from the saddle of the pass he looked out over a vast patchwork of glistening water and stands of trees and grass.

He followed Frémont on down the east slope of the Gavilan, into the steaming golden marshes of the San Joaquin, where the wild birds were settling in to breed and nest and raise their young. There, not much to Sohrakoff's surprise, Frémont stopped and made a camp, a big camp, where he clearly meant to stay for a while, and began sending scouts out.

It was raining, off and on. Every day more ducks and geese were flocking on the broad marshes east of Frémont's campsite, and at night sometimes their racket kept Sohrakoff awake. The whole valley was sodden, streaming, a treacherous bog. The San Joaquin River itself pushed four courses across the valley, through tangles of willows like nets, through stands of tule reeds and prairies of wild oats, where herds of antelope kicked and ran and chewed their cud and the wild mares grazed with their new foals. Sohrakoff worked his way around Frémont's camp, trying to see what the Americans were doing, got bored, and went off toward the Sierra, hunting horses and keeping a watch out for Indians.

After three or four days of this he came down through a draw on a river feeding into the San Joaquin and nearly rode into an enormous camp.

They were not Indians. The men who slouched around fires sputtering in the rain wore leather hunting shirts and carried bowie knives and flintlocks. They were as American as Carson and Frémont, and there were more than fifty of them, and they had been there for a while, waiting. Sohrakoff decided he had found what Frémont was looking for.

It came to him that Orozco had made a mistake. It was one thing to call Frémont unimpressive when he had only twelve men. Now he had sixty, Missouri men, all mounted, all armed with American guns, by California standards a considerable army. Sohrakoff swung his horse around, although the night was coming and the rain was beginning again, and went as fast as he could ride back toward Pacheco Pass.

Orozco had confessed the day before and done penance through the night, and he went to Mass at daybreak in the chapel of the Mission San Juan Bautista and received the Viaticum. The Host like a white flame burned him pure from the inside out. Nothing in the Church or the Mass interested him save this, the supreme mystery — that God should give His flesh to be eaten by sinners.

When the rest of the worshipers had left he rose and went out through the side door into the brick courtyard and the hazy sunlight between rains.

As soon as he came out to the courtyard General Castro turned toward him. Pico, gaudy in a yellow jacket, stood behind Castro, and three of the general's aides, men who usually were content to stand behind the don's chair handing him napkins and glasses. Orozco saluted his commander.

"Well, Major," Pico shouted, "they came back!"

Castro was smiling, not pleased, his eyes small above the rounds of his cheeks. He said, "Major, this is becoming unpleasant. I'm told that Frémont seems to have returned."

"I heard that last night," Orozco said. He was taking off his white gloves; it was very hard to get fine white leather, and these gloves were already almost too worn for dress.

Castro said, "You should have told me."

"You were asleep. There is no hurry, General."

Pico charged up beside them. His face was flushed. "Give me twenty lancers!"

"You'll need more than that," Orozco said. "They've picked up a considerable reinforcement."

"How many?" Castro asked swiftly.

Orozco folded the gloves and put them in his belt pouch. "They crossed through Pacheco Pass with more than sixty men."

Pico wheeled on General Castro, his hands fisted at his sides. "General. I beg you. Give me the honor. Let me do it."

Castro cast him off with a shiver. "Go and order them out," he said to Orozco. "Get them out or we will have to fight them." His jowls quivered. "Is that clear?"

"Yes, General."

Castro's head swiveled toward Pico. "General, if it please you, you may take command of a squadron of my lancers."

"Sir!"

The general's hard, glittering glare found Orozco again. "You are to use Colonel Pico's troops at your discretion. Get those Anglos out of my department, Major."

"Yes, General," Orozco said.

30 🖎 THE RAIN HAD STOPPED. Dark clouds still lay over the eastern half of the sky, but the west showed bright blue, streaked with shafts of sunlight. Long wraiths of mist trailed up from the flat green meadows of the valley. Major Orozco leaned both hands on his saddlebows and stared away toward the long line of hills to the east, where the notched gray rocks of the Sierra del Gavilan burst up through the oaks.

"Very well, let's go down there. Lieutenant Chavez, you will translate." Orozco glanced over his shoulder at Pico. "There will be nothing this time but talk. Colonel, do you speak any English?"

"No," Pico said.

"Neither do I." Sohrakoff of course was fluent, but Orozco had already sent him elsewhere. Chavez, who had some English, would do well enough. "Let's go."

The air was steamy from the rain, but the clouds were breaking up and scudding away and the sun was brilliant, harsh to the eyes, cooking the odors of soil and grass out of the damp earth. Orozco rode at the head of the column, Pico on his right and Chavez on his left, up through the draw, toward the Anglos massed along the creekbank, with the two horns of Hawk Peak beyond them, the highest mountain in the Sierra del Gavilan.

When Orozco approached them Frémont's men were breaking camp, loading their gear onto a train of packmules. Seeing him come, they stopped what they were doing — rough-edged, shaggy men covered in rags and hides — and walked forward toward him. He raised his hand to the lancers to hold them back, and with Pico and Chavez he rode up to the edge of the wet ground along the creek.

The Anglos crowded the opposite side of the stream; they had trampled down the brush that grew along it. They all had rifles. Some of them looked like Indians. In their midst stood a man in a blue United States Army coat with brass buttons, who hailed Orozco in English.

Chavez's voice was high with tension. "He says he's Captain John Charles Frémont of the United States Army Corps of Topographical Engineers and he has passports from New Helvetia."

Orozco let his reins slip. His horse was edgy, snorting at the rank smell of the mules, and he stilled it with his weight and his legs. The Anglos cradled their rifles in their arms. They kept no military order, and only Frémont wore a uniform, which made them hard to read; but they were still an army, a familiar beast. He gave a quick look beyond them, noting the loaded mule train, and brought his eyes back to the Anglo officer in the blue coat.

Captain Frémont had a very bold and commanding air, almost too mighty. Orozco said, "Lieutenant Chavez, inform him that Don José Castro, commandante-general of California, has revoked his passports."

Chavez chattered away in English. Frémont's Missouri men were listening in a rapt silence. Most of them were gathered in behind the Anglo captain. Off to one side there stood a short man in buckskins, his red-brown hair hanging loose down past his shoulders; the ten or twelve men who surrounded him showed him a deference in the very way they stood. Orozco guessed that he was the scout who had Sohrakoff's hackles up like a wolf.

Frémont spoke again, with rhetorical flourishes, and clearly he was addressing his own men as much as Orozco, screwing them to a higher pitch. In the packed ranks of the Missouri men behind Frémont, several rifles veered toward Orozco. His gaze went to the short man again, who did nothing, who said nothing, but who stood there like a little king. Chavez was speaking.

"He says he's an officer of the United States and we have insulted him by demanding he leave. He won't bend to the empty threats of cowards and he's not going to leave, he says, until we apologize."

"Apologize!" Pico lunged forward. Orozco swung toward him and the younger man stopped, his mouth tight, staring at the Anglos. Hot color flooded his cheeks.

Frémont was talking again, this time directly to Orozco, and he pointed up at Hawk Peak behind him. Chavez turned, his eyes wide, and his high, excited voice ran like counterpoint over Frémont's.

"He says he's going to move his camp up there, onto Hawk Peak, and raise the United States flag here, and we can be damned, sir, until we apologize."

Pico erupted in a yell; his horse jumped, and Orozco flung one hand out and got hold of the other man's near rein. Across the creekbank the whole of Frémont's army suddenly rushed a few steps forward. Orozco leaned his face into Pico's. "Do not respond to this. I told you, nothing but talk now. Get back."

"But they —"

"Get back!" Orozco thrust his horse on past Pico's, between him and the Anglos. Some of the Missouri men spoke Spanish; he could not tell Pico now that Frémont was making a mistake.

The Anglos were watching them both like the bait in a trap. Frémont strode forward again, bellowing, strutting, shouting defiance at them. He wanted to draw an attack. He needed the excuse. Sohrakoff's guess was close, but wrong. The scout did not command here. Nobody was in command here.

Pico said, under his breath, "Major, let's go back for the rest of the lancers."

Orozco twisted in his saddle, sweeping one final look over the Americans. "Tell him, Chavez, that he has twenty-four hours to leave California." He wheeled his horse and galloped away up the draw, knowing that Pico would chase him.

Where the ravine widened out onto the flat valley floor he reined in. Pico rushed up beside him, his face taut. "Don't wait, Major. Attack them now, before they get to the top of the hill."

Chavez cantered up to them, stopped his horse, and turned to look back. Orozco shook his head at Pico. "Let them go. We haven't got the men or arms to attack them." He scanned the valley that lay behind him, the Monterey road winding off through the flat green, and the long, wooded approach up Hawk Peak before him.

Frémont had handed the game away. With the strongest army in California he had chosen to pull back into a corner and wait for Orozco to make the next move. For all his fight-talk and strut, the Anglo captain had no belly for it.

His men did. If this broke open, they could run through California like an earthquake.

Pico was scowling at him, one fist on his hip. "This looks pretty bad to me, Major. I don't see why you let this happen like this."

"Shut up," Orozco said. "I see no purpose in giving you lessons in tactics when you lack basic discipline. Pay attention. Go back to the mission. Take command of all the lancers there, which is about twenty-five men. Advise General Castro to call up the others and to bring every uniform in San Juan Bautista out here, no matter what fills it. There are three pieces of ordnance at the mission and he should bring those, too."

"What are you going to do?"

"Why don't you watch me and find out? We will bivouac here, across the Monterey road. General Castro may need your help in arranging the details." He dismissed Pico with a salute, which the don ignored. To Chavez, Orozco said, "Make me a camp."

Pico was glaring at him. "You can't order me around. I out-rank you."

"General Castro gave orders to me to deal with this situation, Colonel. Not to you."

For a moment he thought Pico would argue, but the don had no men here. By himself he had less confidence, and he wheeled his palomino horse and rode off at a lope toward San Juan. Orozco beckoned up one of the lancers to shadow Frémont and make sure he made his way safely up onto Hawk Peak.

Kit said, "You can see almost to Monterey, anyway."

Behind him stood the jagged gray rock of Hawk Peak. Before him the long fall of this hill swept away toward the flat valley, green in the distance. The round, wind-rolled heads of scrub oaks covered the slope; here and there a manzanita tree thrust a long crooked limb up into the sun, a bright orange streak through the green glossy leaves. Above the trees that covered the slope, a hawk soared, teetering on the updraft.

Toward the north, on his right, beyond the green sweep of new spring grass he could see the red roofs of a mission, a little village gathered in its lee. From it the valley swept down around the foot of this slope and off toward the ocean, a broad open highway straight to Monterey. He turned to Frémont, beside him.

"That's where we ought to be going, Captain — to Monterey, not up here."

Frémont said, "We can't act like bandits. If war has been declared, then we can march. In the meantime, we're here, ready, waiting. We'll build a fort here and raise the flag. If they attack us, then so be it. We'll start the war."

"Damn it," Kit said, "you mean, they'll start the war."

He turned to look up at the peak behind him. Water gushed from crevices in the rocks there, trickling down in a dozen little streams. Below it the hilltop stretched out into a broad saddle, studded with trees, a meadow full of grass, although at this time of the year the grass would not keep the horses fat.

In the meadow below the peak, the new men, the company

they had just met in the San Joaquin, were building a wall out of some fallen logs. It looked like a kids' fort.

Kit turned to Frémont again. "This ain't no way to fight. Let me take our ten men and raid Monterey. Once things get started nobody will much care who shot first."

"No," Frémont said. He swung toward Kit, drawing himself up tall. "We'll raise the flag, Kit, and they'll have to do something. They can't just stand there and let Old Glory wave in their faces."

Kit growled at him. He felt tied up, hand and foot, wrapped around and around with Frémont's scruples; his arms strained, the muscles tense, as if he could burst free somehow. He went on down into the meadow and tended his horses, cleaning them up and hobbling them out to get what they could out of the grass, and saw to his guns.

Basil Lajeunesse came up to him. "I need the flag."

Kit had brought a flag in his gear. He rolled up his gun pack and stowed it and opened the other side of the saddlebag, where the flag lay under his spare clothes. "You know, we ought to be raising this-here flag in Monterey."

"Yeah, well, Kit, frankly" — Basil lowered his voice — "I'd follow you into the ocean, Kit, and know if I just kept going, you'd get me up the other side. But Frémont's another horse altogether."

This was the whole problem. Kit dug out the flag, folded and wrapped up in oilcloth. They took it back across the meadow, to the tree that Luke Maxwell had trimmed of most of its branches.

The rest of the men clustered around, their voices high, excited. Kit swept a look around at them. Besides the men he had been trailing with for the past three months, men he had known for years, there were all these strangers now, some sixty or more of them. Their commander was a greenhorn surveyor from Philadelphia named Kern. Their guide was old Joe Walker, whom Kit hated. He turned to watch Basil climb the tree with the flag.

The tree began to bend under Basil's weight; finally he stopped, ten feet below the tip, and hooked his leg around the trunk and lashed the flag on. That done, he hacked off the top of the tree and climbed down again.

The flag hung a while, snagged on the rough ends of some of the branch stubs, but the wind came up and caught it, and the flag flapped out straight, and all the men yelled.

Kit grinned up at it, shading his eyes. Looking at it made him feel better. Maybe this would come to something after all. To Frémont, beside him, he said, "Ever since the first time I saw this country, I wanted that flag flying over it."

Frémont was chewing his lip. He stared up at the flag a moment, turned, and scanned the meadow. "I wish we knew if the war's begun. Come over here and look at this."

He led Kit over to the edge of the hill, below the rocky spur of the peak, and pointed north, in the direction of the mission. There were some people coming toward them down in the valley, a steady stream of horses and carts.

"God Almighty," Kit said. "They're actually going to fight us."

"Is it an army?"

"Well, it's gonna be, eventually," Kit said. "I'll take some men down tonight and scout it out."

"No," Frémont said. "No. Stay here. I don't want to make any mistakes now."

"Captain! What do you breathe for?"

Frémont's lips clamped together, his eyes narrow; he clung to the scraps of his authority. "Stay here! That's an order."

Kit clenched his fist, his muscles burning. Frémont had the uniform. There was power in the uniform. Before he did anything he could not undo he walked off across the meadow, his knees stiff.

Kern, tall, red-headed, slab-shanked, was ordering around his men, building the fort. The ten men who had come down with Frémont considered themselves above that kind of work and sat around Kit's fire passing a jug of the liquor Sutter made on the Sacramento. Kit went up into their circle and sank down on his heels.

Basil held out the jug to him. "What'd Frémont say?"

Kit said, "Forget Frémont. We can do it without him."

Basil gave an uneasy laugh. "Sure, Kit. All eleven of us."

"I'm telling you, we can do it. Those goats up at Sutter's, they hate the dons. When they hear we're mixing it with them, they'll be coming down to help us out with every gun on the Sacramento. All we got to do is light the fire."

"What about Frémont?"

"I'm telling you, fuck Frémont!"

He looked from face to face, but they would not meet his eyes. "Kit," Basil said, slowly, "you can't talk like this. This is mutiny."

"I'll fuckin' mutiny, all right," Kit said.

Some of the other men murmured, uneasy, stirring, their gazes shifting from one side to the other. Luke said, "Kit, I signed on with Frémont and the United States Army."

The half-breed, Denny, said, "Keep your hat on, anyway, damn it, Kit. They'll come running at us, sooner or later. You saw that greaser in his fancy yellow jacket — some of 'em ain't chicken, they'll come, and we'll blow 'em to pieces."

"No," Kit said, "Frémont will kiss them."

Some of the men laughed. Basil said, "Come on, Kit, for chrissake, we're stuck up here on top of this hill with a lot of greasers piling up in that valley, just waiting to swarm us. Let's not get fighting ourselves. Besides, there's Kern's men."

Kit rubbed his hand over his face. Suddenly the hilltop was too small; he wanted to explode in all directions. He was sitting on a keg of powder, but he could not find the spark to set it off. He reached for the jug. "Jesus Christ," he said, and took a long pull of Sutter's whiskey.

31 GENERAL CASTRO ASKED, "Could you hit them from here?"

Major Orozco shook his head. "Not even if we had gunpowder." He turned to watch a column of lancers gallop by. Pico was drilling the horsemen in the broad meadows below Hawk Peak, forming them into lines and charging the length of the meadow and reforming again to charge back. Behind them, in rows, other men waited, not really soldiers: the Indians from the mission, the local rancheros and vaqueros, children and women.

Castro stroked his chin. His belly had been hurting him since this began, as if Frémont's camp were tucked up under his rib cage.

All day long his own people had been arriving down the road from Monterey, from San Juan Bautista, from Natividad and San Lucas, and Orozco had been camping them on the valley floor, where the Anglos on Hawk Peak could see them all. Now he was supervising the assembling of the two four-pounders and the swivel gun that they had brought from the mission, although there was no powder and no shot.

His bony brown face impassive, Orozco sat in his saddle, watching the three laborers struggle to screw down the trunnions that held one cannon into its truck. Castro looked up at the horns of Hawk Peak, where Captain Frémont and the United States Army waited, armed with rifles that actually fired.

Orozco straightened again, his hooked nose aimed away down the Monterey road. "Well, at last," he said, under his breath, and Castro lifted his head.

The Monterey road wound away toward the south, a long strip of dust through the spring green. The stirring feet of the men marching in all day long had lifted its surface a few yards into the air, a thin, drifting veil of pale brown; through this now two riders were galloping, taking shape out of the dust. Their horses struggled merely to pick up their hoofs, their heads drooping. Coming toward Castro and Orozco they dropped to a walk, their flanks flapping with their panting breath.

One of the riders was Orozco's Russian. The other, to Castro's astonishment, was the United States consul, Thomas Larkin.

The Boston merchant was as weary as his horse. He slid

down from the saddle as if putting his feet on solid ground were all that would ever matter to him again. He took the battered hat off his head and dropped it. Dust powdered his well-tailored dark jacket, his side-whiskers, his eyelashes. He wore a pair of ill-fitting chaparejos over his trousers, but on his feet were a city man's shoes, scraped from the stirrups.

He straightened and stood there stiff as a green hide. General Castro said, "Well, Mr. Larkin, I suppose you realize you and your country are in a lot of trouble."

Larkin took a napkin from the inside pocket of his jacket and wiped his face. "So I understand. Tell me exactly what's happened." He blew his nose.

Castro lifted his arm to point to Hawk Peak. "Captain Frémont has raised the United States flag on my territory. I am preparing to remove it, and him, by force if necessary."

Larkin was dusting himself off; his sunburned face was peeling. "I've never been much of a horseman," he said to Castro apologetically. His gaze went past the general, out to the meadow, where Pico's lancers were charging over the grass, and around to the three little cannon lined up beside the road; he gave a long stare to Major Orozco. Finally he turned to Castro again. "Let me talk to Captain Frémont."

Castro said, "I intend to begin my operations against him tomorrow. You have until then to do what you can."

Larkin folded his napkin and put it in his pocket. Just standing was clearly painful to him, his body wretchedly misused after life in a chair. He turned slowly to look around him for the man who had brought him here. "I'll need another horse."

"Right here," said Sohrakoff, and rode forward with a fresh mount. Larkin struggled up into the saddle. Sohrakoff said, "Do you want me to go with you?" Like all the Californios he was watching Larkin's ineptitude on the horse with pity and contempt.

"Is the way marked?"

"There's a wood road straight up. That's how Frémont found it."

"I'll go by myself," Larkin said. He kicked the docile little mare around and started down the draw; after a few yards he managed to excite the horse into a slow trot. Castro watched him jog away behind the trees. Orozco turned toward his Russian, and the barest glance passed between them. The Russian ambled off, not exactly following Larkin.

In the silence, his stomach no sweeter with the knowledge that now he had to wait again, General Castro swung toward his underling. "This had better go well, Major."

"Yes, General." Orozco's black eyes glanced over him, cool, remote. The lean face turned to watch Larkin, his horse back to a walk, trudging away out of sight into the scrub oaks. Sohrakoff had already disappeared.

Castro licked his lips; he wanted to end this now, before it got worse, and just waiting made it worse. But he had no idea what to do. Orozco did know, or seemed to know. Castro forced himself to patience. If this went wrong he would make Orozco suffer for it, he would throw all the blame onto Orozco; therefore he had to let the Indio major have his chance. Castro rode off to do what Pico was doing, drilling their makeshift army to soak up the time.

The valley below Hawk Peak was filling with soldiers. Frémont, his hands behind him, paced up and down along the edge of the hill staring at the enemy camp below. Kit knelt on the ground to one side of him, taking sights with his rifle on the tiny figures in the grass.

"Kill one," Frémont said. "That might incite them to attack."

Kit grunted at him. "They're way out of range."

"They're yellow," said Basil Lajeunesse. He came up beside Frémont, his hands on his hips, surveying the slopes below them. "Look down over there." His hand shot forward, pointing.

The road up here wound back and forth through the trees; along it, half a mile down, a small white horse was trotting across a stretch of meadow.

Frémont wheeled briskly toward Lajeunesse. "Go find that man and learn his business."

The tall mountain man stalked off on his errand. Frémont hitched his shoulders under his uniform jacket. He had seen the right thing to do at once. Lajeunesse had obeyed him at once. That shored up his nerves a little.

Two of the hill's numberless hawks swooped back and forth over the tree-covered slope. Off at the far end of the meadow a flock of jays was fighting. Frémont walked away from the hillside, off a little toward his fort. He was waiting for the spirit of America to fill him, to make him great enough to fulfill her destiny, but so far all he was feeling was a giddy flutter of panic. He wished desperately that he knew what was going on in Washington, where by now surely the war had been declared.

"I hate not knowing exactly what's going on," he said.

Kit was squinting along the barrel of his Plains rifle. He said nothing, having said entirely too much already. Down there, on the valley, more soldiers were riding up to the Californios' camp; under a haze of yellow dust some ox-drawn carts moved up alongside the troops.

Frémont turned a searching look on the grassy hilltop he was defending. The little fort of logs had no roof yet. The men were spread out over the hill gathering firewood and cutting down trees. The mules and horses grazed in the meadow below the gray rock spur of the peak. Everything looked orderly and purposeful. So far everything had gone well. Things were going well now. Then out of the brush on the side of the hill Basil Lajeunesse rode, with the man on the white horse behind him.

It was Larkin, the American consul in Monterey. Frémont straightened; down his spine ran a cold finger of anticipation. Certainly now he would have the command to proceed. He strode through the thick grass toward the two men.

"Larkin," he said, reaching his hand out. "Welcome to Fort Frémont."

The consul dismounted stiffly from his horse. He wore leather leggings over his broadcloth trousers, but his coat was filthy and he had no hat. He got hold of Frémont's hand and pulled him away from Lajeunesse, away from the other men, off to standing near the foot of the flagpole, and gestured up at the flag.

"What are you trying to do here?" His voice was curt. "Exactly what is it you are trying to do?"

The flag was cracking out flat in the high breeze. Frémont glanced at it and turned back to Larkin, from whom he had expected some other greeting, more in the way of enthusiasm and support. He said stiffly, "I am defending the honor and the flag of the United States of America, Mr. Larkin."

Larkin's face shone, unevenly pink. His eyes looked like green-brown glass. "You come into California, attack and insult people, and claim to be defending your country's honor?" He gave a sort of raw-throated, desperate laugh.

Kit had drifted up close to them; three flintlock pistols stuck out of his belt. Larkin warned him off with a look and stood so close to Frémont his breath heated the captain's face as he spoke.

"There is no war yet with Mexico. We need no war. We can get California without a fight. Everybody is sick of the dons' endless bickering and thievery. There are more Americans living here every year. Hudson's Bay is moving out, Sutter's leaning in our favor, Vallejo also. Even in the south we're winning friends and supporters." He pushed his face in toward Frémont's, and his lip curled. "The only thing that could take California away from us is something like this."

"All you politicians," Kit said contemptuously. He was standing off to one side, his hand on his hip. "You've had your chance. You're taking too long."

Larkin gave him a single harsh glare and swung around to Frémont. "Who's in command here?"

"I am," Frémont said, his voice booming.

"Then get out and leave this to me."

Frémont's mouth shut again. He turned and put his back to Larkin, looking down on the valley. Larkin came up beside him, taking a cylindrical leather pouch from the pocket of his coat.

"If you will not consider the use of reason, Captain, please consider the use of this glass to observe what is going on below." He pulled a telescope out of the pouch and handed it to Frémont.

"Thank you," Frémont said. "Mine broke, near Walker Lake." He extended the tube and put his eye to it.

It took him a few moments to adjust to the glass; then he was seeing the bunched yellow-green leaves of the trees below, then brown faces above white coats, sitting in heavy Mexican saddles. Their horses stood in even ranks, dozing, the grass cut and brown beneath them. On the men's belts were long, curved sabers like scimitars.

Larkin said brusquely, "By the road. The guns."

Frémont trained the glass on the road. Beside him, Kit murmured something and put up his hand to shade his eyes.

"Cannon," Frémont said. His stomach turned into a knot.

Larkin said, "Yes, exactly. The longer you stay here, the more men, the more guns, the more power they will have to throw against you."

Without the glass Frémont could no longer see the three little cannon down there. His eyes hurt, straining, and he swallowed a sudden spurt of bile that had come into his throat. Still, they were far out of range.

Kit said, "We could use the telescope, Mr. Larkin."

"I'm not giving you anything," Larkin said in a brittle voice. "You are destroying years of my work."

Frémont said, "We've gone too far now to back down, Larkin." He glanced at Kit, needing some help, and Larkin got in between them.

"Are you in command," he said, "or is this filibustering buckskin auxiliary in command?"

Frémont said steadily, "We're of a single mind here, consul."

"Really." Larkin's mouth twitched. "How comforting that must be. But Washington surely believes your chain of authority is more orthodox. Your scout here will get off for following orders. You, however, will be court-martialed." Frémont jerked, startled. Larkin turned on his heel and strode off toward his horse. Veering past Kit, he snarled, "You damned freebooter." Frémont turned his eyes back to the guns in the valley below him.

Kit said, "You should have taken the telescope from him."

The three little guns were invisible. They were very far out of range. Frémont said aloud, "I think we can discount the guns."

He pulled on his beard. The guns made no difference. It was the assault of his own doubt that was overwhelming. This high hill where he had thought himself safe, this natural fortress of rock, was dissolving out from under his feet. He sank down on his hams, watching the tiny rows of men galloping across the valley below, his mind and his belly both overturned.

Larkin on his conspicuous white horse, moving slowly up the middle of the wood road, made a good diversion, and Sohrakoff shadowed him almost all the way, close enough to see the flag, to hear the sound if not the words of the Americans arguing. Going back, he lost patience with the consul's slow pace and circled on past him, reaching the valley well ahead of him.

At the edge of Orozco's huge, empty bivouac, where now in the twilight more campfires were burning every moment, Pico met him. Most of the lancers were gathered around the front row of fires, cooking their dinner meat over the coals. The rest of Orozco's crowd, vaqueros and servants, were scattered out through the darkness, tending the fires that made them seem three times as numerous as they were. The wind was rising, sweet with the spring rain. Sohrakoff dismounted and took the saddle off his horse.

Pico said, "How close did you get?"

"If I'd had a gun, like him, I could have shot him." He was hungry. Seeing the scout had rasped his nerves raw again. He could not forget the gun muzzle aimed at his face, and the feeling that there was nothing he could do but obey it.

Pico followed him to the nearest campfire. "Lead me up there tonight."

"I don't have a gun. And he does." At the fire, three or four vaqueros, each wearing some part of a uniform, were roasting a newborn kid on a spit; Sohrakoff dumped his saddle and sank down on his heels beside them. One of them held out a leather flask, and he took it and sipped and got a stomach-whacking jolt of apple brandy.

He did not want the scout dead; he wanted the scout afraid, and knowing it was Sohrakoff who made him afraid. He wanted to stand face to face with the American and get back what the scout had taken from him, over the gun sights, at the meadow north of Monterey. Twisting, he looked back over his shoulder, up toward the dark mass of Hawk Peak, thrusting the horizon up into the stars.

In the deep twilight, Larkin had finally reached the bottom of the wood road. The white mare trudged on down toward San Juan, the consul not noticing Sohrakoff there in the meadow. His shoulders slumped. Perhaps he was tired, or maybe Frémont had only laughed at him. Maybe Orozco had made a mistake.

Pico squatted by the campfire, his eyes intent. "We can run their horses off. Poison their water, set fire to the grass."

"It's too wet to burn." There had to be some way of getting his revenge. Reluctantly he pulled his gaze away from the dark mountain and faced the campfire again, where one of the vaqueros was slicing up the goat. With a murmur of thanks he took a chunk of the sweet, tender meat.

Pico said, "Remember what I said before? Come work for me. The life's hotter in El Pueblo, anyway — more to your fancy, I'd think, than this monastery." His voice dropped; he glanced at the Indians in their ill-fitting uniforms and spoke in an undertone. "What do you owe to Castro? Leave him, take orders from me, and I'll pay you, now, anything you want, to lead me up that hill."

Sohrakoff hated Castro. "What will you do when you get there?"

"I'll decide when I see it."

That was how he played poker. That was why he lost at poker. Suddenly this was running clearer, and Sohrakoff said, "I don't work for Castro, I work for Orozco."

"I don't see any difference. Neither one of them pays you."

There was a difference. Sohrakoff wiped his mouth, reaching

for the flask of brandy. Orozco did pay him, in a better coin than Pico would ever have. "I'll take my orders from the major, Colonel."

Pico stared at him, his face rumpled in the firelight. "What if he's wrong?"

Sohrakoff shrugged. "Then he's wrong."

The *abajeño*'s mobile lips twisted into a frustrated grimace. "I have to do something. I'll go crazy sitting still."

Sohrakoff chewed more goat meat; he wiped juice off his beard. His saddle lay behind him in the grass, and he reached around into the back pouch and pulled out a deck of cards. "Do you have any money?" Around the fire, at the sight of the cards, the vaqueros all moved a little closer, suddenly keen.

Pico growled at him. But he settled cross-legged beside the fire. "Deal."

Frémont was pacing up and down along the hillside; he had dented a path into the grass. The sun was setting, and the wind smelled like the ocean, like the coming rain. Up from the Pacific a gray fog was creeping; already it had buried Monterey, rolling in along the lower slopes of the hill, curling in under the trees. Kit could feel the damp chill in the air, the fog's first cold touch.

He smelled this going bad. With every hour there were more soldiers down in the valley; he guessed two hundred greasers with long knives now between him and the cannon, between him and Monterey. Dawdling up here, he was losing his chance. And yet he could not find a way to move.

Frémont came striding back toward him. "Without a declaration of war I have no authority to do this. If Larkin had been willing to support us —"

"Larkin's a whore for words," Kit said.

Some of the other men drifted up to join them. Luke Maxwell lit a cigar and passed it off to the next man, and the fragrance of tobacco floated in the air.

Basil Lajeunesse took a step forward. "I ain't no soldier, Kit.

I don't take much of a shine to being some place where people can shoot at me but I can't shoot at them."

There was a mutter from the other men. Steadily the whole population of Fort Frémont was collecting around its namesake. The night was drawing in on them, and the cold wind was seething through the pine trees on the top of the hill. The flag snapped and cracked like a whip, the mast quivering.

Kern spoke, the Easterner, who still tried to shave every day. "As fast as those Mexican soldiers are showing up down there, they'll have a thousand men by tomorrow night."

His guide, big Joe Walker, coughed in his chest. "I think you birds done got yourselves in a trap here."

Kit walked in through the middle of the powwow, sweeping his gaze around them, pulling them into his way of thinking. "We'll go down there tonight and roll those guns over. They can't hit anything up here from down in that valley anyway. Listen to me."

"Is there a war on?" Kern asked. He swung his gaze toward Frémont. "Is there a war?"

"We don't need no declaration of war." Kit walked toward him. "Forget the rules. We can take this whole fuckin' country right now, just like they did in Texas back in '36."

"What this reminds me of," somebody else said, "is the Alamo. And all those men died." There was a low, alarmed mutter through the crowd.

"It won't go like that." Kit turned toward the voice. They were silent around him, watching him, and he wheeled, looking for men he knew, men who would follow him. Kern's men stared back at him blankly, most of them strangers. Walker gave him a slow sneer. Kit spoke to Basil and Luke. "If we strike now, quick, before they get any more strength together, we can take Monterey in three days."

Frémont stood up. "Or we could all wind up dead. Or court-martialed, and in disgrace." The wind was rumpling the sleeves of his blue uniform coat. He turned to face the men. "We're Americans. We have a certain moral responsibility —" The wind rose with a shriek, and on the tree the flag whipped and snapped and suddenly tore loose and blew flapping to the ground.

Somebody yelled. Half the men got up to look at the fallen flag, and Basil turned toward Kit. "You know, I think that's an omen."

Kern turned around, bellowing, "All my men, pack up!"

Across the meadow, in the dark, already the men were moving. They had decided; the wind had decided for them. The campaign on Hawk Peak was over. His jaw clenched, Kit stood watching them scurry away from him and knew he had lost.

Frémont came up to him. "Get us down off this hill, Kit. Tonight."

Kit stared past him, unwilling even to look at him. "You crayfish."

"That's an order, Kit." Frémont went by him, his head high.

Kit stood still for a long time, seething, and at last went on down the meadow to retrieve the flag out of the muck.

32 🗡 IN THE MORNING, rain was falling in a steady gray downpour. Orozco walked out onto the flat ground on the top of Hawk Peak.

The ground was trampled into a swamp, and most of the trees had been hacked down and trimmed and piled together into a rough square near the middle. By the foot of the stone outcrop on the peak, a thread of smoke still struggled up from a campfire. Bits and pieces of gear lay all over the place — a boot, a scrap of cloth, a blanket, a crushed tin cup.

Pico galloped up the meadow, an unruly column of his lancers pounding along behind him. They had charged the hill that morning to find Frémont gone, and now they were hurtling back and forth over the top of Hawk Peak, making it California again with their horses' hoofs. Pico was furious that he had seen no action. When Castro rode over toward Orozco the *abajeño* don swerved to join them.

Castro was smiling, his face smoother, the hard lines gone from around his mouth; probably his stomach was feeling better. He put up his hand in a salute to Orozco. "Congratulations, Major. Done well."

Pico thrust his head forward, outraged. "He didn't do anything!"

"The best strategy," said Castro, "is always to do as little as possible." He nodded to Pico. "Gather up the debris. We shall display it in Monterey, tokens of our victory."

Pico rode off, bellowing orders. When the *abajeño* was out of earshot, Orozco turned to General Castro again.

"I need something for Sohrakoff."

"Why? He already does what you want." Castro made an overall shrug of his body, looking away.

Orozco said, "I'll lose him if I can't pay him."

"What do you want me to do, Major, give him citizenship and commission him in the army?"

"Yes," Orozco said. "That's precisely what I want."

Castro snorted at him, frowning. "Sergei Sohrakoff will be an outlaw until he dies, Major. It's clever of you to use him, but don't try to do anything more. You may break him to harness, but you'll never get him into the holy water." He swung away, moving fast now. He would pay Sohrakoff nothing, not even a word. Orozco went slowly back down the hill after him.

"Pico's gone back to El Pueblo?"

Orozco smoothed the sand table out into a flat plain and began to draw the road to Brussels on it. Slumped in the chair in the corner, Sohrakoff swung one leg up across the other, his ankle on his knee.

"Yes, he left. Not enough excitement here for him, he said."

Orozco built the long east-west ridge of Mont Saint-Jean onto the table. "Why didn't you go with him?" Under his fingertips the coarse beach sand was cool and gritty. "I asked Castro for a commission for you and he refused." His belly still seethed at Castro's rejection.

Sohrakoff said nothing.

"You should have gone with Pico, who would surely hire you. In fact, he probably made you an offer, didn't he."

Sohrakoff slouched deeper in the chair, batting his spur rowel around. "Pico just likes to fight. You know how to win. If anybody is going to get us through this, it will be you."

"Sohrakoff. An unexpected breadth of vision."

"What are you doing there?"

"Waterloo."

"Really." The Count leaned forward, his interest engaged. "You'll let the beloved emperor lose?"

Orozco put on some trees and hedges and reached under the table for his box of soldiers. He said, "The odd thing about kriegspiels of Waterloo is that if you play the battle strictly by the rules, Napoleon almost always wins."

"Then the rules are wrong."

"Reality doesn't need rules. Rules are a human failing." He put Napoleon before him, with the Old Guard.

He went on placing his soldiers, his eyes on his hands. They had been lucky at Hawk Peak, but the incident itself was a warning shot. This was only the beginning. Somewhere beyond the mountains, beyond the searing desert, other men were marching and making decisions that would change everything, and which he would not know about until the consequences were rolling over him. He put a piece of quartz on the table, to stand for Wellington, and began to make the moves he could control.

33 🦋 "HELP ME." Sutter unrolled the proclamation up against the wooden gate of the fort, and Catharine reached out to hold the corners while he nailed them. Her gaze flew over the paper.

It was copied out by hand, in ornate letters, but at least it was in English. Catharine read the first few lines and let out a yell.

Sutter thrust a folded newspaper at her. "I got this in Yerba Buena too. There's going to be a war with Mexico. Maybe there already is a war with Mexico. And Frémont has lost the first battle."

Catharine clutched the newspaper, struggling through the convoluted language of the proclamation. The rough hang of it was that Don el General José Castro, the commandante-general of California, hereby announced his magnificent victory over a band of Anglo freebooters at Hawk Peak under the command of John Charles Frémont, United States Army.

"Jesus holy Christ." This was John Bidwell, leaning in over her shoulder to read down to the bottom.

The proclamation went on to summon all true-hearted Californios to stand to arms and prepare to defend themselves and their country; all those who were not such true-hearted Californios should prepare to leave at once or be driven out.

"That's us," Catharine said.

"Yes, I think so." John Bidwell stood back; there was a steadily growing crowd around them, pressing in to read the proclamation. Sutter had already left, striding away across the courtyard toward the stairs to the office.

"What do you suppose Frémont did?" She looked up at Bidwell. Somebody reading the proclamation began to swear, and other voices rose, angry, excited. Catharine remembered the newspaper and unfolded it. "Well," she said, "that's why. Texas is entering the Union." This was a Baltimore *Sun,* two months old. By now anything could have happened. "I knew something was going on when Frémont was here last winter."

Bidwell said, "They've hung us up here like a straw target." He strode off across the yard toward the office stairs; Catharine followed him, leafing through the newspaper. After months of travel the paper was ripped and frayed almost to pieces. The editorial gloated over the annexation of Texas into the Union as the addition of another slave state, tipping the balance in the Congress in favor of the South. She pounded up the stairs after Bidwell.

Sutter was sitting at the table; Manaiki was serving him a dish of eggs. When Bidwell and Cat rushed in the Swiss don gave them a long look and reached for his fork. Manaiki went off with her platter. Politics did not interest her.

Bidwell said, "Captain, whatever it was Frémont did, he cooked us, you know, just like tossing us into the fire."

Chewing, Sutter grunted at him. He reached for the cup of coffee in front of him. "Calm down. What're you worried about?"

Catharine went up to the side of the table. "What are you going to do, Captain?"

Sutter drank coffee and wiped his mouth. He looked solid and square and steady as the furniture. His eyes poked at her. He said, "Nothing. I don't have to do anything. I'm a good honest citizen of California and I'm staying here, with my dependents and family and helpers and all that, and doing what I'm good at, as you say, which is farming. In a few weeks we are going to harvest the biggest wheat crop in the history of New Helvetia, and I'm going to need every set of hands to bring it in and thresh it. I want you to go get Zeke Merritt." Zeke was at his cabin in the west country.

John Bidwell said, "You don't think we're sitting in a pig's pot of trouble, Captain." His voice sang like a plucked wire.

"Yes, I do. But we can get through it." Sutter nodded to him. "Go fetch Zeke. We're going to need some Indians for the harvest."

"Yes, Captain." Bidwell went out.

Catharine sat down on the bench, watching Sutter eat. "What else did you hear in Yerba Buena? What did Frémont do?"

Sutter pushed his plate away. "He marched his army up the hill and marched it down again. There's some kind of rhyme about that, I think."

"Have you heard anything about an actual declaration of war?"

"No. Nothing, yet."

"Captain," she said, "we can't just sit here and let them close on us from all sides."

Sutter's eyes widened, and his gaze slipped away from hers.

His hand went up to his chin whiskers. "The United States is going to take California. Nothing will change that. I don't want to think about that anymore. Come over here; I need you to write some letters for me."

"Captain —"

"Cat, damn it, I'm just doing what I can." He glared at her. In the harsh look of command there was a sort of pleading. "Come write these letters." She got up, subdued, seeing him afraid, and did as he wished.

34 ☙ A FEW DAYS LATER, in a fine misty rain, Frémont reappeared, leading far more men than he had left with. They camped on the American River, and most of the people in the valley took some excuse to get over there and talk to him. Everybody knew that there was a war either already on with Mexico or about to be. Sutter told Cat that Zeke Merritt had argued with Frémont for nearly two hours one night, trying to get him to lead them all over to Sonoma and seize General Vallejo, but Frémont would not go.

"There's been no declaration of war," Sutter said. "Not that he knows of, anyway. That's what he says." He was dealing out the hands for a game of whist; the other two men had not come in yet.

"He's not being noble," she said. "He's afraid of what somebody else is going to think."

"All that matters right now," Sutter said, "is getting that wheat crop reaped and threshed." The door opened, and Sinclair and Flugge came in, and they played whist.

Frémont moved his camp up the valley a little. Kit was catching and breaking horses. Zeke and a crew of men from Sutterville went out and rounded up some Indians and brought them back to the fort, where Sutter gave them each a shirt and a sickle and drove them, with everybody else, out to the wheatfields.

The grain stood to Cat's waist, the spiny heads bowing down under the weight of fat, shiny golden kernels; there was so much of it that Sutter called in even the settlers far up the valley to help, and they came, men and women and children, glad to pay him back for a fraction of what he had done for them.

Day after day, from dawn until dusk, they gathered in the wheat and dragged it to the threshing yards, where they poured it on the ground and drove herds of horses through it. The sharp hoofs of the horses slashed the husks off. They scooped up the grain and winnowed it in big Indian baskets, tossing it into the wind, on and on, over and over, until their arms and their backs ached and there seemed nothing in the world but wheat.

By the time the last of the golden kernels were stored up in sacks in the shed, Frémont had moved his camp again, this time up to Lassen's ranch, near the great snow peaks in the nave of the valley. He was leaving California. When Sutter heard of him next, he was marching into the Klamath country of southern Oregon. Still there was no word of the beginning of the war.

35   A FEW DAYS after Frémont rode off to the north, a rider galloped through Sutterville and up to the fort, shouting that a huge army of Castro's men was marching north through the lower valley. Zeke Merritt and John Christenson and Pablo Gutierrez leapt on horses and raced off to scout the oncoming enemy, and everybody else crowded inside the walls and walked on the ramparts, their hands cluttered with guns, and talked and drank and waited.

Zeke came back after dark with a string of seventy horses. There had been no army, only a few vaqueros and a single Mexican Army lieutenant taking a *cavallada* south to General Castro in Monterey. Sutter drove the disappointed crowds out of the fort and lectured Zeke for stealing the horses, and they all went to bed.

A few mornings later, however, a launch flying the American flag sailed up to the embarcadero on the river. Word of its coming had run ahead of it along the riverbank, and when the launch pulled up to the first of Sutter's three wooden wharfs, nearly everybody in Sutterville and the fort beyond it was waiting on the bank.

Sutter himself stood on the wharf, with Cat behind him, as the launch drifted in beside the piers. The crew wore blue navy shirts, with stars on their collars and the name *Portsmouth* on their caps. In the waist of the launch stood a short man with a chin square as a brick; his face sloped back from his upper lip toward a receding blond hairline. Catharine did not recognize his uniform, a red and blue tunic with white belts and a stiff-brimmed cap.

He stepped out onto the wharf, and his cold blue eyes went over the people waiting for him. Sutter moved forward, his hand out.

"I'm Captain Johann Sutter."

The young man looked beyond him, searching through the crowd with his eyes. He ignored Sutter's friendly outstretched hand. "Where is Captain Frémont?"

Sutter lowered his hand to his side. "He's gone. He went north, a few days ago."

From the crowd Zeke Merritt called, "Hey, there, what's the news on the war?" and a general yell went up.

The blond man ignored that also. He spoke to Sutter without deigning to look at him. "I have to reach Captain Frémont as soon as possible."

Annoyed, Catharine got in front of his outthrust jaw. "Who are you?" she said, and when he moved, haughty, shifting his gaze beyond her, she stood in his way again.

Sutter took her by the arm and dragged her back. "She has a point. Who are you, mister?"

The blond man faced him, surly. "I am Archibald Gillespie, sir, Lieutenant, United States Marine Corps. I am here looking for Captain Frémont, and I request that you assist me!" He

snarled the last few words as if he had said them already several
times.

Zeke called again, "The war's started with Mexico, hasn't it?"
and again from the crowd on the muddy shore behind him
there went up a shout.

Sutter said, "Come with me, Lieutenant." He walked down
the wharf toward the shore, Gillespie on his heels.

The crowd divided to let them pass. Sutter plunged on
toward the fort, Gillespie on his heels; Catharine went over to
Zeke.

As Sutter walked through the crowd he plucked men out of
it. "Neale, Sigler. I need you." The two men fell into step behind Gillespie.

Catharine watched them go with a tremor of excitement. She
turned to Merritt and said, "This is it, Zeke." The crowd was
still packed around the wharf, some staring after Gillespie, most
talking together, knots of men, their voices gradually building
toward a general cacophony. She looked up at Merritt again.
"What are we going to do about it?"

Merritt was chewing his lower lip. His eyes had a manic glint.
"Let's go talk to the Captain," he said, and strode off toward
the fort.

Sutter had Gillespie away to the north in less than half an hour
after the arrival of the *Portsmouth*'s launch. As soon as he had
gone, the office began to fill up with people. The room was
already packed when Catharine came in. Sutter sat at the head
of his table, one foot up on the tabletop, a glass in his hand. She
started toward him and came face to face with Ben Kelsey.

"Ben!" She threw her arms around him; he was warm and
smelled of tobacco smoke. "What are you doing here?"

Kelsey clapped his arm around her and walloped her on the
side a few times. "Frémont sent us." Another man moved up
beside him, square-shouldered and broad-backed, with a graying spade beard, and Kelsey said, "You know Bill Ide."

She said, "I know everybody. Hello, Mr. Ide. What's this
about Frémont?"

Kelsey scratched in his beard. "He come through about a week ago telling us all there was Indian trouble and we should report here. Then we come down here and there's no trouble, just talk."

"What about Nancy and the babies?"

"They're home. The babies are some bigger, Cat. You should come up and stay with us."

"Maybe I will when this is over."

Somebody passed Kelsey a cigarette, and he took a drag and handed it on. "When what's over, Cat?" Two blasts of smoke funneled out of his nostrils.

"Some marine officer came through here today chasing Frémont. Mexico's at war with the United States."

On the heel of her words, Sutter's voice rose, roundly calling them all to listen. With Ide on her left and Kelsey on her right, she moved toward the table; the rest of the crowd pushed in around her. Those who got there first took the chairs, and the rest stood behind them. Cat went up to the chair on Sutter's right, where Zeke Merritt was sitting, and made him get up and give her his place. He moved over and half sat on the table.

Sutter waved his hands at them, to get them all to be quiet. His voice rose, as even as a schoolmaster's. "Now, we all know that something is going on between the U.S. and Mexico; they've been growling at each other over Texas for years." Merritt filled his glass and the Swiss don stopped to moisten his lips. "Now there's been a war declared between the U.S. and Mexico. That would seem to be the likely conclusion, anyway."

Above Cat's head, Zeke roared, "Likely, hell! It's sure." A dozen other men raised their voices in a roar of agreement.

"A war," Sutter said, looking from face to face, "that I mean to stay out of."

The passion in them dimmed. Zeke leaned toward Sutter, his hand on the table in front of Cat.

"Why? We got guns."

Sutter said, "I have been through this before." He smiled at Catharine, a mirthless flexing of his lips. "I have seen the folly of my ways. My advice to all of you is the same: stay out of this."

Cat leaned back, watching the faces of the other men. Sutter's resignation slowed them only for a moment. At once they turned to one another, nodding back and forth and talking themselves into another shape.

"Where's Frémont now?" said John Bidwell, at the far end of the table.

"Up somewhere north of Peter Lassen's place." This was William Ide, on Zeke's left. "Gillespie maybe won't even find him, if he's gotten into the Klamath country. That's a thicket up there."

Catharine said, "Frémont is a distinctly fragile reed. Whatever it is he's here for, I don't think we can depend on him being able to do it, or on whatever it is he does do being in our interest. He's already hung us up once with the dons."

Zeke growled, behind her. "That Gillespie's another one. Every time I see anybody connected with the U.S. government it reminds me why I'm in California."

There was a gust of laughter over this, and men pushed closer to the table. Zeke moved up beside Catharine, put both hands on the table, and braced himself over it, his big graying head thrust forward.

"Captain, you're out of it?"

"Yes, I am," said Sutter.

"Then I say the rest of us go over to Sonoma and arrest General Vallejo," Zeke said.

Catharine sat up straight, startled. Sutter said, "Whoa, now."

John Bidwell moved forward a few steps. "That's more like it. Zeke, you're the general."

Kelsey said, "If there's a war, Vallejo's the closest don to us, and we'll have him in our laps in a week. Zeke's right, strike first. You can deal me in."

Around the table the others pressed forward, nodding, their voices loud. Catharine glanced at Sutter, impassive in his chair.

"You ought to think twice about this," she said quietly. "It won't be good for any of us if we're conquered."

Sutter grunted at her. "The dons aren't going to conquer us."

"The dons!" she said. "The hell with the dons. I'm talking about the United States."

Sutter's lips pushed together into a thoughtful purse. For a moment she thought he might change his mind, but then he said, "First you tell me not to fight, now you tell me to fight." He laughed, reaching for his glass. "I'll stay and watch."

Cat's heart was galloping. Around her the other men were boisterous, their voices crackling, their faces harsh and eager.

Kelsey said, "Everybody has to have a gun. We need powder, shot —"

Every man in the room was on his feet now. The door banged open. Rising from his chair, Ide reached for his hat. "We can pick up a few people on the way. There's Todd, we can go by his ranch, and Semple."

"Down to the yard," Zeke shouted. "Everybody gather down there soon's you're armed and got your horse."

Catharine said, "I'm going with you."

Sutter reached out and grabbed her arm. "No, you're not."

She wheeled around toward him, clawing at his grip on her arm. "Damn it! Somebody has to look out for our interests, if you won't."

He let go of her, but he frowned, and the look held her a moment, better than his grasp. He said, low, "You better hope you're doing the right thing, Cat."

She put her hand on her wrist, where he had held her, and looked around. The men nearest the door were already pushing out, their voices rumbling. The stair outside boomed under their feet. There was a whoop in the yard, like a wolf howling.

She went up to Zeke Merritt on the threshold and got in his way. "I've been here longer than a lot of you, and worked harder than most of you. I'm going if I have to walk."

The room was fast emptying. Bidwell started around them toward the door. His face was red with high humor. In passing, he gripped Zeke's arm. "Bring her. You know she'll do the job. I got a gentle mule she can ride."

Zeke nodded to her. "You're in, lady."

36 ✠ IN THE GRAY FALSE DAWN Mariano Vallejo
woke. One of his chamber servants was bending over him, murmuring, "Don General, oh, Don General —"

"What is it?" The don of Sonoma pried open his eyes.
Dreams still colored his mind; the warmth and darkness of his
curtained bed enshrouded him. His wife snored on beside him.

"Don General. Outside —"

His wife muttered, "Husband, the light is on," and rolled
away.

"Be still, dear one." Vallejo swung his legs out of the bed.
The servant was waiting to put a silk dressing gown around his
shoulders. The Indian's eyes were shiny with fear; yawning,
Vallejo went to the window overlooking the plaza.

What he saw went through him like an electric shock. "Wake
my brother," he said. Peering out the window, he counted the
men riding into the plaza below. At a gesture his servants hurried up to help him dress.

His brother Salvador tramped in, pulling his shirt on. "What
is this?" He came up beside Vallejo and looked out the window,
and an oath exploded from him. "What is this?"

"Sutter's men," Vallejo said. "I recognize the big one there.
How many men have we here?"

"Eighteen," said his brother. He was staring out the window,
unmoving. Vallejo stooped to look over his shoulder.

In the broad, treeless plaza, a swarm of Missouri men were
spreading out, their guns across their saddlebows. There were
more than twenty of them. They took up positions around the
plaza, covering every building along it; two of them waited at
the entrance on the far side of the square, rifles in their arms.
The big man, his head hidden by a shapeless brown hat, walked
up toward the front door of the Casa Grande.

"Zeke Merritt," said General Vallejo.

His brother straightened. "Shall I summon the men?" From
below there was the thunder of a knock on the door.

Vallejo was chewing rapidly through this. For weeks he had
heard rumors of wars, but everything had seemed too far away

to matter. Now it was walking up to his house and pounding on his door.

"No," he said. "They're too well armed, and we are too unready. I am going down there now to speak to them." He rubbed his palms over his unruly hair, thinning at the crown. "You will do exactly as I say in this, no matter what your own opinion."

"Naturally."

Mariano looked around the room. His sword hung on the wall; he considered taking it down, but against a Missouri man with a gun a saber would only be a provocation. He turned to his wife, sitting up in the bed behind him.

"Get the children together, and stay up here," he said, and went out to the stairway and down the stairs to the front of his house, toward the impatient banging on the door.

Vallejo received his importunate guests in the hall at the front of the Casa Grande, where he did most of his business. This was a huge room, large enough for a crowd of men, with a rubbed oak table in the middle and a sideboard and some chairs; the windows along the front were still shuttered, but some light came in through an open window at the far end of the room and the pale walls held it, so the room was bright enough. Vallejo sat down at the head of the table and nodded to an Indian servant, who opened the door. Salvador Vallejo stood at his brother's right hand.

Zeke Merritt tramped forward; his brows were pulled down over his glowering red-rimmed eyes. Behind him came another Anglo, armed with a rifle.

"Remember me, don?" He spoke in Spanish.

Vallejo lifted his head and gave him a cold stare. "With considerable distaste."

Merritt stood with his feet apart, planted, his rifle hooked in his elbow, his other hand a fist. "Well, I'm about to give you more of a distaste." He twitched his head back toward the tall man behind him. "This-here is Bob Semple, and I'm Ezekiel

Merritt. We're taking over here, Don Vallejo. You're under arrest."

Salvador let out a grunt. Mariano Vallejo only raised his eyebrows. "Well," he said. He kept his voice smooth, almost bored. "Let me offer you gentlemen something to drink. Sit down; we'll talk about this."

"I'd like a drink," Bob Semple said. "We done rode two days straight, getting here."

"Sure," said Zeke Merritt. He pulled one of the carved chairs away from the table. "We got forty men outside. Don't try anything." Laying down his rifle on the sleek oak tabletop, he sat down straddling the chair.

"Salvador," said Mariano, "how many are there actually?"

"I counted twenty-four," his brother said.

"That's enough," Zeke said. He laid his hand on the rifle. His dark eyes drilled intently into Vallejo.

"I suspect you are right," the don said. Behind Merritt the Indians padded into the room, bringing cups and glasses and several jugs of brandy. "You did say you were thirsty."

The Indians in their white shirts moved silently around the room, serving as they had been taught to serve; with no more presence than shadows they put a cup before each man and set a jug at each end of the table.

"Is the United States at war with Mexico?" Vallejo asked.

"If it wasn't before," Zeke said, "it is now." He reached for the cup in front of him.

Cat Reilly slept for hours after they reached Sonoma, lying with her head on a saddle and her body curled up inside the buffalo coat. The glare of the noonday sun woke her up. She yawned, stretching, gave a long, keen look at the soaring three-story tower of the Big House, and turned to John Bidwell, who was sitting nearby, reading a book. "What's happened?"

"Nothing," John said.

"Nothing. How long ago did Zeke go in there?" She stood up, shading her eyes.

"Four-five hours ago." He shut the book, his forefinger holding his place. "Thing is, we sent Bob Grigsby in about two hours ago, and he hasn't come out either."

Cat looked around her. Bleached in the summer sun, the broad plaza was scattered over with the individual camps of the men from New Helvetia. Most of them sprawled in the dust, dozing or talking; along the far edge of the plaza, where the wall of buildings opened up to the valley beyond, somebody was riding along on sentry duty, his rifle in his arms. Some local people had come out of their houses to stare at the Americans, and a few of the bolder ones were peddling tortillas and brandy and eggs; several of the men from New Helvetia had gathered around a woman with a basket. In the windows of other houses, behind the screens, there were clusters of faces. The quiet was like a density of the air itself, sluggish with the heat.

William Ide and Ben Kelsey came back from the peddler woman, their hands full and their cheeks stuffed. Kelsey said, "Here, grab this," and turned so that Catharine could take the jug he carried pinned under his elbow.

Ide said, "Any sign of Zeke or Bob Grigsby?"

"No," John Bidwell said. "It's too damn quiet, too. Look up there."

He nodded up at the flagpole in the middle of the plaza, the green Mexican flag drooping from its peak in the windless air.

"We've been here since dawn and that flag is still flying there. We're not making any progress. Maybe they have Zeke prisoner."

Ide said, "Somebody ought to go in there and find out what's going on."

Catharine said, "That's a good idea." She walked a little toward the Big House, peering at the shuttered windows. "Come on."

Ide hitched his suspenders up. "Hold on, now, missus, we got to do this in order. Kelsey and you and I will go in. John, you keep an eye on things out here. If we don't come back out pretty soon, all of you better come in after us." He turned to Kelsey. "Got a weapon?"

"Yeah."

"Missus?" He looked her over, paternal.

Kelsey said, "She don't need one. Come on."

They walked down through the plaza toward the blocky tower of the Big House. Cat raked her hair back with her hands. The stillness unnerved her. Surely there would be more to a revolution than this. Behind Ide she went up to the front door and found it open; the hallway was jammed with Indian servants doing nothing.

When the Americans came in, the Indians fled away down the dim red-tiled corridor, a flock of white shirts and pattering bare feet. Ide strode on ahead of Catharine and Kelsey to the first door on the right.

"What's going on here? Where's Zeke Merritt?" Ide walked into the room beyond. Kelsey and Catharine followed him.

"Welcome, all of you," Mariano Vallejo said. "Come in and have a drink. Dr. Semple seems to be having some difficulty with his diction. Perhaps you can help."

Bob Semple sat at the table about a third of the way down from Salvador Vallejo, a piece of paper on the table before him, a pen in his hand; he stared owlishly at the three newcomers, his head weaving slightly.

At the far end of the table Zeke Merritt sat with his head down on his arms, snoring. Bob Grigsby slumped in another chair; his face showed complete absorption in a reality other than theirs. The air smelled sharply of brandy.

Cat went around the table to look over Bob Semple's shoulder; he had covered both sides of the page with script but crossed it all out. While she tried to read through the marks, he reached for his cup on the table before him, said sadly, "I just can't find the words," and folded quietly forward, his head in his arms.

"Have you been doing this in Spanish?" she said. There was more paper scattered all over the floor behind the chair, most of it also written on. She searched for a clean sheet and sat down.

Ide went forward to the side of the table. "Zeke," he said, "you're impeached." His dark eyes, hooded in seams and wrinkles, went to the paper under Catharine's hand and then to the man at the head of the table. "You're Don Vallejo?"

"I am Mariano Guadalupe Vallejo."

"My name's William Ide, from Massachusetts originally." Ide held his hand out to Vallejo, who took it with only a moment's pause. "We'll have to do this in English. I don't speak Spanish. Are you surrendering?"

"If you require it," Vallejo said, "I cannot but agree, since you have the guns."

Ide laid his rifle down on the table, pulled a chair back, and sat down, his hands neatly folded before him. He looked at Salvador. "This is your brother."

"Yes. He will concur in everything I —"

Behind them, in the corridor, there was a bang and a crash and the Indians scattered away into the depths of the building.

With Bidwell leading them, half a dozen of the Americans charged into the room behind Vallejo, some pushing to the right and some to the left. Catharine stood up. Zeke Merritt's big Hawken Plains rifle lay on the table in front of her, and she put her hand on it.

The crowd was surging into the corridor. She thought she heard feet on the stairs. The doorway into this hall was so narrow that the men fought to get through, and they were shouting, and some of the men already in the room were pulling open the cabinets in the sideboard.

Ide climbed up onto the table. "Hold up. Stop!"

In the uproar nobody heard him. A chair fell over. A window shutter broke and the sun streamed in like a veil of white light. Vallejo wheeled around, his face bright red. "They're looting my house!"

An American voice bellowed, "Where's the gold?" Wood splintered and crashed. "Somebody said there was gold!"

Catharine picked up Zeke's rifle. They had to stop this, at least long enough to talk, and she aimed the big gun at the wall and swung the hammer back, surprised at the smooth, light pull. Her finger hardly touched the trigger. The gun went off before she expected it, with a roar that hurt her ears and a recoil that drove her back down into the chair. On the wall, a huge crater opened in the adobe, showering dust.

The shot broke the din. Every man in the room crouched down, ducking, and in the sudden silence, Ide yelled, "Hold still! Listen to me!"

Their faces wheeled toward him. He walked up and down on the table, shouting at them like a schoolmaster.

"I didn't come all this way just to have this thing fall apart like this. Stand up still and pay attention! We have Sonoma. We have the Vallejos here, we're writing up the proclamation, all we got to do is figure out what to say. But we're going to do it right."

The men were watching him, attentive. Catharine put the Plains gun down on the table again. Ide was still pacing along the tabletop, his boot soles squeaking in the silence.

"Bidwell! Take three-four men and scout the house. No looting. Anybody steals anything, anybody tries to turn this into common brigandage, I'll throw him in jail." His gaze switched to Vallejo. "You got a jail?" Vallejo nodded.

Bidwell was already moving toward the door, calling men out of the crowd as he went by. The Indians stuffed the corridor beyond the door; they flocked away as he passed and then rushed forward again to peer into the room.

"We need a flag," Ide said. "You, Todd, make us a flag."

Todd was one of the men they had gathered in on the ride over from New Helvetia. He lifted his head. "What kind of flag?"

"An American flag," Ide said.

"No!" said Cat.

They gaped at her. She climbed up onto the table beside Ide.

"We can't do that. We're all Americans, but Sutter isn't; a lot of people in California are not American, and that flag won't do for them. We need our own flag. We need a California flag."

Ben Kelsey called out, "We need our own country, all the way."

"Hey," somebody else said, "I'm an American, that's good enough for me."

"So am I," Ben said. "But she's got a point. If the United

States walks in here with guns blazing and takes over, we lose everything."

There was a mutter from the other men. Ide stepped forward. "All right. We need our own flag. Our own country. Then we can ask to go into the Union, like Texas did, and they have to agree to our terms. They have to let us keep what we've made here."

"There you go," Ben Kelsey shouted. "The California Republic!" From the rest of the men there came a single-throated yell.

Cat climbed down off the table. Somebody whacked her jovially on the back. She flung a smile down the table to Ben Kelsey, who gave her a crisp nod; his eyes were bright. The other men were passing a jug, and another whoop went up.

"The California Republic!"

Ide nodded down to the Kentuckian, William Todd. "Make us a flag, sonny." His gaze traveled over the people remaining in the room. "We got to write a proclamation. Anybody have any ideas?"

They were silent for a moment. Then somebody behind Cat said, "Free and equal, that's all you got to say." The rest of them murmured in agreement.

"All right," said Ide. He turned to Cat. "You can write this down, missus."

"I'm ready," she said.

Late in the afternoon they came out into the plaza, and all the Americans gathered around the flagpole. Ide lowered the Mexican flag and attached the flag of the California Republic to the halyard.

Rooting around in a chest in the back of Vallejo's house, Todd had found a big piece of white muslin and a strip of red flannel. From the red flannel he cut a star, which he put in one corner of the flag with a saddlemaker's awl, and sewed the rest of the red flannel along the bottom. Above that he wrote CALIFORNIA REPUBLC; when somebody pointed out to him that he had misspelled it, he put a large *I* in between the *L* and the

C. Above that he drew a large animal standing on all fours, facing the star.

"That's a bear," he said, and it looked as much like a bear as anything else.

Ide read the proclamation, which said only that the Americans had come to California with peaceful intentions and now the dons were trying to run them out, and that out of self-defense and the need for order they were proclaiming that California was now a free country, where all people were equal and the government would serve everybody equally, the first president and commander in chief being William Ide. Ide folded the proclamation and ran the Bear Flag up the pole.

The Americans whooped. Turning to one another they began to shake hands and pound each other on the back. Kelsey flung an arm around Catharine. "We done something here, Cat. I'm not sure what, but we done it."

She said, "Yes, I think so, Ben." She put her hands out to John Bidwell, who hugged her.

"Whatever happens," Bidwell said, "it won't be the same again." He smelled of horses and wood shavings. She held on to him longer than she had to. He rubbed his cheek against her forehead.

Behind him Zeke Merritt stood, staring up at the flag. She said, "Zeke, I have your rifle."

"Hunh." He peered down at her; his face looked as if it had been put together from pieces. His hand pawed at his beard. "Not sure I want it now — heard some female shot it off." In the beard his stained teeth showed.

The people of Sonoma were coming out of the buildings along the plaza. Quietly they gathered along the edge, Indian servants in their white shirts, Californios in their reds and yellows, their embroidered black, peering up at the new flag, at the twenty-four Americans in their booming self-congratulation. After a while Bidwell climbed up on a chair and read the proclamation again. Above them the new flag wobbled in the wind.

Catharine watched the local people, wondering why they did not cheer, why they did not join this. Maybe they were still unsure of what was going on. When they understood what was happening, that now they were free, they would join the Bear Flag too. The California Republic. She looked up at the flag rolling and flapping in the wind, and her chest swelled with satisfaction.

By the window his brother wheeled around, still angry.

"Mariano, they are not raising the American flag. It's some other stupid rag they have up there."

"Be quiet," said General Vallejo. "I told you, I will handle this."

In the doorway from the corridor, something moved, and he looked and saw Catharine Reilly on the threshold. Without waiting to be invited the woman walked into the room, her hands clasped before her; she was as rough and wild as the men, but she was a woman still, and from what he had seen of her before, he thought he could trust her.

She said, "General Vallejo, you sent for me?" She sounded surprised. The green eyes were wide and clear.

"I did, Señora. If you please, I present my brother Don Salvador Vallejo."

Salvador muttered something at her over his shoulder. He was not adjusting well to this. General Vallejo, who understood the necessity of adjustment, drew Catharine Reilly over to a corner, where they could speak.

He said, "You know my brother and I are being arrested and taken to Sutter's Fort."

"Yes," she said. "John Bidwell will escort you." Her skin was brown as a peasant's.

He said, "Mrs. Reilly, I would be most grateful if you would take my wife and children under your protection while I am gone."

Her face opened, her eyes bright with surprise. "General, I promise you, we aren't going to hurt anybody." In her low, throaty voice there was an undertone of indignation. She licked her lips. "Where are they?"

"Upstairs. I have spoken with my wife; she understands what is happening here. But I will feel more easy if I know they have you here to champion them."

She said, "I will." She put her hand out to him. "I'm sorry, General. I promise you, your family will be safe."

"Thank you." He shook her hand, which she obviously expected, an Anglo rite confirming an agreement. Her gaze slipped past him to his brother, still standing there with his back to her; between her thick black eyebrows, above her nose, two vertical creases appeared.

She said, "I hope you have an easy ride, General." Without any more than that, she turned and went out of the room.

Salvador said, "How can you talk to these people?"

"Because I have to," said General Vallejo. He moved uneasily around the room, his hands together, a guest in his own house. There was no value in wasting his time in anger. It was nothing, this incident, this Bear Flag, this humiliation, only the first ripple of the rising wave that he had known for years was coming. What mattered was to endure it until that higher crest was by. He paced across the room again, unable to be still.

Cat had not gone up the stairway into the second story of the Vallejo house before. One hand on the railing, she went to find Vallejo's family.

Most of the servants had retreated here, and the upstairs corridor was full of them. She wanted to tell them that they were free now, but if they came at her with a lot of questions her Spanish would give out quickly. They moved back as she passed, their eyes following her, saying nothing as she went by, breaking into a hum of voices when she was beyond them. At the last door she stopped, her muscles gathered, and knocked.

An Indio woman opened it. Without a word she backed away, and Catharine went by her into a wide, sunlit room full of women and children.

They all shrank away from her, the children running into the midst of the women. Massed against the far wall, they stared at her. She cast a quick look around. This was a sitting room, with a fine Oriental carpet on a plank floor, stools and chairs, and the women's work all around — sewing kits and embroidery in hoops, a basket full of uncarded wool.

One of the women, tall, older than Catharine, came a few steps toward her. "You are Mrs. Reilly?"

Catharine summoned up her little Spanish. "I am Cat Reilly. Are you Señora Vallejo?" She glanced at the faces packed along the wall, their black eyes staring at her, and lowered her gaze again to this woman before her, who was not tall, as she had first thought, but only held herself so well she seemed to be.

"I am the wife of Don Mariano Vallejo," she said proudly.

"He asked me to . . ." Catharine staggered along with her scraps of Spanish. ". . . help you. I —" She had arranged for them to be fed and to keep their servants around them; none of the Americans seemed to be bothering them. She had no words to say this with. She said, "I will help you."

"Curse you," somebody else cried, which was a word she did know.

Doña Vallejo moved back a step, startled, and put out her hand. From the group along the wall an old woman marched toward Catharine, her face a wedge, driving her words in. "Curse you, curse you, curse you —" The general's wife got her by the shoulders, whispering something, and the old woman struggled angrily to free herself, still snarling at Catharine. Doña Vallejo's voice turned louder, abruptly, and the old woman shut her mouth and turned and walked back in with the others. They closed around her like wings.

Catharine swallowed. She felt as if she had been pelted by stones, and she ran her hand over her face and back across her hair. Doña Vallejo was watching her with a patient, bitter stare.

"What do you need?" Catharine asked her.

"My husband," said the other woman. "I need my husband here."

"He will be safe," she said. "Nothing bad will come to him."

The face before her cracked like a nut. For an instant the woman looked at her with a fierce rage and contempt. "It already has!" With an effort Doña Vallejo reshaped her expression; her skin was soft and fine and pale. Her eyes glittered with hatred, like the old woman's. "Thank you very much," she said. "You may go now."

Catharine went out. She was stupid to let the old woman's outburst bother her; these people would be much better off now, all of them, they just had to get used to it. She went down the stairs into the ground floor of the house, where a lot of the Bears were loitering, waiting for something else to happen. At the foot of the stairs Bob Semple folded his length against the railing post, drinking from a bottle of wine.

"Where'd you get that?" she asked.

"In back. Hey, Vallejo's got a lot of good stuff here." He held the bottle down to her. "Have a swig, Cat."

The kink of alarm worked its way a little deeper into her. They were, imperceptibly, looting this place. Nevertheless she took the bottle and drank, to steady her nerves.

37 ✍ NORTH OF SUTTER'S great valley, where the mountains loomed up into peaks and crowns covered with snow even in the summer, the forest grew thick and dark and damp, cedars and firs through which the trails of animals and Indians burrowed like the dismal tunnels of trolls. The land was tipped on edge, rising sheer from the narrow bottoms of the river canyons into jagged ridges like rock blades, knifing the sky. Pushing into this new country, this wilderness, Frémont collected specimens and drew pictures and made notes on the wildlife, the plants, and the rocks, and turned his back on California.

The men he had met in the San Joaquin, Ned Kern's men, had split off from Frémont's expedition at Peter Lassen's ranch under the mountains to seek a trail east over the high desert. Frémont now had only fourteen men with him, the best of them, Kit and Basil, Luke Maxwell and Alexis Godey, the Delaware Indians who were the same as the whites in dress and talk and actions, all but their skins. In spite of the dank cold and the miserable gray skies Frémont's spirits had improved.

The other men clattered around the camp, getting ready for the night; they had staked the horses and mules out along the edge of the river that ran sluggishly through the dark trees. Kit was coming up from that direction, a bucket of water in one hand, his saddle against the other hip. Overhead, the jeering and fluttering of a flock of crows busied the high branches. A mosquito hummed in Frémont's ear, and he swatted at it.

Basil Lajeunesse went up past him to the fire and reached down to feel the coffeepot. Frémont put his notebooks away in the case. "Is that going to be ready soon?" The first flavor of coffee reached his nose. He stood up, his knees creaking in the dreary damp.

"Captain!"

"Over here." While he was searching around him for his coffee cup, one of the Delawares came panting up through the barred twilight.

"Captain, there's somebody here."

Frémont straightened, his hands at his sides. Beyond the Delaware two strangers were stumbling forward through his camp.

"Who are they?" A tingle of alarm ran down his spine.

"Captain Frémont?" A slight man in a filthy uniform climbed across a rotting log to reach him, his hand held out. "I am Lieutenant Gillespie, U.S. Marine Corps, sir."

Frémont clutched the hand stretched toward him. "Good to see you, sir! How far you've come — Basil, some coffee — Lieutenant, what's the news?" His belly clamped up against his backbone. He knew what the news was.

Gillespie slapped a mosquito on his neck. His face was lumpy with insect bites and patchy with fatigue. Through the trees the other men were gathering, and he cast a quick look around at them and took a packet wrapped in oilcloth from his coat. "These will explain, sir." He stepped back and unfurled a weary salute.

Kit surged forward, swiping at the letters. "Damn! Tell us what's the news! Has the war started?"

Gillespie stood slumped, as if a hook held him up by the nape of the neck. "The war has begun. General Zachary Taylor has invaded Mexico. When I passed through Mexico on my way here, all the way across, I saw troops moving north to the Rio Grande."

Kit and the other men gave a yell. Frémont clenched his fists behind him, his heart pounding. He had thought this gone by, and now here it was before him again.

Kit was on fire. He wheeled toward him, his fists cocked. "Now, Captain!"

"It's too late to break camp tonight." Frémont gathered himself. His duty was there. He had to go back; he was an officer in the United States Army. In Gillespie's oilcloth packet surely were orders sending him to war. Evenly he said, "In the morning we will turn back to California." There would be no order telling him to hurry.

Kit roared. He flung one arm around Basil Lajeunesse and the other around Luke Maxwell. "The Angel done talked to Captain Frémont! O' course by now the fuckin' war is over. Captain, send somebody for Ned Kern and get those other men back here."

Frémont glanced at Basil and Luke Maxwell, both taller than Kit, flanking him like the lion and the unicorn. Before these men, before Gillespie, he had to hold his command. He said, "I'll give the orders, Kit."

Kit said, "Send for him!"

"When I choose!"

The scout's face twisted, his gaze on Frémont like a barb, but Basil caught him by the arm. Murmuring in his ear he pulled him off. Kit turned on his heel and strode away toward the horse lines, his friends trailing after him. Frémont sat down again, his mouth dry, and his chest tight.

Gillespie sank onto the log next to him, wiping his face on a handkerchief. "If you don't mind, sir. That's a long, hard ride."

"Yes, yes, at ease, Lieutenant. You did very well. Give me the letters."

The marine held out the oilcloth packet. Somebody brought him and Frémont each a cup of coffee. Gillespie said, "Are there Indians around here?" He yawned.

"Klamaths," said Frémont. "We passed one of their villages a few days ago." The Klamaths had been fishing in the river for salmon; they had traded with Frémont's men but had refused to guide them on, and their sharp dealings over the salmon had made everybody angry.

Inside the packet were his orders, letters from the Secretary of State, from the Secretary of the Navy, from his father-in-law, Senator Benton, from his dear little wife, Jessie. He held them all in his hand for a moment. When he looked up, Archie Gillespie was asleep, still sitting on the log, his head drooping on his chest.

Frémont opened Benton's letter first. The first line of it read, "You will now surely be in command of California . . ."

The piece of paper rattled in his fingers. His ears and neck burned.

Night was coming, a thickening in the air, as if the dripping, entangled trees exhaled some dark fume into the space between them. He crept closer to the fire. The men were bedding down around him; somebody moved Archie Gillespie down into the shelter of the side of the log and put a blanket over him. Frémont read the rest of the letters by the firelight, bending down to hold them in the faint red glow.

The official letters all said the same thing, the same phrases, "to secure the lives and property of American citizens against aggression," "to support American military forces wherever possible." Everything that could be safely written from a distance of three thousand miles, by men ignorant of the situation — which meant nothing useful.

Kit came up to him, stretching. "I'm going to sleep a couple hours. Make sure the sentries are posted." He nudged Frémont's knee with the toe of his moccasin. "Does that make it easier, Captain? Think you can do it now?" With a wave of his hand he tramped away.

Frémont's packs and blankets were tucked in under the spread branches of a cedar tree behind him, but he did not go crawl into that shelter to sleep. He hunched down in the warmth of the banked fire. His belly hurt.

Somehow now he had another chance at California, if he

could only keep Kit under control and aim him in the right direction. Now he had official sanction. Glory awaited him with all her riches. Yet half of him pulled back, like a raped bride, unwilling to do it twice.

Down by the river a mule nickered. He got up, more for the ease of moving than anything else, and drifted off through the camp. The night's clammy cold made his skin ache. The horses and mules stood quietly at their lines, unmoving; perhaps he had heard nothing. He went back up to the fire and sat down again.

The letter from his wife was really no different from the others. She talked of her Glorious Hero and the Great American Cause and Destiny Made History, all in her beautiful handwriting that reminded him of the tendrils on grapevines. There were a few little notes about his daughter, Lily, who was four now, who would not remember him, tiny girl in her blue organdy pinafore. He kissed his wife's signature.

Out there, on the far side of the camp, there was a thunk. Frémont jerked his head up; then, off to one side, Kit yelled, "Basil?"

"Get your guns," Frémont shouted, and dropped belly first to the ground; crawling like a worm, he lunged toward the cedar where his rifle was. Through the trees a lot of men were running toward him, and now he could hear the swish-swish of arrows.

Before he pulled his rifle to his shoulder, the men around him were firing, the light, spitting bang of muskets, the louder, flatter shot of Hawken rifles. He swung his front sight around, laid it on a figure running through the trees ahead of him, cocked the hammer, and pulled the trigger.

He never saw if he hit anything; even hunting buffalo he was never really sure he killed anything. Lying halfway under the shelter of the cedar's branches, he scrabbled around for his pouch and horn, poured powder into the rifle muzzle, measuring it as he had learned to do in the dark by counting to two. He dampened the ball in his mouth and spat it in after, banged the butt of the rifle against the ground to seat it, laid the rifle down again and thumbed a percussion cap onto the nipple under the hammer, swayed the front sight back and forth across the forest until he saw what looked like an Indian, cocked the action and pulled the trigger. He did this over and over, while in the dark around him other men screamed and guns went off and the fires crackled and exploded, until Kit yelled, "Stop!"

Frémont stopped. He put his head down against the rifle's greasy stock and shut his eyes, panting as if he had run across the plains.

Slowly he got up, the front of his clothes soaked from lying on the ground, and went down to the nearest fire. Luke Maxwell knelt there in the mud, coughing. He choked out, "Got him right in the head, right in the head, and split it like a melon."

Other men moved up through the darkness beside them.

"Crane's dead. He took five arrows." Crane was one of the Delawares.

"Where's Kit?" Frémont looked around for the scout. "Who's dead? Crane and who else?"

Luke wiped his mouth. "Basil Lajeunesse."

"Oh, no."

"Cracked his head open with an ax, Captain."

"Anybody else?" Frémont moved around, counting heads. Gillespie showed up, shivering in his blankets, haggard. Somebody had put the coffeepot on the fire, and the aroma floated through the air.

"Denny, the half-breed. You see that Indian leading them? God, what a charge."

"Damn, he took six, eight shots."

Frémont went off through the trees to the next fire. The attack had come from the far side of the camp, along the bank of the river; all the dead men were lying there near the picket string of the animals. So the mule had nickered after all. Frémont looked down at the sprawled, bloody bodies of his men, his chest clamped tight with remorse. Kit walked up to him, stooped, and laid his hand on Basil's arm.

When he straightened, he was staring into Frémont's face. "I told you to see those sentries were posted."

"They were posted," Frémont said. "Denny was the sentry —

there." He pointed to the middle of the three dead men. He had to defend himself against that steady glare; he forced away his guilt. He looked Kit in the eyes and made a deal with him: Basil for California. "Let's pack up and get out of here. It's not more than a few hours before daylight, anyway. And send Luke to catch Ned Kern."

He could see only the shape of Kit's face in the dim light of the fire, but the scout's eyes glinted. Finally Kit said, "Whatever you say, Captain." His voice was heavy with contempt. Stooping, he bent over his friend again. Frémont went away to organize the men.

38 ✤ CAT GOT UP and left the room. The men's voices rose behind her, arguing again, louder than before. She stood a moment in the passageway listening to them, to Zeke, roaring about guns and scouts and powder, and to Ide, insisting on writing everything down, and to half a dozen others. All they did was talk. They spun every decision down fine as a thread, tangled it up, and then worked it all out again, over and over; they never got to the end. She went out of Vallejo's house into the quiet twilit plaza.

Sonoma still surprised her. She had not expected a place this size, with more people than at Sutter's Fort, maybe more than in Yerba Buena, living in the adobes that enclosed this broad square. She walked out across the plaza toward the flagpole. On all sides, lamps burned in the windows of the houses; she heard people laughing and talking.

Since they raised the Bear Flag men had been streaming in to join them. There were more than ninety Americans in Sonoma now, and they had taken over several of the buildings. Some had been empty, some not. The dispossessed families had moved in with neighbors. There had been no real trouble, all the local people having fallen into General Vallejo's attitude of complaisance.

None of the locals had joined the Bear Flag. She wondered if under their bland surface of acceptance they were hoarding up curses, like the old woman's, and against her will she was realizing how this would have seemed to her, had it been Sutter's Fort and not Sonoma.

She went by a gate in the blank wall of a house, and through the grillework saw, for an instant, shapes moving back and forth. Those were the people who belonged here. There were Californios all around her, and they had to be dealt with, but half the Americans couldn't even talk to them.

She went out to the south edge of the plaza, where the guns were. Rummaging through the Vallejos' armory, in the old mission barracks that was now used as a stable, Zeke Merritt had found eight brass cannon, in pieces, but with their trucks and hardware piled around them. In another room were a heap of old muskets and a keg of gunpowder. The eight big guns were now lined up along the front of the Sonoma plaza, facing south, toward General Castro. There was enough powder and shot to fire each one of them once. Cat went along behind them, from one cold, gleaming barrel to the next, and stood by the last one looking south, down the dark valley.

She wanted to go back to Sutter's Fort, where her work was, had wanted to go with John Bidwell, when he took the Vallejo brothers away, but she could not. She had to stay here, waiting for General Castro's counterattack.

In taking Sonoma the Bears had, mostly by accident, made the best use of their strength. They had removed the Californios' only base north of San Francisco Bay, so that the vast waterway of the bay and the delta now lay between them and the southern dons, a better defense than a hundred big guns.

Maybe the dons would simply let the Bear Flag have the north. She doubted that. Eventually they would mount some retribution, and she knew who would be leading it.

John Christenson rode around the outside corner of the building, his rifle slung in the crook of his arm. "Hey, lady."

"Hey, Chris. Everything quiet?" she asked.

He rode past her. "Like a church."

She watched him pass by. In a few hours she would ride her stretch of patrol duty, too. She had insisted on it, screaming at Zeke when he tried to go on about women's place; she had to have something to do. She wanted to be in Sutter's Fort, working, playing her piano, not here, where she was idle so much, where the men all looked sideways at her. Here where what she had thought she had done was turning out to be something quite different, where everything was making her think about a man she wanted to forget. But she had begun this, and now she could wait here to see what became of it.

He had told her this would happen. Bitterly she was awakening to a wider sense of it; there was more going on here than she had thought. He had said that. She folded her arms, looking down the valley, waiting for Castro's army.

39

SUTTER WENT UP to the Feather River, looking for a site where he could try again to build a sawmill. Most of the men of New Helvetia had gone off to Sonoma to join the Bear Flag, and the wheat crop had been reaped and threshed, giving him some open time. The harvest had been tremendous, yielding thousands of *fanegas* of wheat to pay the Russians, to placate his other creditors; it seemed to him that the work of building New Helvetia was finally beginning to take hold. The future spread out before him as wide and sunny as his valley.

The first warmth of summer was gilding the flat country along the river. Off to his right the tops of the Sierra floated above the haze, a thin, jagged line of white, like the edge of a higher world. He had a road to follow now, his settlers' road, rutted with tracks, and around him, now and again, he passed one of their cabins, or the road to it, or saw their smoke — his people, in his kingdom.

All along the Sacramento River the Indians were gathering for their summer dances. He had let his Indians go for a while, since there was no work, so that they could join the festival too. Brush huts stood like little hives in every curve of the river bar, children played in the mud, fish weirs rippled the shallows. As Sutter rode by, the Indians turned and stared at him; they all recognized him, so that his name trailed him up the river like a wake.

He spent the night at the Feather River fork and in the morning went on, keeping a watch out for a good place for the sawmill but looking also for signs of the camp he knew was here somewhere. Lassen had sent him word that Frémont was moving south again; talk was that the mapmaker was somewhere around the buttes to the east of the river here. When Sutter crossed the fresh trail of several bunched horses headed toward the hills, he left the river and followed.

The buttes stood on the flat river valley like chunks rolled down off the top of the Sierra. As he came closer he saw a column of smoke rising over the high humped shoulder of the nearest hill. He rode around through the drying grass and came into a little draw.

"Hold it! Call out!"

He reined in, not seeing the sentry; the mouth of the draw was choked with oaks and brush. The smoke rose beyond it, up between the steep, wind-blown flanks of the hill. "It's John Sutter. I want to see Frémont."

One of the Delawares walked out of the brush. "Hello, Captain. Come along with me." He turned and put two fingers in his mouth and whistled, and from the far side of the draw a long, shrill whistle answered him. Sutter rode after the Indian back up the draw.

With a creek running along one edge and the steep hillsides sheltering it, this canyon was a lake of grass, riven by the shallow, sandy courses of old flood channels. Frémont's men were camped along the creekbank from near the mouth of the draw to the creased hillside at its head. Their horses and mules were beating the high grass down in swaths. Sutter rode along the sprawling camp, aware of their stirring interest; a lot of them stopped what they were doing to follow him.

He rode up to the main campfire, under a tree, and Frémont and the marine lieutenant, Archie Gillespie, came forward into the sun to meet him. Kit Carson stayed behind in the shade, watching intently, his hat brim pulled down over his eyes.

Sutter dismounted, jovial, his hand out to the Americans. "Hello again, gentlemen."

Frémont and Gillespie both stood there with their hands behind them and stared at him. Frémont said, "Are you here to spy or to capitulate, Colonel Sutter?"

Sutter's hand fell to his side. For a moment he was quiet, collecting himself in the face of this unexpected hostility. When he spoke he kept his voice even.

"I assure you, Captain Frémont, the Mexican flag no longer flies at Sutter's Fort." He looked from Frémont to Gillespie's scowling face and beyond them to Kit Carson. "You haven't heard about the revolution?"

Frémont's lips parted. Gillespie said, "What revolution?" From behind them Carson barged in between them.

"What revolution?"

Sutter smoothed his mustache between thumb and forefinger. "Some of the Americans seized Vallejo's stronghold at Sonoma. They've raised their own flag, the Bear Flag, and proclaimed a republic. California is free, gentlemen." He had to smile; their faces twitched and hardened as he spoke as if his words struck them. Carson wheeled and tramped away across the camp to stare at nothing.

"Who?" Frémont said.

Sutter said mildly, "Some of the American settlers." He folded his arms over his chest; if, as he suspected, this was beyond his control, beyond anybody's control, at least he could amuse himself watching the others dance.

Frémont shouted at him, "Who? Answer me!" His face was pale as fish skin, his eyes sleek.

"Zeke Merritt. John Bidwell, William Ide, Cat Reilly, Bob Semple. Ben Kelsey. Twenty-four of them altogether."

Carson paced around with a restless energy, his arms moving, his glance raking the camp. The two officers stood still, deferring to Carson, which Sutter thought curious. The buckskin man circled back toward the Swiss don. "What about you? What are you in this?"

Sutter pulled on his mustaches again. He glanced at Frémont, who was letting this scout take command, and said, "Captain?"

Frémont said, "Who leads this republic? You?"

"I believe William Ide is their president. I have no part in it. I want none." Sutter glanced from one to the other, seeing them all still dismayed and angry, and said, with a wicked satisfaction, "Surely you respect the right of other Americans to do as they have."

Frémont lifted his head. The skin over his cheekbones was shiny; behind his feathery mustaches the thin line of his lips was like a seam. "Colonel Sutter, you may leave."

"As you wish," Sutter said. He turned to his horse, eager to be gone.

In a brittle voice Frémont said, "That bunch of drunks from Sutterville took Sonoma."

Kit said, "Damn them. They got more sand than we do." He looked around at the other men, and his voice was almost gentle. "We marched around and made a lot of noise, and they just rode over there and did what they had to." Most of the other men had drawn up within hearing, their faces taut. The redheaded Easterner, Kern, stood a quarter of the way around the circle from him, hands on hips.

Archie Gillespie said, "What's this about another flag? They're all Americans."

"They're not." Frémont strode back, his face working. "Sutter is Swiss; there're a lot of German settlers too. Anyhow, that bunch is just cussed enough to want to stand by themselves."

Kit said, "We all know what we're gonna do, now."

At that Kern bridled, his fair face paler than usual under his fresh tan. A lot of his men stood in a clump behind him. Frémont's men shifted away from them. Nobody said much; they avoided looking at him. Kit went around the circle again, measuring them.

Frémont said steadily, "What do you propose, Kit?"

Kit swung his arms at his sides, pumping himself, judging the men around him. They had no lust for this, not after Hawk Peak. He knew what they needed, a good fight, a bloodletting, to bring them all together. He turned toward Frémont. "First, we have to cover our backside. There's Indians gathering all along the river; they don't mean us no good. If we leave them here behind us, as soon as we're gone they'll turn on all these white people up here." He nodded to Frémont. "First we take out the Indians."

Frémont said, "And then?"

"Then we go down to Sonoma and give these Bears a real flag to fight for."

40 ∰ MIDWAY THROUGH THE AFTERNOON Kit slowed his horse and stopped. His shoulder socket throbbed. Behind him with a whoosh a brush hut caught fire; the wet wood screamed for a moment, a thin flute wail. The rank smell of green willow burning floated down the river in a coil of black smoke.

Up past the bend another flurry of shots rang out. He wiped his face on his sleeve, felt the slime on his cheek, and realized that his leather shirtsleeves were soaked with blood.

Archie Gillespie rode up to him. "Are we done now?" The marine's eyes popped, his mouth hung open, drawing huge gusts of air down into his lungs; he had lost his hat and his yellow hair stood on end.

"Yeah," Kit said. "We're done."

They were still shooting up there, though. Those who had

kept on using their rifles were wasting powder and taking too long. Early on, Kit had switched over to a Mexican saber he had picked up at Lassen's, a better weapon for this work. Now he lifted up the long notched blade and watched the blood drip off it and threw it down point first into the sand, like a marker. His horse shied, snorting, from the steel twang.

Back there still somebody was shooting. Kit looked back, his hands braced on his saddle pommel.

The Sacramento's bed stretched away from him, a vast trench cleaving through the yellow plain; its upswept, tree-crowded banks curved away north toward the Feather River fork. Saplings and weeds sprouted up on the bare gravel, in the shelter of old shoals. The river itself, summer small, ran off to his left, out of sight behind a thicket of willows.

Beyond the bend, the smoke rose in columns into the air, like a row of great wind-blown trees, as far as he could see. Just below the bend, on the sand, lay a tangle of bodies.

He had ridden for miles along the river, shooting first, until he got tired of having to stop and reload, and then hacking with the saber, and with each brown skin he saw he thought of Basil Lajeunesse and slashed hard to make the blood leap. Now the rage was fading in him, and he felt cold and slow and old and sick.

Ned Kern drifted in among them, saying loudly, "We had to do that. To protect the whites. Didn't we. They were painting themselves for war. Weren't they." His voice shook. There was blood in his hair. He had ridden as hard as any, ripped and struck as hard as any. Now when the lust was shrinking in him he could not bear what he had done.

Kit said, "Shut up, Kern." He did not know why the Indians had been painting themselves, but these were Diggers, who never fought.

"Yes, sir."

The rest of Frémont's men were riding toward Kit along the river bar, no longer yipping and howling. As they slowed they threw down the last of their torches. A few of them also dropped clubs, and the others were stowing away their rifles.

They crowded in around him, looking furtively at one another, and what they saw drove their gazes down, toward the ground, or to the sky, and nobody spoke.

In the reeds along the river, where a lot of the Indians had fled, the Delawares were taking scalps.

Frémont jogged his bay horse up toward him. Frémont alone wore no badge of blood. He rode clean and fresh down the river bar, in among men splashed with blood and stinking of the work that had put it there. Frémont's face was stony, expressionless, behind the mask of his mustaches. His horse side-stepped, nervous at the stench of dead Indians, of burning huts.

Ned Kern said to him, "We had to do that." His voice shook.

The captain reined in, his eyes steady on Kit. "Have you done what you wanted?" His voice was carefully even, uninflected, as if he were bored.

Kit said, "Call up the rest of the men."

Frémont without question laid the rein against his horse's neck and cantered back up the river bar, swerving to avoid a body in his path. Kit turned to Gillespie.

"It's his fault. If he'd done it right at Hawk Peak we'd never have been here in the first place. If he'd done it right at Hawk Peak we wouldn't have to prove now that we mean what we say."

Gillespie shook his head. "Kit, I never meant to question anything."

"Good," Kit said. "I like to hear that. Say that again sometime." He swung his horse around, following Frémont back toward the rendezvous.

Sutter had heard the shots behind him as he came down the river, and he turned his horse and rode north again. When he saw the black smoke rising he spurred his weary horse hard. The river spread across his path and he drove the horse in at a gallop, and halfway across the wide, rippling shallows the horse shied so violently that Sutter went off into the water.

He caught the horse, its cupped nostrils blowing, its ears switching, its nervous hoofs churning up the water, and only then saw what had spooked it. In the reeds and rocks that packed the middle of the ford there was a body.

It was an Indian child, a girl, maybe four or five, and freshly killed. One arm was gone completely and a deep slash had torn her open from belly to collarbone. Sutter got on his horse and swung around to go upstream.

Around the next bend there were more bodies, borne down on the Sacramento currents and trapped in the reeds and the driftwood. He got off his horse to look at them and found bullet holes in some of these, along with the unmistakable wounds of sabers.

He understood now, better than he wanted to. The smoke was climbing into the sky. He thought he could hear men screaming and yelling up there, around the curve in the broad river bar.

Stooping by the Sacramento, he washed his hands in the cool water. His back crawled. He went to his horse and mounted, and for a while he fought with himself; he told himself it would do no good to go up there, to denounce Frémont, to weep over dead Indians. But in his heart some voice had begun to scream, and it would not stop, even when he mounted up and turned his back on this and rode away south toward his fort; it would not stop, it would not stop.

41 AFTER THE MASSACRE on the Sacramento, Kit moved fast. He led the sixty-odd men of Frémont's expedition across the river, veered to pass by Sutter's Fort, and headed west, stopping only to eat and sleep a few hours, working his way into the unfamiliar hills, following deer trails and creeks. None of them had ever been to Sonoma. Kit missed by a wide margin and instead got them to San Rafael, on the coast of San Francisco Bay.

The mission was deserted, although there were still blankets on the beds and horses in the corrals. Frémont walked out across the short grass toward the bay. Behind him, to the west, the flanking hills rose up dark and steep; before him, the glistening blue water stretched toward a distant flat shore. Sheer rust-red boulders stuck up out of the water, here and there, as if they had dropped in from the clouds.

Archie Gillespie sauntered down toward him. "A beautiful piece of country." The marine folded his hands behind him, looking around.

"The geology is very confusing. An abundance of wildlife." Frémont's head turned, his attention caught on something white moving into the edge of his vision.

A small boat was sailing along the coast, coming toward them. As they watched, the dinghy's sail luffed, and the boat drifted up into the mouth of the creek below the mission, one of the passengers paddling it the last few yards. A man in the bow leaned out and caught a jetty and pulled the little boat up to the mission's dock. The three passengers got out and reached down into the boat for their baggage. Their fancy tight jackets and cartwheel hats marked them for Californios. Kit stood at the top of the rutted yellow path through the grass, watching.

Frémont turned away. "Let Kit handle this," he said.

Gillespie said, "Kit seems to be handling everything."

Frémont gave him a sharp look. The marine was staring away across the bay, his face bland.

The three Californios dragged saddles out of the boat and started up toward the mission, then saw the Americans and stopped. Kit ambled down to meet them and spoke to them in Spanish, a language Frémont did not know. That was why it was best that Kit handle this. He glanced at Gillespie again, wanting to make this point, but the marine was drifting away to get a better view of the water. "Where is Yerba Buena from here, sir?" he called back.

Frémont followed him across the slope, tunneled with gopher holes and their drying mounds. "That way. You can see the hills above it."

"Have you been to the presidio?"

"When I passed through Yerba Buena in January." Gillespie

knew nothing of California; Frémont was his clear superior here, and his confidence billowed. "Green boys manned it then, and the cannon were full of spiders."

The shot that rang out behind him startled him. He spun around into the blast of two more shots. The three Californios lay sprawled on the sand by the bow of their beached dinghy. Kit was turning a flintlock over in his hand. He stood there, his back to the dead men, and reloaded his guns.

Frémont swallowed hard; he raised his eyes to look at Gillespie and started to rush in with an excuse for this.

Gillespie's expression stopped him. On the ruddy face of the marine was a lively admiration. Frémont shut his teeth together and looked away.

Kit came toward them. "We can't very well take prisoners," he said. His gaze shifted from Frémont's face to Gillespie's and back again; he gave both men a bland smile and walked away up the slope, toward the mission.

Gillespie said, under his breath, "My God. The man's an Alexander."

Heavily Frémont tramped away, after his scout.

42   GILLESPIE SAID QUIETLY, "Kit seems to know exactly what to do. What do you think he plans for Sutter?"

They were riding up through the valley toward the mountains, toward Sonoma at their foot. The moon had just risen, spreading its treacherous blue light over the flat land; the mountains were a flat black jagged line against the northern edge of it. The vast crowns of the oaks scattered on the silvered grass caught the light and blended into it, while beneath them lay vast pits of black shadow, like openings into the underworld.

Frémont said, "Kit is not in command. This is my command. We just work very closely together, have for years."

Gillespie murmured something, smiling. He nudged his

horse along, keeping pace with Frémont. The rest of the men, in no particular order, were drifting along to Frémont's right and behind him, following the road up toward Sonoma. Kit was over somewhere to his right, he hoped out of earshot.

Gillespie came at him again. The marine was determined to show Frémont he understood the real order of things.

"What do you think Kit will do about Sutter? From what you've told me, he's probably just as much of a traitor as these oafs up ahead of us."

"Traitor," Frémont said, startled. "These men aren't traitors."

The young marine snorted at him, contemptuous. "If they had a chance to put the Stars and Stripes up over California and they put some other flag up instead, I say they're traitors."

Frémont turned away from Gillespie, who wanted even more trouble. Ahead, under the dark looming wall of the mountains, lay the moonlit walls of Sonoma. Frémont raised his hand. "Come on, that way's good food and a place to sleep." He lifted his exhausted horse into a lope.

The men closed in around him, driving hard the last few hundred yards to the end of the road. Kit galloped up on Frémont's left. The geometrical shape of the adobes at Sonoma stood clearer against the dark hills, the square edges of buildings, the high upthrust of the tower. There, by the gate, something glinted. A torch, maybe, a watchlight. Frémont steered toward it. On the other side of the gate, now, another light swung.

Kit roared, "Those are slow matches! Rein in, rein in —"

Frémont sat back hard in his saddle, and his horse stopped cold; the other men rushed up around him, a horse banged into his, and a tail swiped his chest. Kit galloped back and forth across the road in the moonlight, shouting.

"Hold up! Don't shoot! We're Americans!"

From the gate into Sonoma there went up a yell. "It's Kit! That's Kit Carson — hold the cannon!"

Frémont's arms felt cold under his jacket, the skin quivering uncontrollably. His mouth was dry. He glanced at Kern, still on his right, whose eyes shone white in the moonlight, and lifting his hand he led his men at a sedate jog down into Sonoma.

William Ide said, "Lucky you sung out, we damn near shot y'." This seemed to amuse him much more than it did Frémont.

Frémont took his hat off. They went into a long room at the front of the big house, and Ide lit some candles. Several others of the Bear Flaggers came through the door behind them, farmers and workmen, each man with a rifle or a musket. Frémont looked them over, half contemptuous, half amazed.

He said, "You did a fine job, Mr. Ide. A fine job."

Ide had a graying spade beard, a placid, easy face, a pair of shrewd dark eyes. He said, "You mean, we're doing a fine job. You see any sign of an army coming this way?"

Kit strolled up the side of the room, stopped to finger an old bullet hole in the wall, and came toward Frémont. "No. No army. Just us."

The room was rapidly filling up with Bear Flaggers and with Frémont's men. Ide said, "That's a relief, I suppose. You boys are coming to join in, I gather?" His voice was mild as milk, but his sharp, clear eyes moved from one to the other.

Gillespie nudged Frémont in the side. Over Frémont's shoulder the marine lieutenant said, "We represent the United States government. You men may think you're in charge here, but now —"

"But now you think you ought to take over," Ide said.

His voice was still easy, but his arms rose and folded over his chest. Gillespie poked Frémont again.

Frémont said, "We ought to talk about this." Through the tail of his eye he saw the crowd swelling into the room, and he said, "Without guns."

Up past the long table in the middle of the room came Zeke Merritt, vast and rumpled and red-eyed. "What's going on here?" Behind him was a short, slight figure Frémont was startled to see here. He nodded to Cat Reilly.

William Ide turned toward the crowd, lifting his arms up, and said, "We got to talk, here. It'd be best if everybody laid their guns down. Zeke, help me get this table out of the way."

Kit nudged Frémont in the back. "Go on out," he said, low-voiced. Frémont went away the length of the room, toward the door, his hands together behind his back. Kit drifted after him. He was scratching in the stubble of his beard, his pale eyes abstracted. In his belt he carried three pistols. Casually he strolled out into the long corridor, got Frémont by the arm, and pulled him into the small room across the way.

There was no lamp, and the shutters were closed over the windows. Frémont moved into the dark, out of reach of the light coming in through the door. "There's a lot of men here."

Kit said, "You go back in there and talk pretty to them. Get them to see things our way."

"Right."

"If you have any trouble, just keep talking."

"Right."

Frémont went out to the corridor, where a steady stream of Bear Flaggers was moving in from the plaza. Kit stayed behind; Frémont did not turn to see what the scout did or where he went. He pulled his uniform coat straight and combed his whiskers with his fingers. In the big council room before him voices rose in loud, boisterous talk. Frémont moved on into that room.

At the far end Gillespie was already standing, his hands in his pockets, his shoulders hunched. He watched the crowd gathering before him with a look of baffled anger. Frémont went by him, facing the blank wall, and tried to think out what he was going to say.

The room quickly filled with Bear Flaggers. Filing in the door, they laid down their arms on the table and moved up toward Frémont, young men and older ones, talking with Kentucky voices and New England, Ohio and New York, dressed in hunting shirts, in battered farmer's overalls and hand-cobbled boots. Their voices swelled, loud, competing, and there was some laughter. The room was much hotter than it had been a moment before, and some of the men along the long wall began to open the shutters that covered the windows. Archie Gillespie, slapping his hands together, stepped up beside Frémont. "Can you handle this?"

Frémont looked around the room for faces he knew — Ben

Kelsey and Zeke Merritt and Ide, Ridley, Grigsby, Semple. Cat Reilly, watching him steadily from one side. The room was packed now, men standing shoulder to shoulder from the windowed wall to the edge of the oak table, their hard, direct faces aimed at him. Frémont told himself that his country needed him, and that put some strength into his voice.

"As most of you know, I'm Captain John Charles Frémont, of the United States Army. I'm here first to congratulate you men. You've done what Americans have always done — you stood up for your rights, you defeated the foreign oppressor, you raised the flag. What you've done here in Sonoma will always be a glorious moment in the history of the United States."

Ide stood in the front row, his face bland. "Meaning you want us to quit now."

In the packed room behind him voices simmered. Frémont lifted his hands. "It's the American flag that belongs on top of that pole."

"That's our flag," Zeke Merritt rumbled. "We put it there, and we'll keep it there. Look, Frémont —" Zeke moved up into the front of the room, his elbows cocked, his head thrust forward. "I got a proposition for you, now. You kick in with us, and we'll let you into the Bear Flag Republic."

At that the men behind him gave up such a shout that Frémont's ears hurt; he stepped away from the blast of sound. His heart was socking the inside of his ribs. He went forward toward the Bear Flaggers again.

"You men are Americans! What did you come to California for, except to make it American? And when they attacked you, wasn't it for being American?"

Somebody in the back said, "Personally, I come here to get the hell away from people telling me what to do, like you're doin'!"

They howled again, dangerously exuberant. Yellowed by the candlelight, the air of the room was thick with smoke and so many close-packed bodies; a drop of sweat ran down Frémont's side under his shirt.

"Listen to me. This is much bigger than you think —"

With a rush, Gillespie strode past him, bellowing. "You can't keep this stupid republic, you clods. There's a navy fleet headed for California now, if it isn't already anchored at Monterey. There's an army coming overland from Texas."

"Let 'em come," one of the Bears roared, and across the tossing swarm of heads a score of fists struck up into the air.

In the wind of this uproar the marine lieutenant stepped back, his mouth clamped grimly shut. His eyes glittered. Frémont pushed him away toward the wall behind him. "Stay out of this!"

Gillespie's protruding jaw thrust out like a pike's; his pale eyes examined the Bear Flaggers with brimming indignation. Frémont wheeled and walked the few feet toward the rebels' front rank. They jeered at him, boisterous. Then through the door at the back of the room Kit came walking, and through every window along the wall, suddenly, Kit's men were leaning into the room, their rifles in their hands.

The crowded room fell slowly, utterly still. The faces of the Bears turned one by one toward Frémont. Kit walked the length of the room, up beside Frémont, and turned.

He said, "This time, I ain't taking chances. You're with me or you're out. Now I want to know who's with me."

None of them moved for a moment, and Frémont let his breath go. In the windows the rifles bristled, and the Bear Flaggers stood there with empty hands and their mouths hanging open. Then Cat Reilly stepped forward. She went straight at Kit, her wide green eyes like jewels and her voice ringing, loud. "What are you trying to do? You couldn't stand up to the dons at the Gavilan, but you can walk on us. We should have shot you."

Kit stalked down toward her, grinning. His feet boomed on the floor. He looked nowhere but at her. He sauntered around her, and the men in the crowd drew back from him, giving him the space he wanted, so that when he turned his back on them and faced her she was isolated from them, standing small and alone between Kit and Frémont. He said, "I killed a lot of people lately, Cat. It's getting real easy."

She stared straight back at him. "Oh. Is that why it feels as if there's a knife in my back?"

Kit's grin widened, as if she amused him, which she probably did. He hitched his belt up, lifting his voice to the men behind him. "We're all Americans here, and we're going to do what's right, we're going to put the Stars and Stripes up on that pole, and then up on every flagpole in California. I want to know who's with me."

She wheeled around; her eyes came to Frémont. "Stop him."

Frémont froze. The pleading look in her eyes struck him like an arrow.

She said again, "Stop him."

Frémont said, "Somebody put this woman under arrest before she gets herself shot."

Kit said, "Leave her." He put his hands on his hips, facing her, his mouth curled into a mirthless, nasty grin. "Anybody else?"

Behind him the Bear Flaggers stood in silence; they kept still for a while under the guns clustered in the windows. Finally Zeke Merritt said, "Hell, Kit. I wanted you in this from the beginning."

"Yeah," said another voice. "Count me in, Kit," and now three or four spoke at once, and now ten or twelve. In a mass, they moved in behind him, all their exuberance drowned in their submission.

Kit nodded at the woman before him. "Nobody, see. Nobody but you. Gillespie, take her."

She said nothing more and only stared at him until Archie Gillespie went up and grasped her arm and pulled her by force out of the room.

43 ⚑ KIT SAID, "Cross your hands on the horn," and when she did not, he pulled her hands together in front of her and lashed her wrists to the pommel of the saddle with a piece of rawhide.

"Damn you, Kit," she said, humiliated.

"I told you, I'm not taking any chances." He pulled the reins forward over her horse's head and led it away toward the front of the plaza, where a dozen other riders had already gathered, the men he was leading to Sutter's Fort.

On the pole in the center of the plaza, the Bear Flag still fluttered and snapped in the fitful breeze. Her head turned, her gaze directed up at the flag, and she said, "Wait."

He stopped and faced her. "What? I'm in a hurry."

She did not look at him; she stared at the flag. Frémont had come out of Vallejo's house, trailing Archie Gillespie and William Ide and Zeke Merritt. The mapmaker was carrying a package under his arm. Cat said, "I promised Don Mariano that I would look after his family. They're upstairs in the Big House, there."

Kit said nothing. At the flagpole Frémont stopped and nodded to Ide, and the older man went by him and lowered the Bear Flag. As the red and white cloth came down Zeke stepped forward and gathered it into his arms.

She lowered her eyes to Kit, looking him in the face. "I want you to make sure nothing will happen to them."

Impassive, unsmiling for once, he stared at her a moment, to let her know he did not feel compelled, and then dropped the reins and walked over toward Frémont.

The captain was reeling the American flag up to the top of the pole. Archie Gillespie saluted it, so stiffly at attention he seemed to vibrate. Zeke and William Ide were busy folding up the Bear Flag. Kit tapped Frémont on the arm and spoke to him; Frémont, taller than Kit, had to stoop to listen. Kit strode back across the plaza and took the reins of Cat's horse.

"All right," he said. "But that's all."

"That's all," she said. He led her away across the plaza.

Kit said, "This place looks pretty quiet." They had forded the river south of Sutter's Fort; the sun slid through the haze in the peak of the sky. Ahead of them Sutter's Fort looked small and unimportant, a hump on the sweeping golden plain with its dark studs of trees.

"They're all in Sonoma," said Luke Maxwell. He looked around at the fading campground of Sutterville, where new grass was springing up through the black pits of old cook-fires.

"Keep an eye cocked," Kit said. "If there's any shooting, I'll take Sutter. Each one of you mark somebody else."

He got the reins of Cat Reilly's horse in his fist and snugged its head up close against his thigh. He said to her, "Keep your mouth shut."

She said nothing, watching him with a steady hatred. He led them on at a lope toward the fort.

The gate was open; nobody challenged them. Kit let his horse drop to a walk as it went into the yard. Off to his left some little children were jumping rope in the sun, and they stopped to gawk at him. A hammer chimed rhythmically on iron over in one of the smithies. Otherwise the yard was empty. Kit rode over to the foot of the stair up to the office and let go of Cat's horse, spreading his fingers, limbering his hand. His men ranged themselves around him.

"Sutter! Hey, Captain!"

The door opened; they had been waiting, then, they had seen him coming. They were already cowed, and this was all but done. Sutter walked out onto the landing. "Well, Carson, I thought you'd get here eventually." His voice was hollow with a false challenge.

John Bidwell appeared behind him in the doorway. Kit craned his neck, trying to see beyond him into the office. "Anybody else up there with y'?"

"General Vallejo and his brother," Sutter said.

"Hey, hey," Kit said, grinning at him. "They're supposed to be prisoners of war. Like you. You're under arrest, Sutter."

The Swiss wobbled as if the wind swayed him. Bidwell stepped forward past him to the rail. "You rotten son of a bitch, Kit."

Sutter grabbed him by the shoulder, pulling him back. "No,

damn it — stand clear." He turned a taut, white face toward Kit. "I'll surrender. I don't want any trouble."

Bidwell twisted toward him. "Captain, he can't do this." His gaze swung around again, past Kit, to the woman on the horse behind him, as if he had just now realized she was there.

"Cat. What's going on?" His voice was tight, cracked, a rough edge of desperation in it. His dark eyes aimed at Kit. "Why is she a prisoner too?"

She said, "The Bear Flag's gone, John. They took us over. Frémont's in command at Sonoma. You might as well give up."

Bidwell said, "Jesus." Sutter came past him, down the steps, his hands lifted.

Sutter said, "There wasn't anything anybody could have done."

Cat said, "We should have shot them when they rode up to Sonoma."

"They'd have killed you." He leaned heavily on the table, his face slack. They were sitting in his room, in the west end of the fort, where he was jailed. She had tried to get him into a game of cards, but he would not pay attention to anything. He was half drunk; Manaiki came into the room with another jug and put it down beside him.

"How could they have killed us all?" Cat said. "We should have stood up to them. He was bluffing."

"No, he wasn't. He'll shoot anybody who gets in his way." Sutter's voice strengthened; he lifted his head, his gaze sharpening. "They killed a hundred Indians, up on the river, getting their sights in. They shot three men down by San Rafael just for being Californio. Don't you dare think he was bluffing."

"A hundred Indians," she said. "What Indians? Why?"

Sutter stared at her a moment. His shoulders slumped again, his eyes going dull and his face withdrawn, and after a while he shook his head and looked away.

She put her hand on his shoulder. "Captain."

"There wasn't anything I could have done," he said.

"What Indians?" she cried.

"Our Indians," he said. "My Indians. They were up on the

river for their summer dances. You know how they danced. Kit and the rest of Frémont's men went through them like reapers."

She sat back, her hands flat on the table, and stared away into the dimness of the room. Manaiki moved through the shadows.

"There wasn't anything I could have done," Sutter said again, in a leaden voice.

"No," she said. "If we were going to do anything we would have had to start a long time ago."

She got up and walked out of the room, out the door, and across the yard toward the central building. There was a string of horses tied up in front of the blacksmith shop, and the smell of bread flooded the air around the bake oven. The oak tree's great green head of leaves shaded the whole corner there; Manaiki's sister sat under it, out of the sun, doing some sewing. Down in the other yard the children were singing a rhyme and jumping rope.

There seemed only peace and growth and goodness in it, and yet it was cankered and something evil had been nurtured in it, or come with it, and she had done this evil, this unspeakable, horrible thing, helped in it, she herself.

Her feet felt like dead lumps. She clomped up the stairs to the office and stood there on the landing, where she had shot the vaquero's horse, and looked away over the valley.

She loved it. The golden haze of the broad valley, slung between the soaring peaks of the Sierra and the lower, tighter folds of the coastal ranges, the dirty white walls of the fort itself, and the people who lived here, and their lives here — she loved it all. She had made a new world here.

Doing it, she had destroyed an old one. In moment after moment, she had hardened herself to it rather than give up what she wanted. Made reasons to defend what she wanted from the fact of what she was doing to get it. Frémont's slaughter of the Indians was only one step further on, and she had made it inevitable.

After a while she went into the office. There was nobody in the room; Kit was out gathering horses, and John Bidwell was keeping to himself, somewhere, grieving. The Vallejo brothers were locked up. She went to the piano and sat down, but she could not put her hands to the keys, she could not sound a note, not for hours.

Finally, in the twilight, she began slowly to play her feelings into something she could endure. She started with Mozart, Purcell, Scarlatti, long strings of notes, arpeggios, scales and runs and octaves, music of order and place and harmony. The room grew dark, and she played in the dark. Then the door opened behind her. Kit came in.

She put her hands down, a tremor running over her, the breath of rage. He lit a lamp and put it down on the table and pulled a chair around to sit at the end of the piano bench.

"Keep playing," he said.

She played a Beethoven romance. He lit a cigar and puffed on it, while she got to the end of the piece, and when she was done, he offered the smoke to her. "No," she said. "Even the smell makes me sick."

In the lamplight his eyes glittered. "I keep forgetting you're just a woman." He stuck the cigar back between his teeth.

"What, are you looking for a fight?"

"I could stand some excitement. Play some more, I like it."

She began the rolling thirds of a sonata, watching her hands. "Why did you do it?"

"You did it wrong," he said.

"Who are you to judge that?"

Abruptly he swung his arm down over the keyboard, between her and the piano, and thrust his face almost against hers. "You did it wrong, baby. I made it right. That's all." He leaned his weight down, and fifty notes banged, a raucous jangle. "That's all."

Her body throbbed. In the muddle of her passions she found no clear thought; she wanted to smash him, to hurt him back, but if she touched him, she knew, he would make her suffer. He was staring at her. He knew everything she thought. She lowered her eyes to the keyboard and played Beethoven. He puffed on the cigar.

She said, "I want to go away. The launch is leaving tomorrow for Yerba Buena. Let me go on it."

"I can't do that without an order from Captain Frémont."

"Damn it, don't try that with me. I know who you are."

He looked her over, through veils of cigar smoke; with an impatient jerk of his head he flipped his hair back. "If you just want to get away from me, you might as well stay here. We're leaving pretty soon anyway, as soon as Frémont arrives. And you ain't going nowhere that ain't ours. The Stars and Stripes is flying now in Yerba Buena. And in Monterey."

"Monterey." The name sounded in her ears like a door shutting.

"That word came this morning." He was watching her with an unblinking interest, his eyes flat and colorless and predatory as a rattlesnake's. "The navy sailed into Monterey a month ago. Took it without a shot fired. We're going down there to meet some commodore and mop up. California belongs to us. Play some more."

She turned back to the keyboard and began the sonata again, its brooding sentiment like a weight on her mood. Through it she sifted what he had just told her. She said, "I still want to go."

He said nothing; he sat there in the dark, listening to her and smoking the cigar down. She wondered why he was interested in her when so much else was going on, and decided it was only his relentless will to dominate everything that moved. Finally he got up and went to the door. "If it was anybody else I'd think you was trying to get out of this, but likely you're getting deeper into it. Go on, go to Yerba Buena. You're just a woman. There's nothing you can do." He walked out.

44 ✠ THOMAS LARKIN'S HOUSE in Monterey was a huge, two-story adobe with a redwood verandah running all the way around it; it was the biggest house in Monterey, and unlike the others, it had a tiled roof that sloped up to the gable on all

four sides. This made it look so much like a Massachusetts house that Catharine stood and stared at it for a while before she went to the door.

Inside, the house was loud and packed with people. The central hall opened on both sides into public rooms, the one on the right serving as Larkin's mercantile store, and the one on the left, smaller, as his consular office. He was in neither place. Looking at the frantic men hurrying in and out, Catharine began to think she had no business being here.

She went out to the verandah and sat down on a bench. She had brought her bag in from the beach, and now she set it at her feet on the gray floorboards of the porch. Out in the harbor she could see the ship that had brought her here from Yerba Buena, the *Moscow,* whose Captain Phelps owed Sutter a favor. It was only one of a score of ships cluttering the long shallow bay of Monterey, and it was small and nondescript, compared especially with the sleek, black-hulled American ships of war at anchor in the north end, the ships that had taken Monterey.

She sat on the verandah, her courage ebbing. A stream of men bustled in and out of Larkin's house, most of them in uniforms but many in the dark clothes of townspeople. Some looked like Californios, others were fair, and there were Negroes and some Indians. A few stood on the verandah arguing, mostly in Spanish. In the street other men hurried up and down, and many as they passed Larkin's called out to someone on the verandah and waved.

Monterey was bigger than she had expected. She felt ashamed of being there, a placeless woman in worn-out clothes, among all these other people who looked so important and so busy.

After a while, bored, she stowed the bag under the bench and went out to walk around. There were real streets here, not like the footpaths of Yerba Buena, and the houses stood in rows and blocks, surrounded by adobe walls that enclosed the large, sunlit yard. In the street beyond Larkin's there were several other handsome large houses, although none as big as his.

She went down toward the beach, past some smaller, older adobes; chickens rummaged through the garbage in the street outside, and she heard the high giggle of a child. A woman in

an arched doorway smiled at her. For a few minutes she followed a *carreta* of firewood, with a little brown boy sitting on
top, who watched her with huge black eyes.

Everywhere she saw uniformed men strolling around in
groups. She caught some of them staring at her and stayed away
from them, wary.

She went along the beach, through the fish market there,
where women in shawls poked crabs and clams and tuna into
their baskets. The roar and crash of the sea made a constant
background. Some of the fishermen were building a fire on the
beach; the wind whipped at it, making the flames roar. In her
childhood when her grandfather had been alive they had gone
out often onto the shore for clambakes; there was some standing
adult joke about shucking votes along with the clams.

The beach curved away from her, its slope traced with the
delicate edges of wave shores, of old tides, the crackling shells
of tiny things under her feet. Out in the blue water there were
mats of bull kelp floating, like seaborne gardens. She passed the
wreck of a ship lying on the sand; there was nothing left of it
but a few wooden ribs and a spine, worn silver.

North of that, inland, was another market, in a square
bounded by ruined adobe buildings, with a fountain in a stone
basin. In the middle of this square the Stars and Stripes flew
from a white flagpole. A man in a marine's uniform stood duty
at the foot of it.

She went through the market, looking over the heaps of vegetables displayed in baskets and carts. The vendors called to her,
friendly, competing with one another for her attention; when
her broken Spanish stumbled, they waved that off, unimportant,
and brandished peaches at her, crooned to her seductively over
the gray-green bulbs of artichokes bigger than her head. When
she held up her empty palms and remembered how to say she
had no money, then they lost interest.

She sat down on the stone rim of the fountain and watched
the bustle in the plaza.

Nobody here seemed to care about the war. When a group of
blue-shirted sailors walked in, the Montereños called and waved
to them as they had to her, holding up their fruit, their strings

of chilies, a hat, a splendid shawl; they saw these men as prospective buyers, not conquerors. The sailors themselves seemed on holiday, strolling around, unarmed, wide-eyed, leisurely.

She sat there in the sun, watching the children play, trying to understand the Spanish words she overheard. A group of girls came to the fountain and filled buckets, and their eyes glanced over her. She felt the quick stab of their notice like little claws taking her apart, her poor clothes, her broken shoes.

She wondered what had happened here, why they had surrendered without a fight. They did not seem to care. Maybe it made no difference to them who ruled them, as long as they could grow their peaches and sell their onions and artichokes. She went back toward Larkin's, and her gaze fell again on the big ships in the harbor, their hulls pierced with gunports. She saw no guns in Monterey itself. Finally, having nowhere else to go, she drifted back to Larkin's verandah and sat down, staring at her hands, her thoughts morose. She had thought she knew these people, but she had known nothing of them at all.

"Mrs. Reilly?"

She looked up, startled, into the hazel eyes of Thomas Larkin.

Larkin gave her a bedroom in the second story of his enormous and already overcrowded house; he was endlessly busy and she hardly spoke to him. A few days after she had moved in, she went out to sit with him and his family and watch John Charles Frémont and his army ride into Monterey.

The whole town had come out for the event, lining both sides of the road, which wound along the beach a while before it curved up into the hills. The shoreline rocks were covered with children and seagulls. In among the white coats of the Montereños were clumps of blue, the uniforms of the sailors off the ships. A British warship had sailed in since Cat's arrival, H.M.S. *Collingwood,* and the lime-suckers were clustered in two neat lines directly across from Cat, staring down the street, their voices booming.

The sun climbed; Larkin's wife began to complain of the

heat, and she waved a little fan; she called to friends she saw, and sent her Indian maid to take a message to the French consul's wife, down the street. Then, from the north, there came the first tiny crash and whistle of a brass band.

The crowd hushed to an electric expectation. All heads turned to look along the road. Far off the tinkle of the band sounded, and now, up there, the first cheers.

Cat clenched her fists in her lap. Her heart pounded; she was taken back, irresistibly, to the Fourth of July on the Boston Common, patriotic hearts beating to the pulse of drums and horns, and now, here again, three thousand miles away, here came the parade.

The band marched first, two ranks of glittering horns that tooted and blared, and two men with drums. The men playing wore caps with U.S.S. *Congress* on the front; they were off the huge ship of war in the harbor, Commodore Somebody's ship. There were two commodores currently in Monterey. After the band marched Archie Gillespie, his chest out like a pigeon's, carrying the American flag.

The Americans all cheered as it passed by; Larkin stood, his hand to his breast. Catharine lowered her eyes. She felt like a traitor, like an outcast. Then, after the flag, Frémont rode alone.

He was mounted on a gray horse, and she stiffened, her teeth in her lip; it was Sacramento, Sutter's horse. Abruptly she was burning with rage, her eyes scalded, her skin shivering as if with a fever. He rode past her, his head high with pride, wearing a polished uniform coat, and the crowd cheered him obediently, some even knowing his name.

After him came his army. His own men were there, but mixed in with them, more numerous, was the Bear Flag Republic.

Almost at once she saw Zeke Merritt, riding along slouched in his saddle, and John Christenson, with a jug propped on his thigh, and gray-bearded William Ide in his suspenders, Ben Kelsey and his brother Jack, and even John Bidwell. Past the British in their trim and proper uniforms the Bears came, raw, brash men in half-laced leather shirts, in long-fringed boots, knives hanging on their thighs, pistols stuck in their belts, shaggy as beasts, their faces bold and lively and free. To see them again, to see them from the outside, roused her to a torment; her throat was full, her heart quaked; she had to fight the urge to call out to them, to wave her hands, to run in among them again. She clenched her fists, instead, in her lap.

The crowd's voice gathered, thunderous, rolling toward some frantic pitch, and she lifted her head, wondering what they saw.

Their applause deafened her. All up and down the road, they surged forward, cheering and yelling and waving their arms, and down along the road, ignoring them all, Kit Carson rode.

He was grinning, as always, broad and easy, a feather stuck in the band of his hat, his russet hair hanging lankly down over his shoulders. His reins loose, he leaned back in his saddle, his feet thrust out before him, as if he sat in a chair. Talking to Luke Maxwell, who rode on his left, as if there were no deafening acclaim, no tumult all around him, he passed by her down the road, and the people broke rank and rushed after him, screaming to him, begging for a glance.

Catharine sank down, exhausted. Beside her, Larkin leaned in. "You see how things are going."

She said, "Somebody has to tell the truth about this."

He nodded to her. "We'll see what can be done."

Commodore Sloat bent forward over the table. The room was utterly quiet, although it was crowded with American navy officers. Sloat fixed Frémont with a cold stare.

"Let me understand this. Without orders, without proper authority at all, you came into this country, riled the local government to the point where they expelled you, incited the settlers to rebel and proclaim their own republic, and then subverted that republic to yourself?" His head swung toward the man standing at the window behind him and brought his gaze back to Frémont. "I think your conduct has been disgraceful."

Frémont swallowed down the sudden dryness in his throat. He was aware of the other men around him as if their looks were thorns. He said, "I was doing what seemed right, sir."

"As an American officer I am ashamed," Sloat said. The table's glossy surface was littered with papers; his hands moved, pushing the pens before him into an even line. "I can only thank Mrs. Reilly here for her testimony, for coming all the way with her witness, a long journey for a man, much less a woman alone."

Frémont could not look at her, off to one side, with Larkin behind her. When he first came into this room and saw her here his heart had shrunk to a pebble in his chest, and what she had said had rolled over him like a landslide.

Sloat said, "In my opinion you have disgraced the flag and the army, Captain Frémont."

He looked around, over his shoulder again, at the man by the window.

"However, regrettably, my illness disables me from this command. Commodore Stockton here will replace me. He will deal with you, with, I hope, the censure and dishonor you deserve."

Sloat got up; his thinning gray hair was scraped back over his head, and he ran one hand over it and picked up his hump-topped commodore's hat from the table. He did look ill; his lips were pale and his eyes watery — or perhaps it was his obvious distaste for this command.

He said, "Captain," and saluted. With a slight nod of his head toward the window, he walked out of the room, and several of the junior officers lining the wall followed him.

Frémont looked down at the carpet he was standing on, feeling sick to his stomach. He knew the men around him watched him with contempt. Ahead of him now lay a court-martial, conviction, and disgrace. Suddenly his whole soul twisted in an agony of hatred for Catharine Reilly, who had done this to him, destroyed his career, for the sake of a few Indians and a home-made flag.

"Captain Frémont," said the man who stood in the window.

Frémont lifted his head. The new commander of the Pacific Fleet, a looming shadow against the brightly lit window, had turned to face him. "Commodore," Frémont said, "Let me explain this. It wasn't the way she says it was."

"I've read your report," said Commodore Stockton, and came forward from the window; the light of the lanterns swept up his body and shone on his face. "You've raised Old Glory in Sonoma and Fort Sutter and at Yerba Buena, which I think excellently done, excellently indeed. In fact" — he reached in among the papers on the table and slid one toward Frémont — "I have signed a brevet promoting you to major."

Frémont said stupidly, "Sir."

Catharine Reilly stepped forward, fierce. "Commodore, in the course of raising the flag in all these places he killed hundreds of people — unarmed, unresisting people."

Stockton tucked his hands behind him. In contrast to Sloat he looked the book picture of a commanding officer. His woolen navy uniform was brushed like velvet, the brass buttons shining; the commodore himself, handsome and clean shaven, with a jutting jaw and direct, intense eyes, gave off a fragrance of power. He looked down at the woman before him as if she stood no higher than his shoelace. "As for Mrs. Reilly's testimony, I feel we can discount it as the ravings of a hysterical woman."

She went straight at him, three steps, her voice keen as the scream of a hawk. "There were pieces of bodies floating down the Sacramento for weeks."

"Mrs. Reilly," he said, cool, looking elsewhere, and she swung herself up in front of him and shouted into his face.

"They arrested Sutter, who saved and succored every American in the valley. There would be no Americans on the Sacramento except for Sutter. The least you can do is order them to let him go."

"Mrs. Reilly, let me remind you that this is a war, and you are quite out of place here."

"A war!" She flung her arm out to point at Frémont. "Then why is it he did all the killing, and all the victims were unarmed?"

Stockton said, "Mr. Larkin. I resent this."

Thomas Larkin stepped up behind her, grave, neat in his townsman's clothes. "Mrs. Reilly has her rights, Commodore."

The commodore glowered at him. His jaw jutted out. His

voice came clipped and even and cold. "So does the United
States. Since we began on this continent, every time we've faced
an enemy, the Indians in our midst have turned on us. They
fought against us for the British in '12 and during the Revolution and before that for the French, time after time, until finally
we had to drive them out of the east. That will not happen here.
We shall eliminate them here, now, in the first place, before they
turn on us." He glared down at Catharine Reilly standing stiff
before him. "You may go, Mrs. Reilly. I have no further interest
in your opinions."

Frémont stepped forward. "Commodore, maybe you should
place this woman under arrest. For her own good."

She ignored him, staring at Stockton, her black brows tucked
down, her lips thin and tight. The commodore straightened,
giving thought to Frémont's suggestion, and from behind Cat,
Larkin lifted his voice. "I advise you to be prudent in your dealings with Mrs. Reilly, who is handsomely represented in the
Congress."

Stockton said brusquely, "Then get her out of here."

She turned toward Frémont. "This isn't over," she said. "You
can lie and lie and lie but the truth won't change. You'll have
to pay your debt to it in the end." She walked toward the door,
through the crowd of officers, and nobody there spoke a word
until she was gone.

45 AFTER DARK, Monterey boomed with parties,
with music and dancing, at the house of the French consul and
at the houses of merchants and in the big new customs house.
The streets caught the overflow, the sailors noisy with drink and
the shore steady under their feet, the rich Montereños on horseback, the Americans trooping everywhere, groups swarming
from house to house with pole lamps to light their way, their
boisterous celebrations drowning the ceaseless thunder of the
surf.

Larkin went to all these parties. Catharine walked instead through the town toward the plaza.

The market had closed up. In the old church at the far end, she could hear people singing, but the square was deserted. A racket from the west side of the wall drew her around to the lane there. One of Larkin's servants had told her that this was where the men came to gamble.

In the alley outside the wall a score of lanterns burned, some hanging on the adobe and some standing on the ground. All the voices here spoke Spanish. They clustered thick around a shallow pit where the high, agonized screams of dying chickens sounded, and gathered in little groups along the wall to play cards, to throw dice. They were farmers, mostly, barefoot, in worn, shapeless clothes. She could smell horses and blood, aguardiente and stale piss, but she saw no brazen-haired men with blue eyes, and she went away again, avoiding the crowds and the light, back to Larkin's house.

Larkin was saying patiently, "Commodore, everything depends on the outcome of the war in Mexico. There's no reason to fight here any more at all."

Stockton made some unworded, contemptuous sound in his throat. "I know the Mexicans." The commodore loved a crowd; his voice swelled like organ music to fill all those extra ears. "I was stationed in Galveston for several months. These people only fight an enemy whose back is turned. Isn't that true, Carson?"

Kit muttered something, his hat tipped down over his eyes, shading out the light of the overhead lamps. He upended his glass and put it on a bench behind him. Stockton irritated him.

Actually they all irritated him, the officers, with their shiny buttons and their salutes and their up-and-down order. Stockton, for instance, thought that he was in command of California, when he held only this little part of it and Kit had taken the whole north; but Stockton had gold braid on his hat, and that made the difference.

Larkin was another, smooth, slippery, whom he did not trust, a dealer in words and smiles. Larkin was going off through the crowd, talking to everybody, making his way toward the door. Kit wished he could leave as easily as the consul.

They were standing around in the fandango room of the customs house. Fancy lanterns hanging from the ceiling lit everything to a soft yellow. There was a good fiddler playing, and on the far side of the room people were dancing. Indian servants passed around glasses and jugs of wine and brandy, and the long tables at each end of the room were loaded with food. If they had left him alone, he wouldn't have minded so much being here.

But they all wanted to meet him, now another, Stockton turning to introduce some woman, somebody's wife, who bubbled and leaned on him; she smelled like roses. She grabbed his arm like an old aunt. He fended her off, and Stockton, practiced, courtly, collected her away from him.

Bidwell was over by the door. Kit liked Bidwell better than most and was headed that way when he saw Frémont over there too. Kit turned his back.

That trapped him with Stockton again, the commodore's voice booming at him. "Isn't that true? The Mexicans won't fight, as long as we keep their faces to the floor."

Kit said, "Hell, they never fight. You can't make 'em fight." Stockton was much taller than he was; Kit kept his eyes at his own level, which always bothered big men.

"Larkin wants me to sign a truce." Stockton stooped a little, trying to catch his eyes. "I think that's small-minded. My plans are these, sir — I want to raise a thousand men in California and sail them down to Mazatlán and march on Mexico City. I'll end the war by Christmas. What do you say to that? I'll be military governor of Mexico in '48 and president of the United States in '52!"

"Yeah, sure, tell it to Frémont," Kit said. He had to get out of here, and he started around Stockton, toward the door through which Larkin had escaped.

The commodore reached out his hand and caught him by the arm. "You're the man I want to talk to, Carson."

Kit jerked around, rotating his arm out of the commodore's

grasp. "I don't want to talk to you," he said softly. "And that's what matters."

Stockton drew back, his shoulders square, his face stiff with wounded pride and reasonable fear. His throat worked up and down. Kit walked away, on through the room, circling around the dancers, to the verandah on the outside.

From here he could see out across the bay. The lights on the ships pocked the dark. The air tasted salty, damp, with the faint, sour tang of the shore wrack. The wind sang through the pine trees on the headland south of the customs house. He half sat on the rail at the end of the verandah and felt around in his coat for a cigar.

Into the yellow wedge of light spilling out the door a man walked, looked around, saw him. It was Frémont. He paused, thinking it over, and finally came slowly up the wooden porch toward Kit. "Everybody is talking about you. Somebody just said you're as famous as Wellington."

"Who's that?" Kit said. He folded his arms over his chest. He knew who Wellington was.

"An English duke. You should have locked Cat Reilly up with Sutter. She's down here making trouble."

"I saw her when we rode in."

"She threatened me, the bitch! You should have left her in the desert."

Kit's temper flashed. "Shut up."

Frémont said hastily, "Of course, I meant that figuratively."

"You didn't mean it at all."

Frémont played with his mustaches, looking elsewhere. Kit climbed over the railing and dropped down to the sandy yard in front of the customs house, where their horses were hitched up to a rail. His officer was watching him morosely from the verandah. Kit climbed into his saddle and ambled away down the street.

He left the noise behind, the lights, the thousand competitions of the crowd. In the dark, alone, he felt a little better, but not much. The war was over now, the good part anyway. From here on, it all looked too easy, no real fighting, just a lot of mouthwork and paperwork. Too much brass, too much muscle spent polishing the brass. He thought: Time to move on.

But now he had come to the edge.

He rode down past the road, down to the beach, to the end of the continent, until he had nowhere left to go.

The beach curled away into the dark, the sand a faint, pale sweep above the black water. The crash of the surf felt good to his ears, like the mist on his face, soft and cool. He nudged the horse out into the sea, where the waves came up and broke against his boots. A bird screamed at him. He leaned his hands on the pommel of his saddle, staring west, and let the restless surge of the ocean dissolve his temper in its cleansing, renewing chaos.

This was all going sour on him; he was beginning to wish he had left the Bear Flag flying.

Too late now. He was getting to be an old man — that was being old, when you looked back and regretted it all. He spurred the horse, trying to move it out into the ocean, maybe even swim in the high-piled surf, but the horse stiffened its legs and snorted, frightened, and flung its nose up, and he let it bound away back to the shore.

Frémont said, "Oh, well, he's always strange around crowds of people. I think personally he hates everybody."

Gillespie laughed, misunderstanding, or rather, liking what Frémont had said about Kit without considering what it meant about himself. He was looking around the room with a hawk-like intensity. "I'll bet you half these people aren't on our side. You know that, Frémont? Half at least of these people are enemies of the United States of America."

Annoyed, Frémont grunted at him. So far everything was going very well; Stockton was even suggesting that John Charles Frémont would soon be acting governor of California. He wanted no more enemies. What Cat Reilly had said to him fretted like something buried under the skin, and Kit had refused to exorcise her for him, which aggravated it. He took another fortifying sip of brandy.

"That Larkin," Gillespie said, "for one of them."

Frémont laughed, thinking that the marine was making some kind of joke. "Larkin is the American consul here. He's a special agent of President Polk."

"That's what I mean," Gillespie said. "You can't trust anybody."

"I don't think —" Frémont turned, looking for Larkin, but did not find him in the crowded room. Luke Maxwell was coming toward him, circling across the sleek waxed planks of dance floor, the reflected lantern light blazing in pools on its surface. Behind him, the fiddles suddenly struck up the merry opening notes of a reel, and there was a cheer from the dancers. Frémont turned back to Gillespie. "What's the latest plan now? I understand they're negotiating a truce."

"God," Gillespie said, "I hope not," and Luke Maxwell walked up to them.

"Cap'n."

"Major," said Frémont patiently.

Maxwell, a little late, saluted him. "You know where I can find Kit?"

"He left," Frémont said, and returned the salute. Gillespie was watching them through the side of his eyes. "A bad case of crowd rash. What is it?"

"You mind that brassy-haired Californio horse-dealer spy Kit almost shot that time? He's here in Monterey."

"Well," Frémont said, "they paroled a lot of Castro's officers when Sloat took the place. I don't see any harm in that."

Gillespie turned his full attention on them. "What's this? An officer of Castro's?"

Frémont said, "Come on, Lieutenant, you're going to find plenty of Californios in Monterey." He laughed, pleased with this profundity, but Gillespie scowled at him and turned briskly to Luke.

"You saw this man?"

"Not me, somebody else did, but you can't miss him," Luke said. "He's the only blond-haired, blue-eyed greaser I ever seen, and he's a real snoop."

"Then he shouldn't be hard to spot," Gillespie said, and smirked at Frémont. "Come on, Maxwell, let's go hunting."

Thomas Larkin said, "I told you, the names have changed. Sloat is gone now. Commodore Stockton is in command of the Pacific fleet, and Commodore Stockton has so far refused to agree to anything at all. I'm relying on General Castro's legendary patience to give me time to work something out."

They sat in his upstairs study, between walls lined with the elegant striped wallpaper that had come all the way from France, and lit by the silver lamps his mother had sent him. The two big open windows let in the sound of the surf.

Count Sohrakoff as always had pulled his chair around so that his back was to the wall. He sat slumped down, truculent, dusty, his blue stare accusing. "Frémont is in Monterey," he said. "General Castro has no patience left. There are two hundred and fifty armed horsemen here now, besides all the guns and men off the ships. While you're talking truce, they're piling up on us."

Larkin raised his hands, patting the air, trying to keep this down where he could manage it. His voice quickened. "I'm asking Commodore Stockton to agree to a cease-fire as things presently stand, with General Castro in possession of the interior of the country and the American navy holding Monterey and San Francisco Bay, pending the outcome of the war in Mexico." He tried to keep the pleading out of his voice, the desperation. "I can't hope for more than that."

Sohrakoff said, "Castro would probably agree to that." His shoulders shifted in the chair, restless. His hat rode on the back of his head; he wore a loose red Russian shirt, with full sleeves and no collar. "What about the Bears and Frémont? They're the worst of them." There was a knock on the door.

Larkin stood up, surprised; he had thought nobody else was in the house. He leaned both hands on his desk and spoke firmly to the closed door. "I'm busy. Come back later."

Instead the door opened, and Catharine Reilly walked in.

The consul blurted out, "Mrs. Reilly. If you please, I must ask you to leave," and stopped. Neither she nor Sohrakoff was paying any attention to him.

Sohrakoff had risen to his feet in one supple, startled move. At his sides his long-fingered gambler's hands closed and opened again. "What are you doing here? Are you part of this?"

She took two steps into the room; the door swung shut behind her. "I was in the Bear Flag," she said.

"Damn you!" Sohrakoff stalked away from the chair, toward the middle of the room, and wheeled and glared at her. "What are you doing here?"

"I want —" She stood where she was, her eyes never leaving him. She was having trouble with her voice, soft and shaky. "I tried to stop Frémont in Sonoma, and I came here to try to stop him here."

Larkin pushed himself in between them. "We can stop this all, now, if we merely agree not to fight. The issue will be resolved in Mexico and Washington, not in California, as any rational man must see, and we can make peace here, with little damage, now, since nobody has been killed yet."

"Except those three people in San Rafael," she said. Her words quaked with a bitter, half-choked anger. "And a couple of hundred Indians. I suppose that's nobody."

"What Indians?" Sohrakoff came up the room, his body tilted toward her. "What Indians?"

Larkin saw how the words stuck in her throat; they came slow and grudging from her, as if they hurt. "Frémont's men massacred the valley Indians. Before he took over the Bear Flag."

Sohrakoff was still a moment, his face blank; he gave a little uncontrollable shake. "He killed them all?"

"Not all. A lot of them. To frighten us. To frighten Sutter."

"You people are cannibals!"

"Count," she said, "give me a chance."

"You roll around eating everything you can reach. When you've eaten everything else you'll eat yourselves up." His hands jabbed at her. "What chance are you giving any of us?"

"Count, I didn't do it!"

His hand rose again, softer, and fell to his side. "Why did you come here?"

"Looking for you," she said.

He shook his head. "It's too late, Cat. It's too late now for us." His head jerked up; in a rush he backed away from her, turning toward the open window behind him. "What's that?"

Larkin hurried to the window and put his head out into the cool, moist air. The lanterns along the eaves of the verandah cast a deep yellow glow across half the street. From the landward side, a troop of men was crowding forward through the light, toward his front door, carrying rifles. Their leader, hatless, marched toward the front steps; Larkin recognized him at once.

"Archie Gillespie." He turned back into the room, nodding to Sohrakoff. "You'd better go. Take the back stairs."

The Count's eyes blazed. "This is my country," he said. "I live here. And I won't run anymore." He started toward the hall.

Cat Reilly stepped into his way. "Count, they have guns."

"I don't care." He brushed by her, headed for the door.

Larkin's neck tingled with a presentiment of catastrophe. He got out of the room one step ahead of the Count and hurried down the dark hall to the stairwell.

There was a light burning on the landing, and another hung on the wall below, beside the front door; the two globes of light shone a dim figure eight along the steep, narrow rise of the steps. Even before he reached the top of the stairs, heavy knocking sounded on the front door. Sohrakoff came along after him; the consul glanced over his shoulder and saw Mrs. Reilly following them both.

At the top of the stair Larkin turned and faced the Californio. "Don't start any trouble. This is my home. My wife and children live here." Then, below, the door crashed open.

Hatless, a pistol in his hand and another in his belt, Archie Gillespie marched in the front door. After him swarmed half a dozen of Stockton's sailors and three or four Bears, all fairly well along in drink. Larkin in a rush went halfway down the stairs and planted himself, facing them; his throat was dry, and he wet his lips with his tongue.

"Why are you bringing this mob into my house, Lieutenant?"

Breathless, the marine jerked to a stop at the foot of the banister, his cheeks bright red. His eyes glittered. "Somebody saw a Californio spy come in here, consul."

"Are you looking for me?" Sohrakoff's voice rang out from the head of the staircase.

Gillespie gave a visible start. He took a step to one side, peering by Larkin up the trough of the stairwell. "You're the one," he said. He swung his hand out, gesturing behind him. "Stay back! Leave this to me."

Larkin moved between him and Sohrakoff. "He's unarmed, Lieutenant. And he has every right to be here."

The Count said, "Get out of the way, Larkin." He was coming slowly down the stairs into the brighter light of the door lamp. The cartwheel brim of his hat framed his face. It was so quiet that Larkin could hear the clink of his spur rowel. The consul backed up, turning, to keep the two men together under his eyes. The crowd that had followed Gillespie was packed into the narrow space between the foot of the stairs and the door.

Sohrakoff had one hand on the banister, the other loose and open at his side; his gaze was locked on the American marine. He said, "I'm walking on down and out this front door, gringo, and you're going to watch me do it."

Gillespie aimed the pistol at his chest. "I'm saying you're under arrest."

Sohrakoff answered that with a snarl of a laugh. "You can't arrest me. This is my country." The tread of the stair creaked under him. He went by Larkin, slow, his attention riveted on Gillespie. "I live here. You're the ones committing a crime here."

The marine's jaw muscles bulged. The muzzle of the pistol tracked Sohrakoff's steady, slow approach. Sohrakoff reached the bottom step. Less than a yard separated them, the gun between them.

Gillespie said, "I'll give you one more chance. You're under arrest. Put your hands up or I'll shoot you."

Sohrakoff said nothing. He gave Gillespie a long sideways look and went down past him, his back to him now, and started toward the door.

In Gillespie's hand the gun swiveled, the muzzle aimed between Sohrakoff's shoulder blades. He reared the hammer back
with his thumb. The click released Larkin, who lurched forward, but before he could reach the marine, somebody else was
there.

"Stop," said Frémont. "Let him go."

Gillespie, startled, twitched his head up, and Frémont put out
his hand and took the gun from him. The crowd, raptly silent
until now, burst into a low mutter of comment. They parted
down the middle to let Sohrakoff walk out the door. When he
was gone they pushed onto the verandah after him.

Frémont reversed the pistol and gave it back to Gillespie. "I
think you ought to wait for orders, Lieutenant." His voice was
low and very steady. He glanced up the staircase, toward the
hall above, and went on out of Larkin's house.

Gillespie growled, "You were lucky this time, consul." He
thrust the pistol into his belt and followed Frémont away. Larkin went to the door and shut it. He looked up at the dark
hallway at the top of the stairs, but Mrs. Reilly was gone now.

When he was sure that the crowd had left, that Gillespie had
left, he went back upstairs to his study.

The lamp had been trimmed down to its lowest light; Catharine Reilly stood by the window. When he came in, she turned
her head, noted him, and aimed her gaze out the window again,
toward the street.

"That's a man, Mr. Larkin," she said.

Larkin went around behind his desk and sat down. "I hope
less desperate than he seems."

"What was he doing here?"

"Well, actually, Gillespie was right. He was spying." He
leaned across the desk and trimmed the lamp higher, to put
more light on her. "Forgive my curiosity, Mrs. Reilly, but how
long have you known him?"

Staring out the window, she said, "Since before Sutter ate the
Indians."

"I'm sorry. What does that mean?"

She faced the light, her hands together before her. "What happened here? How did they take Monterey?"

"Back in June, even before you raised the Bear Flag, Commodore Sloat sailed in with the warship *Savannah* and two others. He had definite word that the war had begun, but he was a gentleman, and he anchored out there for a month while I tried to work out some arrangement to save everybody. Then one day with no warning he sent in two hundred fifty troops and took the place."

"They made no defense?"

"There was nothing anybody here could have done. The *Savannah* alone mounts fifty-four guns. From the bay she could have hit everything here with eighteen-pound shot and leveled it all in a few hours. Castro as always did the prudent thing: he withdrew out of range. Orozco surrendered Monterey; they paroled him. I've been trying ever since to conclude a truce. Commodore Sloat was at least willing to listen. Commodore Stockton is a different man."

In her lap one of her hands gripped the other. "You have to make that truce. I want to help you. Let me help you."

A weary smile twitched across Larkin's mouth. "Mrs. Reilly. It's not up to me or you, it's up to Robert Stockton."

She turned and stared out the window again. "What are we doing here? Why are we doing this to these people?"

The consul made no answer.

46 🖾 LARKIN WAS ADMITTING to himself that the situation did not look promising. Stockton had finally agreed to meet with a representative of General Castro's to discuss the truce, but he had chosen to do this in public, on the beach, in the excitement, the extremity, of a crowd. Whatever he said and did here would be for the crowd and would not be recalled.

The commodore had set the stage with attention. His men

had hauled in eight of the guns off the *Congress,* huge thirty-
two pounders couched in black trucks like great brass lions
squatting behind him on the coarse pale sand. The American
flag flew above them, and on either side, ranks of the marines
from the *Congress* stood at ease, their uniforms fluttering in the
stiff wind off the Pacific.

Beyond the marines, and on the beach and the road, half of
Monterey was gathered, watching, when at last Castro's envoy
arrived.

The envoy, Larkin saw with some relief, was Jesús Orozco,
who could be depended on to keep his head. After Hawk Peak,
Castro with great ceremony had promoted him to colonel and
hung masses of gold braid on his shoulders. He dismounted at
the road and came down the beach toward Stockton, his dress
uniform flawless, his boots and shako shining, a scabbarded saber at his side, four lancers trailing after him. When he stopped,
they formed a rank behind him. He saluted Commodore Stockton.

Stockton did not stand. In a chair brought in from his ship
he sat with his legs stretched out, relaxed. Lieutenant Gillespie,
who spoke fair Spanish, came up to translate, and the two officers passed the amenities back and forth. The crowd was very
still. Beside Larkin, Catharine Reilly was watching Orozco with
absorption.

Orozco stood at perfect attention, speaking in a dull voice.
He showed no interest in the row of huge guns aimed at him
over Stockton's shoulder, and he showed no insult at Stockton's
lounging in his chair.

This refusal to be ruffled obviously annoyed Stockton. He
said abruptly, "No need to go further with this. I have no interest in a truce. I am here to subjugate California."

Gillespie translated this with relish, louder toward the end.
Orozco never looked at him. His face perfectly composed, he
was staring at Stockton. He said, "No one has offered any resistance. You came at us without provocation, in overwhelming
force."

"No resistance!" Stockton raised his eyebrows. He sent his
bold, full-bodied voice rolling out over the crowd. "Yet Major

Frémont brings me word of Indians incited to massacre, of cowardly assaults from ambush."

"Major Frémont," said Orozco, without a quiver of feeling either in his voice or on his face, "manufactures the truth."

Without translating, Gillespie rushed up into the Californio officer's face. "Are you calling him a liar?"

Orozco said nothing to Gillespie at all. He stared at, or past, Stockton, and the silence grew, and finally Gillespie turned, looking baffled, and translated the remark for Stockton.

The commodore twitched in his chair. "I see no reason to endure insults against a fine American soldier. This discussion is now ended. No truce." He bobbed his head at Orozco. "You can crawl or you can run. That's your choice."

Gillespie gloated his way through this, smiling. Orozco stood without moving, his face blank, his black eyes like beads.

Stockton said, irritated, "This one is too shiny. Isn't he on parole? Gillespie, tell him he can hand over his bright little sword."

Gillespie said, "The commodore orders you to surrender your weapon."

The crowd murmured, and beside Larkin, Catharine Reilly caught her breath; he glanced at her, saw her still watching Orozco, her mouth half-open.

Orozco said, "The conditions of my parole allow me personal arms, Commodore."

"We gave parole," Stockton said, "to soldiers. You're not a soldier. Soldiers fight, they defend their countries. They don't stand around in fancy uniforms polishing their swords."

Gillespie, as he turned this into Spanish, gripped the hilt of the sword and jerked it out of the scabbard. He swung it free, and the sun caught it in a single blinding flash. Orozco did not move. The sword flew in a high, high arc out over Monterey Bay, to splash into the water beyond the surf.

"You're not a soldier," Gillespie said, his voice as loud and crackling as the sound of the flag whipping in the wind. "You don't deserve a soldier's respect."

Catharine Reilly moved, and Larkin looked at her again, but she had only folded her arms over her chest. She was frowning at Stockton, her wide mouth warped with dislike. The crowd was muttering, and behind Larkin people were moving up, edging closer. Spanish voices rose, puzzled, angry. Larkin glanced around, and saw the stunned faces of the people near him. Even the Anglos were amazed at this venom.

Stockton saw it too. He crossed one leg over the other. "Lieutenant, that's enough."

Gillespie backed up, the fair skin of his face flooded with color. As if he had savaged himself, his own uniform looked suddenly disheveled and awry. Orozco stood before them, his long face still, his black eyes unblinking.

Stockton said, "You're dismissed," and his hand started toward his forehead: then he realized he was saluting, and he stopped. Orozco gave him as crisp and military a salute as he would have given General Castro, turned precisely, and walked away. The four lancers flanked him and they marched away through the crowd.

The commodore slouched in the chair. "Well, now we can get back to work," he said loudly. The crowd was leaking away; Gillespie stepped back and stood there like a toy, waiting to be wound up again. Larkin let out his breath slowly, and his shoulders went slack under his coat. Everything he had built since he came to Monterey seemed to be sinking into the sand. When he looked, Catharine Reilly had gone. Heavy-footed, he went away toward his house.

General Castro pulled his gloves on. "I'm leaving you half the lancers. A few of the other officers have elected to stay behind also." His voice was brisk, loud, as if they stood on a parade-ground, as if he were still in command. As if he were marching down the street, and not running away to Mexico. "I'll try to raise an army in Sonora. Perhaps Mexico City can supply us with some artillery."

Orozco said, "Yes, General."

Castro glanced across the courtyard, toward the columns of mounted men waiting to escort him on his flight, toward the three cannon packed and ready to flee with him. In the sunlight

their brass barrels gleamed like false gold. All along the three
closed sides of the courtyard, beneath the eaves of the red-tiled
roofs, Castro's servants and minions watched in silence. Only
the racket of the birds in the trees disturbed the quiet.

The general's gaze returned to Orozco.

"While I am out of the country, you are in command of California. Take whatever advantage you find in the situation;
maintain your position as well as possible."

Orozco said, "Yes, General." He spent no more interest on
General Castro, who after a few moments would effectively
cease to exist.

"God help you," General Castro said. He saluted, turned to
his horse, and mounted.

Orozco took a step back, out of the dust, and watched the
commandante-general of California jog his horse up to the head
of his little escort. There he lifted his hand, and the whole little
army marched away. As they passed out the gateway the long
lines of white-shirted servants broke and ran, some hurrying
toward the gate, crying out farewells, and others rushing back
into the mission buildings. Many of them crowded into the
church.

Orozco walked back toward the barracks. In the white plastered wall there was a small gate; he let himself through it into
the lane beyond. A row of fragrant trees grew along it, their
heavy leaf masses rumbling with bees; between the gnarled
trunks he could look down across the head of the Salinas Valley,
pale and soft in the summer sun, toward Monterey.

California was his command now — his.

He would have to stop wearing the uniform, which made
him too conspicuous. Since he had given his parole to the Anglos, fighting against them would make him an outlaw in their
eyes anyway. He had to draw back, collect the men left to him,
find some aerie and watch and wait a while, see what broke
where the Anglos stepped and what caught fire when they
rubbed too hard. He had certain advantages: he knew the
ground, he had a few good soldiers. He had the benefit of the
Anglos' own ignorance and confusion.

He continued to look across the valley, remembering the marine's insults, the shrill of his sword leaving its scabbard, the
blinding flash of the blade through the air. They thought they
had thrown him down, as easily as that. Instead they had freed
him. They thought this war was over. Instead it was just beginning. He went on down the lane, past the trees, into the open
air.

A week after Stockton refused the truce, in the beginning of
August, the commodore loaded Frémont's men and his own on
board the *Congress* and the *Savannah* and sailed south, to take
control of El Pueblo de los Angeles, the only town of any size
in California. That afternoon, while Larkin was sitting in his
study, using the fresh quiet to pull his thoughts together, Catharine Reilly came in.

She said, "Mr. Larkin, I have to talk to you. I won't be long,
I promise."

He sat back in his chair, looking her over. She had been living
in his house now for nearly two weeks and she dined with him
every evening, but they had hardly spoken since the night she
found Count Sohrakoff here. Larkin had kept some watch on
her, through his servants; he knew she went around the town
as boldly as any man, which had worried him a little at first.
His servants were fascinated with her, making up gossip about
her, none of it as extraordinary as the truth.

She did not look extraordinary, a small, slender woman
wearing a frayed muslin dress, her mass of black curls caught
in a ribbon.

He said, "Well, Mrs. Reilly, have a seat. I hope I can be of
some service to you."

"I owe you a lot already," she said. She sat down in the chair
across the desk from him, sweeping her skirt smooth with one
hand. "You've taken me in like an orphan. I wish I could repay
you."

"No trouble at all. Stay as long as you like. In fact, I am
hoping, now that Frémont is gone, you'll consent to let me show

you off to Monterey society. It's not often we have a grand-daughter of a senator here."

She harrumphed at him, her mouth curling at the corners. When she smiled she looked much younger; he realized suddenly that she was only twenty-four or twenty-five.

His curiosity poked him. "Have you had any further contact with Count Sohrakoff?"

"No." She lowered her eyes; in her lap her hands curled together, one inside the other. "You heard what he said. That's over." She raised her gaze to his face again, unsmiling. An untidy coil of her hair trailed across her cheek. "Where is Orozco?"

"I haven't seen him since the interview with Stockton. General Castro has fled south. I have serious doubts that either Orozco or Sohrakoff went with him, but they are certainly no longer in Monterey or San Juan."

One hand rose to finger the long tress back behind her ear. "What will happen now? Is the war over?"

"Stockton will take the south — El Pueblo, San Diego, Santa Barbara. When that's done, California will belong to the United States."

"The southerners won't fight either."

"They have nothing to fight with, Mrs. Reilly. They have no guns, they have no armies, and probably they have no leaders, because the dons of the south have run too. Stockton, with the crews of his ships and Frémont's battalion, has an army as large as the entire population of El Pueblo."

"Then it's better if they just give up."

"Yes, it is." He leaned back in his chair, wondering how much to tell her; the advantages of having another knowledge-able mind to discuss this with overcame his natural caution. He said, "Unfortunately the company Stockton is sending to garrison El Pueblo will be under the command of Marine Lieutenant Archie Gillespie."

"Gillespie," she said. Her eyebrows jerked down over her nose. "Can't you do something about that?"

"No, apparently not."

Now she was watching him intently, her upper body in the

thin, worn dress tilted slightly forward, her hands fisted together on her knees. "Gillespie in command. Where is Stockton
headed?"

"As soon as they have the south he and Frémont will sail
back to San Francisco Bay and the Sacramento, where Frémont
will raise an army of one thousand men, to make Stockton emperor of Mexico."

She cackled out a mirthless laugh. "I can't see Kit going along
with that."

"No," Larkin said. "I don't know what he's doing. I don't
talk to earthquakes, and I don't talk to Kit Carson."

She said, "Without Kit Frémont will do nothing."

"You know them better than I do." He lifted his shoulders
in a shrug. "They seem foolishly overconfident to me. If there's
going to be any resistance, it will be in El Pueblo, where most
of the Californios are, and which is a fairly rough place anyway.
But they are leaving Archie Gillespie in command with only a
small garrison."

She said, "And you don't know where Orozco is."

"No."

Her gaze strayed. On her knees her hands opened and
pressed together, palm against palm. Finally she said, "Mr. Larkin, will you help me get to El Pueblo?" She faced him again.

He said, "Why do you want to go there?"

"A lot of reasons."

"You still want Sohrakoff."

"He's the only honest man in California."

"The price of his honesty could be very high. Perhaps your
life."

Her wide mouth tightened into a smile. She said, "Other
reasons. I started this, somehow. Somehow, I'd like a chance to
fix what I did. I'd like to prove we're more than cannibals."

Something moved, in his thinking, to fit together with this.
He nodded at her. "I would, too. Very well, then. Perhaps we
can work together. I'll do better than help you get there, I'll
give you a letter to Gillespie introducing you as my agent. Also
some letters to other people, friends of mine, down there. How
is your Spanish?"

"Terrible. I keep trying to talk to people and they keep on not understanding me."

The hall servant had reported that actually she was learning very fast. Larkin smiled at her. "Well. We have a little time. You certainly don't want to go down there while Stockton is still there. You need some new clothes, too."

47 🖾 EL PUEBLO DE LOS ANGELES lay in the southern desert some twenty miles from the sea. It had no harbor. The *Vandalia* dropped anchor off the beach, in the lee of a steep-sided, flat-topped point that swung out to the north and west. Inside this slight protection from the wind, the sea ran in to a long white beach and a stretch of low cliff, whose top was the edge of a plain that ran back toward the notched blue crests of barren mountains.

Between the ship and the shore lay a quarter of a mile of shallow, pale blue water, flowing in long swells that broke well before they reached the beach into a sudsy lather that slopped up and down the pale sand. Cat and the four other passengers off the *Vandalia* rode in a longboat to the beach; the oarsmen leapt out in the surf and hauled the boat up to the dry sand, the passengers clinging to the gunwales and bouncing on the thwarts.

Above the tide line on the white sand was a single building of adobe, the flat roof covered with black tar. Here a tiny withered man rented horses and carts; he expected her to ride in the *carreta,* but she made him give her a horse instead.

They followed a road that led them first through a ripe-smelling marsh, where stands of reeds fluttered with birds, and then climbed to a broad savannah of grass and wild mustard, high as her head, sweeping away to the east. The track followed the bank of a little river, at this season running a thin trickle down the very bottom of its broad sandy bed. The horses soon outdistanced the *carreta.* The other riders were all men, who ignored her, except to stare at her when they thought she wasn't looking.

She watched the hazy land ahead of her for El Pueblo, her thoughts churning.

As Larkin had foretold, the south had yielded without a struggle. After a month's glorious conquest Frémont and Stockton returned north to San Francisco Bay and the Sacramento Valley. The trouble Larkin had been looking for in southern California had not yet appeared. He had said again, when he put her on the ship, "Maybe nothing will happen." But with the little stack of letters he gave her, he had held out a horse pistol. "Take this."

She had started to reach for it and had then drawn her hand back. "No."

"My dear Catharine, this could be dangerous."

"No," she had said. "I'm not going to shoot at anybody." He had put the gun away.

Now the little caravan climbed up a short, steep slope to a flat, wide, grassy meadow, and at the far edge of that the plain rose again, like going up steps. Beside the trail now and then they passed white bones, curved rakes of ribs, cow skulls, in some places great piles of them. Off to the north there were some low buildings in a fold of a hillside.

They were coming into a vast bowl in the lap of the mountains. The road ran a thin crescent strip through the sandy grass, and in the distance the flat, even plain broke in a confusion of sharp angles and white walls, low and humble against the gaunt blue slabs of the mountains. That was El Pueblo de los Angeles.

Adobes. It was not so different, then; she took heart. They rode in through the fields, brown earth ridged with old furrows, stubbled over, here and there the withering vines of melons and sheaves of dry corn plants bound together like poor people's dolls. She watched some pigs rooting through the dense, dark earth. In the distance the sun glittered on water, maybe another river.

They crossed the water as they went into the town; it was not another river, but an irrigation ditch. The hoofs of her horse boomed on the plank bridge over it. Before her the near roof-lines of houses broke the distant blue haze of the mountains. They rode on between blocks of adobe walls into the aroma of chilies and corn tortillas, the faint smell of tar, the overriding sweet odors of offal and garbage, the muddled sounds of the city.

The journey ended in the plaza, a broad, open square where the dust was pocked with countless footprints. On three of the sides stood big adobe houses with balconies and tiled roofs; the narrow windows in the walls facing the plaza were shuttered and barred. The high, scalloped front of a church stood on the fourth side, its plaster pierced with holes for bells.

American headquarters was down the Calle Principale from the plaza, in another part of the town. The Stars and Stripes flew on a pole rigged in front of a long, low adobe with a wooden gate beside it opening into a horse yard. Sitting on a keg in front of the open gate was Zeke Merritt.

He saw her and bellowed. Hulking, he rose to his feet and lumbered out a few steps into the sun, squinting, his eyes red-rimmed and bloodshot, his graying hair on end like that of a dissolute, overaged sun god. "Cat. What're you doing here? Hey." His arms spread and he engulfed her.

She laughed, her face pressed to his vast, stinking bulk. She had been unsure of her greeting and it felt good to be taken in.

Zeke watched her, his dark eyes narrow, his hands on his hips. "I done heard some bad things about you, Cat. Captain Frémont didn't sound too pleased. What'd you say in Monterey?" He got a chaw out of his pocket and bit into it, tore loose a chunk, and began working it down to the proper consistency with his back teeth. "What're you doing here?" He spat.

"I'm working for the consul, Larkin." She patted his stomach. "You don't think I could stay away from you forever, do you?"

"Frémont didn't like Larkin much either. How's it all going up there? They gonna take Mexico? When can we get outta here?"

"You're not happy here, Zeke?" She followed him in across the horseyard and through another gate into the house.

A short passageway through the building took them into an open courtyard, with roses planted along the edges; crowds of people stood here, waiting, talking in low voices, Californios, in their flat-brimmed hats, their short jackets and high boots. Among them the bearded American who strode down the walkway by the wall looked out of place.

He stared at her, recognized her; it was one of the men from the Bear Flag. She said, "Hello, Bob," and he muttered something and went off by her.

Zeke said, "This way," and led her down a corridor, from which doors opened into sunlit little rooms.

"Cathy!" John Bidwell bounded out of a room she had just passed and strode up to her, his arms out. "Cathy. What are you doing here? Is the war over?"

She hugged him. "Not that I know of. What are you doing here, is what I'd like to know. I thought you hated Frémont." He smelled familiarly of tobacco and horses.

"That's why I came as far from Frémont as I could get." He rumpled her hair. "Well, God damn it. Good to see you. You bring anything to eat?"

"Anything to eat?" she said, startled, and looked at Zeke.

The big man shrugged, his black brows furling down over his nose. "Getting hard to find grub," he said. He nodded. "There's Gillespie."

She swung around. They were ten feet down the corridor from an open door, where several men stood with their backs to her. She drew in a long breath and let it out again, pulled herself up as tall as she could, and wended a way through the men to the threshold of the room.

Inside, several men were arguing in loud voices that they had worked too hard already and wanted time off. She knew most of them, Bear Flaggers, Sutter's men, John Christenson among them. One man wore a blue uniform; so Gillespie did have some regular soldiers here.

Gillespie himself marched up through the uproar of voices, hatless, his yellow hair bristling. "This is a war — I'm not sleeping either, damn it!" He saw her. His face fell open with surprise. "How the hell did you get here?"

In the back of the room, John Christenson said, "Jesus, it's Cat Reilly."

"Thomas Larkin sent me here." She held out the folded papers introducing her.

"Hey, Cat, is the war over yet?" somebody called, and she waggled her hand at him.

Gillespie took the papers. She looked around again, from face to face. "Where's Kit?"

The marine jerked his gaze up to her. "He's gone. He's got the dispatches announcing the conquest of California, and he's taking them to Washington."

"Washington!"

"He says he can get there in sixty days." Zeke had come in behind her. "We all got cash riding on it, one way or another." The other men rumbled, breaking into smiles. "Some of us got other than cash." There was laughter, and in unison they turned to leer at John Christenson.

She faced Gillespie, who was reading her letter of introduction. "What's this about your not having anything to eat?"

Another of the Bears said, "It's there. I say, tear this place apart until we find their cache." The other men growled, a rumble of baffled discontent.

Gillespie thrust her papers into the breast of his uniform coat. "That's no business of yours, Mrs. Reilly. As I remember, you behaved in a most questionable manner both in Sonoma and in Monterey. Whatever your business here for Larkin, do it and get out. Merritt, see she has proper quarters. I can't spare a guard. The rest of you, come with me now, and no more mutiny or I'll throw you all in irons."

He marched out, brisk, and reluctantly they trudged after him.

"Send all these people home!" he shouted, out in the courtyard. "I'm not hearing any more petitions!"

"He has fifty men," Cat said to Zeke Merritt, "and he wants to chain them up."

The big man sighed sadly at her. "This here soldierin' life ain't what it's talked around to be, Cat."

He led her out of the office and off through the adobe, looking for space for her to stay; the other men overflowed the place,
their gear scattered along the walkway and through all the little
rooms. They had scratched words on the walls and hacked up
the dirt floors to make fire pits and pissed in the corners.

Zeke said, "Whatever you done in Monterey, Cat, don't do it
here. We got enough problems." He pitched boxes and a saddle
and a stack of moldering blankets out of a room in the southwest corner of the adobe. "Clean this up a little, maybe."

"This will be fine," she said. "Why is there nothing to eat?"

"Goddamn greasers are hoarding everything."

"Zeke, I rode up through rangeland to get here. There should
be cattle all over. You should at least have meat."

He leaned against the wall; his eyebrows wiggled. "Maybe.
We don't."

"Were there cattle on the range when you got here?"

"Yeah, I guess so. Lots of horses, too, and now they're gone."
He stuck his thumbs in his belt. "You know the greasers.
They're so damn touchy, any little thing — anyway, they don't
just blow up in your face like ordinary people, they hold it in
and let it stew a while."

She looked around at the bare little room; there was a window, a rag covering it, and she went over and pulled the rag
down. A stream of dusty sunshine flooded in. "Are you having
any other kinds of trouble?"

"Naw," Zeke said. "We're handling it." He hitched his pants
up with his thumbs. Brown tobacco juice stained his beard.
"They're still greasers. They don't fight, they just get mad, like
I said, and sulk."

"Zeke, it sounds to me as if they're doing more than sulk.
They're driving off your meat, they have Gillespie going without sleep and the rest of you mutinous."

The big man shook his head. "I'm not paying that much
attention, you know, I just want to go home, Cat." His voice
was plaintive. He straightened, his hands swinging loose. "I'll
get your trunk. You'd best find a broom or something." He
ambled out toward the door; as he went out of the room his

hand slid out and stroked her arm. "Glad you're here, lady." He walked out, leaving her to stare frowning into the dusty sunlight.

In Monterey they had slaughtered cattle every Saturday; today was Saturday, but in El Pueblo there was no cattle drive. Maybe they had another day for it. She walked around the little city for a while and found no market either.

The plaza was deserted, even now, in the middle of the day. The people who went into the church seemed to sneak in around the corner. All the big houses at the sides of the plaza were empty; she guessed they belonged to rich people, who had someplace else to go when the Americans moved in.

There were still plenty of Californios here. She stood on the bank of the irrigation ditch and watched a steady file of men and women and children moving back and forth between the town and the surrounding fields. In the ditch, two men with shovels were digging the silt out of the bottom. A great hump-backed brown sow with four or five half-grown piglets waddled away into the field across the ditch from her, her trotters sinking above the ankles into the rich, worked earth, stubbled like a three-day beard.

A *carreta* heaped with dried cornstalks rumbled across the bridge over the ditch. She stretched her gaze away over the fields and the tiny figures working in them, all dwarfed to nothing by the huge valley, sweeping up at its edges into blue-purple rock cliffs thinly spotted with brush. Through it the river's low, sandy bed curved down from the north past the town, several little streams running through stands of reeds and grasses. Behind her, in the town, the church bells began to ring. In the ditch below, the two men stopped working at the sound and crossed themselves.

She walked back through the plaza and down a side street, cluttered with the shacks and hovels of poor people. There was no grass, and only a few little trees; lines of white stones set the yards of the little huts off from the street. A goose shrieked at her from one yard. Half a dozen ragged little boys, hot-eyed, sauntered toward her with elaborate unconcern, broke into a run two steps from her, and banged into her; she wheeled out of their way, and they were gone into an alley, a derisive scream lingering with their dust.

In the next street there were a few little shops, all closed up, like the houses on the plaza. Some women passed her, draped in shawls, their shoes clicking. Under their shawls they carried market baskets and the baskets were full. She saw peaches, smelled warm cornmeal. Lingering in the shadow of a little tree, she watched a while, to notice how they came and went.

Across the street, a man in a dark hat knocked at the door of a cobbler's shop and was quickly let in, although the door seemed to be boarded. On the worn adobe wall above the door was the shop's sign, a painted boot. A few moments later the man in the hat was coming out again, a pair of shoes under his arm.

She took off one of her shoes and broke the strap. Going to the door, she knocked.

The door opened an inch. The dim face beyond said, "No, no," and started to close it. She stuck her hand into the space and held the door.

"Please. My shoe is broken. Please." Under pressure her Spanish was dissolving. "Please help me."

"No — no —" But he would not shut the door on her hand; he pushed at her fingers.

"Please."

The door sagged open. A broad brown face stared coldly at her. "Come in."

She went into a cupboard of a shop, deeply scented with tanned leather and neat's-foot oil, like the leather shop in Sutter's Fort. The cobbler perched on his stool, her shoe on his knee, and patched the strap together with a dozen stitches of his awl, his hand moving with practiced grace, a small delight to watch.

She said, "Why didn't you want to let me in?"

"Gringos don't pay," he said.

She paid him. "Thank you," she said, and left.

Walking back toward the Government House, she thought

that the Angeleños seemed to be going on as usual, in the spaces around the Americans. Maybe she had been too quick to see trouble; maybe there was nothing happening here but simple resentment.

She found Zeke Merritt in a sunny corner of the yard, trimming the hoofs of a lanky buckskin gelding. He wore no shirt; long dark hair covered his shoulders and back, his belly and chest, like a pelt. She leaned against the wall beside the horse.

"Do your boots need mending?"

He made a disagreeable noise. "Wish I was to home. I could likely get horseshoes, too." With the curved knife he trimmed a white curl off the side of the hoof.

"Go to the cobbler's down in the last street north off the plaza. Black Alley, I think it's called."

"The hell with that. I ain't asking these greasers for nothing."

"Zeke, do it."

He straightened, his jaws moving ruminatively; he aimed a long brown stream out toward the dusty yard. "Got anything to eat?"

"No. I was just thinking about that."

"Hang around, I scrounged some good stuff this mornin'." He stooped, reaching for the horse's left hind leg.

She settled back against the wall, her arms across her chest. "God, you are the hairiest thing."

He leered at her. "Keep y' nice and warm, lady. You oughta try it."

"Oh, no. God knows what hides out in all that fur. Tell me the routine around here."

He picked out the inside of the horse's hoof with the tip of the farrier's knife and trimmed the overgrown and ragged frog. The rank smell of old horse hoof reached her nose. "Ain't much. We're supposed to muster out in the morning and watch little Archie raise the flag, which I don't do, and we ride around at night, keeping the curfew."

"Does he send out patrols?"

"Up and down to San Pedro, like that. Lead this nag around for me."

She led the buckskin horse around the yard while he watched how it put its feet down. Several other men in a group came out of the house and took mounts from the string dozing hipshot along the shady wall; John Christenson whistled to her, and a couple of the others waved.

His chores finished, Zeke took her to the room he shared with Bidwell and Christenson and gave her some sausage and cheese and apples and a jug of brandy. She dosed the brandy liberally with water, and still her head thickened. The room had a dirt floor, buried under the men's cast-off clothes and gear. Three rifles hung on the wall beside the one window, with their powder horns and bullet pouches; Zeke took the pistol out of the waistband of his pants and laid it on the head of his bed.

Christenson came in, a saddle over his shoulder, and slacked it down to the floor. "Anybody for a game?"

"Deal 'em out," Zeke said.

The tall man kicked clothes, a bridle, a sledgehammer, out of the middle of the floor and put a stool there. His long blond hair hung in a braid down his back. John Bidwell and two men from the next room disposed themselves around the stool, and Cat slid down to sit on the foot of the bed.

"I'll take a hand. What's the stakes?"

All of them turned to her and released the obligatory tomcat yowl.

She said, "Sorry, boys, I've got money, and lots of it." Bidwell, smiling wide, began to deal. "I like to hear that, Cathy. Let's spread it around a little."

"Tell me more about Kit taking off for Washington."

Zeke belched a laugh. "Bet him ten dollars cash American he wouldn't make it."

"That's three thousand miles in sixty days," Bidwell said. "Half of it through the worst desert in the world. Not even Kit can do that."

"Just wish I could see him settin' in the White House with Pres'dent Poke." Christenson was staring at his hole card. "I bet he don't even change his shirt to do it, just set there like one of us, talkin' to the pres'dent." He gave a high cackle of laughter and pushed a piece of money into the middle of the stool. "I'll open."

The other men hooted at him. "You better hope it takes him sixty-one days, or you got to explain things at home pretty fast."

Bidwell turned to Cat. "Chris bet him his wife."

"What?" Her eyes opened wide.

Zeke guffawed. Christenson said, "Hell, I tole him: just once, and he can put a bag over her head while he's doing it."

They all roared. Cat stared across the table at the tall man. "You pig, Chris."

"Hell, Cat, he'll lose. She'll never know."

"You're still a pig." She had a deuce in the hole and a nine showing and she folded the hand over. Compared to whist, poker seemed mindless to her, which was probably why she was no good at it. "What's going on up at Sutter's Fort?"

The man on her right dropped a piece of Sutter's tin money into the pot. "Ain't called that no more, Cat. Calling it Fort Sacramento now."

"Those bastards. Where's Sutter?"

"He's there," Bidwell said. "They had to let him out, had to beg him to work for them." He dealt the cards face up, the little boards slapping on the wooden top of the stool. "Couldn't run the place without him. He isn't the same, though."

"He should have refused," she said. She spread a broad, accusing look around them. "You should all have refused."

They murmured at her. Bidwell now had two jacks showing, and the rest of them quickly bailed out. Bidwell took in the money; Christenson reassembled the deck and dealt the next hand.

Cat leveled her stare at Bidwell's open, guileless face. "You'd adjust to anything."

"You have to see things straight, Cathy. It was all going to happen like this anyway. What we did in Sonoma, the Bear Flag, all that, we couldn't have gone too far with that."

"No," she said, watching the cards fall. She sat cross-legged on the edge of the cot, her skirts tucked around her feet. "Especially not with Kit holding forty guns on us."

There was an uncomfortable little silence. They wanted to

remember that differently. The cards fell in their soft rhythm, forming columns on the cracked flat stool. Finally Zeke said, "Kit done what he had to do, and he did it the best he could, fast and clean. Got to give the son of a bitch a little credit."

"I don't have to give him a pile of horse manure," she said, and Christenson jeered at her, and the other men all laughed.

"You're just pissed off he tied you up," Zeke said. "That was a compliment, seems to me. Never bothered to tie none of us up. You got that other heart there, lady?"

Before her now she had four hearts showing; he had a high pair, the only other money hand in the game. She did not refer again to her hole card, but gave him a long, bland look. Their eyes met. Slowly he smiled at her, and she worked to keep her face still; but in the wicked gleam of his eyes she saw that somehow he knew she was bluffing. With a flourish he dropped a piece of silver into the pot.

"Let's look at it, lady!"

"God," she said. "Real money." She pushed her hand in.

Zeke crowed. "Women can't play poker, Cat. You can't fool me, not ever."

A foot scraped in the doorway. Archie Gillespie said harshly, "What's going on here?"

Christenson and the other man from the next room twisted to look at him, but Zeke was hauling in his winnings and Bidwell was shuffling the cards and they ignored him. Cat smiled at the marine's ruddy, perpetually angry face. "Just playing the game, Lieutenant."

Gillespie stepped into the room. "Are you aware," he said portentously to Bidwell, "that this woman is probably a spy?"

"A spy," Bidwell said, and bubbled up a disbelieving laugh. His dark eyes gave her a quick survey, up and down, and returned to Gillespie. "For who?"

Gillespie's jaw clenched, the muscles bulging. His fist clenched. "You slut. This is no place for a woman. If you cause me trouble here, I swear, I'll treat you like a man."

"Really," she said. "When did you learn how to be a man?"

The others chuckled; Christenson gave a low, derisive whistle. Gillespie's eyes popped. He took a step into the room, and

Zeke murmured, "Now, now, Archie. She may be a lip, but she's our lip."

Gillespie hesitated. They all stared at him, waiting, relaxed and easy; she saw that Zeke was the real leader here, and even Gillespie knew it. He turned and went out of the room.

Zeke's elbow jabbed at her. "Deal."

In the morning Zeke went to the cobbler in Black Alley and, after some argument, was let in and bought a new pair of boots. The following day the shop was open.

48 ✄ GILLESPIE'S MARTIAL LAW was iron-fisted: he forbade any public gatherings except a single Mass in the morning in the church, and he had closed the cantinas and the gambling shacks on Wine Street, forbidden the sale of liquor, and allowed no fires after sundown, not even cooking fires. The Americans patrolled around the city all night long, watching windows for the glow of a flame; John Bidwell told her that in the first days of the occupation they had smashed down doors and put fires out. It was easy to see why the Angeleños were hostile.

Probably they had other reasons, too. Zeke was breaking into the big houses along the plaza during his night patrols, which was why he always had something to eat. Cat discovered this by following him as he rode through the dark city.

But the curfew, also, was unenforceable, at least with the number of men Gillespie had, and especially if they were all like Zeke and spent the time on their own business. After dark, on foot and quietly, she went around the city and saw people everywhere, going from house to house and in and out of the church; she smelled food cooking, heard, once, the shriek of chickens:

they were even putting on cockfights. Gillespie was wasting his time.

Half the people for whom she had letters from Larkin had fled El Pueblo. Abel Stearns, however, had remained. He was an American, a merchant who had settled in El Pueblo long before, built his business there, and married a Californio woman. She went to see him at his adobe mansion down the Calle from the Government House. Like Larkin in Monterey he operated his mercantile out of the front rooms of the house, but the business was shuttered and the doors closed. A servant let her into a long, narrow room in another wing.

In spite of the summer heat, the room was pleasantly cool. Three big windows on the west wall let in broad strokes of light; there was a carpet on the floor, which was paved with planks, and the two big chairs by the fireplace were of mahogany, the seats cushioned in plump, figured velvet. The lamps had shields of pierced tinwork. Pieces of embroidery hung on the walls.

A Spanish guitar sat jauntily in one of the chairs. She picked it up and held it on her lap. Tentatively she ran her fingers over the strings and sounds came out, but she could not make the sweet and subtle music that the Californios drew from it. Slowly she picked out a scale.

Abel Stearns came in, tall, dressed in Californio clothes, his long, thin face ending in a broad jaw that gave him the look of an unhappy mule. She introduced herself, and he listened to her for a moment and shook his head.

"I won't open my store again until martial law is lifted."

She lifted one hand, palm up, pleading. "Gillespie is being extreme. If you can help get things back to their usual course —"

"Mrs. Reilly." As if somebody pulled a string behind it, the long face before her tightened into a disapproving scowl. "If you want to get things here back on course, get rid of Archie Gillespie, and fast."

She said mildly, "Is there so much urgency? Do you happen to know an officer of Castro's named Jesús Orozco?"

"Orozco." The question surprised him. He lifted his head, his neck stretching up from his high white collar. "Is he here?"

"I don't know. I'm hoping to find out."

"I think if I saw Jesús Orozco now he would spit in my face," Stearns said. "You and the rest of that pack in the Government House had better hope he's left for Mexico with General Castro."

"Do you know an aide of his named Sohrakoff?"

That name slid off him, catching no interest. The merchant shook his head. "No. I can't help you, Mrs. Reilly. I'm sorry." Grudgingly he nodded at her, giving her a crumb. "If Orozco is in El Pueblo, the priest would know it. Orozco is a very religious man."

"Is he," she said, startled. "Well, thank you, then."

"Which does not make him merciful," Stearns said. "You may wish you had not found him, if you do."

She wondered what he knew that he was not telling her. He took her up through the dark and shuttered storerooms of his mercantile and held the door for her.

"Larkin should never have let this happen," he said. His frown made his horse face look mournful rather than angry. "He should never have let it happen like this. There will be trouble now for years between us and the Californios, for years and years." He nodded to her. "Good day, Mrs. Reilly."

She went off to the church, on the north end of the plaza. The dark, narrow building smelled of incense. The worn earth of the floor was rippled from the passage of generations of feet and knees. Up at the altar, before an iron rack of candles, some bowed figures knelt, and she turned in another direction. Going along the side of the building, she looked at the scenes of Christ's Passion painted on the walls.

The work was crude, flat, without shading or detail. The faces of the Roman soldiers, of the crowd, of the man who helped Christ carry the Cross, of the two thieves, were all brown — Californios, Indio, here and there an African. The face of Christ was white as pot clay.

She realized that someone was coming toward her, and turned to see the priest in his black robe. Before she could speak he said, low, "It is the custom for women to cover their hair in the church."

"I'm sorry," she said. "I didn't think. Could we go outside? I'd like to talk to you."

"Certainly." He gestured toward the side door, and they went out into a covered walkway along the churchyard.

She turned north, to walk along the side of the church. "My name is Catharine Reilly. I work for Thomas Larkin, the American consul in Monterey."

The priest said his name; he was French. She had heard that he and another Catholic priest had come here only by accident, having been thrown out of the Sandwich Islands by Protestant missionaries. His soft voice was noncommittal, almost listless. "How may I be of service to you, Mrs. Reilly?"

"I'm looking for a friend of Mr. Larkin's, Jesús Orozco."

"I know no one by that name."

His voice was flat, indifferent. He was lying, without even bothering to put a good face on it.

She said, "What about a man named Count Sohrakoff?"

"I've never heard of him, either."

They had come to the end of the walkway. Behind the church on the naked desert lay a graveyard, a field of long mounds, some marked with wooden slabs; down at the back and in the middle were a few graves set off inside little wooden railings on knobbed standards like bedposts. Beyond that the barren land rose in a sudden jerk up to a steep hill.

She faced the priest again, determined to break through his resistance. "I want to end the war, Father."

His face was bland, asexual, bloodless. "The war is over, Mrs. Reilly. You won."

"The war is only beginning," she said, "and it will go on forever, and nobody will win, unless we find some way to make peace."

"I don't understand what you're trying to say."

"And you've never heard of Jesús Orozco," she said.

"Never."

She lifted one hand and let it drop to her side. "Thank you, Father."

"Good day, Mrs. Reilly."

She went away down the covered walk; talking to people here was like running headfirst into walls.

In the last shade at the edge of the plaza, she stood looking into the blast of the sunlight, the long, low lines of the adobes under the furnace lid of the sky. Nothing moved in the square, in the dusty houses. Yet there was no peace in the silence.

To move forward into the sun took an effort from her, an investment of her will. She went down the Calle toward the Government House.

Later that day she went down Black Alley. The cobbler's shop was closed again. She knocked on the door and nobody answered. There was no one in the street this time. She thought they were watching her from the windows. She felt their eyes all over her like the points of knives. Her head down, she walked back to her room.

One of Gillespie's patrols galloped in a few days later with a prisoner; in a racket of excitement the marine lieutenant called John Bidwell and Zeke Merritt into his office and shut the door. The other men drifted off toward the courtyard. Cat went into the room next to Gillespie's, a storeroom, where she had already quarried out a chink in the corner of the wall behind a tilted stack of wooden beams. The hole opened into one end of the marine's office.

She sat down on the floor, her ear to the hole, staying small behind the stack of beams in case anybody looked in from the corridor.

Through the hole some of the things said reached her only as indistinct rumbles, but Gillespie's voice came clear and louder; he was probably walking toward her. She wished she could see into the room. The wall was thick, the hole like a telescope with no lenses, the view dollar-sized.

Gillespie said, "He was trying to eat this when we caught him. It must be important."

"Read it, then," Bidwell said, grouchy.

"Damn it, I'm trying! It's in code. Somebody get a pen."

Zeke's voice muttered something she could not make out.

"Damn you, Merritt, you drunken sot!" Gillespie's voice had a high machine whine. "I got it! It's easy. Caesar's code. I learned this at college."

He was still a moment, and Bidwell said, "Any word from the commodore? We should get him to buy some food from Sutter and ship it down here to us. The *Vandalia* is still in San Pedro."

"Shut up," Gillespie said stridently. "This is important, I told you. There's an army moving up from Mexico to attack San Diego."

Zeke's voice rose again, the words run together into a mash of sound. She took her ear from the hole in the wall and put her eye to it, but all she could see was the opposite wall and the corner of a chair.

Bidwell said, almost idly, "While we're sending the *Vandalia* to get some food we can pick up some gunpowder, too." There was more rumbling from Zeke.

"All you two think of is your bellies," Gillespie said. "Listen here. This Mexican Army's due to arrive behind San Diego in two weeks. I told Stockton to leave a garrison in San Diego." Gillespie's voice was jubilant; he had found an enemy, somebody to attack.

Bidwell said, "What if the note's a fake? The dons go in heavily for things like that."

"No. He was trying to keep us from finding it. And it's in code."

"I'll go to San Diego," Zeke said. He had come much closer.

Bidwell laughed. Now his voice abruptly decomposed; she looked through the hole again. The light was gone from the far end. Somebody was standing in front of it.

They were arguing, their voices loud, the words impossible to make out. She clenched her fists, her teeth on edge. Then abruptly whoever was standing there moved away, and John Bidwell spoke clear as an angel into her ear.

"This stinks, Lieutenant. Don't believe that note. Why would they attack San Diego first?"

"It's closer," Gillespie said. "And there's a harbor there. You're not military. This is typical of the Mexicans — they only fight an enemy whose back is turned." His voice quivered a little. "At times like this I always ask myself what Kit Carson would do."

In the next room, Cat shut her eyes, smiling; she felt a sudden rush of sympathy for Archie Gillespie. John Bidwell said, amused, "Sure. Kit can't read. Forget the note, Lieutenant. Let's go out and scout some of these outlying ranches and try to find some cattle, and send the *Vandalia* to Monterey."

Zeke said, "Maybe there's something decent to eat in San Diego."

Gillespie said curtly, "You're dismissed, both of you."

Feet rasped on the floor. "Come on, John," Zeke said.

"Lieutenant," Bidwell said, "you been in California three months. I been here four years. I'm telling you, you're making a mistake."

"A mistake, is it?" Gillespie roared. "All right, Bidwell, if you know so much, you go to San Diego! If I'm making a mistake, why then, you'll do just fine, won't you."

Zeke said, "John, come on," urgently.

"You're dismissed, Bidwell," Gillespie said.

"Whatever you say, Lieutenant." Bidwell left, and Zeke followed him.

After the door shut, Gillespie said, "Damned volunteers." Cat got up and went quickly out of the room.

The sultry heat made the midday unbearable, and while the sun was high El Pueblo was quiet as a desert, but in the evening, in the early morning, all through the city, little groups of people began to collect. Gillespie rode out with his men and their guns and broke up these knots of bodies, but as soon as he had dispersed a crowd on the Calle another formed in the plaza, or in an alley, or in Wine Street around the empty cantinas. These little crowds did not fight; as soon as Gillespie and his men appeared, the people fled and turned up somewhere else.

Cat went into the back of the storeroom where they had put the captive courier. He lay on his side, his head in the shadows, his bare feet in the sunlight coming through the window. They had taken his boots off before tying his ankles. He was asleep when she came in, but he woke immediately, hitched himself up to sit, and glared at her. There was a bruise on his forehead. They had roughed him up a little, bringing him in.

"Thirsty?" she said. She had brought a jug of water laced with aguardiente and some tortillas and peaches.

He said nothing. His harsh stare watched her, hostile, as she stooped in front of him and lifted the jug up for him. For a moment, his head back, he scowled at her and made no move to drink.

"Please," she said. "Don't be a fool. Drink it."

He was young, and very handsome in spite of his bruises, with wonderful long mustaches and wide-spaced, expressive black eyes above a large, shapely nose. He put his mouth to the lip of the jug and drank, and she fed him the tortillas and the peaches, one bite at a time, wiping peach juice off his chin with a rag.

"What's your name?" she said.

He said nothing.

"Do you know Orozco?"

Nothing. His face was blank. They had captured him somewhere out on the valley floor near the Mission San Gabriel.

Her fingers were sticky and she rubbed them on her skirt. This next was delicate. She said, "Do you have to urinate?"

A flush spread across his face, and his gaze dropped.

She said, "I can't take you out of here or untie you. You'll have to let me help you. I'll get a pot."

She found a pot in another part of the storeroom and helped him stand up and undid his trousers for him and held the pot while he pissed in it. It took him a while to get the stream going, his face red as a rose, his eyes averted. She took the pot away and emptied it in the privy. In the morning she tended him again, and the next evening too, but she never got him to say a word.

John Bidwell said, "Come with us, Cathy." He pulled the knot tight on the pack hitch. The mule groaned.

Standing on the other side of the pack from him, she shook her head. It was barely sunrise and already the air was warm; his face shone with a fine mask of sweat. "Larkin sent me here, not to San Diego." Cat agreed with him; the note was a fake. Whatever was going to happen would happen here.

Gillespie stalked toward them. The front red-trimmed flap of his uniform tunic hung open. "She's going back to Monterey as soon as the *Vandalia* is done taking you to San Diego." He sneered down at her, his lip curled. Quickly he turned back to the men. "Now listen, Bidwell, don't you try any of your Californio tactics. If there's trouble, shoot first."

Zeke Merritt tramped out of the building behind them, a pack slung over his shoulder, his rifle in his hand. "We'll handle it, Lieutenant." His horse waited in the middle of the horseyard; the rest of the men going south with them were waiting in the street, just outside the gate.

Gillespie said, "I've given you half the gunpowder. We'll get Monterey to send some more. Pick your shots." He stalked away, swaggering, his hair a field of damp spikes.

Bidwell turned to Cat again, urgent. "Do that. When you go back — make sure we get supplied, Cathy." His dark eyes searched her face. "You got anything to eat for now?"

She jerked her head toward Zeke. "I have Captain Merritt's cache. That will last me a few days." She put her hands on Bidwell's arms. "Be careful, John. Don't shoot anybody."

His hands clasped her arms. "I'm going to worry about you," he said. His head jerked toward the disappearing Gillespie. "Do what you can."

"I'm trying." She went into his arms and then turned to Zeke, at the gate onto the street, and took a moment's shelter in his warm embrace. "Watch out for each other."

Zeke murmured something in her ear. His mouth pressed

wet against her cheek. Turning to his horse, he mounted up, and with Bidwell started out the gate. She stood there a moment watching them go off down the street. Twenty men trailed in a disorderly line after them.

Hastily she followed Gillespie back in through the Government House gate. "What about the courier?"

"I haven't had a chance to talk to him yet," Gillespie said. "Get away from me, damn you. I'm busy."

"Aren't you even going to feed him?"

He spun on his heel and shouted into her face. "I haven't eaten all day! When I eat, he'll eat! Get out. The next time I see you I may slap your face off, you whore."

"Oh, that's original." She folded her arms over her chest and watched him stride off down the corridor, shouting for Christenson. A few minutes later he rode out with the twenty men remaining to him, to chase away a crowd in the plaza.

She went to the storeroom. The courier watched her approach with the same furious, harsh outrage that Gillespie used on her. Now that John and Zeke were gone she was alone in the middle here. She had brought a knife; she bent down and began to saw through the ropes that bound the young man's feet.

He grunted, surprised, and his face loosened up. He asked, "What are you doing?"

She said, "I'm letting you go."

"Why?"

The ropes parted. He kicked out violently, both feet together, and flung the bindings off and stood up. His beautiful dark eyes burned at her. She said, "Turn around," and he did. She cut the ropes around his wrists, and he wheeled and lunged for her. She backed up in a rush, the knife blade aimed at his balls, and he stopped. She nodded at the window above him. "Go that way. Everybody's gone but they'll be back soon."

He said, "Why are you doing this?"

She said, "I hate to see helpless children suffer." He turned to the window, boosted himself up on his arms over the sill, and went away.

. . .

Later that day, when she went to her room, her trunk was open and her bed had been fussed with. She realized that somebody had rifled through her belongings. That night and the next she slept in a corner of a shed, hidden behind some empty kegs.

Two nights after John and Zeke went to San Diego, John Christenson did not come back from a patrol; at dawn they found him, beaten to a bloody rag, in the plaza.

The racket they made bringing him in woke Cat, and she came out of the shed to watch them carry Christenson down the corridor. When he saw her Gillespie roared at her, "Here, come do something womanly for once — take care of him!" She followed them into the room where she had played cards with Christenson and Zeke and Bidwell.

They laid Christenson down on one of the cots. He moaned. Cat said, "Bring me some water, then," and sat down on the edge of the bed next to him.

Her nerves were already tight, and the smell of old blood aroused a nameless churning fear in her. The room was full of men; the heat made the air thick. She unbuttoned Christenson's shirt and unbuckled his belt and stood up again.

"Somebody help me pull his clothes off."

The other men were milling around the corridor outside and pushing in the door for a look, their voices high and loud. They seemed charged, overheated, aimlessly eager. When she had Christenson undressed she felt over his arms and legs and found no breaks; his chest was dirty but undamaged. His spectacular injuries were all on his face. Whoever had done this had wanted a display and had gotten it. She searched around the clutter on the floor for a rag, found a torn linsey-woolsey shirt, and sat down beside the blond man and began to wipe his face off.

Gillespie leaned over her to bellow at Christenson. "What happened, damn it? Who did it?"

Christenson's eyes were black and swollen shut; his nose looked like a pork sausage; the front teeth in his lower jaw were caked with dark blood. His voice came feebly through the mush of his lips and tongue. "Dropped on me off the roof."

A voice in the back of the room muttered, "Greaser bastards." Somebody brought Cat a bucket of water, and she dampened the cloth and scrubbed the blood off his forehead and cheeks and mouth.

"All right," Gillespie shouted. "All right! Now, we'll handle this. Everybody go get a gun."

"You idiot, Archie," Cat said. She wiped Christenson's eye and he whined, trying to get away from her ministrations. She had never liked him much and she took no pity on him now, pinning his head down with one hand and rubbing briskly with the other. "Hold still, Chris, I'll be done in a minute."

Gillespie was giving orders in a crisp voice. "Oliver, get me that priest."

Cat said, "You know, Archie, somebody did this on purpose."

"Shut up." He struck at her, a contemptuous backhanded slap that banged her shoulder. "Now, listen to me. Everybody get armed. We're going to drive these greasers back into their hovels and keep them there for three days. Got that? Get me the priest!" He bulled his way out into the corridor; most of the men followed him. She finished mopping up Christenson, thinking, unwillingly, of somebody who might still owe Christenson an old grudge.

"Chris," she said, "who was it?"

"I dunno." He groaned, his head rolling to one side. She brought him some brandy and helped him drink it and tucked a blanket around him. "Cat," he mumbled. "Thanks."

She sat there beside him a moment, feeling useless. They were all sliding deeper into a terrible danger, against which such small, soft helps as this would be nothing.

He whispered, "Gimme another drink, lady."

She held the jug for him and stroked the blanket up under his chin. "Go to sleep, Chris," she said, and went out and shut the door.

Gillespie wrote a proclamation for the priest to read from his pulpit at the next Mass, confining every citizen of El Pueblo to his home for three days. Nobody was to leave even to get water or food. The priest protested briefly, in his tired, limp voice, but he took the proclamation.

The Mass was held every morning very early, before the farmers went out to their fields, before the day's heat began to sizzle. Gillespie and his men, with their rifles, went into the back of the church, behind the congregation, to hear the proclamation read. Cat watched from the plaza.

The wide, dusty irregular space was already shimmering with the warmth of the sun. Beyond the curled eaves of the church, the hill rose, brown and pale brown, and past that the purple-blue ridges of the mountains. It seemed a barren, ugly place.

Yet these people had raised this town here, built lives and a community. Her mind went poking at it, curious, trying to find a way in. She was beginning to get a sense of them, the colors and flavors of their lives, the sounds of their city, their way of understanding: enough to know she knew nothing. Enough to want passionately to protect them, and to be afraid of their will to defend themselves. In the church now, there was a sudden many-throated yell.

She straightened. Gillespie and his men were backing out of the church. Their horses waited along the edge of the plaza, and with their guns on their shoulders they mounted up and rode away, down the Calle that left the plaza at the church, off toward the Government House. For a moment nothing happened.

A few people began to dribble out of the church and stood, staring away down the Calle, while others moved into the doorway behind them. Their voices rose, angry. As the crowd behind them grew, the people in the front sidled out into the plaza.

Usually after the Mass these people went quickly off, to their homes, their shops, their fields, but now they spilled out across the dusty plaza and clotted into groups and stood talking. Somebody climbed up on a wall down the way from Cat and began to shout and wave his arms, and the people clustered around to hear him. The crowd swelled up the plaza toward Cat.

At the back edge of the crowd, a woman saw her; a set of

wide, dark eyes fixed on her. Turning, the woman let out a yell, calling to somebody in the crowd, waving and pointing toward Cat. Cat gave way to a surge of panic. Whirling, she ran away as fast as she could go, back toward the Government House.

49 ☙ ALL THROUGH THE DAY the city was quiet, but as the daylight and the heat faded, people began to gather in the street outside the Government House. Gillespie sent out men to drive them off, and they fled, but as soon as the men returned inside the wall the crowd was back, larger and louder. Steadily their numbers swelled. Even when Gillespie's men shot at them, it did not keep the crowds away for long, and the Americans were running out of gunpowder.

Just before sundown Gillespie gave up trying to drive the crowd away. He posted the twenty-five men of his command along the walls, their guns loaded and ready. His control of El Pueblo had shrunk down to the boundaries of the Government House.

Cat went into the room where she still kept her clothes and put on her riding skirt, which was comfortable to walk in. She packed everything else in the trunk and shoved it under the bed. She had eaten very little all that day, and some food remained in the cache Zeke had given her; these men here might need it more than she would, so she left the half-dozen pears and the sausage and the last two flasks of brandy on the bed. She left the room and made her way along the covered walk toward the gate into the horseyard.

The sky was darkening to a clear purplish blue. Above her, on the roof, the men of the garrison were setting up, stringing themselves along the wall, where the top of the building made an inside rampart for them to sit on. They carried what food they had up there with them, canteens of water, their blankets.

By the far corner two rifle barrels stuck up into the air against the sky like a tripod.

As she neared the gate somebody yelled to her, and she dodged out of the way of two or three loose horses, white-eyed and twitch-eared, who trotted by her into the inside courtyard. She went quietly through the gate into the horseyard beyond.

Gillespie was walking up and down, giving orders in a crisp voice. She stayed out of his way, although she doubted he would try to keep her here. They were driving all the horses into the inside yard. Some of the men were carrying armloads of hay out of a shed along the back wall; others were hauling water. She went up the ladder there, onto the tarred roof of the hayshed, climbed over the wall, slid down until she hung by her arms, and dropped.

The fall jarred her. She huddled there a moment, her legs throbbing. Out here in the two corrals a dozen more horses and some mules stood in a quiet, dark mass in the gloom. The crowd had not spread around behind the Government House, not yet. She could hear the distant murmur of voices, but she saw nobody else out here, nothing save the horses.

Out past the poles of the corral fence, the field stretched flat and still toward the next street; the moon would not rise for hours. She went around the outside of the corral and started quickly out across the grass toward the south edge of the city.

She would walk down to San Pedro and wait for the *Vandalia*. Maybe the ship was already there, and she could get some help for Gillespie and the other Americans. In any case she was not staying here. She waded through the high bunch grass of the field toward the blocky shapes of the houses ahead of her, and as she rounded the edge of the gulch she heard behind her the crunch of a footstep.

She broke into a run, circling the rim of the gulch, heading for the street. A quick glance over her shoulder showed a man running after her, twenty feet behind. Her arms pumping, she raced toward the row of shacks and small adobes that marked the street.

Quiet feet padded swiftly after her. She dashed down the lane between two plastered walls, jumped a heap of garbage, turned left at the street, and ran diagonally across it toward the mouth of Black Alley. The man crashed through the lane behind her, kicking aside the garbage and the litter; she moaned, frightened, and strained to go faster, driving her feet against the ground.

The street was empty. Ahead of her at the next block of houses, a dog began to bark. With every step she took, a sharp stitch bit into her side. The man coming after her was only a stride behind her; she could hear his harsh, labored breathing, the rasp of his clothes as he moved. She whirled to face him, and when he slowed, his arms out to snare her, she saw he was the handsome young courier.

Her heart jumped. She feinted to the right, and when he leaned that way she dashed around to her left. He lunged, and one hand got hold of the back of her shirt, ripping it. She spun away from his grip and ran back toward the block of shabby little houses, and out of an alleyway another man sprang at her.

Startled, she flung her hands wide and swerved, and from behind her two long arms encircled her waist.

She whined. A white panic wiped her mind blank; she flailed out with her whole body, hurling herself with all her strength from side to side, kicking and clubbing at him with her fists and feet. He hoisted her up off the ground, one arm around her waist, and struggled with the other to pin her right hand. His voice bellowed Spanish in her ear. "Help me, Rico —"

She kicked back, and her heel hit something hard. He yelled and loosened his grip. The other man had a blanket in his arms; he was coming at her, the blanket spread out to engulf her. She drove her elbow into the chest of the man behind her and tore with her nails at his hands and broke free.

The blanket swirled over her like a net. Panicking, she stooped down, leapt away under the edge, and ran again, and after three steps something caught her feet and she went face first into the street dust. The blanket swept down on her. She rolled and they flung the blanket over her again. They gathered her up, her head wrapped in the smothering wool, her arms swaddled and useless, her legs hobbled, and carried her away.

Terrified, she bucked and heaved against their grip, but they had her tight, carrying her along, and all she did was half strangle in the blanket. She slumped, worn out, and then a trickle of air ran down her throat. Slowly she drew in a breath.

A door slammed. She was inside somewhere, and the men holding her put her down on her feet with a jolt. There was a smooth floor under her. The blanket pinned her arms against her sides. She reeled, dizzy, and then the blanket was jerked away from her face and a voice roared in her ears.

"Here, Count, is this what you wanted?"

She blinked, dazzled, the fresh cool air washing over her, the blanket still wrapped tight around her body, and looked across a little room into his crystalline blue eyes.

"Yes," he said. He came a step closer to her. There was a light hanging from the ceiling, which glittered on the brassy nimbus of his hair. "Did she try to escape?"

"Over the wall." Beside her, the courier laughed. "You were right, we needed the blanket. She fights."

Sohrakoff was watching her with a fixed stare. "She's scared. Aren't you, Cat."

She said, "You did this. You dragged me in here." For an instant, with all her strength, she strained uselessly against the blanket.

"You're too valuable to let run loose," he said. He raised his hands out to his sides and moved toward her slowly, his voice a drone, as if he were talking to some horse he was breaking. "Nothing will happen to you if you cooperate with me."

He had known she was here and made no effort to reach her until now; she was nothing to him. A cold fear coiled in her belly. He was coming at her, his hands out. She shrank from him. "Don't touch me." Trapped in the blanket, helpless, she watched him come closer, and every hair on her body stirred.

"I have to see if you're carrying anything interesting. You can let me do it, or he can hold you while I do it, either way." He reached out and started to unfold the blanket, watching her face.

Her jaw clenched. She tore her gaze from him, and he moved in and pulled the blanket down and began to feel over her with his hands. The courier was watching from one side, his face lascivious, and she said, "I helped you, and you did this to me."

The young man's lips twitched. Sohrakoff laughed. His hand slid impersonally down her thigh. She looked quickly around the room, guessing they were in a house somewhere, and tried to judge how far they had carried her. Certainly not past the plaza. A straw rug covered the dirt floor, and there were a table and some chairs at the far end, with a lamp standing on the table. Sohrakoff felt along her sides. Her forearms began to hurt; she had scraped them, falling in the street. She stared at the courier, whose face had slipped a little when she accused him, and gave him another push.

"Gillespie wouldn't have fed you. You'd have suffered a lot worse if not for me."

Sohrakoff said, "Be quiet." He went off, back to the table, and lifted one of the chairs into the middle of the room. "Sit down."

"What do you want?" she said, not moving.

"I'm going to ask you a few questions." He went to the other chair and turned its back to the corner and dropped into it, crossing one foot over the other knee. "If you sit down, I'll let you have something to eat."

"I can't help you," she said. "I won't betray them. It's still my country, even if they are a damned pack of wolves."

"Sit down and I'll feed you."

"There's nothing I can do to help you anyway."

"Why did you let Sarbulo go?"

She glanced to one side, toward the young man with his extravagant mustaches. "Stupid of me, wasn't it."

"Maybe. Don't be stupid now. Sit down and I'll feed you."

She was hungry. She had been hungry for days. After a moment she went to the chair and sat down.

Sohrakoff nodded to Sarbulo. "Go get her something to eat. Some wine, too."

He left, purposeful. Sohrakoff shifted in his chair. Now that they were alone together the distance between them seemed to shrink, to thicken, a charged place.

"Where's Frémont, Cat?"

"Is that what you want?" She shook her head, tired, her hands between her knees. "You want to know the wrong things."

"What are the right things?"

"How to stop this."

"I'm trying to stop it. I have every intention of stopping it. When did you learn to speak Spanish?"

"I'm still trying."

"Why did you leave New Helvetia?"

She lifted her head. "There is no more New Helvetia. They're calling it Fort Sacramento now, and Frémont is riding Sutter's horse." Her voice quavered. Her vision blurred to a fog. She glared into the haze, determined not to cry. She was tired. She was finished. Putting her hand up to her face, she pressed her fingers against her eyes.

"If you hate Frémont so much, tell me where he is." His voice was a quiet, reasonable wheedle.

"You're not doing much better than he is." She rounded on him, angry. "You're only making it worse."

The door opened. Sarbulo brought in a red glazed dish of tortillas and meat and a little potbellied jug, which he set down on the table. The smell of the meat and the toasted corn overwhelmed her. Under their eyes she went up to the table and began to eat, her hands shaking. Sarbulo brought the chair and she sat down; he poured wine into the cup.

"Cat, where is Frémont now?" asked Sohrakoff again.

She chewed down a mouthful of tortilla, reaching for another. "Don't worry about Frémont. Kit's gone. Without Kit Frémont won't do anything."

Her appetite had her mastered. Even as she talked, she was eating like a glutton, with both hands. Her body drove her while the little god Mind rode on top and thought it did everything.

"It doesn't matter. They don't need Frémont." She gulped the wine. "You can't win, it doesn't matter that you should win, you can't."

She belched. Suddenly she was sick to her stomach, and she

wiped her mouth on the napkin that had covered the tortillas. After days of eating scraps she was filled by a few bites. Her head felt large and soft and loose.

"Even if Frémont never gets south of the Sacramento, there are all those men on the *Congress* and the other ships, all those guns, and they'll send more and more until they roll right over you, just the way they rolled right over us. Make peace now, and go on from there, because it's all you're going to have, and if you keep going like this, you won't even get that."

He said, clipped, "Gillespie thought he had won here, didn't he."

"Yes, damn you." She twisted in the chair, facing him, her fists between her knees. "And you led him right into this, didn't you, you worked him into this — what's going to happen to these people, now that they're in a full-tilt rebellion? What happens when Stockton comes?"

"Where is Stockton now?"

"In San Francisco Bay," she said. "With all the ships, and all the guns in the world."

"How much gunpowder does Gillespie have in the Government House?"

She bit her lip. "No," she said. She huddled on the chair, tired, feeling sick from eating so much so fast, and wished there were more wine.

He said, "I want you to tell me what Gillespie has."

"No," she said.

"I can make this really hard for you."

"No," she said.

From behind her a hand fell heavily onto her shoulder, and she startled, her skin going rough and cold.

"Are you going to beat me up now?" she said. "Like Christenson?"

Sohrakoff's voice was flat. "Don't touch her." The hand left her shoulder. He said, "Tell me what I want to know and I'll leave you alone."

She said, "Some of those people are my friends." Across the space between them, the abyss of the war, she said, "Don't do this to me, Count."

His face altered. For a moment he sat slack in the chair, one arm hooked over the back and the other hand fiddling with his spur. He said finally, "I know enough to do what I have to do, anyway. Do you want anything else to eat?"

"No," she said, relieved. "Please. Let me go now."

He gave a low, hoarse laugh. Getting up, he nodded to the young man behind her, and said, "You'd better get some sleep, Sarbulo. We have to move in before dawn."

"Let her go," Sarbulo said. "She talked, some, at least."

Sohrakoff came up beside her and put his hand on her back. "She's better off here. Don't let her infect you." He pushed her, not gently, toward the door. "Move."

"Where?" she said, her feet planted, and the hand on her back shoved her forward.

"Move!"

She went out the door.

Sohrakoff said, "Don't try to run. You're safer here than outside."

She prowled around the room, her arms hugged against herself. She was barefoot; her clothes were torn. He watched her from the doorway. He had expected her to be afraid. He had not expected this other thing, this anger.

In front of the window, she turned to face him. "Safe. Until you decide I'll do what you want if you hit me?"

"I didn't beat up Christenson."

"But you ordered it." Her head jerked toward him. "Didn't you." She walked again around the little room, past the saddle-bags slung over the chair and the saddle tipped against the wall, the bed below the window. Her hand flicked out at the deck of cards scattered on the table, and she wheeled toward him. "This looks like your room."

"It is my room."

"What makes you think I want to be in here?" she said, between her teeth.

He leaned up against the wall and folded his arms over his

chest. "Come on, Cat. You were smart enough to leave Gillespie when you saw he was trapped. Smarten up a little now."

She turned her back on him, her head bowed. He went out the door and shut it, took the padlock out of the hip pocket of his pants, and locked her in.

50 ♛ OROZCO said, "I don't want a fight, Count. Don't make me use Pico."

Sohrakoff pulled his cinch tight and brought the stirrup down. "Gillespie may not give up."

"We'll see. Don't let him kill you."

The Count gave a low laugh. It was still dark, an hour before daybreak. He got into his saddle and swung the horse around, fishing with his toes for the stirrups. "If he kills me, don't let him surrender."

Orozco said, "Do it properly." He walked across the yard toward the house. Sohrakoff went out the gate into the plaza.

They had come into the city four days before, when Gillespie split his troops, and had taken over an adobe townhouse on the southwest side of the plaza that belonged to the Pico family. Besides him and Orozco there were thirteen men left from Castro's lancers; the rest had gone with the general into Mexico. These men were waiting in the plaza now, at the end opposite the church, along with Sarbulo Varela and about a dozen of his friends, some on foot and some already mounted.

Andrés Pico and his personal army, forty men, were outside the city, but Orozco and Pico were already fighting over the command. If Pico won the battle for El Pueblo, Orozco would have to let him take over. Sohrakoff had no desire to get orders from Andrés Pico.

Sarbulo had seen him come out the gate and jogged over to meet him. "What did you do with the woman?"

"Damn you! Forget about her, pay attention to this. Do you have the torches?"

"Yes."

"You and I go first, and then the others, when the bell rings. Straight?"

Sarbulo thumbed his sweeping black mustaches, his eyes wide. This was new to him; Sohrakoff had met him at a fist-fight, and he was a good brawler, but following orders made him nervous. He said, "Let's get going."

Sohrakoff circled his horse around, counting the men in the plaza. Orozco's orderly, Chavez, raised his hand to him, and he waved back. The sky was steadily brightening. The Count turned into Black Alley and Sarbulo trotted up beside him, holding his rein hand high, like all southerners. Sohrakoff faced forward.

He had told Sarbulo to forget about Cat Reilly, but he himself could not forget her. He had work to do; today they took El Pueblo or they lost everything — but he kept thinking about her, locked up in his room now, his prisoner.

He pulled his mind away from her, made himself think about what he had to do.

They left their horses in the lane and went quickly down through the Sanchez Gulch toward the back of the Government House. The ravine was full of old cowbones. A field of tall grass ran from the edge of the gulch to the adobe wall around the building. A few horses dozed in the two corrals at the back. The thrushes were singing and fluttering through the meadow. The night had never gotten cold enough to drop any dew, and the ground was paper-dry.

Sarbulo murmured, "What if they see both of us?"

"Do you have a tinderbox?"

"Yes. What if —"

"Shut up," Sohrakoff said. "Don't talk. Don't think about it. Just do it." He pointed away down the gulch. Sarbulo hesitated, then went off. Sohrakoff watched him a moment, wondering if he was going to carry this through.

The sun was coming up. Sohrakoff boosted himself up onto the top of the gulch and trotted down across the field. As he went, stooped and quiet through the grass, he watched the straight black line of the wall against the pale sky.

Down by the corner, the line of the wall bunched up suddenly and moved. Sohrakoff dove headlong into the grass. A gunshot cracked out, and the bullet sang off the ground a yard behind him. He got his feet under him and bolted into the shelter of the pole corral.

A man yelled in English on the wall. Sohrakoff pulled down two of the poles in the fence and went into the corral. The three horses were standing stiff-legged, snorting, their ears pricked up; when he ran toward them they scattered, their quick hoofs hammering on the ground, two going right and one left, and he ran with the two on the right and got the inside one by the mane.

On the wall a voice called out, "Over here! I need another shooter."

With one hand fisted in the long mane, the other on the horse's nose, Sohrakoff guided it toward the gap in the fence, and the other two horses saw the opening and galloped out past him. There was another shot from the wall, but he did not hear the bullet.

That helped: this sentry was a bad shot. He knew some who would have hit him by now. At the gunshot his horse bolted, and he let it drag him along a few steps, out of the corral, and opened his hands and dropped flat into the grass.

The rising sun suddenly broke over the top of the San Gabriel Mountains and spilled its warmth and light across the valley, and the wall he was watching turned from gray to pale gold. Down behind him, in the plaza, the church bell began to ring. Sohrakoff lifted his head slightly, looking for Sarbulo, and saw nothing. He wondered if the Angeleño had turned scared.

Out there, in the street, there was a shout.

Sohrakoff got up and ran toward the second corral, where there were more horses, and on the wall above him the sentry stood up and his rifle swung. Sohrakoff dove for the cover of the corral post. The rifle cracked and the bullet kicked dust just beyond the stretched young shadow of the post. Sohrakoff reached around to pull the top rail down.

Up on the wall the sentry was reloading. Sohrakoff hunkered down, lifting the bottom pole out of its socket, looking around for Sarbulo. Then around in the front of the Government House a volley of shots rang out, and a roar went up from the crowd.

The sentry wheeled, looking that way. Sohrakoff darted into the corral and ran the horses out; he still saw nothing of Sarbulo, and he was cursing him for an *abajeño* coward when he saw a stick sail into the air and hang an instant in the sky, just above the corner of the wall, before it fell into the horseyard of the Government House.

Out in the front of the building, more guns chattered. The crowd wailed; Sohrakoff, standing in the cover of the corral post, could see people running away along the street. Gillespie's men were driving them off. Then suddenly a great triumphant cheer rose, and in the street the people running stopped and turned and looked around.

With a whoosh flames rocketed up from the corner of the wall above Sarbulo, who was throwing another torch into the blaze he had already built. On the wall by Sohrakoff the sentry backed off, recoiling from the heat, and the fire leapt and crackled and spat, growing steadily along the tarred roof of the building inside the wall. The sentry turned suddenly and ran along the back of the wall, toward the main part of the compound.

The crowd was surging along the street, screaming. There was another shot, and then no more. Sohrakoff ran down to Sarbulo, in the lee of the wall. "Here — help me!" said Sohrakoff.

Sarbulo's face shone. "It worked!"

"Not yet!" Sohrakoff pulled him away down the wall, on the far side of the fire from the sentry, toward the front corner of the horseyard. "Give me a boost."

Sarbulo laced his fingers together. Sohrakoff put one foot on them and stepped up, Sarbulo lifting him, and hooked his arm over the top of the wall. He was too close to the fire, which was spreading fast, and the heat washed over him, crisping his hair. He swung himself up and over the wall and dropped, feet first, into a trough full of water.

A gunshot cracked. The fire was blazing forty feet high now out of the roofs of the haysheds at the back of the horseyard. Sohrakoff sloshed out of the trough and crouched behind it. The fire was driving the Americans off the back wall and out of the horseyard; the last two of them ran through the gate into the main part of the building, and the gate slammed. On the roof above them, a man with a rifle stood up, aiming at Sohrakoff.

Seeing the man on the roof, the crowd howled, and a volley of stones pelted down around him. He ducked. On all fours Sohrakoff scurried down along the wall behind the trough, toward the gate that led out onto the street.

The gate was buckling in under the pressure of the crowd outside, so that at first he could not get the bolt off. Another gust of stones rattled against the roof and the wall beyond him. Sarbulo ran up next to him; together they fought one end of the beam up out of the bracket, while the crowd, whooping and howling, swept the roofs beyond them with showers of rocks and dirt. More men were climbing in over the wall. They heaved the bolt up and off, and Sohrakoff leapt back, and the crowd poured in past him, howling, and attacked the inner gate.

Sohrakoff wheeled, looking for Sarbulo, saw him in the crowd, and lunged for him. "Talk to the gringos — tell Gillespie he can surrender if he walks out in fifteen minutes."

Sarbulo plunged into the crowd, fighting his way through toward the gate. Sohrakoff backed up, out of the way. The crowd surged past him, roaring. Nobody was shooting now. He realized that from the waist down he was soaked; his boots squelched. He laughed.

The ringing of the bell woke Cat. She sat up, hearing people shout outside, and went to the window.

It was filled with little panes of glass; this room had a wooden floor, too. The window opened on a narrow alley between the house and another high wall; she could look down to her left and see part of the plaza, where a crowd had gathered, mostly women, their heads covered with shawls, and children. They seemed to be clustered in front of the church, peering down the Calle.

She walked around the room. She had slept in her under-wear, and her shirt was too ripped to be put on again. She dumped the saddlebag over, making a pile of clothes and a hal-ter and some dice and some Indian beads, and took a red shirt out of it and put it on.

It was too big. It smelled like sweat. She rolled up the long, full sleeves until her hands stuck out, and she put on her riding skirt. While she was fastening her shoes, there was a shriek from the plaza.

She rushed back to the window. Down past the opening of the alley, men were riding two by two, men carrying lances; they wore no uniforms except short leather jackets, but they rode like soldiers. As she watched, a don came by on a palomino horse, his saddle spangled with silver. The crowd shrieked in greeting.

She already knew that the door was locked. She picked up the chair and used the legs to smash the window in. The broken glass scattered across the deep windowsill and into a stand of dry weeds that clogged the alley. She climbed carefully out over it and went down to the crowd in front of the church.

The mob of women was pushing down the Calle toward the Government House. As they got close enough to see the build-ing, a high-pitched roar went out of them, and they broke into an eager trot. Cat ran along with them, craning her neck. She could see the black smoke rolling up from the building; flames nibbled along the roofline there. She got out to one side of the crowd, where she could run faster.

A mob surrounded the Government House. The lancers were forcing a path through them, but the going was slow even for mounted soldiers. Cat could see the heads of Gillespie's men up there like crenelations on the walls, but nobody was shooting. The crowd had broken into the horseyard; they spilled around behind where the corrals were. She ran up into the back of the mob and began to shoulder and elbow and slide her way through toward the front.

Halfway there she came up behind the lancers, and following them was faster. The mob pushed back to give the soldiers room, and the lancers spread out in two ranks in the street in front of the gate. Cat went up to the wall beside the gate.

Its two wings stood flared wide, the people jammed into the space between and beyond them. By the far side there was a man on foot, watching. When she saw him she backed off, toward the lee of the wall, and his head turned and he looked straight at her, through the boisterous crowd.

It was Orozco. She had seen him only twice before, in the gaudy blue lancer's uniform; now he wore a close-fitting black jacket, plain narrow black pants, as if he would deny his body any reality at all. She pushed backward, trying to escape his attention, but his gaze followed her. Somehow he knew her. She swallowed once, unnerved, wanting to get away from him; then the don on the palomino rode up and diverted him.

"I hope you have left the final assault to me, Colonel."

"I don't think we'll need one, General Pico." Orozco nodded. "Look there."

The crowd began to yell, a low murmur at first, but its voice gathered and swelled to a roar that hurt Cat's ears. She stood on her toes looking around, wondering what they saw.

Up the flagpole in the courtyard of the Government House, a white flag was fluttering. Archie Gillespie had learned just in time how to fight like a Californio.

The crowd kept up its victory cheers for a while. Orozco stood still by the gate, the don beside him on his yellow horse. Once, watching them, she saw Orozco's eyes stab at her again. He had not forgotten her. The red shirt made her obvious. She stroked her hand down the front of the shirt, wondering where Sohrakoff was, and she looked in the gate and knew he was in there.

They had done this. This time they had won. Through the cold fear in her gut there burst a treacherous leap of triumph.

Sarbulo fought his way up through the mob to the gate. "Clear the way — we have to clear the way!"

Orozco spoke to the don, who backed up his palomino and

gave sharp orders. The lancers spread out over the street. Slowly the mob pushed back, emptying out of the horseyard. Cat slipped inside and pressed herself against the wall, in the angle of the gate, out of the way.

The inside gate opened, and Archie Gillespie led his men out of the Government House.

His uniform was dusty; his face was set, stony, and pale. After him the other Americans came on foot, leading their horses, their hats pulled down over their eyes. They carried no guns. They filed out of the courtyard toward the gate, and the crowd let out a derisive yell.

At the screech of the mob, Gillespie's head rose an inch. He struggled with his pride, crossing the threshold of the gate, and then Orozco stepped into his way.

"Remember me, Lieutenant?"

Gillespie's head jerked up, and his face flooded with color. Orozco leaned toward him.

"Remember me, Lieutenant? You said I wasn't a real soldier, remember?"

Cat, watching, gave a quick glance at the other Americans, standing still and quiet by their horses; in their midst, John Christenson's face looked like raw meat. Quickly she scanned the crowd for Sohrakoff but did not see him. Everybody was watching Gillespie, who stood in his tracks, his mouth shut, and his face grim, while Orozco leaned over him, talking into his ear.

"I just picked you off, soldier, like a ripe peach. You tell me who the real soldier is. You had overwhelming force, and I had nothing, and I beat you, damn you, gringo, like a damned dog." He stepped back. Gillespie's face was pale as wax, his lips bloodless. Orozco said, "Get out of my city."

The marine walked forward, stiff-legged, his shoulders squared. The don gave an order, and his lancers swung around, forming a corridor through which the Americans could march. The crowd bunched in tight around them, just beyond the lancers, and now suddenly they got their voices back. They whistled and jeered and called names at the Americans marching by, ran along beside them, flung dirt at them, spat at them. Thus Archie

Gillespie left El Pueblo de los Angeles, surrounded by the hoot-
ing mob.

Sarbulo came out the gate. "They broke their guns. We got
some gunpowder."

An old woman walked up past Cat, an old woman with
white hair under a shawl. "I have a gun," she said. She put her
hand out toward Orozco.

Sarbulo ignored her. "We found some other things, too —
they tried to burn some papers but didn't get them all in the
fire."

Orozco pushed him back. "What?" He was looking at the
old woman.

"I have a gun, sir." She smiled at him, her hand out, a little
brown withered hand that stroked the air between them. "The
holiday gun. It was in the plaza. We used it for special occasions,
to fire salutes." She seemed to be apologizing for this wanton
use of a weapon. "When they came I buried it in my garden."

Orozco said, "Take me there. Wait." His head swiveled, he
shot another look at Cat, in the angle of the gate, and turned to
Sarbulo. "Find the Count." Cat turned and went away down
the street.

She had no place to go. She would not follow Archie Gillespie
on his march to San Pedro. She walked around the city for a
while, taking in the abrupt and tumultuous change in it. Quiet
before, empty, now the streets teemed with people, the shops
were popping open, a market had appeared at the edge of the
plaza. Children ran everywhere, shrieking and leaping. In the
middle of the plaza a man with a fiddle and two men with
guitars were playing and people were gathering to dance. Men
and women flooded in and out of the church; here and there,
suddenly, a group would erupt in wild cheers. The church bell
rang steadily.

They saw her, they knew who she was. They stared at her,
their eyes hostile, pushing at her across the space between them
and her; some of them came after her, cursing her and calling
her names. Once somebody threw a stone at her. She stayed at

the edge of the plaza, a wall behind her, understanding now something more about Sohrakoff.

By noon the plaza was full of people celebrating. Several groups of musicians were playing, and everybody was dancing. The women had spread rugs on the ground and brought out baskets of food. Cat stood by the corner of Black Alley watching.

Sarbulo rode up to her on a bay horse. He had a garland of daisies around his neck, and his mustaches were braided.

"Mrs. Reilly," he said, "we found something of yours."

"What?"

"Come along with me." He dismounted and led her and the horse a little way down the plaza and in through an open gate to the courtyard of a big two-story adobe.

This was where she had spent the night. She had not seen the front of it before, but she knew the room he took her to. With a flourish he presented her with her own trunk, now standing in the middle of it. "El Conde says this is probably yours."

"El Conde's very clever," she said. She went to the window; the glass had been cleared away and a grille of worked iron fastened over it. Through it, looking down the lane, she could just see some of the dancers in the plaza.

He came into the room after her. "If you don't want him," he said, low, "I will protect you." The door slammed.

She spun around. He was right behind her, too close, she could not get away from him, and he put out his hand and fingered a curl of her hair.

His eyes were hot and bright. She remembered how he had watched while Sohrakoff was searching her, and his gaze went over her now like Sohrakoff's hands.

She struck his arm aside. "I protected you once, remember? And I'm still waiting for you to repay that. Get out."

The greed in his eyes cooled a little, and he lowered his hand. Her breath short, she went by him, into the middle of the room, and could not keep from glancing at the door. With one forefinger he swiped at his mouth and his sweeping mustaches. He gave her another, softer look, and strode out of the room. She went back to the window, looking out to the plaza and the rejoicing people of El Pueblo.

The old woman's gun was a brass four-pounder. They dug it up out of her garden and poured the sand out of it, and Sohrakoff and a carpenter fit it onto a pair of cartwheels. Orozco stood watching them make a sponge and a ram for it.

"How much powder did you find?"

"About four pounds," Sohrakoff said. He knelt in front of the gun, his shirt soaked with sweat, sliding the new sponge into the bore. "About eight shots, if I measure it right. Did you look at those papers?"

"No. What are they?"

"I don't know. I can't read English. I only know the Russian alphabet. Reading isn't my long suit anyway."

Orozco took his hat off again and flattened his hair back with his hand and put the hat on again, exactly straight. The heat was like a club. He wished he were back in Monterey, where the wind blew sweet and cool off the ocean. "We need this gringa to cooperate." He wondered if he would ever see Monterey again.

"She could do it."

"Starting tomorrow we have to recruit every man in the area into an army. Form companies, drill them, arm them with whatever we have. Can you make gunpowder?"

Sohrakoff sat up, his arms over his knees. His hair hung in damp, dark ringlets past his ears. "Sulfur, saltpeter, and charcoal. That's all it is. Unfortunately it's very hard to make it explode instead of burn. You have to wet it and then dry it out and crumble it so it's the right texture. And saltpeter is going to be hard to come by." His arm hung over his knee. His hand was battered. "Give me six months and maybe I could figure it out."

Orozco gave a little shake of his head. "We haven't got that much time."

He had no idea how much time they did have. Beyond El Pueblo, he knew nothing.

"What will this shoot?"

"Stones. Bullets, nails." Sohrakoff stood up, pulled the long tail of his shirt out, and wiped his face. "I've got a couple of people sewing up bags full of shot for us."

"Good. Are you done here? Come show me these papers."

51 🐾 BY NIGHTFALL the plaza was a tumult of bonfires and horse races and dancing. Cat stood by the window watching; she had tried to get out of the room and could not. In the evening, with the sun going down, the door opened and Sohrakoff came in.

He said nothing to her at first, which warned her. He poked around in his gear for a while, staying on the far side of the room. She kept her back to him, her eyes aimed out the window, but she saw nothing; her attention was directed behind her. Finally he drifted up toward her. Her nerves quivered.

He said, "You should stay out of the street. You'll get hurt."

"I hate being penned up," she said. "Is Gillespie gone now for certain?"

"Pico took him to San Pedro." He was close behind her, within reach of her. She could not look at him. He said, "We found a lot of papers in the Government House. They're in English. None of us can read English. I want you to read them for me."

"I can't do that." Her voice shook.

"They betrayed you. What the hell loyalty do you have to these people?"

"It's my country."

"What about this country? Don't you have any love for this country?"

"Oh, Christ, Count, leave me alone." She went by him

toward the middle of the room, and he followed her and got her by the arm and held her.

"Look at me. Why won't you look at me? Because you know I'm right."

She looked at him, and their eyes met, and then she was in his arms, her mouth hard on his.

"Oh, God —"

His arms went tight around her, his hands gripping her. The kiss ripened. His body pressed against her, warm against her; she tipped her head back and his lips went to her throat. Through his shirt, she felt the swelling muscles of his upper arms. She put her hands on his chest and pushed at him and turned away from him.

She said, "I can't. I can't."

He grabbed her by the shoulders and turned her around again. "Oh, yes, you can."

His mouth came down on hers again, open and eager, and he pinned her against the wall, holding her with the weight of his body. Her hands between them, she twisted her head away from him, afraid now, and he felt it and stepped back and let her go.

"Damn you," he said. "I don't want to hurt you. I'm not going to rape you. I love you. I told you that once before and it didn't matter then, and it won't matter now — you're a stupid, selfish little bitch and I wish to God you'd never come here." He walked out of the room.

She sat down on the floor and stared at the wall, her face hurting, her chest hurting, as if she were being torn in half.

There had been a dozen people shot in the siege of the Government House; two of them died. Orozco went to the Masses and to the burials. He had the priest summon the men at the Mass, and in the plaza he began the long process of drilling them into soldiers.

The second morning after he took back El Pueblo, he called a council in the parlor of the Pico townhouse where he was headquartered.

José Antonio Carrillo came in first. He had ridden up from

San Diego with the news that he and Flores had driven the Anglos out of the harbor there. Pico came on his heels, talking as usual, and they went to the shady side of the room. Even indoors the heat was a constant pressure. Orozco sat behind the table at the end of the room and watched the other men come in.

Pico sprawled in a chair, his long legs stretched out before him. His voice boomed. "We should give up El Pueblo. You can't hold it. Split us into flying columns and we'll raid them to death."

Carrillo sat down on a stool. "That's a disaster." Soft-looking as a monk, he was a general of cavalry, a son of the family that ruled Santa Barbara and a dozen great ranches. He and Castro had been implacable enemies. He smiled on Orozco. "What's happening in Mexico? Any news at all?"

"Nothing."

"That's what matters, and we will never hear anything. We could win a thousand fights here and lose it all there." He got a cigar out of his pocket and bit the tip off and looked around for somewhere to spit it. From behind him one of his juniors came up with a hand cupped.

Sohrakoff slunk in, black with the filthy mood he had been in for days, and went into the back, past Orozco, and sat down.

Orozco leaned on the table. He had been talking to the *alcalde* and the *jefe* of El Pueblo about calling the General Assembly; he knew they should make an attempt at maintaining a normal government. Pico was wrong. The Californios had to hold the capital; if they turned into guerrillas the Anglos would ignore them, make them outlaws, run them down one at a time like wolves.

Sarbulo Varela, flamboyant in a red jacket and a huge sombrero, walked through the door, noisy, with some other men. After them was Chavez, the box of documents on his shoulder; he carried it up to the table in front of Orozco and put it down heavily. Orozco looked beyond him and saw Catharine Reilly.

She stood in the doorway, her face pale, her hands clasped before her, two soldiers behind her; when she came in every man there turned to stare at her. She walked the length of the room toward Orozco through an electric silence.

She faced him steadily, her eyes wide. At the last moment her gaze slid sideways for a second, toward Sohrakoff.

She seemed frail as a piece of driftwood. Her thick, curly black hair drew her head back with its weight. She came up to the table and stood there, her eyes green shadows.

He said, "Mrs. Reilly, you know who I am?"

"Yes, Colonel."

He glanced at the room full of silent, staring men. "This woman was Sutter's clerk. She was one of the original rebels under the Bear Flag, and she is an agent of Larkin's. She can be very useful if we can persuade her to be."

"I can't help you," she said at once. Her voice was louder.

"What's this?" He leaned out and flipped open the iron-bound box of documents. The loose papers filled it.

She glanced at the box. "Congratulations, Colonel, you have Gillespie's mail."

"I want you to read it to me."

Her speckled eyes slid sideways again, toward the corner, toward Sohrakoff. Along her narrow jaw the muscles tightened. Orozco leaned his elbows on the table. "No," she said, facing him. "I can't read it. I can't help you."

"They certainly gave up any claim on your loyalty when they betrayed you at the Sacramento. Why not enjoy a little revenge?" He sat back, studying the effect this tactic had on her, and saw her shy violently when Pico lurched up off his chair.

"Take a quirt to her," the big man said. "When she feels the lash she'll do it."

After the first jump she was still, frowning straight at Orozco, her mouth twisted; the threat scared her, but not enough. In the corner behind Orozco, the chair creaked. Sarbulo Varela strode up between her and Pico.

"No! This is beneath our honor, to threaten a woman like this." Sarbulo's face radiated a passionate indignation. "All she is doing is what any of us would do if the enemy took us."

"Sarbulo," Orozco said, "sit down. General Pico, I need her to cooperate. You sit down also."

"If she was in the Bear Flag," Pico said, "she deserves the quirt anyway." There was a low mutter of agreement among his and Carrillo's officers. But he sat.

"Yes," Orozco said to her. "You did this to us. You could make some restitution." He watched her face, waiting for some sign of weakness, some wince, some guilty start, that would give him an opening.

"I know my sins, Colonel, better than you do." Her voice was low, and now there was a throaty growl to it. "I would do you no favors, helping you. Those papers can't tell you anything that will win this for you. The odds against you are impossible. All you can do is prolong the war."

He said, "Sometimes that's the object, Mrs. Reilly. There are no ultimate victories. Everybody loses, finally. What really matters is whom you choose for an enemy, and what you choose to defend."

Her eyes widened. She understood that. Her gaze slipped toward the corner again, and her lips parted and she took a deep breath, and looked around the room, at all of them, and back to Orozco. "That's very noble of you, Colonel, and it's easy, when nobody is dying."

She moved in, closer to the table, and put one hand on the oiled mahogany surface, and he realized, surprised, that she was going on the attack.

"When you took the Government House, you let Gillespie go. You exacted a flashy public revenge, and let them all go. That's a California war. In Texas ten years ago, when they took prisoners, they shot them. That's a real war."

"I know what war is, Mrs. Reilly."

"Do you," she said. "In Mexico now they're fighting a real war. At some place called Resaca de la Palma last spring they fought a battle. It was an absolute rout. The Americans lost thirty-four men. The Mexicans lost twelve hundred."

Orozco sat back. All around the room the other men stirred, whispering, their words cracked and sharp and hard. She stood there a moment, staring at Orozco, and he smiled at her. "Well struck, Mrs. Reilly. A very good play."

"God," she said, "you're like obsidian. This isn't a game. You're talking about wasting all these lives on an abstraction."

"I'm talking about defending my country, which is your country, too, and you will do nothing."

"Everything I do I destroy. I don't want anybody else dying because of me," she said. Then they could all hear the feet running down the hall toward them. Orozco stood up.

In through the door a man burst, dusty and panting. "General —" He rushed at Orozco. "The gringos are coming. There are two ships at San Pedro and they're landing men."

A yell went up from General Pico. Carrillo swore, and among the other men there was a sudden gabble of talk.

Orozco lifted his voice. "Be quiet."

They stilled. Everybody looked at him, waiting for his orders.

"General Pico, get your lancers and ride down to San Pedro. General Carrillo, stay with me. Sarbulo, ring the militia out, the men we drilled today. Count, can we use the gun?"

"Yes."

"Good. Bring it. Chavez, where are you going?"

"To get your horse." Chavez looked startled. The other men were rapidly filing out the door; Sohrakoff shouldered his way in among them and they backed up quickly to let him go by. Carrillo moved off to one side to talk to his second.

Orozco turned to Cat Reilly. "Can you ride?"

She raised her wide eyes to him. "Yes, sort of."

"Good. I think you ought to see this abstraction, Mrs. Reilly." He got her by the arm and moved her along ahead of him. "Chavez, find her a horse."

52 ✒ THE SULTRY HEAT brooded under an opaque sky. The wind rose, fitful and quirky, swirling up the dust; even here, up on the hill inland of the beach, Orozco could hear the

pounding of the waves, an angry, sullen surf, churning up trouble. He got off his horse, not wanting to be an easy target, and sent it off with Chavez down into the draw.

Carrillo had come with him, and two of his juniors. Carrillo said now, "There they are."

"I see them."

"I estimate over two hundred of them, Colonel; this could be a quick end to our revolt."

Orozco did not bother answering him. The gringos had landed on the beach in good order, from two ships that now sat a little way off the shore, in the lee of the point. One was the *Vandalia,* which had no guns; maybe the other had no guns either. Orozco squatted on his heels, watching the gringos march up through the salt grass at the edge of the beach and on toward the long, flat-topped ridge before them.

He was watching from one end of this ridge. Sweeping off to his left, to the south and east, the crest of land ran like a broad, flat step; deep draws gouged the slopes, slippery with long silvery grass. His army was milling uneasily along the top of this natural wall.

Sarbulo Varela had brought out fifty of the militiamen, most of them mounted, armed with willow spears; they got off their horses now and stood at the center of the ridge, directly in the gringos' line of march. Sarbulo strode among them, working them into even lines, vivid in his red jacket. Pico had dropped back a little and was leading his forty lancers down into a gulley between Orozco and Sarbulo.

Beyond Sarbulo, now, back on the flat savannah, half a dozen horsemen were galloping up toward the height, raising a tremendous cloud of dust; Orozco could not make out the gun, but he could see Sohrakoff leading them, his hat gone.

Below Orozco, the river's valley cut a shallow trough back through the plain. The river itself, summer thin, was a glassy trickle along the far side of the wash. Closer, the gringos walked steadily on toward the Californios.

The dingy sunlight glinted on the Anglos' rifles. The men marched in a square formation; some of them wore uniforms, heavy green tunics like Gillespie's marine uniform, and some wore dark blue shirts, which he thought might mark the sailors off the ships. They had no horses, which was going to make all the difference.

Outside the square, on either side, ten or twelve men paced along, in no uniforms, in no order, and at the head of the group closer to Orozco was a man with yellow hair.

"Gillespie," Orozco said, and shook his head. "They are persistent."

Carrillo said, "They certainly are. Here comes this woman, for another case."

Orozco looked around. Catharine Reilly was kicking her horse up the grassy savannah toward them. She rode astride; Orozco had never seen a woman fork a horse before, and he found it extremely lewd. She rode very badly, awkward, slow, which also provoked him.

They had outdistanced her within moments of leaving El Pueblo. Yet she was going to be here to see it.

"Chavez," he said, "have you got the flags?"

"I have everything, Colonel."

"Good." Down there the front rank of the gringos was narrowing the space between them and the foot of the slope. Orozco lifted one hand. "Tell the Count to charge."

When she reached the height where the officers were, the south wind blasted up into her face like a furnace, stinging with sand. The sky was yellow. Out over the ocean, above the two little ships with their naked yards and masts rocking in the violent swells, the clouds were building into towers, miles high, black at their bases, their tops boiling up in white curling bubbles. Cat's horse stopped.

Before her the land fell away in a long brown sweep, and over the low ground a vast block of men moved steadily inward. Her muscles tightened. At the threshold of her hearing the even tramp of their feet sounded. The wind blew her hair into her face, and she scraped it back with her hand.

The Californios were strung out along the top of the ridge, a thin, ragged row of men; the square of the Americans looked much bigger, more organized, and now a bugle sounded and down there the square stopped.

Then along the ridge came a whirl of dust, five horsemen going at a flat gallop down the slope, into the face of the American advance. After them on ropes they pulled a little cannon that bounced and bumped on the uneven ground like a toy.

The Californios wheeled to a stop, perched on the slope, and one of them flung himself out of his saddle. Cat's hands fisted. It was Sohrakoff. Even from here she could see the corona of his hair. He knelt behind the little cannon.

The Americans' square faced him. The front row dropped to one knee, the next row stood over them, and all at once the long rifles swung down off their shoulders and pointed up ahead of them. There was a shout and the rifles cracked and then the cannon went off.

The reports of the rifles were tiny, like sticks breaking. The cannon was only a little louder. She saw no effect from the rifle fire, but the cannon shot blew in the middle of the Americans, blasting down the standing men as they stood shooting, bowling over the kneeling men as they reloaded, and left a swath of bodies like bits of fluff across the ground.

All over Cat's body the skin jumped and tingled. She clutched the pommel of her saddle, her breath stuck. Down there, he was dashing around in front of the cannon, swabbing it out with a long-handled sponge. Another man leapt from his saddle and helped him reload while the bugle sounded behind them and the Americans charged.

On the slope around the cannon the Californios' horses bounded and reared in a frenzied panic. The steep ground slowed the oncoming soldiers, and the little cannon jerked down, aiming straight into them, and the Americans saw it and dropped flat, and the cannon banged again. The puff of smoke blew off in an instant in the wind. This time no bodies fell.

"Where the hell are you, Pico?" Orozco murmured, beside her. "Chavez, give him another signal."

Sohrakoff's horsemen whirled around and galloped up the hill, and the little cannon flew away after them. Sohrakoff was still on foot, the last to go. One of the others held his horse's reins, and he ran five long steps and hurled himself across the saddle. The horse bolted away, over the pale grass toward the height of the ridge. Behind him on the slope the Americans leapt out of the dirt and clawed their way after him, forty men staggering and stumbling up the hill.

Out of a draw to the left, abruptly, Pico's lancers charged.

Cat whined. At a dead gallop the horsemen with their lances lowered slashed into the unready extended flank of the Americans, and the whole square broke. The lancers' column tore straight through it and across and off away over the grass, and there were men lying in the grass, twisted bodies, and people screaming.

She stood in her stirrups, scanning the ridge, her heart a painful mass in her throat. Among the shifting, stirring mass of men along the top of the ridge Sohrakoff wheeled his horse. Behind him his five riders dragged their little cannon along at the ends of their ropes, the wheels banging over the ground.

On her right Carrillo said, "What are they shooting in the cannon?"

"Some kind of grape," Orozco said. "Stones, I think."

The American bugle shrilled its manic, seesaw notes. On the flat ground below the hill the dark uniforms pulled together swiftly into even rows again. On the top of the ridge, among Sarbulo's screaming militiamen, Sohrakoff turned his horse into the slope once more and his men plunged down after him, the horses straight-legged, sliding on their haunches over the sheer grassy hillside, flinging up scarfs of dust that the wind tore away.

In the square, the rows of rifles leveled, regular as stitching; she could see an officer raise his arm to order the fire, while on the slope ahead of them, the five horsemen skidded to a stop again, and Sohrakoff was out of his saddle and down behind the gun.

Now suddenly from the south Pico led his lancers in again, racing down toward the square of soldiers.

"Not yet, you idiot," Orozco said, under his breath, and Carrillo laughed.

The Americans wheeled toward this new threat, and Pico

swerved, pulling his men back in a stream, scaling the sheer rise of the ridge; the rifles crackled. A horse went down hard. The rider scrambled away across the grass. On the slope, the little cannon cranked around, its blackened barrel like a finger pointing. There was a small boom.

The shot sprayed the center of the line, and again the bodies were flung down like rags, and she heard, again, the thin wails of pain. Her hand went to her face. Frantically she searched the hillside for Sohrakoff. On the slope they were hauling the cannon off again, and the Americans were charging after them. Without Pico's lancers to cut the Americans off, they were running straight up the slope toward Sohrakoff, and she screamed at him, beating her hands on the saddle. Her horse jumped sideways, snorting.

Out there on the grassy hillside, Sohrakoff scurried away, the gun already bucking and flying up the hill at the ends of the lassoes. The Americans were swarming after him. He ran for his horse, and the man holding the horse for him suddenly flung the reins down and whirled and fled.

Orozco gave a harsh growl. Cat screamed again, and her horse reared. Sohrakoff's horse, terrified, raced away from him across the windswept grass. He ran after it, and three Americans behind him dropped down to one knee and got their rifles up to their shoulders.

Sohrakoff's horse swerved, trying to escape the steep slope before it. For an instant it was wheeling back toward him. He threw himself at it. Behind him the Americans shot, and the horse staggered, but Sohrakoff had hold of a stirrup, and the horse reared up and bolted again, the reins flying, straight up the hillside. It dragged Sohrakoff three steps and he scrambled into the saddle, and the horse carried him away into the midst of the Californio army.

Her throat was raw. Her hands hurt. She slumped, empty.

A bugle was blowing, over and over, the same desperate notes. Half the Americans were still scaling the steep slope of the hill, fighting the slippery grass. The others dropped into their even ranks again, below them, on the flat. Along the top of the ridge, the Californios gathered, and in their midst the little gun rolled forward. The Americans on the slope flung themselves face down and began to crawl backward down the hill.

Below them, the first rank of riflemen fired, and the Californios shrank back from the rim of the hill. While the front rank reloaded the second rank stepped up, ready, but did not shoot. There was a sudden stillness. The Californios spread out along the hilltop, stooping, crawling along the ground. She could see some of them picking up rocks. The bugle was blowing again.

Carrillo said quietly, "The officer with the artillery is very good."

Orozco said, "He'll do."

She had lost him. Her gaze searched the packed bodies along the top of the ridge, hunting that frizz of orange hair. Her horse shifted and flung its head up, and Orozco said something, impatient, and Chavez came over and held her bridle. Still she had not picked Sohrakoff out of the crowd of men on the top of the ridge. Her mouth was dry; her eyes burned.

Then he was swinging up into sight again, mounting another horse. She shut her eyes a moment. The muscles of her arms fluttered.

Orozco said, "They're retreating."

Down on the flat, the American square was moving slowly away toward the beach again. They had taken up their dead and wounded; their last rank walked backward, guns ready.

A roar went up from the Californios on the hill. Half of them plunged down the slope, shouting and cheering and shaking their fists. They stooped for stones and pitched them after the retreating gringos. When the Americans raised their rifles the Californios turned and raced for the top of the hill again.

Cat lifted her head, feeling the wind suddenly cold and damp on her face. A great ledge of cloud was clamping down over the southern sky. The first hard drops of rain hit her.

"We won," Chavez said. His voice swelled to a bellow. "We won!"

Carrillo said, smiling, "Congratulations, Colonel, very nicely done."

Cat straightened, empty of feeling. In the roaring, cheering mass of men that swarmed along the hill toward her, she could not see Sohrakoff. She rubbed her hand over her face. She turned toward Orozco and met the hard, expressionless black eyes.

"Do you still think I can't win, Mrs. Reilly?"

Now she began to tremble, as if everything in her body were coming loose; the battle was something shapeless and terrible before her that she was struggling to fit her mind around. In this tumult the only thing left standing was the force of Orozco's single-minded will. She said, "You're a master of the game, Colonel."

He turned to his orderly, who had brought up their horses. "Keep her under control." Precise, exact, he stepped up into his saddle and rode away. Tamely she followed the orderly in the other direction.

53   "WHAT WAS THE BILL?" Sohrakoff asked. He was filthy; he smelled like gunpowder.

"I don't know. Maybe twelve dead, all theirs." Orozco glanced at Carrillo. "What would you estimate, General?"

"Eight, twelve dead, at least that many wounded. A very bloody battle, for California," Carrillo said. He got a cigar out of the inside pocket of his jacket. "And all of them on the right side." The junior officer just behind him was already fumbling with his tinderbox.

Orozco lifted his head, looking for the rest of this. On top of the grassy ridge behind him, Pico's lancers formed two long, irregular columns; the militiamen had gathered around the gun in the center of the line. Their voices rose in another ebullient cheer. Chavez had taken the woman up onto the road to the beach. The sky to the northeast was blue, but overhead the

clouds bundled, steel gray and sooty black. The first huge drops
of rain were falling.

A few yards to his right, Sohrakoff wiped his face on his
sleeve, his eyes vivid against the dirt. "What do you want me to
do now?" His gaze shifted, aimed past Orozco's shoulder; he
had seen the woman over to the west. His horse stepped nervously sideways. "What's she doing here?"

"Being educated. One of your crew needs disciplining."

"Sarbulo is doing that." The Count swung toward him, bad-
tempered. "If you let Pico touch her —"

"Yes, yes," Orozco said. "You and Sarbulo will duel for the
honor of flaying me."

Pico himself, the next problem, was riding up to them now,
smiling, his palomino horse sweat-darkened to the color of gold
money. He swept off his sombrero. "You see, Colonel, what
happens when you finally let me fight."

Orozco edged his horse over against Pico's, shoulder to flank.
"I see you don't listen to orders. I saw you come roaring down
that hill two shots too early. Don't tell me you know how to
fight."

Pico's face gathered into a red knot. "You can't talk to me
like that."

Orozco leaned into him, nose to nose. "This is my command.
Do what I say or get out." He kept his spur against his horse's
side, pressing his mount against Pico's rangy palomino; the big
man was staring stonily at him, his jaw set, but his dark eyes
narrowed and his horse gave way, and Orozco forced it to take
another step, making it crabwalk across the top of the ridge.

"Well?"

Pico's head twisted, looking somewhere else. "Yes. Colonel."

"Good." Orozco backed his horse up. The rain was starting
to fall faster. The little patch of blue in the northeast had vanished behind the roof of the storm. He slued in his saddle, casting around for Sohrakoff, who rode up beside him.

The Count said, "I have to go see to the gun. The wheel
broke."

"Is there any more powder?"

"No."

"Send it back to the city, but you stay out here and meet me at the Dominguez ranch later. Now I'm going to take a ride down to the water and set up a faster coast guard."

"Yes, Colonel."

Sohrakoff rode off, circling to avoid Pico's men, who were gathered in a disorderly mass on the road back toward El Pueblo. Orozco could see that Pico was certainly going to be more trouble. In the other direction, to the west, Carrillo and two of his officers were waiting on the road toward the beach, with Catharine Reilly and Orozco's own lancers. He loped up on his horse to join Carrillo, near the head of the line.

The don had appropriated Catharine Reilly; she went along beside him on her nag. Orozco edged his horse around to put her between him and Carrillo. A gust of rain swept over them, and the air turned cold and clammy. Carrillo put out his arm as if he could drive the rain off her.

"You need a coat. It will be worse by the ocean."

Orozco said, "Let her suffer." He shot a hard look at Carrillo, to warn him off, and lowered his gaze to the woman on the horse between them. He said, "Still an abstraction, Mrs. Reilly?"

"There's always more killing," she said. "Every time, more people are going to die."

"Then why are you helping these murderers and plunderers against us, when they already have every advantage?" He held his voice down, he kept still, patient, no need to lean on her, to batter her like a Pico. He said, "This is the man you love, fighting for his life, and you will not help him."

She shut her eyes. Her head turned a little, deflecting him. She said, "What do you want from me, Colonel?"

"You said Stockton was in San Francisco Bay. Are all his ships there?"

"Most of them." Her voice was almost indifferent. "I think the *Cyane* is still at Monterey."

"How many men can they raise in the north?"

Her hand moved, picking at a loose piece of the rawhide that wrapped the saddlehorn. "The most we ever had under the

Bear Flag was one hundred. Maybe another couple of hundred men, if they take absolutely everybody."

"Is that all they have? Stockton's men and whatever they can raise here?"

"There's another army coming overland. In the south somewhere."

"Where?"

"I don't know. I heard — overheard — Gillespie talking about it. Through the desert." She turned to look at him again, remembering. "The Gila Trail." Her face seemed to clear, as if some struggle had ended, and she glanced back over her shoulder toward the battlefield.

"How many men in this army?"

"I can't remember. Horse infantry."

"Dragoons. Remember. How many?"

"I don't really know." She brought her attention back to him again, the rain against her face. "I can't remember everything. You can find somebody to read those dispatches. The general is named Kearny."

"All right." He nodded to her. "Go."

She picked up her reins; Carrillo held his horse back two steps, and she pulled the nag awkwardly out of the column. Slapping at it with the rein ends, she pushed it into a lumbering gallop, back across the grass toward the battlefield.

Carrillo watched her, his face rumpled, the cigar tilted in his fingers, gray ashes scattered over the front of his coat. "Is she a prisoner or is she not?"

"She's Sohrakoff's," Orozco said. "He'll handle her." For a moment, though, she had belonged to Orozco. He had cracked her open and taken what he wanted from her. The keen pleasure of that surprised him.

Carrillo said, "No army could cross the Gila Trail. The desert will make nothing of them."

"Maybe," Orozco said. "I'll send Pico down there to keep watch for them." Which would remove one rock from his belly.

He thought now he was probably seeing the whole of the board. None of it was particularly encouraging. Still, he had come this far. And today he had fought two battles and won them both. He picked his horse up into a canter, going down the road toward the white maelstrom of the ocean.

One of the little gun's wheels had broken during the battle and they had fixed it, but now it lay in three pieces on the ground. With the butt of an ax and some wedges Sohrakoff pried off the trunnions that held the brass barrel in its makeshift truck.

Around him was the flat grassland, creased by the road to El Pueblo and the banks of the river. All up and down it the militia was celebrating, clustered in little groups that occasionally burst into whoops and shrieks; some of the men had wine or aguardiente. He called over the nearest three of them. Sarbulo was riding toward him across the flattened grass, up from the river, where they had taken the horses to water them.

Sohrakoff showed the three militiamen how to pack up the pieces of the cannon. Sarbulo leaned down from his horse, smiling wide at him. "Manolo apologizes." The smile crackled into a laugh. "Or he will, when he wakes up."

Manolo had panicked in the fighting, had left Sohrakoff on foot in front of forty riflemen. The Count grunted something. He himself had panicked; but he had been lucky. Out on the grass he saw something moving.

"What's the matter with you?" Sarbulo said. His eyebrows arched; high color still glowed in his face, vivid from the fighting. "We won. We beat them. You should be yelling and getting drunk and dancing." His head turned, his gaze following Sohrakoff's, off across the sunburnt yellow grass.

Up the road from the beach a brown horse was trudging along. The wind blew the heavy long hair of the rider, who sat small and clumsy in the saddle. The road curved away, but she did not follow it; she kicked the horse down over the trampled grass toward Sohrakoff and stopped fifty feet from him.

Sohrakoff turned back to Sarbulo, on his horse beside him. "Don't be a fool, Sarbulo. We used all the gunpowder. Maybe we can find more, but likely not. And we did not beat them. The south wind beat them. They knew their ships couldn't hold the coast in this storm, so they called their men back and left. When the wind changes, they'll come on again."

Sarbulo shrugged that off; it was not real yet. While the wind blew he was a winner. "What are you going to do about her?"

Sohrakoff gave a quick look over the men trying to pack the cannon and then set off across the grass toward the brown horse. Most of the militiamen were already spilling away down the road toward El Pueblo. The rain fell in a light scatter of drops, but the sky to the south was the color of gunpowder. Sarbulo followed him over to Cat Reilly.

"Orozco dragged you out here, and now he expects me to drag you back? I'm not going. Sarbulo can take you."

She said, "I want to go with you."

Surprised, Sohrakoff lifted his head, looking into her unsmiling face with its steady green eyes. An American, one of them. But this one he could get to. "Wait here," he said. "I have things to finish." He turned and walked away, back toward the three men and the brass gun and the packhorses.

When he thought about the battle all he remembered was the hot brass barrel of the gun and the blast and the bodies flopping and flying. His hands stung with powder burns; his hip hurt, and his left knee, where he must have fallen when the horse dragged him. He hated the Americans more because he had killed them. He took Sarbulo over toward the militiamen who had finally gotten the gun barrel slung between two packhorses.

"Take this all back to El Pueblo. Put the gun up somewhere; maybe someday we'll have more gunpowder."

Sarbulo said, "I'll do it." He palmed Sohrakoff's shoulder, nodding to him, solemn. "You were a hero today. Try to enjoy it."

"Christ."

Pico was riding up toward him. Sohrakoff glanced around at Cat Reilly, who had gotten down from her horse and sat in the lee of its shoulder, staring in another direction. The fighting had left a sour stiffness in his muscles; he still wanted to hit somebody. The palomino came to a restless stop and danced in a circle, and Sohrakoff took the hand that Pico stretched out to him.

"Ruso, I'm going."

"We had a good fight there, General."

"Tell Orozco. He is all up and down me, for nothing. I'm going down to Santa Isobel."

"To Santa Isobel! Why are you going down there?"

"Something your woman told him." He raised his hand, and his horse spun around and galloped away, toward the columns of his lancers already riding out to the south.

Sohrakoff collected his horse and went over to Cat Reilly; she saw him coming and pulled herself clumsily up into the saddle, and they rode on down along the flank of the ridge where the militia had watched him make Orozco look brilliant. The rain was falling harder. He had lost his hat before the fighting even started, but the cold wetness felt good on his hair. It was going to be a long storm.

Side by side they went down to the southeast and crossed the river and climbed up the steep southern bank. She said nothing; she had enough to do staying on the horse. When they were walking along the flat ground beyond the river, he turned to her and said, "What did you tell Orozco?"

She said, "That there is another army coming, up through the Gila Trail."

A white heat broke over him. He rounded on her, furious. "You people are like a disease! You never stop coming — some kind of filthy scum, washing up over everything —"

She was saying, under the torrent of his words, "I'm sorry, I'm sorry," and then she stopped talking and stared down at her horse's neck, her cheeks red.

"You're dirt," he shouted at her. "You can't live where you're supposed to so you scum up everybody else's."

Her gaze lifted; her eyes were wide, calm. The rain washed down her face, over her bare arms. He wiped his arm over his mouth. He felt stripped to a gray, exhausted, spiteful anger, an ash of despair.

"I killed a lot of your people today. Doesn't that bother you?"

"Yes," she said.

"I never killed anybody before. It feels as if I owe somebody something." He braced his hands on the saddle, trying to box this up in words, to pack away this onrush of guilt and fear. "I lose even when I win. The more I try to hold on, the less I have. The deeper I get into this, the less I understand."

She said again, "I'm sorry."

"How can you be sorry?" He lunged at her, shouting at her again, their horses shoulder to shoulder, his body canted over her. "You're not losing anything. You're winning! You're winning! And I'm killing all these people and you're telling me you're sorry."

She said nothing, her face still with a weary, patient resignation, and he realized he was out in the desert in the rain, screaming at a helpless woman.

She looked as if she had just walked up out of the ocean, her hair slicked down, her skin shining; her soaked dress clung to her. He reached behind his saddle and got his serape. "Put this on."

She wrapped the blanket coat around her. They started off again, down a trail that led them over the grasslands. To their right through the rain a stand of trees showed as a dark blur. The long slope before them blended in the steely mists to one long shadow.

He said, "Why did you give in to Orozco?"

"He let me see you damned nearly die," she said.

"So you gave him what he wanted. That's why he'll win the war."

She said nothing. The trail edged down a steep bank; her horse slipped and she grabbed for the horn, her hand jerking on the reins.

"You can't ride," he said. "I've seen three-year-olds who ride better than you."

At that she laughed; she raised her eyes quickly toward him, her wide mouth curled. His body quickened a little. He pulled the reins out of her hand and led her horse along, down through a dry wash choked with old willow trees growing along the ground like snakes of wood. He spoke to her over his shoulder.

"Up ahead of us there's an old empty ranch house — that's where we're going." The trail climbed up over the top of the wash, and on the broad, declining slope before them the old adobe house took shape out of the rain, a low, irregular box in a cluster of fences. "This is a good place. We stayed here when we first came south. The house is tight, there are beds, we left some food. Orozco will meet us here in a little while."

On the hillside above the ranch he reined in, looking the place over, and when he knew it was deserted he rode down and through the yard to the corrals in the back. Beside him she jounced along, holding on to the horn of her saddle. The rain was beating on them now, rushing off the roofs of the buildings in sheets and torrents, running puddles through the yard. In an angle of the fence, where the L-shaped wall of a shed cut the wind and the rain, he dismounted.

She pulled the serape off and draped it over the saddle and slid down to the ground, and he kissed her.

She kissed him back. He was hard already, and he pushed against her, to make her feel it, and her hands slipped in between them, unbuckling his belt.

His blood burned. He pulled her into the shed, yanked her skirts up, and took her against the wall, fast because he didn't know how long they would be alone, and beautiful because she came back at him just as hungry, just as hot, sucking on his tongue, thrusting against him, until he thundered off, peal after peal, leaned on her jelly-legged and shuddering, his face against her rain-soaked hair. He closed his eyes, reconnected.

He said, "I love you, Cat Reilly."

She murmured something below words. Her arms curled around his waist under the tails of his shirt, and she nuzzled him.

"You're mine now," he said. "You understand that?" He fingered back a thick curl of her hair. Outside he could hear horses coming.

"Yes, Count," she said. She tugged her dress down over her thighs. Her nipples showed against the wet fabric of her dress, the swell of the underside of her breast. He put his hand over it. His.

"Go in there and look for a room where we can spend the night. With a bed. Make sure the bed has a mattress."

She went off through the rain toward the ranch house. Sohrakoff pulled his pants up and walked the other way, out toward the yard, where Carrillo and the lancers were crowding toward the fences and Orozco was just dismounting from his horse.

54 ❧ BROKEN HAND FITZPATRICK, guiding General Kearny's army, had come about as far as he thought he could get — to Socorro, on the bank of the upper Rio Grande, somewhere deep in northern Mexico.

Here there was water, and some grass on the rolling dry hills, and Kearny's three hundred dragoons had made camps along the river's east bank, above the wells and the three adobes of the town. A string of horses stood like a fringe along the edge of the water. There had been some rain recently and the Rio Grande was running well, not so full of mud as usual, in places almost clear.

Broken Hand had never been west of Socorro. All he knew of the trail from here on was what he had heard. West of here there was no water for two hundred miles, until you came to the Gila River. Then there was nothing but the Gila River and bare red rock and the blinding sun, for three hundred miles more.

He went over toward General Kearny, who was standing by one of the huge slant-sided wagons, signing an order. "General," he said, "we got to talk this over."

Kearny handed the order board to a shavetail, and above two rows of brass buttons his boyish, ambitious face swung toward Fitzpatrick. "We aren't going fast enough. We're behind schedule."

Fitzpatrick put one foot up on the hub of the wagon wheel and leaned his forearm on his knee. "I can tell you flat out now, General, we're never gonna make it." Something moved in the distance, behind Kearny's head, and the old mountain man looked sharp. "Holy God," he said, and stood up straight.

A line of horsemen was flying down the steep brown slope toward the river. There were a dozen of them, wearing buckskins, whooping and shouting like Indians. They were not Indians. Unaware of that, Kearny's dragoons, seeing them, shouted, wheeled, and swarmed toward their camps. Kearny himself spun to confront his scout. "What's this? What's this? Bugler!"

"Cool off, General," said Broken Hand. "They're white. Sort of." He backed away from the wagon, watching the oncoming riders, who let their charge drop to a lope and then a jog. They spread out along the west bank of the river and stopped. Their horses lowered their heads to the thin sheet of water. All along the opposite side of the Rio Grande, Kearny's dragoons stood gaping at them.

Opposite Fitzpatrick a big bay horse jogged down to the water and waded out halfway across. The man on its back called, "Broken Hand! Where you takin' these soldier boys?" He sat slouched in his saddle, his feet out straight, his long russet hair hanging down his back, and across his face his wide mouth stretched into a grin that raised the hackles on Broken Hand's neck. He had never gotten on well with Kit Carson.

"We're headed for California, Kit, there's a war on, horse, haven't you heard?"

"War's over, Broken Hand." Kit nudged his horse into a trot and splashed the rest of the way across the river. The big bay carried him up the near bank toward Fitzpatrick. In the shade of the brim of his battered hat Kit's eyes were pale as mercury. His gaze flicked from Broken Hand toward the general behind him, around the camp, and back to the other buckskin man. "You're too late, Broken Hand, we done took California already." He reached down and slapped his palm against one of his saddlebags. "I'm carrying the word back to Washington."

Behind Broken Hand there was a growled oath. Kearny stamped up past him. "Who took California?"

Kit pushed his hat back. "I did." His voice was cat-sleek. His grin widened, showing his teeth. "And a couple of navy boys and their ships. But I took most of it. Even if they ain't never gonna say so."

"Who the hell are you?" Kearny asked, skeptical.

Fitzpatrick said, "General Kearny, meet Kit Carson."

"Carson."

In the packed ranks of the dragoons who were crowded around watching, the name multiplied into a little army of whispers.

After a moment Kearny asked, "What navy men?"

"Sloat. Stockton. Major Frémont." Kit wagged his head at the camp around him. "You ain't gonna get there with this outfit anyway, General. You might as well turn around and go back to Fort Leavenworth."

The general's round, young face was taut with baffled anger. He stared west, as if he could pull himself to California by sheer strength of will. Broken Hand said, "You just come over the Gila Trail?"

"Eatin' horses the whole way," Kit said. "The rest of it oughta be a circus ride."

"Get any fightin' in California?"

"Not much."

Kearny swung toward them. "You came over the trail here. You look in pretty good shape."

"I'm an easy keeper," Kit said. He examined the general with condescension. His lips twitched.

Under this look Kearny bristled like a woods pig. He glared at Kit and glared at the way west. "When did you leave?"

"Left Angeles September fifth."

"So it took you a month," said Kearny. He swallowed, his throat working up and down, and he brought his unblinking, angry glare up to Kit on the horse before him. "Take me to California."

"Hell, no," Kit said. "I'm going to Washington and tell the president it's ours. Thirty days from now I'll be sitting in the White House sipping tea."

"No, you won't," Kearny said. His voice shook. "I order you to guide me to California. Fitzpatrick can take your dispatches."

Kit straightened, his hands on his saddle pommel, his smile gone. He said, "The hell with you."

Kearny said, "You're an army scout. I'm your superior officer. The president ordered me to California and I'm going. I'm ordering you to take me and my men to California."

Kit said nothing. Fitzpatrick folded his arms over his chest, fighting off the urge to smile; suddenly this was working out very well for him. He said, "I'll go to Washington."

Kit gave him a look of compacted fury. "The war's over," he said to Kearny. "You got no reason to go."

Kearny said again, "The president ordered me to California."

Kit pointed away the northeast. "My wife is two days' ride that way."

Kearny said, "Two days and however long it takes you to get me to California. Or don't you think you can do it?"

Broken Hand's smile broke loose and crossed his face. Kit pulled his hat off and gave Kearny a white-eyed stare. Slowly he passed another long look around Kearny's camp, the hat clenched in his fist, and brought his eyes back to the general.

"All right. You pick one hundred men, leave the rest here. Three hundred horses. Leave these fuckin' wagons, pack everything on mules. You can bring the howitzers but pack 'em, and if I say we drop 'em, we drop 'em. You got that?" He beat the hat across his knee, knocking off the dust in a powdery cloud.

"I've got it," Kearny said. "We'll march in the morning." Kit put his hat back on and reined away.

55 ☙ DAY AFTER DAY, through the autumn, the farmers of El Pueblo planted their winter crops in the broad fields around the city and picked apples in the orchards, and then they went back into the plaza and Orozco drilled them into soldiers.

The people from outlying ranches came in, some mounted, some on foot, and he taught them to march, to obey orders, to read flags. By the beginning of November he had raised an army of over six hundred men, virtually every male Californio south of Santa Barbara, and they all knew something at least of what they were doing.

They carried lances made of willow, shields of hide, lassoes of horsehair and hemp. They had a few old muskets but no gunpowder. This did not seem to bother them. They shouted as they marched, exuberant, even after weeks of drill, and from the pulpit of his church the priest preached to them that God was on their side and so they would surely win.

Catharine stood in front of the church watching sixty white-shirted farmers march up and down the plaza with sticks on their shoulders, and asked, "How can you say that to these people? How can you lie?"

The priest said, "Is it a lie? Surely God will not let the right fail in this."

She said, "You told them whatever Gillespie wanted you to tell them, too. You could guide these people better than anybody. Wasn't it Pope Celestine that Dante wouldn't even let into hell, because he shirked his vocation?"

The priest gave her a sneer as muted as the rest of him. "I have heard unpleasant names for your vocation, Mrs. Reilly. Such as whore." He walked away into his dark church.

Cat stood watching the men march. She knew the prevailing opinion in El Pueblo was the priest's: God would save them. God, thus far, had shown some reasonable interest. In October, after the Battle of the Old Woman's Gun, the wind had blown foul for two weeks; then the air lightened, and the American ships had come back, with the *Congress,* Stockton's flagship.

This time Orozco had good warning. When Stockton's men began wading ashore through the long blue shallows, Orozco lined up every human being in El Pueblo along the heights above the beach, shouting and marching. Behind them he drove herds of horses and cattle, to stir up the dust, as if there were an army of thousands awaiting Robert Stockton and his men.

Stockton brought several hundred men ashore, but he landed no guns, he had no horses, and he never moved inland. Orozco wrote him an invitation to fight, tied it to a dog's tail, and chased the dog into the Americans' camp. The Californios loved the exploit, but the commodore ignored it. After a week on the beach, with the Californios howling and galloping night and day along the ridges above them, and without horses of his own to make any reconnaissance, Stockton loaded his men back into his ships and sailed away.

He sailed down to San Diego, where John Bidwell and Zeke Merritt and their twenty men, driven out in September, had clawed their way back onto the shore. On the high ground above them, the Californios under Flores and Carrillo kept them penned against the waves, raiding them, attacking their water supplies, and setting fire to the town, but they held on to a few buildings, and Stockton went in to their rescue.

Once again, God, or California, made a fool of Robert Stockton; when he tried to sail into the harbor the *Congress* ran aground on the bar, and the last word Orozco had heard from San Diego was that they were still trying to float her off.

Now out there in the yellow dust ten rows of farmers strutted and shouted and waved sticks in the air. Cat went out into the city.

To accommodate Orozco the market had moved into the little irregular space at the foot of the plaza. Cat made her way through the thin crowd that sat or stood along the side of the open ground, watching the men march. On the balconies of the great townhouses, people stopped talking and watched her as she passed. She went down into Wine Street, where the cantinas were open, loud, spilling their crowds out to the sunshine. On the corner was the big shanty where Sohrakoff went sometimes to gamble, and even now men crowded into it, milling around in the street before it. She swung wide to go by them at a safe distance. At night Wine Street roared, full of drunks and gamblers, cockfights and fistfights and other diversions; then Sarbulo Varela was king, and not even Orozco cared to interfere.

El Pueblo was full of idle men, with nothing to do but wait to fight. The women, as always, worked around them, carrying water, chasing children, feeding them, dressed in the bright colors they favored, desert colors. Cat walked along the broad, dusty street, past blocks of adobes; the air was flavored faintly with wine and corn and aguardiente and chilies. Ahead there grew a stand of palm trees, their trunks draped in skirts of old, dead leaves, their crowns erupting into clutches of green fans like forty-fingered hands. The uproar of the cantinas fell behind her. Beyond a wall a guitar was playing, a nimble run of notes and chords, somebody practicing the same thing over and over; in her mind she tried to play it on the piano. Two women came toward her, jugs of water from the *zanja* on their heads, making them tall as towers. They watched her suspiciously as she went by.

They tolerated her, for Sohrakoff's sake, whom they loved, but they associated her also with Gillespie, and in their faces always she saw their dislike.

Halfway down Wine Street she crossed the *zanja madre,* the irrigation ditch, flowing loud and deep after the recent rains, and turned to walk along the edge of it. Once she left Wine Street there were fields of new-plowed ground on either side of the ditch, the dug earth dark and damp; she passed a man and a woman and a row of children going along the furrows, planting seed. She wondered what they were growing, maybe corn, although that seemed out of season. They moved together a few steps and then stooped together, like dancers, patient at their slow, enduring work. She remembered the cannonfire blowing holes in the ranks of the soldiers, and her gut churned. She came to the end of the Calle and turned left and walked back along it through the city.

The San Gabriel Mission stood surrounded by orchards on the flat dun plain of the valley; a low fence of willow poles rimmed the courtyard of its church. Along the fence were hitched a horse and two mules and a few *carretas,* waiting for the local people attending Mass.

Cat loitered at the gate a while, wondering if she should have come here. She left her horse by the fence and went uncertainly forward. A strange, magnificent plant grew at the front corner of the church, a fan higher than her head of huge, stiff, spiny leaves; she stopped to stare at it. On ten-foot spikes its ripe fruits hung, long black berries dangling from white stems. Some had fallen onto the ground below, and the wasps were eating them. The edges of the leaves shredded away into a fringe; the whole plant gave off a faint tangy smell.

She could hear voices inside the church, and footsteps; she felt as if she were violating something by being here. Beyond the giant plant there was a garden, and past that more adobe buildings, their walls honey-colored, their roofs red-tiled against the stark blue sky.

Somewhere out here Sohrakoff was trying to make gunpowder. She had gotten into an argument with him that morning; he had walked out.

She drifted down the yard, closer to the garden, peering toward the buildings just beyond it, where she thought she could see people moving. Wondering what she was going to say to him if she did find him. What he might say to her.

Then there were footsteps behind her, and she turned, and he was coming across the yard toward her.

"Cat." He came up to her. "Somebody told me you were outside, but I didn't believe it. What are you doing here?"

She said, "I wanted to see you." Relieved, she saw he was not angry. She turned toward the plant again, a safe, cool subject. "What's this thing?"

"Yucca," he said. "Soapbush. They don't usually grow down this low. The monks must have transplanted it." He reached her side and brushed against her, his hand light, tentative. "Why did you come out here? Just to see me?"

"I wanted to apologize," she said. "About this morning. I shouldn't have said it."

"You just said what you think." His hand stroked up her back, and his fingers caressed the nape of her neck.

She leaned back against him, and his arm slid around her. "You weren't that broad-minded this morning," she said.

"I lost my temper. Come around to the garden."

They went back through the mission to the garden, where a huge old grapevine grew over an arbor along the side of the church. The grapes were gone and the leaves withered, and the fat stock, with its loose, flaky bark, was pruned down to the new shoots. Under it soft, dusty rags of sunlight hung down to the earth. He took hold of her hand and they walked along toward the end of the arbor. Neither of them said anything. They had been talking too much lately, too loud.

On one side of the arbor the garden was laid out in spaded beds; there were some trim rows of herbs, some low shrubs. A row of buckets stood on the walkway, and a wooden rake. On the other side, between the grapevine and the church wall, uneven rows of wooden crosses stood, marking graves. Sohrakoff stopped in the shadows midway along the arbor path, and she turned to him and kissed him.

He smelled like sulfur and smoke. There were pieces of lucifer match behind his ear.

She said, "Has it gone off right this time?"

"No," he said shortly. "Don't start that again."

She could think of nothing else. She saw him as a bomb, full of powder that he was trying to explode. Plunged back into the silence they went down through the shadowy tunnel of the arbor. At the end was a wall of plastered adobe. Holding her hands, he turned around and leaned his back against the wall, as he always did. They kissed again.

"What are you going to do?" she asked.

"Keep trying. I can't make the mix flash, I need saltpeter to feed it oxygen. Nobody can find me any saltpeter."

Reckless, she said, "How long will you keep trying?"

He let go of her with a little shove. "I told you, don't start that again."

She said, "I love you, Count."

He reached for her and she moved in close to him, her head tucked under his chin. His fingers laced through her hair. "You're crazy, then," he said, "because there's no future with me."

She pressed her face against him, her arms around his waist. The dusty air smelled acrid. Out in the sunlit garden somebody was working, the steady scrub of a hoe or a shovel on the dirt. A multitude of muffled voices in the church all spoke at once.

He said, "You smell good."

She laughed. "You stink."

His arms squeezed briefly around her; in his voice she could hear him smiling. "I'll wash it off later. Stay out here. It's quiet out here."

"Whatever you want, Count."

"We'll find something else to talk about."

He stroked the back of her neck. She kept her mouth shut, since everything she said went the wrong way. His touch was a sweet comfort; she let it swallow the moment, more real than the war. In the church a bell rang.

People began to move out through the doors, midway down the arbor. As the crowd milled toward them Sohrakoff took her hand and they walked out to the path through the garden, circling into the sunlight, the beds of herbs and vegetables. The people from the church flowed out across the garden and into the courtyard, and Sohrakoff walked quickly to avoid them.

As they came to the front of the church, she saw some horsemen coming up the road.

"Orozco," Sohrakoff said, taut. "He has General Carrillo with him. Something has happened." He let go of her hand and strode out past the last of the churchgoers.

Cat followed him toward the gate through the willow fence. Orchards grew along either side of the road; the wide, flat floor of the San Gabriel Valley stretched off toward the mountains. The dust of the summer bronzed even the air. Orozco on a chestnut horse trotted up the last few yards toward them. He reined in and dismounted. Behind him came Chavez, his orderly, and another man she recognized, a small, balding man who was not supposed to be here, General Carrillo.

Orozco spoke to Sohrakoff, his voice perfectly even, his face impassive. "The gringos have taken back San Diego. They brought the big ships in and they're landing guns and men."

Cat hunched her shoulders up. Her throat was tight and her skin prickled. Sohrakoff said, "You knew that would happen. What do you want me to do?"

The colonel stood stiff and straight, and he made no answer yet to the Count; his black eyes came looking for her, the only enemy he could reach. "On his way here General Carrillo captured a courier. Chavez, give her the dispatch."

She swallowed the tension in her throat. A thrill of warning went down her spine. She moved off a little way from Sohrakoff, and he turned and watched her. Behind Orozco, Lieutenant Chavez swung down from his horse and came toward her, holding out a piece of yellow paper. General Carrillo still sat in his saddle, his round face bland, staring at her. She lowered her eyes to the paper; for a moment, struggling with herself, she could not make out the words.

Then the sentences jumped at her. She dropped the note. "I'm not going to read that."

Orozco walked two steps toward her. She knew him now; in spite of his self-control she could see the fury in every move, and she flinched away from the blast of his bad temper. He said, "You don't have to. We've already read it. It's an order to Frémont, who is somewhere north of here dawdling. Stockton wants him to get his army down here or Los Angeles will be *leveled to the ground* before he arrives." He stooped and picked the note up and thrust it at Chavez.

Cat folded her arms over her chest, her heart thudding. Up her throat and cheeks a gritty heat climbed, as if there were dust in her blood.

Sohrakoff came up beside her again, his arm curling around her. "What do you want me to do?" he said again to Orozco.

"You have to bring Pico back here."

"What about Kearny?"

"Forget about Kearny. Stockton will be here very quickly." Orozco turned his head, looking over his shoulder. "You're dismissed."

Carrillo and Chavez rode off across the courtyard toward the church. As soon as they were fairly gone Orozco wheeled on her. "You soulless little gringa, you're still one of them."

She lowered her eyes. Stockton was exaggerating, as he did everything — he could not level El Pueblo. A moment after thinking so, she wondered if she was deluding herself. Sohrakoff said, "Leave her alone. Is Pico at Santa Isobel?"

He was going. She gripped his hand, as if she could hold him here. Under her fingertips she felt the knobs of his knuckles. Her stomach hurt suddenly.

Orozco said, "As far as I know. Take this horse; it's very strong."

"Just a minute." He turned to her. "I have to go do this."

She said, "Yes." Blindly she lifted her face, and they kissed, not long, not there with Orozco watching them. Her voice came out a croak. "Be careful."

His hands pressed on her shoulders. "Whatever happens, stay with Orozco." He bent to kiss her again, his lips dry and soft. He turned to the other man. "Take care of her. Whatever happens."

Orozco made no answer; he was looking elsewhere, the flat plane of his hat brim throwing a curved shadow on his face. Sohrakoff went off toward the chestnut horse. She folded her arms over her chest, watching him gather the reins and vault up into the saddle, the horse dancing under him, and he turned onto the road and put the horse into a steady jog south.

Orozco was standing there, staring at her. She did not look at him; she watched her lover ride away, and said, "Why did you send him? Why not Chavez, or Sarbulo?"

"Because he always does what I tell him."

"He's your friend and you send him into the teeth of whole armies who will shoot him on sight."

"Would you rather he go to God on a rope? That's where we'll all end if they catch us alive."

Her eyes ached. Down there on the dun-colored road he was already almost too small to see. Chavez crossed the courtyard past her, leading the red bay horse that Sohrakoff had ridden here.

Orozco took the reins from the orderly and drew them through his fingers. "Find her horse. She'll go back with us."

Chavez saluted him and went away again across the courtyard. Down on the road, Sohrakoff was gone. She shut her eyes.

Orozco's voice shocked her. "You denied me. I think you should reconsider your loyalties, because you're their enemy now too, and to them you're just as damned as we are."

She wheeled toward him, for the moment hating him as much as he hated her. "More of your stupid game, Colonel? You didn't need that letter read. You just wanted me ashamed."

He pulled the leathers between his fingers, staring at her, as if he owed her no more words.

Her temper ebbed a little; she understood his anger better than she cared to. She said, "I am ashamed. Where is Frémont?"

"Well north, apparently, and moving at his leisure. You were right — he's not going to matter."

Chavez led up the little brown mare, and she turned toward the saddle. She could not find a way to move, to act, or even to think. Every moment was taking Sohrakoff farther away. She was pulling apart, stretching, struggling to keep hold, but he was farther and farther away. Her side hurt like an open wound. Standing before the horse she put her hands up on the heavy bulge of the saddle pommel, and abruptly Orozco stepped over beside her, set his hands on her waist, and lifted her up sideways on the saddle.

His strength startled her. That he had touched her at all startled her. He turned away at once, not looking at her, going to the red bay horse, his back to her. Against their will Sohrakoff had pushed them together, made a bond between them. She swung her leg across the saddle pommel, to sit astride, and followed him out the gate, past another yucca like a living crown of thorns.

56 GENERAL KEARNY was jubilant. He twisted in his saddle, looking away from Archie Gillespie in front of him, and his gaze searched out Kit, off to his right.

"You were a little premature, I think, Carson? California seems to require a little more conquering than you thought."

Kit ignored him. The last month with Kearny had rubbed him to a blister. They were drawn up on a grassy slope, somewhere east of San Diego; behind him were Kearny's one hundred dragoons, and in front of him were Archie Gillespie and another fifty riders, better mounted and much fatter than Kearny's men.

Kit cocked his head to one side, looking slantwise at Gillespie, who had just told him what he had never expected to hear, and said, "You lost Los Angeles. How did you do that?"

"Lieutenant, you may form a column," Kearny said crisply, "and take up the forward march."

Gillespie shouted his men into lines, and they started away down the broad, barren slope. It had been raining off and on all night and the wet ground gave off a vapor like a sweat into the air. Gillespie swung his horse around to ride beside Kit; their stirrups clashed.

Kit wheeled on him. "What happened?" he asked again.

"That fancy colonel, up in Monterey? The one with the sword?"

"Yeah," Kit said. "What about him?"

"He drove me out," Gillespie said. He scratched in the stubble of his blond beard.

Kit swiveled toward him, surprised. "He attacked you? Where'd he get an army?"

"He didn't really have an army." Gillespie shook his head, looking away. "He set me up like a drunken duck and picked me off. Made me think about a lot of things." He nodded. "Here comes somebody."

Kit looked where Gillespie was looking. It was early in the morning still. Kearny had marched them through the night, pushing toward San Diego; the army was moving down across the slumped, treeless hills in two ragged columns. A rider was galloping toward them out of the west, and Kit shaded his eyes and saw it was one of the outriders. He turned and looked back over Kearny's army.

He had brought them across the desert faster than he had ever made the passage before, less than a month crossing bare rock with nothing to eat for a man or a horse, not a blade of grass, not an insect, nothing but the blazing sun. None of the men had died, although they had eaten a lot of their horses. At a backcountry ranch they had rested up a little and gotten more horses, but these remounts were poor, and the men were worn down to leather and bone. He swung toward Gillespie again.

"Where's Stockton now?"

"He's marching on Los Angeles from San Diego with eight field guns and six hundred men."

"We may get some kind of a fight out of them yet."

"Maybe," Gillespie said. The scout galloped up toward Kearny, and the general turned and beckoned Kit toward him.

Kit rode in beside Kearny. The general was as gaunt as an old fencepost; out of a piece of saddle leather he had made a sun visor for his dragoon's cap. The scout saluted him and turned and saluted Kit, too, which annoyed Kearny.

"Get to it, boy!"

"Sir." The scout swung his arm out to point behind him. "There's a whole herd of riders up ahead of us, in the next valley. They ain't Indians and they ain't us, so I reckon they's them."

Kearny asked, "How many?"

Kit put his hands on his saddle pommel and scanned the broad, featureless hills again. Riding down over low ground like this bothered him; he wanted to be on the high line, where he could see farther and stay above any trouble. In the west the sky was murky, and the wind swept the grass down. He thought it was going to rain some more.

Where there were Californios there would be horses. He could get a better horse, maybe, if they could run down these greasers.

The scout was telling Kearny, "I couldn't count 'em, sir. They don't keep order. Maybe a hundred."

"A hundred," Kit said. "Not a chance." He gathered up his reins. "I'll go look."

Kearny flung one arm out. "Stay where you are, Carson." He nodded to the scout. "Where exactly are they? How are they riding?"

Kit stood in his stirrups. "There." He pointed ahead of them.

As he spoke, all the rest of Kearny's army saw them, too, and gave a yell. Ahead of them on the next ridge, a line of riders had suddenly appeared, black shapes against the yellow sky, galloping up over the ridge. On the peak they wheeled to a stop, their horses leaping and shying, boldly looking over the Americans below them. The silhouettes of their cartwheel hats made them look a little like giant insects.

Kearny's army let out a bellow and surged forward, their first burst of excitement carrying the general's horse on a few steps. Kearny flung his arm up. "Hold on! Keep in order — forward at a trot!"

The bugler put his brass to his lips and sounded the advance. Kearny and his army started off down the grass, moving at a dog trot, and up there on the ridge the Californios sped away like birds taking to the air and vanished.

Gillespie said, "General, you'll never catch them — they may not fight, but they ride like centaurs."

"Their horses are in better shape than ours," Kit said. "If I was you, General, I'd unpack the howitzers."

Kearny's face worked. A red glow of excitement showed in his cheeks. "Will they attack?"

"No," Kit said. "Unholster the guns, General; you can hit them with the guns, maybe." Behind him, Kearny's dragoons called back and forth to one another, their voices buoyant. After the long march now finally they were going to see some action.

Kearny was staring into the west, where his enemy had disappeared. Abruptly he turned, decisive. "All right. We'll hold hard while we get the howitzers out."

His bugler sounded another order, thin wavering notes in the wind. Kit reined his horse off to one side, checked the two pistols in his belt, and pulled his rifle out of the scabbard under his left stirrup fender. He ran his gaze around the whole horizon again.

Gillespie had shouted his men into order; he rode up beside Kit. "What do you think? Will there be a fight?"

"Like fighting Indians," Kit said. "As soon as we see them, charge. Hit 'em as fast as you can, because they'll run like hell."

He checked the load in the rifle and hung it in the crook of his arm, looking up at the lowering sky. The weather was going to make it more complicated. Kearny's gunners had unpacked the howitzers and were assembling them onto their wheels and harnessing the mules. The dragoons broke into four columns; most of them still had their carbines slung.

The wind was rising, fresh in Kit's face. The bugle sounded the advance, and he eased his horse forward into a jog. Gillespie was back, riding along beside him, his rifle across his saddle-bows.

With the howitzers on their trucks trundling along behind harnessed mules, they rolled up toward the crest of the next ridge. A few drops of rain began to fall. Kit tucked his powder horn under his shirt and pulled the shirttail down over the action of his rifle to keep it dry. He rode along just behind Kearny, with Gillespie on his left. After him the dragoons trotted in their columns, pushing on in their excitement, driving their officers ahead of them.

The storm burst on them suddenly. Through a blinding sheet of rain and mist they climbed up to the ridge where they had seen the Californios, but the late sun was already shining, and as they scaled the crest of the ridge the rain had stopped. They moved up over the top of the ridge and looked out over a long, shallow valley that skirted a narrow creek, a sweep of bunch grass pocked with clumps of cactus and outbreaks of rock, now glistening with the fresh, rain-washed radiance of the sun.

The scout cried, "Sir! There they are!"

Kit's horse flung its head up suddenly and gave a ringing neigh. His muscles tensed. Down there along the creek ahead of them were the few scattered brush huts of an Indian village, and all around it were the Californios, scrambling into their saddles, herding loose horses together.

They had been camping there; a dozen smokes rose from their fires. Half of them were still on foot, their horses milling in confusion among the humps of the Indian huts. It was hard to count them, but there were certainly fewer than in Kearny's army, maybe only sixty or seventy men. The general swung around, his eyes gleaming, and bellowed, "Charge!"

The bugler put his horn to his lips. Before the first notes sounded Kearny's army spurred into a full gallop down the hill.

Right in its first stride Kit's horse stumbled and pulled itself up again, running with its head too high, its gallop uneven. He shortened his reins, trying to steady it, with the dragoons thundering down behind him. Ahead of them, on the flat valley floor, the Californios were rushing away out of the Indian village, turning tail. The front of the column veered to follow them. Some of the men like fools shot off their rifles, long before they were close enough to hit anything. The rifle of the man beside him misfired, the powder wet. Then the horse swerved straight in front of Kit.

Kit's mount shied, and its forelegs buckled and it slammed headfirst into the ground, and he went flying.

He plowed into the dirt, shoulder first; he rolled his knees up and his head down, his arms over his head, the earth under him trembling and booming under the hoofs all around him. The army thundered over him. The wheel of one of the howitzers screamed by his nose. A hoof slammed against his thigh and a horse hurtled across him. The sound faded. He lifted his head and saw the dragoons pounding away from him down the slope, and beyond them the Californios were running away.

He stood, his knees wobbly. The stock of his rifle was broken. His horse was dead, its neck doubled under its shoulder. He stood on the slope watching Kearny's men gallop away from him in a wild, disorderly rout, following the Californios out over the valley.

Ahead, the Californios slowed.

Kit yelled; he tossed the rifle away and began to run down the hill, looking for another horse, another gun. He was too far away to do anything now but watch.

Like a dog on a bait, Kearny was hurtling along on the heels of the Californios, his men strung out behind him down the valley. The howitzers were bouncing along useless at a full gallop, and the men were already shooting off their rifles. Ahead of him, the Californios wheeled around to either side and curled back.

Kit, running, heard only a few scattered shots. Most of the dragoons seemed to be struggling with their carbines. Coming from either side, the Californios at a dead gallop closed on the front and the middle of the line. The first few of them swung out the loops of their lassoes. Kit stopped, out of breath.

The dragoons in their ragged line wheeled to face the attack; he saw some of them reverse their guns, swinging them up like clubs, but they were no defense. The lassoes of the Californios unwound through the air like the flight threads of spiders and snared one man after another and yanked them out of their saddles. Before they even hit the ground the other Californios closed in on them with spears and sabers. The rearguard charged forward, and the Californios wheeled on them too.

Kit could hear no shots. Around him the grass was steaming from the rain, the air moist and warm as a fog; inside his shirt, his powder horn knocked his ribs. In wet air like this, guns often failed. Now, suddenly, the Californios were the ones with the range and the weapons.

A riderless horse galloped up toward him. He grabbed for the flying reins, missed, and chased it vainly on a few feet, desperate. Yanking the pistols out of his belt, one in each hand, he started down there at a dead run, while out on the valley floor Kearny's army screamed and died.

57 ✍ THE ONES WHO RAN were easy. Sohrakoff's horse ranged up alongside a dragoon fleeing away back up the slope to the east; his tired mount staggered with every stride. As Sohrakoff caught him the blue-coated soldier leveled his rifle at him and pulled the trigger again. It misfired again. Sohrakoff dropped the loop around his shoulders, dallied the rope twice around the horn, and sat the horse down.

For three more strides the dragoon kept going. The rope sang taut, and his horse raced away out from under him; for a moment he hung in the air. He hit the ground on his back, and from both sides the lancers swooped in on him. He screamed once. Sohrakoff reeled in his rope, his horse jumping sideways, fighting the bit, its ears pinned flat and its neck dripping lather.

Most of the Americans were not running. They held their ground in a long line down the middle of the valley, their ranks pulling together, holding their rifles by the barrels, to use the heavy stocks for clubs. Their bugle began to sound a frantic call. He saw a few of them trying to reload; he saw them raise the guns to shoot, but nothing happened. He hoped it rained again.

At the east end of the valley somebody was screaming, "Gillespie! Gillespie!" The Californios had found their worst enemy.

Sohrakoff galloped up the line, looking for the heavy guns the Americans had brought with them. Ahead of him three Californios with lances were circling a knot of six or eight dragoons, unhorsed and standing back to back, waving their rifles. Two bodies sprawled on the ground in their midst. He built the loop in his rope and rode in on them, not alone, other Californios rushing in from all sides to the kill, and they roped the dragoons off one by one and held them for the lancers.

His body burned, every muscle vibrant and alive. He felt enormous, invulnerable. He fought against this feeling, which was like being drunk, keeping him from thinking about what he had to do. He pulled away from the fighting and rode off again to look for the howitzers.

Archie Gillespie had taken a slash across the back from a saber, some time before, in the first charge, what seemed hours ago but was really, surely, only minutes. He could hear men screaming his name. His breath sawed through his throat, and the vast wound on his back was flapping. He felt no pain; it was strange; his mind moved so slowly, too. He put his hands out again and lifted the howitzer load up into the bore of the gun.

They were screaming and screaming. He tasted blood in his mouth. He leaned on the howitzer a moment, his head numb.

"Sir!"

"Help me —"

"Sir! They're charging again — get down —"

Gillespie sank down on his knees, clinging to the gun. The

men around him grunted and screamed and swore and prayed, their bodies banging against him, fighting against the swarming assault. He groped blindly under the howitzer for the slow match and crept into the shelter of the gun and struggled to light it. The bugle was sounding, over and over, *fall back, fall back*. He was not leaving the gun.

The attack had subsided. He had the match going, and he straightened, gasping for breath, his vision blurred and red.

Dragoons surrounded him with their useless rifles. Blood dripped steadily down the face of the boy beside him. They were all on foot, packed together to defend against the vicious whining ropes that dragged them away to die. There were dead and wounded men sprawled on the ground around him and he stepped on them; he could not help it. Soft squishing under his feet, the crackle of bone.

"Here they come."

A wave of horses rolled down on him. He swung around, setting the match to the fuse. The bugle blew without ceasing; it was sawing at him, like something cutting in his ears, that thin ribbon of sound through the clamor and the roar and the shriek. He leaned on the howitzer, which did not fire, while the dragoons around him beat off the attack once more with the clubs of their rifles, dodging the lethal grasp of the ropes. More of them died. Somebody was praying.

There was another load in the ammunition case. Gillespie wobbled, went to his knees, and crawled around to the bore of the howitzer to clean it out and try again.

The bugler stopped, and Kit kicked at him. "Keep it up!" He had Kearny's arm over his shoulders, the general's head lolling down on his chest, his uniform coat soaked with blood from the wound in his face. The bugler lifted his horn and tootled out his crazy song.

Kit dragged Kearny on toward the growing clump of men around the howitzer. The valley floor around him was a riot of riderless horses and dragoons on foot and the wheeling, murderous charges of the Californios like hawks swooping. He had to get to the howitzer, get everybody to the howitzer. The soft grass hid tangles of cactus that grabbed his legs; a spine ran through his boot into his ankle. By twos and threes the dragoons were falling back toward the sound of the bugle, their faces wild with shock and fear. As they joined him he bellowed at them and hit at them until they circled him, shoulder to shoulder, their rifles raised butt first, and then he headed them across the trampled grass.

Already this pack was too many for the Californios, who had easier game, chasing down the stragglers and the cowards and the wounded. Kit stood a moment, pulling up some strength out of his gut. In the stunned, exhausted mass of men around him somebody was sobbing, "Oh, God, Mom, oh, God." The boy before him abruptly slumped to his knees, his head bowing, a long saber slash gaping in his neck. A hundred feet away two vaqueros wheeled their horses toward an American on foot, who swung his rifle in a wasted arc and went down with a lance through his chest.

"Come on!" He dragged Kearny's arm up over his shoulders again and plodded toward the howitzer, where, once again, the Californios were charging in.

Sohrakoff had dropped his rope and found a saber. He galloped up toward the howitzer, which stood in a clump of rocks near the Indian village, a dozen of the Americans around it struggling to fire it. As he went he tried to bring the other Californios with him, but they were maddened with the killing, heard no orders, did nothing together.

He was as mad as any of them, the blood lust raging, and alone he shortened his horse to a stiff-legged gallop, lifted the saber, and went straight at the little gun and the desperate men around it.

They reared up to meet him, and he drove the horse into their midst, flailing with the saber, down and down and down. A rifle barrel bounced off his hip. His face was wet. His horse reared, surrounded by dragoons clubbing at him with their rifles, with their fists, and he slashed out with the saber. The blade met bone with a thunk like chopping wood. Somebody grabbed his belt. They were pulling him off the horse, into their midst, hands gripping at him. He sank his spur into the horse's side and it lunged and still they held him; a face before him screeched, a red mouth wide, and he put the point of the saber into that mouth and pushed it through.

The horse bounded forward, neighing in terror and pain. He pulled free, away from the dragoons, half out of the saddle, the horse staggering with each step. Its hind end was crippled; fifty feet from the howitzer it collapsed and he leapt to the ground. Pico came galloping up to him.

"Come on, Ruso — let's get out of here!"

"Get me a horse!"

Pico reached down to him; he gripped the other man's forearm and vaulted up behind him, and Pico wheeled the horse around.

The flat ground was sprinkled with dead men. Just east of him most of the Americans had banded into a single mass of men. The bugle shrilled a random frenzy of notes in their midst. They were working like a real army, protecting each other, dragging their dead and wounded and themselves doggedly toward the howitzer, while the Californios were scattered all over the valley, everybody off on his own little war.

"Call them all up," Sohrakoff shouted; he clutched Pico's belt, every jump of the big horse nearly pitching him off. "Make a good charge and we can kill them all and get the howitzer." His vision blurred to a red mist; he swiped with his arm at his bleeding forehead.

Pico said, "No chance! Let's go."

"Damn you —"

The howitzer went off. Sohrakoff heard the low thud of the gun firing more in his bones than in his ears, beneath the uproar of the fighting; then the shell screamed through the air toward him and he ducked, like a child, and the shell hit the ground twenty feet away and exploded.

Pico's horse reared, which saved them. The air sizzled. Like iron wasps bits of shrapnel sang and whizzed around them. The horse went over backward and Sohrakoff landed hard on his side.

He had lost the saber; he rolled over and got cactus spines all through his left thigh. He stood. On the trampled yellow grass nearby Pico sat braced on one arm, his head hanging. The horse still thrashed on the ground, while its body spurted blood from fifty punctures. Pico staggered up onto his feet.

"Come on, you fool." He palmed Sohrakoff's shoulder and shoved him away. "I'm the general here."

The main pack of the Americans had reached the howitzer. They circled it, a wall of their bodies, too many now for the Californios to attack. Sohrakoff suddenly realized his leg hurt, his hands were slick with blood, there was blood all over his face. He limped after Pico. Two lancers rode toward them, reining in, reaching down to take them on their horses, and he scrambled up behind a saddle and they galloped off.

The shot from the howitzer had driven the Californios away. Night was falling. The whole fight had lasted about ten minutes. Kearny was injured, Gillespie was horribly injured, and the next three ranking officers were dead. Exhausted and dazed, the rest of the beaten dragoons clustered in their pack, some moaning, some praying, most silent. They had lost all their horses. Kit shoved and cursed and kicked and begged the men until they gathered up the bodies and dug a quick grave, there on the valley floor, near the howitzer.

Digging the grave took longer than the battle had. Kit kept a watch out, his nerves yipping, his belly a mad seethe; this was not over yet. As soon as the dead men were covered up he began to drive the live ones on, and they dragged themselves and the wounded and the howitzer up the steep slope of the closest hill.

As they were trudging up the hill the Californios came back. They spread out through the valley, herded up the loose horses, and stampeded them toward the Americans. The dragoons held together, waving their arms and shouting, and turned the charge, and Kit managed to shoot two of the animals as they passed by, so they had meat. There was no water. A few of the dragoons had something left in their canteens.

They laid the wounded out on top of the hill and put the healthy men around them. Kit went quickly around checking on their weapons. Some of the dragoons had kept hold of their rifles, but many of them had lost them, and most of the powder was wet and ruined. He reloaded as many rifles as he could and put those men at the corners of the camp. He had no more ammunition for the howitzer.

The Californios surrounded the hill, riding back and forth around the foot of it, watching the Americans through the dusk. Off down the valley a wolf howled. Kit started a fire with sun-dried dung and dead cactus, and the men singed horsemeat over it. The night creeping in on them brought the wind with a cold edge like a saber. One of the junior officers quietly began to organize the camp, putting out more sentries and assigning men to finish cutting up the dead horses and make more fires. Two of the wounded died almost at once.

There were more than twenty men hurt. Gillespie lay on his side, covered up with a horse blanket; his back was torn open down to the pink spongy sack of his lung.

But he was conscious. When Kit bent over him, he said, "Still going, Kit."

"Yeah, yeah," said the scout. "You did a good job, Archie, you saved our tails."

Gillespie's mouth was white with pain, and every breath sobbed in his chest somewhere. "Got to be a real soldier," he said, and shut his eyes.

Kit put one hand on the marine's hair, the only place that was not wounded. "Sleep, damn it, will y'?"

Kearny lay beside Gillespie, breathing hard. He had taken a lance through the cheek. Kit, his forearms on his knees, hunkered down beside the general. It was too dark now to see much of the valley, but Kit could make out the movement of horses pacing by along the foot of the hill, well out of rifle range, if he had had a rifle.

"Like fightin' a fuckin' bunch of Blackfeet," he said.

Kearny made a sound as if he were waking up. "Jesus. What a mess. I could see a court-martial for this. How many dead?"

"I don't know. I reckon it a hundred thirty men up here now, about, counting wounded, and some of them will die. We started out with a hundred fifty something." The wind tasted bitter. It was going to rain. "You got anything that holds water, General, put it out now."

"We have to get marching again."

"You leave now, General, you'll kill half your wounded. Gillespie over there, he'll die, if you move him now." Gillespie would likely die anyway, like a real soldier. Kit looked up at the sky, thickening and moist above him. "I'll walk out. You stay here until everybody who's gonna die dies. Then come along slow and easy and I'll bring you some help."

Kearny's head bobbed. He was looking around him; the light of the little fire showed him the wounded, huddled on the rocks and grass, among the ear-shaped leaves of the cactus. He faced Kit again. In his eyes there was a glint of terror.

Kit said, "When you do march, stay together, General. The greasers, they'll get tired of it, they'll quit, if they don't get blood again pretty soon."

Kearny said, "Yes." His head drooped. "Go, Carson." Kit went.

Another long, thin thread of a wolf's howl went up, out there in the valley. The rain was starting, the first fat drops banging on the brim of his hat. He walked across the top of the hill, toward the west, where the ground was more broken, and began to work his way down the slope, staying low.

The rain came, a sudden explosion of the clouds; this made good cover, and he went straight down the hill, skidding on the grass. As quickly the rain stopped. He crouched in an outcrop of rock, halfway to the valley floor. Below him there were horses moving in the dark. He lay down flat on his stomach and shut his eyes, which made his ears keener, and could hear voices speaking Spanish.

He lay there a while longer, hoping it would rain again. He had walked in some cactus during the fight, and his foot hurt already. It was a long way to San Diego. The wolves were moving in; they would be eating dead Americans before long. Down the slope, Californios went by him steadily, in both directions, talking to one another, their horses' hoofs soft on the grass, their gear ringing and creaking. He smelled sweat. Somebody laughed. The rain steamed back up out of the ground again, getting him wet.

He got tired of waiting. He began to crawl.

58 🗡 THE AMERICANS HAD BURIED their dead, but the grave was shallow, and the wolves were moving down. Sohrakoff and three other Californios piled rocks on the mounded earth to keep the scavengers out of the dead men.

The weight of fear and guilt had settled on him again; he felt that sick dread again. He kept remembering the red, open mouth and him thrusting the saber into it, that wet, red, open mouth.

It could have been him; he could have died here; he almost had died here.

The rain began again, which felt good, cold and wet, like plunging into seawater. In the dark, as he walked away from his enemies' grave, Pico rode up, leading a fresh horse.

"Thanks." Sohrakoff doubled the leadrope in his hand and looked around, trying to remember where his saddle was.

"You're still leaving?" Pico said.

"Yes." He climbed up onto the bare back of the horse and rode off through the dark, looking for his saddle, and Pico jogged along beside him. He was riding the big palomino.

"They have no water up there, no food, they'll come down soon enough. Stay and kill a few more of them with me."

Sohrakoff's horse had dropped near the howitzer. Sohrakoff trotted down the side of the valley, looking for it. The fresh horse was spooky and nervous and hard to rein with just a leadrope; he kept his free hand on its neck, stroking it, and could feel the sweat popping out of its hide. He turned to Pico. "Orozco sent me to bring you back to El Pueblo, not fight here. Are you coming with me or not?"

"Orozco! He's an Indio altar boy. Stay with me, Ruso; we can raid the Yankees to death, like today."

Sohrakoff snorted at him. "Yes, just like today. If Orozco had been here we'd have killed them all, or a lot more of them, anyway, and we'd certainly have gotten one of the howitzers. They're a better army than we are, Pico; they obey orders and they work together."

He could hear wolves in the dark to one side of him, snarling and snapping. He guessed they were eating the dead horse, and he veered toward them.

He twisted toward Pico again. "We could learn something from that. We have a good commander. If we were a good enough army, we could win."

Pico made a contemptuous sound in his throat. "I saw when they had no guns they were nothing."

Sohrakoff shook his head. The wolves scattered away at the approach of the two horsemen; he heard them slavering and whining in the dark, and the horse under him danced, its breathing loud, wanting to bolt. He threw the leadrope to Pico and slid down to the ground. The dead horse stank. He ungirthed his saddle and hauled it out from under the carcass and retrieved his hackamore and bridle.

"I'm going to El Pueblo. Stockton will be attacking there within a few days." He hauled the gear off a dozen yards, away from the wolves. Pico led the horse after him. Behind them in the dark the snarling and cracking and chewing picked up again, the devouring.

"You are a tough nut, Ruso. I'd like to have you with me."

"Then come to El Pueblo." Sohrakoff put his hackamore on the horse's head and the bridle over it.

"I'm not giving up here yet," Pico said.

"This won't matter. If they take back El Pueblo, we won't be any better than outlaws." He saddled the horse up; the saddle was dirty and he rubbed it off with his serape.

Pico said, "I'm not doing anything for Orozco." He was staring away toward the gringos' hill.

Sohrakoff mounted the horse. Up there on the top of the hill the Americans had their fires going again, after the rain. They would move off, eventually, and Pico would not be able to hold them, or even hurt them much, especially if they got the howitzer to fire. They would march together, defend each other, and somewhere out there were more of them, always more of them, with their guns, with their order and their utter certainty they were right.

"Goodbye, Ruso," Pico said.

"Come to El Pueblo," Sohrakoff said.

"Not for Orozco. Not ever." Pico raised his hand. "Good fighting." He went off, and Sohrakoff rode away toward the north.

59 ✠ THE PRIEST WAS no longer telling them that God would win the war for them; now he was saying that God was sending them a trial, to test their faith. The townhouses along the plaza would soon be empty again — the rich people were leaving the city, packing up their goods into *carretas* and onto mules and moving off to ranches in the countryside. The poor people were filling all their water buckets and hiding their food. The shops had closed. Even the gambling shanty was empty now.

The church was full. Armies of candles burned on the altar. Families with blankets and caches of food and water huddled along the outside wall in the walkway and down in the old graveyard, praying.

The priest was still in the vestibule; the Mass would not begin for a few moments. Cat lifted her shawl over her hair and went into the church.

Orozco stood behind the rest of the congregation, a lean black shadow, his hands at his sides. The murmuring voices of prayers filled the church. She went up next to him, and he glanced at her, down his beaked Indio nose.

"A timely conversion?"

"Have you heard anything from Count Sohrakoff?" she asked.

"No."

"You're still going to fight?"

"I have an army and an enemy," he said. "An enemy who despises people who don't fight back."

There were rumors all over the city that Stockton had offered to negotiate if the rebels would turn Orozco over to him. She stood beside him, looking past the massed heads of the worshipers, toward the blaze of the candles at the altar. "How far away is the commodore?"

"Three days, more or less."

She kept her gaze on the altar, washed in candlelight; it seemed an unreal place, a passage into eternity. The two altar boys in their fine embroidered smocks moved around it, carrying a book, a cup, some cloths with crosses sewn on them. Something else she knew nothing about. She said, "You are the Angel of Death, Colonel. The last absolute. And you're going to kill us all to honor it."

He twisted toward her, a suppressed violence in the thrust of his head and shoulders. "What do you know about honor? Get out of here. No. Chavez!" His voice was brittle. "Lock her up." She turned her gaze once more toward the glittering enchantment of the altar and walked ahead of Chavez out of the church.

Stockton was moving up from the south, in good order; Orozco's scouts reported his flanks protected, his supply trains keeping pace, his ranks disciplined. In less than a day he would reach the river that ran down through the enormous flat valley where the Mission San Gabriel stood, two hours' ride east of El Pueblo.

The river, broad and swampy, now running deep from the winter's rains, was a good place to stop him, and Orozco led his army out and set up a camp north of the Bartolo ford. There was still no word from Sohrakoff, and without him Orozco was short-handed and short-tempered; he had a council of his officers late in the afternoon at which with declining patience and ascending sarcasm he argued them into submission, accepting his deployments and his orders at least as long as they stood face to face with him.

The council broke up, the officers dispersing noisily. Orozco went back into the dry, brush-shadowed wash where he had made his camp. The sun was setting and the wide valley lay in a fading haze; the campfires of the army already sparkled in the gloom. He sat down a little way from the campfire, in the lee of the bank, where there was a patch of sand, and smoothed the sand and began to draw in it.

Stockton was marching north across the valley, but when he came to the water he would have to swing to the west to the ford. Orozco estimated that he would reach the river in the late afternoon, so that when Stockton's men turned, the sun would shine in their faces. That favored Orozco and his men, who would have their backs to the sun.

For days the weather had been cool and clear, but all this afternoon the wind had been rising, a hot, sour wind off the inland desert. Even now he could hear it rattling in the brush above his head.

He had seen such a wind before. The local people called it the Santa Ana. Usually it blew for days, and if it blew tomorrow, then it would fill the air with whirling dust, blinding and confusing dust.

The wind was a devil wind, too, working on the nerves like a rasp.

Together with the sun and the wind, he needed luck tomorrow. He was already heavily in debt to luck. He could hardly expect another large increment of it. More likely, as she had said, a lot of people were going to die.

If he could not drive the enemy out of California, he could still force him to pay a price, maybe, higher than Robert Stockton could afford. In the sand before him he traced Stockton's march through the valley.

As he bent over the picture in the sand, through the fitful rustle and stir of the wind, another small sound behind him reached his ears. He lifted his head and saw Count Sohrakoff walk his horse down through the spiny brush that choked the head of the draw.

"Your sentries are lazy," the Count said, and went by Orozco to the fire, where Chavez had put out some meat and tortillas for his officer's dinner. Sinking down on his heels, he began to stuff food into his mouth as if he had never eaten before.

Orozco went down after him to the fire. Sohrakoff looked tired, but he was whole, except for a gash that crossed his forehead. The dust that covered him was the same color as his hair. There was a jug of brandy in Chavez's pack, and Orozco got it out and set it down beside him.

"Thanks."

"What happened?"

"Pico and I ran into a crowd of gringos down by San Pascual and killed a lot of them."

Orozco turned his head and whistled for Chavez. Sohrakoff had wolfed the half-cooked meat and was stuffing raw tortillas into his mouth, dampened with swigs from the jug of brandy. "Where's Pico now?" asked Orozco.

"Still down there. He wouldn't come." Sohrakoff's voice was flat, tired, dull. He said, "We scratched them up, but it made no real difference. Pico's men wouldn't obey him any more than he would obey you. We had an advantage but we lost it."

"You said you beat them."

"We tore them up. Their guns failed. We roped them and stuck them, like hunting bears."

"But Pico would not come back."

"No. I'm sorry."

Orozco said nothing. He longed for Pico's sixty men, tough and well-mounted, and now with a victory in them. But he had Sohrakoff back now, his eyes and hands, the only man he trusted. Chavez walked into sight up the draw, saw them, and stopped short.

"Count." His hand rose in a truncated gesture toward his forehead. "How did you —" He turned to Orozco and finished the salute. "Sir, did you want me?" His eyes veered toward Sohrakoff, drinking the brandy.

Orozco said, "Sohrakoff's won a victory down in the south."

The young man let out a whoop that startled the exhausted horse. He said, "Oh, sir." His arms flapped. "Sir, can I tell everybody?"

"Call Flores and Carrillo," Orozco said. "And tend this horse."

"Yes, sir!" Chavez bounded toward the horse. His gaze stroked over Sohrakoff again. "Well done, sir. Thank you, sir." He dragged away the weary horse; a few feet from the firelight his voice rose in a piercing, excited shriek.

Sohrakoff was still drinking, the jug upended over his mouth. Orozco asked, "Did you see Stockton?"

"I came by his flank this morning. Lots of guns." The Count lowered the jug. In the red light of the fire his face was worn and grim.

Out on the floor of the valley, now, there was a many-throated murmur of a cheer, growing and spreading as the news of the victory reached the army.

Sohrakoff asked, "Where's my woman? I told you to watch out for her."

"She's perfectly safe. I locked her up in your room."

Across the fire the pale eyes blazed at him. "What, did she say something you didn't like?"

"Yes, in fact, she did."

Sohrakoff wiped his arm over his mouth. "She's good at that."

"Leave her where she is. She's under control, she can't run away."

"She won't run."

"Leave her there anyway; where else can you keep her?" Down the draw, he could hear horses galloping; that would be the other officers, come for news. "I need you here. Leave her where she is."

Sohrakoff's head swayed, like a nervous horse weaving. He said, "I'm tired."

"Stay awake long enough to tell them and me what happened."

The dusty wild head drooped. One hand reached for the jug again, but it was empty. The oncoming horses were thundering up into the draw, and out there the whole army was cheering. Orozco went to meet Flores and Carrillo.

They shut her up in the room with a lot of water and food, and then everybody left. The door was padlocked on the outside. Through the space between the door and the jamb she could feel the latch, and she worked on that, sometimes scraping on it with a knife, sometimes hitting it with the knife and a piece of wood for a mallet. The work was hard and there was no way of knowing what good it did, but when she stopped, the silence, the emptiness, drove her back to it again.

In the night she heard Sarbulo Varela, outside the window, calling her name.

She threw herself across the room and up against the iron bars of the grille. "Sarbulo! Where is the Count?"

Down the long, narrow alleyway between this wall and the next, she could just make out his shape in the dark, his horse sidestepping on its toes. The light of the lamp behind her blinded her to the darkness, and she turned and pinched out the flame.

"He's with the army," Sarbulo called. "He can't leave, we fight tomorrow. He sent me instead, to tell you that he is alive still, another day, anyway."

"Alive. Is he all right?"

"There was a battle down in the south. They killed a lot of gringos."

She pressed her cheek against the grille. "Sarbulo, get me out of here. I want to see him. Take me to him." The twisted edge of the bar was cold on her face.

"He says you should stay here, Cat. He'll come for you, he says."

"Sarbulo!"

"He said to tell you he loves you more than anything."

"Sarbulo!"

He was gone. She leaned against the iron bars, watching, but he did not come back.

She left the lamp dark. There seemed no purpose in the light. By touch, her increasing collection of tools spread around her, she dug and scraped and poked and battered around the door latch.

He had told her to stay and wait for him. He had not told her what to do if he died.

Stockton was going to take El Pueblo anyway; she had to stay out of his hands. She dreaded what might happen to her if Stockton's army took her prisoner.

If they took her prisoner it meant Sergei Sohrakoff was dead.

He had told her to stay. If she left, she might never find him again. She might never even know what had happened to him.

She sat in the dark, tired, her hands raw and cramped, the waiting like a slow disintegration. It came to her that she had made this decision once before, when she climbed out of her bedroom window and ran away with John Reilly.

She thought of him for the first time in a long while, with a sudden aching fresh remembrance, a new grief. His gentleness, his kindness, his manhood reduced in his grave to dry bones. She saw the stone she imagined his skull to have become, lying on the sketchpad, the wind curling the pages, a piece of the desert.

He had set her free, brought her halfway across the continent, so that it would come to this, that she would sit in another locked room, waiting for another man.

She was tired, she had to sleep; there was food here and she should eat it. But the turmoil in her gnawed her up, set her mind to jittering even in the dark, coiled her muscles tight; she had to get out of here. She turned to the door again and hacked at it.

60

STOCKTON'S ARMY looked like the armies on Orozco's sand table, a square of men that crept over the floor of the valley, always straight and even, always together. In the middle of the square, triple teams of mules hauled along the brass guns. They would reach the San Gabriel River in less than an hour, and Sohrakoff lifted his horse into a lope and circled around their flank, headed for his own lines.

He rode out into the open past one corner of the square, as he had done before, testing their discipline, and as they had done before, they shouted and pointed at him, but they did not shoot, they did not break rank, they sent no one out to chase him off. They knew he could do them no harm. He galloped his horse down along a shallow wash toward the river, which curled in broad meanders between head-high brush and willow trees like a seam through the flat dun valley.

Halfway across the river, he stopped and let his horse drink, knee deep in the pale water, and from the high brush on the far bank, twenty horsemen suddenly burst down on him.

He wheeled, caught between them and Stockton's oncoming army, but then he saw the leader's palomino horse and stopped. Pico's men hooted at him for spooking. They let their horses jog down to the river's edge. Pico himself rode up through them, the silverwork on his jacket flashing in the sun.

"Hey, Ruso!" In the shade of his sombrero's brim, his teeth showed in a sudden smile. "I think you need some help here."

Sohrakoff trotted his horse through the water to him, and Pico stretched his arm out and they shook hands. Sohrakoff was glad to see him; he punched him in the upper arm. "I thought you were staying out of it, General."

Pico shrugged. His hat had creased his forehead with a broad red dent. "Those other gringos, they got away. One of them walked out and brought back help." His lips still held the smile, but his eyes narrowed. "This doesn't look too good, Ruso."

Sohrakoff shook his head. "It's worse than it looks. Let's go."

With Pico's lancers strung out behind them, they loped up along the north bank of the river, through meadows of spiny bunch grass and the shallow courses of old creeks. Clumps of dusty willows crowded the banks. It was nearly midday. Off to Sohrakoff's right, along an old bed of the river, they passed Flores's sixty-five lancers waiting on the ground, sitting in the shade of their horses. Beyond them was Orozco's militia army.

Vaqueros and farmers these were, and shopkeepers and craftsmen from El Pueblo. As Orozco had taught them they waited in lines, their lances beside them, their hide shields tipped up over their heads against the sun. Half of them had horses, but half were on foot. When Sohrakoff and Pico went by, a thin, ragged cheer went up from them. They covered the whole broad meadow in front of the river, and in their leather jackets they looked like an army.

Ahead, in the lee of a steep rock-tipped ridge, Carrillo's thirty mounted men were gathered in a disorderly mass. Out of their midst three horsemen trotted down toward Sohrakoff, and he reined in where he was, seeing Orozco among them. Pico stopped beside him.

On this low rolling rise they were in the full blaze of the sun, with El Pueblo off to the west and the San Gabriel Mission to the north. Uneven rows of trees marked the old water courses around them. The wind was rising, the dry, nerve-wracking Santa Ana. One hand on his thigh, Sohrakoff twisted in his saddle.

Down to the south, now, he could see Stockton's army inching toward the river, not the individual men but the dust they kicked up, a fume in the wind.

They were not individual men, they were a single fist of blood and iron, aimed at the green, almost unarmed people behind him, who had no idea yet what they were facing. He remembered the howitzer at San Pascual, the shell bursting, the whine and screech of the shrapnel. The horse's body, pierced like a sieve. Leaning his hands on the pommel of his saddle, he stared away toward the yellow dust, while Orozco and his aides jogged up toward him.

"General Pico." Orozco's voice was a harsh, metallic bark, his throat raw. His horse danced, its neck doubled and its teeth grating the bit. "I thought you declined the invitation."

Pico said, "I came, anyway, Colonel. For El Ruso's sake."

Sohrakoff was watching the enemy approach; a weight of despair dragged at him. He made himself listen to Orozco's voice, behind him.

"We have to stop them at the river. General Flores will attack the corner of their square, and then Sohrakoff and I will attack them in the middle and try to catch them in the water. General Pico, you can join General Flores if you'd care to."

Sohrakoff straightened. He cast a look over his shoulder at the lines of farmers with their sticks, and looked forward again, toward the dust. Now he could see the legs moving along through its lower edge, and the sun flashed off the brass barrel of a cannon.

He gave a quick glance at the men around Orozco. Pico was silent, his mustaches drooping, his eyes on the enemy. Flores and Carrillo were looking down. None of them would speak against Orozco, but they wore what they thought like a brand.

Sohrakoff swung his horse around, shoulder to shoulder with Orozco's.

"You can't do this," he said. "We'll all die."

The lean, dark face showed no surprise. "If we all attack together at one corner we can hurt them."

Sohrakoff looked again at the other officers; Carrillo raised his eyes, his face grooved, and gave Sohrakoff a brief, intense glance, like a plea. The Count turned back to Orozco.

"The militiamen will attack if you send them. But when the guns start, they'll run, and the gringos will chase them. It will be a rout; they'll all die."

Orozco's head swiveled away from him, aiming his attention toward Stockton. "Better if we die fighting than let them grind us to nothing."

"No!" Sohrakoff leaned forward into his way. "I won't kill anybody else for no reason. We can't do this. Let them go."

Now Carrillo said, hoarse, "Colonel, I agree with him. We have to withdraw." On his far side, Flores lifted his head and sighed.

Orozco straightened, looking from one man to the next. Like obsidian, she had called him. When his eyes shifted finally to meet Sohrakoff's, there was no feeling, no interest in them, no warmth of recognition, only the black clarity of volcanic glass. The devilish wind shrieked suddenly, like a taunt.

"God gave us a world without justice," Orozco said. "Dismiss them."

Sohrakoff drew in a breath and let it out again. The other officers straightened in their saddles, their faces sliding soft and open with relief. Abruptly they were active, brisk, their hands busy collecting their horses.

Orozco said nothing more. He twisted to stare down the valley toward the river, and his body contracted, his back slumped; he crossed his forearms on the pommel of his saddle and bowed his head down. Sohrakoff faced the other men.

"Pull back, now, quickly. Stay together, go to ground somewhere, send us word of your whereabouts. We'll be at the Dominguez ranch for a while anyway."

Carrillo saluted him. "Nobody but you could have done that, Count," he said. He backed his horse and spun it neatly on its haunches and galloped away toward his men. Flores saluted and left in the other direction.

Pico said, "Ruso, give me the militia."

"Yes, pull them back and make sure they stay out of range. Let them go home if they want. Send me Sarbulo Varela."

The big man nudged his horse around and led his lancers away and gave them orders. Sohrakoff turned toward Orozco again.

"What else?"

Still crumpled forward over his saddlehorn, Orozco was staring away toward Stockton's army. He said finally, "We have to surrender. She'll do it; she came here to do it." Straightening, he turned toward Sohrakoff, expressionless still, not from discipline anymore but from exhaustion and defeat. "Tell her she misjudged me. I'm as rotten as the rest of you." He made no move that Sohrakoff noticed, but his horse carried him abruptly away, swinging around wide toward the west, to avoid Stockton's army. Chavez was already galloping away after his officer.

Sohrakoff stayed where he was a while, watching Stockton's army cross the river, their lines unbroken, neat as woman's work. In the broad, barren sweep of the valley, Orozco was only a black fleck moving swiftly through the dust; he crossed the road that led to the mission, going south. Sarbulo Varela trotted up beside the Count.

"If he had had an army like Stockton's," Sohrakoff said, "he'd have pushed them back to the Missouri."

Sarbulo said, "Is it over, then?"

"Oh, yes, it's over, Sarbulo. Nothing left but the executions." His body felt stiff, bound, the joints locked, the blood cold and sluggish. On the plain behind him, Orozco's army had vanished. The wind tore up the brown dust and whirled it off, erasing their tracks. Now only the bleak, empty plain stood between Commodore Stockton and his victory. "Let's get out of here," he said, and picked up his reins and rode away.

El Pueblo was as empty as an old skull. The night had fallen; he and Sarbulo trotted in across the *zanja,* and the wind harried them along, not a steady blast, but battering, whirling gusts that came from every side, piping a thin whistle, falling off into silence and stillness, and then springing up again to a maniacal screech.

"Go get her a horse," he said to Sarbulo. "Be careful; there may be looters around."

Sarbulo grunted at him. He pitied any looter who came on Sarbulo. Sohrakoff rode across the empty plaza.

From the gate into the townhouse he could see that her window was dark. A thread of panic worked its way through him. Sarbulo had said she wanted to get out. He knew she was afraid of Stockton. His horse skittered sideways across the courtyard, its nose in the air, its ears switching back and forth. A shutter was banging somewhere. She had to be here. He dismounted and went in the side door and cut through the house to the back wing.

The corridor was dark, but a faint light shone in from her room, and the door hung open. The latch had been pulled out of the wall. He banged into the room, and it was empty.

"Count," she said, behind him.

He turned and she came toward him from the corner, her arms out, her breath as harsh in his ear as the Santa Ana. She filled up his arms. She had been crying, her cheek was wet; he stroked his fingers over her face and held her tight against him.

Behind them Sarbulo said, "I have the horses."

In his arms she moved, her voice thick. "What happened? I heard nothing, no guns, nothing."

Sohrakoff let her go, his hands sliding down her arms. "There was no battle. Orozco backed down."

Sarbulo said, "The Count made him back down."

"No," Sohrakoff said. "He made the decision. He knew I was right." She moved toward him again, her hands on his chest, and murmured something. He took hold of her wrists. "Come on, we have to get out of here."

"What are you going to do now?" she said.

He led her back by the hands, out the ruined door. "I need your help. We have to surrender, so that these people can go home. Sarbulo, and Pico and Carrillo. And we have to protect Orozco. What will happen if we ask Stockton for a surrender?"

She walked along beside him, Sarbulo behind them, down the corridor. For a few yards their footsteps were the only sound. She said, "Not Stockton. He'll concede nothing."

They had come to the doorway onto the courtyard, and the bright, serene moon shone in around them, its light sheer to the maddening wind.

Cat asked, "Where is Frémont?"

"Frémont!" Sohrakoff said. "He's in Cahuenga. I don't see what use he'll be."

"He knows the truth. Maybe somehow I can make him honor it." She turned toward him, and he saw, all down her face, the moonlit streaks of tears. "Take me there," she said. "There has to be some justice in this, somewhere."

Frémont and his California Battalion had moved onto a ranch in the pass above Cahuenga, north of El Pueblo, where the ridges of the mountains writhed along toward the sea. A sentry took her up through the yard, past a string of horses dozing in the early morning sun, past a heap of firewood. Down to her right, the slope fell away, dotted with chaparral and cactus, to a meadow where most of the battalion was camped; from the campfires there the smells rose of meat roasting.

The sentry went in to tell Frémont she had come. She stood in the stony yard, her hands clasped before her, wondering what she was going to say. Behind the ranch house the steep slope climbed into the blazing blue of the sky; a vulture wheeled past, waiting for the camp's offal. Away to her left, where the well was, she could hear somebody singing in Spanish.

She could think of no argument that might force any concession at all out of Frémont. The rising had vanished into nothing. Stockton had already entered El Pueblo without firing a gun. Most of the poor people had come back into the city, seeing it was not destroyed, and returned quietly to their lives.

The sentry came toward her again. "Colonel Frémont says you can go in, ma'am."

She went up the steps. The ranch house had a broad roofed porch; when she crossed it her feet boomed on the planks. Somebody opened the door for her. She crossed the threshold into a room where every face was already turned to stare at her.

She smelled tobacco smoke. Her hands were sweating. She went into the middle of the room, toward the dozen men who sat or stood before a huge stone fireplace, watching her approach. In their midst Frémont rose to his feet, coming to a precise, military posture.

"Cat Reilly," he said. His voice rattled. "So you've come back to get in with the winners again."

She stood in the center of the room, in the midst of these men, and looked around at them. She knew them all, Sutter's men, William Todd, who had made the flag in Sonoma, and Long Bob Semple, who had tried to write the proclamation in Spanish, Bob Grigsby, and William Ide, the President of California himself. The Bear Flag Republic: men who had stood mute, in Mariano Vallejo's house, while she faced Kit Carson alone.

She looked from one to the next of them, knowing, now, what she was going to say.

"No," she said. She brought her gaze back to John Charles Frémont. "I came here because it's time you lived up to what you believe in."

Frémont said, "I'm not really a soldier, but I've seen some of it done, enough to know that what you gentlemen did was extraordinary."

They were gathered in the front room of the ranch house in Cahuenga, with several of Frémont's officers standing along the walls to witness the signing of the capitulation. In the middle of the room stood the five Mexican officers. He looked them over, remembering the tall, thin one with the Indian face from Hawk Peak; he had not known until now that this was the same man, who had nearly stolen California back from them.

He spoke no English. Behind him, translating, stood another man Frémont remembered, the only blond-haired, blue-eyed Californio.

Frémont said, "We are honorable men. We want no revenge. We want peace with you. We ask no conditions of you, who are also honorable men. There will be no reprisals, no paroles, no oaths of allegiance. All I ask is that you fight no more against us, and the outcome of the war in Mexico will decide the fate of California."

The tall one spoke Spanish, and the blond man said, "We accept, Colonel Frémont."

"Then, General Orozco, you should sign this first, I think."

The tall, thin one stepped forward, expressionless, and took the pen. Behind him the blond man broke into a broad smile; Frémont wondered if he had said something wrong.

The Indio general stepped back and gave the pen to another man. "General Carrillo."

He signed, and Flores, who had taken San Diego, and Pico, who in ten minutes had destroyed one third of Kearny's army at San Pascual. Frémont signed it for the United States.

He said, "Gentlemen, we're all Californians, and all Americans. Soon, I hope, we'll all be citizens of the United States. Thank you for coming here.

"The California war is over."

Outside, in the sun, Orozco stood on the hillside staring away over the valley and said, "By what right is this pompous bluecoat gringo calling himself a Californio?"

Sohrakoff laughed. Pico came up toward them, his hand out, and they shook hands and said things, and then the *abajeño* general went off toward the column of his men and his waiting horse.

Flores stepped forward. "Thank you, Colonel."

Orozco shook his hand. "You're a good soldier, General."

"Not as good as you are, Colonel. It was a privilege to serve under you."

They saluted each other. Carrillo rode by, and leaned down and gripped hands and spoke, and he too left.

Sohrakoff said, "What are you going to do now?"

Orozco made no answer. He had given up his life to the defense of his country, and now that was done, and he still had life ahead of him; he seemed outraged by this lack of thrift.

They crossed the stony, shadeless yard to their horses, standing side by side at the fence. On the far side of the corral some of Frémont's men leaned on the rail, staring at them. Orozco drew his reins free of the hitch; he put his back to the Bears and faced Sohrakoff.

"This was a lie," he said. "All his high talk about honor. They hate us, we hate them. What can come out of this but more trouble between us?"

Sohrakoff slung his arm over his horse's withers. "We had to come here. Anyway" — leaning on the horse, he smiled at his friend — "for me it's a good lie, you know, Colonel. Sutter ran me out of Ross. The dons kept me an outlaw in California. But now, Sutter and the dons and I, we're all the same, now."

Orozco said, "Yes. You won the war."

Over his shoulder, Sohrakoff glanced at the Bears on the far side of the corral, their faces cranked with suspicion and dislike. Orozco had said it right. His blond hair and his blue eyes, which had marked him for a stranger among the Californios, now made him familiar to the Anglos, a gringo, like them. He said, "There are coves and valleys, up on the coast north of the Russian River, where nobody ever goes. I want to find one of them and build a place of my own."

"With Mrs. Reilly."

"She'll go wherever I go. I want you to come with me too."

Orozco made a weary, disdainful sound in his throat. "I'll ride with you as far as Monterey, anyway. Where is she now?"

"There's somebody she had to see in El Pueblo. I'm going back to get her. You can go on to San Fernando and we'll catch up with you." Sohrakoff swung his reins around his horse's neck. He meant Orozco to come with him; he would work on him all the way to Monterey. He put his hands on his saddle-horn and vaulted up onto his horse.

The priest said, "Why do you want to see that one? He's a savage."

He led her away to the house beside the church, which the Americans had turned into a hospital, putting the priest in charge. Some of the wounded from San Pascual were here, in the big front rooms, and a larger number of men sick with camp fevers and flux. Archie Gillespie was here someplace, recovering from the terrible wounds he had taken at San Pascual; they had brought him out of his bed just long enough to raise the American flag again in El Pueblo.

The priest took her down a shadowy corridor into the back.

"Why did you put him away by himself?" she asked.

"He wanted that," the priest said. "It suits him, too, the black-hearted devil." He pushed a door open for her.

In the room beyond, the windows faced south and east, and the sun had passed by noon; the bare space of the room was full of soft, shaded light. The bed was pushed up against the window so that the man lying there could look out. When she went in he ignored her a moment.

As she came toward him he turned and saw her, and surprise washed over his face.

"What are you doing here?"

He was naked; he made no effort to cover himself; probably the thought never entered his mind. She brought a stool over and sat down on it beside the bed. "I came to see the man who conquered California."

"Go find some general," Kit said.

Under the wasted muscle of his chest, his ribs showed; his belly was hollow, his hipbones were like blades. His feet were wrapped in dirty bandages. He had walked them to the bones, going for help for Kearny's army, and then in the hospital in San Diego a camp fever nearly killed him. He hitched himself up on one elbow, his gaze on her, hostile.

"What do you want?"

"The war's over, Kit. I came to make peace."

She had not been able to find cigars in El Pueblo, but Zeke Merritt had gotten her a cigarette, rolled in a Bible paper. She held it out to him, with a lucifer. He muttered in his throat, still bad-tempered, but he took them. When he had the lucifer flaming, he puffed on the cigarette until the tip glowed and held it out to her. She shook her head.

"It still makes me sick."

He made a sound that could have been a laugh.

She said, "Anything else I can do for you? You don't seem too happy."

"Happy, hell." He snorted smoke. "I want to get out of here. I can't even walk, I puked my guts up for a week, there's too fuckin' many people."

"You brought us all here," she said.

"Yeah, yeah, it was a mistake."

His mood was like a wall against her. She began to wish she had not come. "Well, Kit," she said, "peace." She started to get up, and his hand shot out and gripped her wrist and held her.

"I didn't say I wanted you to go."

She sat down again, reining in her temper, wondering why she had come, why he still compelled her. He stubbed the cigarette out against the wall and laid it on the windowsill.

"What are you doing down here?" he said. "The last I saw you was in Monterey."

"Larkin sent me here," she said.

"Larkin." She could see he detested Larkin. "You have something to do with this capitulation?"

"Something," she said. "I talked to Frémont."

He grinned at her. "I knew you weren't running away, up there at Sutter's Fort. I knew you were still in it. All right." The old wicked gleam was in his eyes, but he was tired, and trapped in a half-wrecked body; he lay back again. He let go of her. "Peace, Cat. Between you and me, peace." Lying back, he reached up on the windowsill. "Thanks for the smoke."

She went out and shut the door behind her. Alone in the corridor, she paused, wondering which way to go; she did not want to walk back through the crowded hospital, through the smell and sight of wounded men.

Then in the rear of the corridor another door opened, letting in a dazzling blaze of light. A shadow formed in the middle of it, darkened, grew distinct, the shape of his body, the wild halo of his hair. She walked toward him, and he met her there and took her hand and led her out to the sun.

Note ✒ The events of this story are history. In the interests of fiction I have tinkered with the scheduling here and there, left out episodes that seemed redundant, and compressed things together. I wanted to honor both the Kelsey-Bidwell-Bartleson crossing of the Great Basin and the Sierra in 1841 and the great winter crossing by Frémont and Carson in 1844, so I combined them. I did some meddling also with the timetable of the Bear Flag Revolt and the Californio Rising.

California's pioneer period is graced with a fine historian, H. H. Bancroft, who had the foresight to assemble enormous masses of documents and personal accounts that are the primary sources for this time. I also want to thank Jennifer Holland, John Ponce, Mrs. Violet Chappell, and Robert Grimes for their invaluable help.

Except for John and Cat Reilly, Count Sohrakoff, and Jesús Orozco, the characters are history. Orozco is a blend of José María Flores and José Antonio Carrillo.

Here is what happened to some of these people.

Johann Augustus Sutter lost New Helvetia in the chaos of the Gold Rush. He died penniless in Pennsylvania in 1880.

John Charles Frémont survived a court-martial after the war and resigned from the army. He sat in the United States Senate for California and was governor of Arizona Territory before he ran in 1856 as the first Republican candidate for president of the United States.

Kit Carson served as a brigadier general in the Union Army and as an Indian agent, sired seven children, and died in bed at the age of fifty-nine.

John Bidwell, the so-called Prince of California, mined during the Gold Rush and ranched in Chico, where he settled. He was a major player in California politics all his life and also ran for president of the United States.

José Antonio Carrillo went to California's maverick Constitutional Convention.

John Christenson married for a tenth time.

Long Bob Semple published the first newspaper in California.

José Flores went back to Mexico and finished his career in the Mexican Army.

Robert Stockton left California and was elected senator from New Jersey. He tried several times to win the nomination for president but failed.

Thomas Larkin died in 1858, rich and well loved, the only real hero of the war.

Ben Kelsey, whose numerous family built mines and ranches at Clear Lake, kept moving, to Oregon, to Texas, back to southern California.

Sarbulo Varela dropped from sight.

Stephen Kearny got Frémont court-martialed but died in 1848, perhaps of lingering consequences of the wounds he took at San Pascual.

William Ide settled at Red Bluff and held most of the important local political offices, and believed to the end of his life that he was the real conqueror of California.

Archie Gillespie died in 1873 at San Francisco, having done nothing remarkable since 1847. Bancroft says he seems "to have lost his grip on life."

Zeke Merritt disappeared sometime before the Gold Rush.

José Castro came back to California after the war and lived quietly at Monterey and San Juan for a while, returned to Mexico, and was assassinated there.

Mariano Vallejo was half-ruined in the conquest, but he had so much to begin with that half-ruined still left him comfortably fixed. He went to the Constitutional Convention at Monterey and was elected a state senator. He founded the city of Vallejo, and the city of Benicia is named for his wife.

Andrés Pico also went to the rowdy, uproarious Constitutional Convention, which forced California's way into the Union as a free state, thus making the Civil War inevitable. It's said that when the constitution was finally written, the delegates would not stop dancing to sign it, so the document was brought into the fandango room and signed there. On this high level California politics have continued ever since.

The Indians of California were slaughtered in the decade following the war, their numbers reduced by as much as ninety percent. The Kashaya people skated along the edge of disaster for years but survived; they now have a *ranchería* on a remote ridge north of Fort Ross on the Mendocino coast.

The Bear Flag continued to be an object of veneration for years, until it was destroyed in the fire after the '06 quake.